# BENEATH A MOURNING SKY

KRISTEN ELLIS KIEFFER

First Edition (2023).



ISBN: 978-1-7342064-8-7

Published by She's Novel Press

Cover design by Miss Nat Mack

Editing by Sara Letourneau and Misha Kydd

*This one's for me.*

# AUTHOR'S NOTE

This book contains subject matter that some readers may find distressing. Visit *A Note on Subject Matter* on page 411 for a detailed list of concerns.

The Waking S
Ifros
CARASTILE
Istanel
ININAZA
Brenmere
ANDITH
ORVEST
The Westmead
TARNA'S CORSI
HA
Geldegat
THE EIGHT REALMS OF THE
Radiant Astral Empire

SAMNE
RNOS
Calas
AVERSERE
Daorender
Arivis
MORSAY
Olska
GITHA
THE WILDS OF DAEGLAND

# PROLOGUE

*Life is full of falls.*

Riders spill from their horses. Children stumble as they learn to walk. Women catch their babes as they tumble from the womb. On occasion, the troubled pitch themselves from rooftops or rock faces in the hope of ending a more visceral fall. But it's not the fall that matters. It's the landing. Or, rather, what results from the landing. Broken bones. Bruises. Tiny scratches that blossom with pinpricks of shiny crimson, or cuts so wide and frightening that they leave even the strongest as queasy as a bairn upon their first nip of whisky.

This was my domain: the wounded, the fallen. Many long years I spent devoted to their care—and make no mistake, I excelled in my devotion. Every suture was my offering, each set bone my song of praise. For my devotion, I was rewarded with a skill of hand and a sharpness of mind that spoke of hallowed greatness—a double-edged sword, for it is said that greatness often breeds blindness.

Perhaps that is why I failed to see my own fall coming.

# CHAPTER I

The lad flinched as my needle arced beneath his skin. His name was Alcom, though at the time I couldn't have told you so. Lady Kelkevie boasted half a dozen fiery-haired sons, and the lass I'd been at four-and-twenty had seen little importance in remembering who was who. As children of the Count and Countess of Tarne, the brothers' noble birth had been enough to satisfy my curiosity, which concerned little more than my efforts to ascend beyond the high glens of Daorender.

"Steady now," I crooned. Sweat dripped down my brow as I cinched the first suture tight against the lad's cheekbone, drawing together the rent edges of his skin.

The hour had already grown late when the Kelkevie brothers had first appeared at Erune's surgery door that night. Upon seeing the bright red wad of cloth the youngest lad was holding against his face, the master healer had tossed more logs into the hearth fire. "What is it this time, lass?" she'd asked, entrusting me to assess the latest of the Kelkevie brothers' long string of recklessly begotten injuries.

"Three bloody gashes," I'd said after peeling the hastily crumpled cravat from the lad's cheek. "They'll need suturing."

"I'll get the kettle on, then," Erune had replied, tossing one more log upon the fire for good measure.

With the hearth now ablaze, I had plenty of light by which to work. The tiny surgery, however, had turned sweltering. As if sensing my discomfort, Erune cracked the casement window open. I drew another stitch as a blessed rush of wintry air cooled the nape of my neck.

"Stars, the lot of you smell ripe as the horses in the stables," Erune said, addressing the other Kelkevie brothers, who had crowded near the threshold of the surgery. "Dare I ask how you injured yourselves this time?"

One of the brothers scoffed. "'Twas but Alcom who set about bleeding himself, my lady."

"Aye," insisted another. "Only Alcom's daft enough to go chasin' a wildcat. We went up the bens to hunt a stag, not to—"

"The *bens*?" The words flew out of Erune's mouth like a bolt from a crossbow. "Without a proper guide? By the Black, you wee fools! There are drifts up there this time of year that would swallow a lad whole."

"But they didn't!" cried a third brother, his shrill voice pitching with pubescence. My ears rang as I tied off the first set of sutures. As I started the next row, my charge began to squirm. Squirming, I had learned, was often a precursor to bolting. Hastily, I set about drawing together the last gash in his skin.

"We were on the trail of a big 'un," the third brother continued. "Nigh on the biggest stag I've ever seen and—"

"Och, you've never seen a stag, you wee dolt," said yet another brother. Perhaps the eldest, judging by the depth of his tone.

And so the argument began. The row held little consequence, as was the way of quarrels among bairns. Rightly, I remember little of what was said that night, save that the bickering had seemed for a time to be interminable.

After finishing with the sutures, I smothered the lad's stitched flesh in a coat of musky calendula salve. Erune then ushered the brothers out of the surgery, bidding them settle their affairs elsewhere.

"Nay, leave that," she insisted as she turned to me, gesturing to the excess suturing thread I was gathering. Firelight glinted off the silver strands of her hair and painted her pale skin a bonny shade of gold. "It's time you headed back to catch your rest, lass. We'll only find ourselves the busier on the morrow."

Had it been another time of year, I might have argued against her suggestion. *A healer is only as skilled as her surgery is clean*, Erune had taught me. But the preparations we'd made for Imbelaine the past few weeks had demanded an intensity matched only by that of the festivities to come. Truth be told, I was worn low as the candles we had burned late into the night.

Gathering my cloak and slim roll of surgical tools, I followed Erune through the bowels of Castle Tarne and out into the night. A chill wind plummeted over the keep, carrying the crisp scent of fresh-fallen snow as it cut through the bailey.

"Tonight, do you think?" Erune mused, appraising the blanket of Stars above.

I followed her gaze. "So the astralaries say. Have we enough prepared?"

"One can never be too prepared, lass. But aye, it will do."

The soft, wet smack of hooves filled the air as a groom led my horse—a sprightly mare borrowed from Clan Larmach's stables—into the courtyard. With a nod of thanks, I fitted myself in the saddle. "I'll be here bright and early," I promised.

Erune's mouth quirked with humor. "I'd expect nothing less of you, lass."


The road to Aversere ran west along the swift waters of the Serenault, the river surging with meltwater from the mountainside. I welcomed the icy breeze that licked up off its surface, numbing my mind to all but the promise of a hearth fire at the end of my journey. Tucking my knees into the horse's ribs, I urged the palfrey home.

*Home.* It was a strange word. As Erune's apprentice, my home ought to have been within the walls of Castle Tarne. But the castle was little more than an overgrown croft, its surgery only large enough to house its resident healer. Apprentice be damned. So I kept my bed in the nearby city of Aversere, at the guildhall where the renowned healers of Clan Larmach gathered to ply their trade. I had been born and raised there, my father having been one of the guild's resident archivists, but the guildhall hadn't felt like home for some years.

Still, I was glad to see the lights of Aversere as I drew

near. The bitter highland cold was wont to sink its teeth into the bones of weary midnight travelers. Never mind that the journey from Tarne to Aversere took less than the time I'd needed to stitch wee Alcom's cheek.

Candlelight flickered in half a hundred windows, visible given that the city bore no battlements. The Daor saw little honor in siege tactics. Disputes were settled as they ought to be: in open fields, under the cleansing light of the sun; or in the dark of invaded keeps, should a laird or lady prove themselves too craven to meet a challenge. As shops and guildhalls rose around me, my pulse thudded in my ears, blood churning against the threat of frostbite as the barren road gave way to the beginnings of a city street. It seemed to grow louder still as I made my way deeper into the city, and I began to worry that the night was colder than I'd realized. But then understanding dawned with sudden clarity. . . .

The sound thundering in my ears wasn't my pulse. It was the drums.

The resounding beat pounded from deep within the heart of the city, heralding Imbela's arrival. I drew my horse around to find the splendor of the Bright Star's red-gold eye peering above the eastern mountains, just as the astralaries who studied the night sky had predicted. To the south, a flame had taken root atop the Sanctuary of Stars, matched in magnificence by the brazier that burned bright atop Castle Highdale's keep in the north. In a matter of minutes, the cry of greatpipes would pierce the air, followed by the shouts of children roused and rapt with wonder. Blessings would spill from the mouths of winter-worn women as the rhapsody of the luminaries echoed through the glen. *Lady of Fire!* the priestesses would sing, their words dark and lilting in the ceremonial tongue of the eight realms. *Bearing the flame of life reborn!*

A thrill chased up my spine. There was a prickle of possibility in the air, ripe as the bright green-gray of a coming spring. Even beneath the acrid stench of woodsmoke, I could smell it. I sucked in a breath as though I might fill my lungs with that thrill, as though I could make it as sure a living part of me as the blood in my veins. For five long months, heavy winter snows had dammed the mountain passes that led west beyond Daorender. But with Imbela's dawning came the arrival of spring. Soon, the passes would clear—and I could leave the highlands behind me. And this time, I vowed that I would.

I led my mare down an alley, taking a winding route to the guildhall to avoid the townsfolk spilling into the streets, their faces lifted to meet Imbela's eye. It was good that I knew the city well. Aversere was a sea of crowded houses and meandering streets, hewn-stone shopfronts and narrow market squares. I weaved my way through the familiar maze of muddied cobbles before passing through the guildhall's eastern gate. A stable girl collected my mare as I dismounted, casting a long look over her shoulder as she retreated into a stall with the horse. The Bright Star Imbela had yet to rise above the rooftops of the inner city, but that hadn't stopped a crowd of healers from gathering in the courtyard. I smothered my disdain with a sigh. I might not have believed in the deity of the Stars and the Dark Between, but I had no wish to be unkind. Still, my jaw ground tight as I waded through what should have been an empty courtyard, eager for the comforts of my room.

Breaking free of the crowd, I hastened up the stairs to

the second floor of the apartment hall. When I threw open the door to my bedchamber, I found Lenghan sitting at the foot of my bed.

My hand flew to my chest. "You wee bastard. Do you wish to frighten me onto my pyre?"

Lenghan laughed. "If you're unaccustomed to finding me in your chamber, lass, then perhaps I haven't been doing my duty by you."

"Oh, aye? And is that what you've come to do? Your *duty*?"

"Well," said Lenghan, arching one blond eyebrow. Rising, he bridged the space between us. We were of a height—Lenghan broad and of a middling stature, while I was tall and lean—and so his lips found mine with uncommon ease. He tasted of woodsmoke, ale, and bright mountain's mint, as alluring as it was familiar. With a self-satisfied humph, he pulled away. "Forgive me?" he teased.

A derisive snort of humor escaped me. If I were being honest, something about Lenghan's casual command of my bedchamber rankled me. Though the rented room wasn't mine in deed, it served as a personal sanctuary. The only place where I could be, for a few fleeting moments, alone.

"Why have you come?" I asked. Setting aside my surgical tools, I drew the woolen cloak from my shoulders and hung it on the peg near the door.

"Is it not enough that I should wish to see you?" Lenghan's hands found my hips. When I cut him a hard look, he snorted. "Fine. I came to see if you'd celebrate with me."

"Celebrate?"

"Imbelaine is upon us, Clìana. Will you not have a bit of fun?"

I envisioned the streets of Aversere—the crush of bodies, the pungent smells, the untempered gaiety. I sighed his name.

"One night," he pleaded, plucking my cloak from its peg. "Give me one night, Clìana. You ken you work too hard as it is."

"Which is why I should sleep."

"Which is why you should dance a reel, aye? Have a nip of cider? If not for your sake, then for mine." He held my cloak out to me. "It would do me good to see you smile, lass."

"*Lenghan*," I said pointedly.

"*Clìana*," he replied.

Instinctively, my eyes fluttered shut. I didn't want to make merry in the streets. I didn't want to pretend at joy while others laughed, danced, drank, and sang. Lenghan knew this. Still, he pushed. Maybe he made his request in hope, from a genuine desire to see me return to some semblance of the carefree lass I'd once been. Or maybe it was something else he wanted. Something—*someone*—to shape and mold to his whim. At the time, I didn't suspect the latter. But even if I had, I doubt it would have mattered. Because for eight long years, I had craved the ache of pain as surely as the rush of a scalpel in hand. To atone for the hurts I could not heal—and to prove to myself that I was yet alive.

With a small nod, I drew my cloak around my shoulders and followed Lenghan out into the night.

✦

I'd never been one for revelry. I didn't care for large crowds or the cacophony of celebration. A walk through the city on market day offered plenty to tolerate, let alone the crush of the Òengar Road on the night of Imbela's dawning. Yet that was where I found myself, my hand in Lenghan's as he tugged me through the heart of the thoroughfare. The air of festivity was a smothering pall. The heat of bonfires licked at each street corner, the thick stench of smoke mingling with stale sweat and the heavy aroma of roasted meats. A peal of laughter cut through the din, chased by the call of a tin whistle. Desperate for reprieve, I pulled Lenghan into the nearest alley, a crooked little space between two jagged buildings.

"What's wrong?" he asked.

I shook my head. "I shouldn't have come."

A deep crease formed between Lenghan's brows before his features softened. "I remember when you used to dance. When we were wee, aye? Your limbs long and graceful, stretched all about. Do you not remember?"

The words stung like the light from a candle struck suddenly in a darkened room. I pressed my hands against Lenghan's chest, as if my mere touch could silence his reminiscing.

"Stars, you're shivering," he said, taking up my hands as if to warm them.

An unnatural flush of heat coursed through me then, prompting beads of sweat to pool at my temples despite the frigid air. When I realized what Lenghan had done, I gasped. "I didn't ken you could—"

"I've been practicing," he said quickly, his deep-set eyes glittering in the moonlight. "I could show you more, if you'd like. I could teach you."

He must have seen the panic in my stare. Instead of waiting for my reply, he pulled me back into the crush of the crowd. Mindlessly, I followed him, too overwhelmed by the unnatural warmth humming through my veins to resist. He bought me a tin of ale from one of the stalls on the street, then an egg-lacquered pastry fragrant with nutmeg and studded with cloves. When the elderly merchant noted the feathers in our hair—each plume signifying one of the healing arts we had mastered—he refused the coin Lenghan offered in payment. Such generosity wasn't uncommon in the streets of Aversere, where the healers of Clan Larmach were revered for their skill. We knew better than to argue and thus give offense.

I felt a wee bit steadier as the food settled in my wame. To my dismay, I couldn't recall the last time I'd eaten. Had I managed a quick supper at Castle Tarne? Or had the Kelkevie brothers kept me from my meal? I had only a moment to consider this before Lenghan led me up a flight of stairs to the gallery that overlooked the city's largest market square. A ripple of tartan caught my eye as we leaned against the balustrade. The center of the square had been cleared for a wrestling match; and two men now circled each other, goading back and forth as they grappled for a firm hold. Spectators pressed closer as the bout intensified, then roared with approval as the larger man heaved the smaller over his shoulder with a grunt. I winced as the opponent's back slammed against the hard-packed earth. Even from a distance, I could tell that the fall had knocked the wind out of him. Metal glinted among the crowd as coins passed between hands and the victor beat his chest in triumph.

I wasn't surprised when another man pushed his way

into the ring. Wrestling was a common sport in the high-lands, where the blood of the Daor burned hot and fierce. There was hardly a wedding, festival, or wake that didn't see a few rounds of friendly brawling. I nestled into my corner of the balustrade as the next round began. A few spectators shouted words of encouragement. Others stood with heads bent low, whispering in one another's ears. Something seemed amiss.

That was when I noticed the disturbance at the north end of the square, where the crowd had begun to part. A finely dressed nobleman made his way through the throng. Tall and broad, his muscular physique commanded attention as surely as his air of importance. Whispers filled the square as he swayed left and right, drunkenly kissing anyone unlucky enough to catch his eye.

"Blessed Imbela!" the man cried, and the crowd echoed the refrain. His face awash with ecstasy, he gathered up a pale-haired lass by the waist and squeezed.

"Och, Ulmhar!" someone shouted in a voice like thunder.

Silence settled over the square. The victor from the ring pushed his way through the townsfolk, heading straight toward the offending nobleman. *Ulmhar*, he had said. No wonder the square had rippled with excitement at the man's arrival. Sir Ulmhar Dalmorie was Bright Lord Dalmorie's nephew and war chief—and soon to be Daorender's new lord protector, if the rumors were true. He was renowned for his skill with a blade, as befit any war chief worth his sword arm.

"BacMannen!" Sir Ulmhar shouted, undaunted by the bear of a man stalking toward him. With another squeeze, he released the lass and raised a hand in greeting. "How do you fare, man?"

"None so well, seeing as your hands are on my wife."

I sighed. There was humor in BacMannen's voice, but I knew the highland way. With or without offense, this encounter would likely end in bruising or bloodshed. Mentally, I recounted the small supply of medical necessities I kept in the sporran cinched around my waist. Little more than a tin of salve, a short length of catgut, and a needle.

"Who? Not the blond lassie, surely?" said Sir Ulmhar, his words bleeding one into another. "I was told you prefer bedding the pigs and the sheep."

"Oh, aye? And who told you that, you wee bastard?"

"You'd be surprised what your mother will admit when she's well-pleased, man."

Laughter rang through the crowd as something between the two men shifted.

"Are you sure you want an audience for it?" said Sir Ulmhar, thumping BacMannen on the shoulder. "Have you no mind for your pride?"

"Enough to bring to blows the man who worries my wife in front of all the town. Eh?"

"Aye. Well, let's get to it, then." Sir Ulmhar grinned like a fiend. Casting aside his weapons, the war chief shed his greatcoat and stripped to the waist before following BacMannen to the center of the square.

"Two coppers on the common-born?" said the woman beside me, holding two gnarled fingers aloft as the men bent low, their hands snaked out in search of purchase. I dismissed her offer. Had I been one to bet, I would have placed twice as many silvers on Sir Ulmhar. Despite his opponent's hulking stature, it seemed a bonny wager.

Tempted, I turned back to accept the offer when a man's cry, low and animal, tore through the square. It was a cry I knew well, one that drove me to action as surely as a war drum beckoned soldiers to the battlefield. Pushing away from the balustrade, I plunged into the thick of the crowd.

# CHAPTER 2

Sir Ulmhar lay groaning in a pool of mud that smelled strongly of whisky. From the broken slats scattered beneath him, I could only surmise that BacMannen had sent him crashing into an ill-placed crate of the drink. But what mattered wasn't the whisky. It was the splinter of wood that now protruded from Sir Ulmhar's eye, its rough surface tinged a putrid shade of orange in the light of nearby braziers.

"Holy Stars!" someone shouted.

"Someone fetch a surgeon!" said another, but there was no need. I'd already trampled down the gallery stairs and cut my way through the busy square, the masses parting as word of the presence of a Larmach healer spread. BacMannen stood above Sir Ulmhar, looking horror-struck. I brushed him aside, dropped to my knees, and took the war chief's face between my hands.

Up close, I saw the lines that spread like fissures from the corners of the war chief's eyes and across his brow. He wasn't as young as I'd first thought, though he'd not yet reached middle age. His skin was taut, and his chestnut hair showed only a hint of gray. When he glanced up at me, his expression was pained but present, the iris a startling shade of blue.

"Still now, Sir Ulmhar. Aye?" I said. "You must be absolutely still."

His hand trembled as it wrapped around my wrist. His calloused grip was slick with sweat. "Do as you must," he urged between gritted teeth. Then his hand fell away, and his uninjured eye went wide and glassy, his head swaying with shock.

Biting back a curse, I tightened my grasp on his face. "I need light—and *space*," I said as the crowd pressed in, no doubt eager for fresh gossip and a glimpse of a Larmach healer at work. "And someone to fetch the bright lord's men."

My orders seemed to rouse BacMannen from his shock. As he barked commands of his own, I returned my attention to Sir Ulmhar. For the first time since Lenghan had whisked me from my bedchamber, the viselike grip on my lungs had eased. In the face of gruesome injury, I came alive, my mind and body fully engaged in this battle between life and death.

Pushing aside a shock of Sir Ulmhar's sweat-slicked hair, I assessed the wound more closely. The sliver was sharp and thin. Its point had pierced the sclera just beside the tear duct, narrowly avoiding the iris but severing a host of tiny veins that left the eye red with bloodshot. This time, I couldn't hold back a curse. Sir Ulmhar was going to lose all use of the eye, if not the eye itself. Still, he needn't lose his life. The sliver tapered to a narrow point where it protruded from the ocular tissue, making it unlikely that the fragment had pierced his brain—at least not yet.

Sir Ulmhar shifted beneath my touch, his chest fluttering as he gasped for breath.

"You must be still, Sir Ulmhar." The hard edge in my voice did little to calm the war chief's rising panic. Low moans bubbled up from his throat as he tried to push himself upright. Each movement was an opportunity for the splinter to sink deeper into his eye socket. Gripping his shoulders, I pressed him to the ground. "You're all right, sir. You're all right. But you *must* lie still."

Swift as an adder, Sir Ulmhar clutched my arms and shoved. I tumbled back, grunting as my elbow jolted against the hard-packed earth. No sooner had he struggled to his hands and knees than his heavy body slumped, his wide eye slipping shut as he sank into the depths of unconsciousness. Lunging, I grabbed him to ensure he landed on his back.

"All right, lass?" Lenghan said, crouching beside me.

A long beat passed as I stared at him, struggling to reconcile his presence at my side. He must have followed me through the crowded square, but I hadn't thought of him since I had first heard Sir Ulmhar's cry. My gaze shifted between Lenghan's face and Sir Ulmhar's body, my skin prickling with suspicion. "Did you—?"

"Aye." The word confirmed what I'd suspected: Lenghan had used his unnatural power to ease Sir Ulmhar into unconsciousness before the man could injure himself further. I studied Lenghan's face, unsettled by his unholy power and the recklessness with which he'd used it—in so public a place, with so much attention upon us. But if

Lenghan feared the consequences of his actions, he concealed his worry. "Best be quick about it now, lass."

The reminder startled me from my stupor. He was right, of course. Even with Sir Ulmhar unconscious, the splinter would have to be removed while we were in the square. Transporting the war chief to a proper surgery posed too grave a risk. The jolting of a wagon would only drive the sliver closer to his brain. Nay, the work would have to be done by hand beneath Imbela's eye—and the sooner, the better.

Forking two fingers, I peeled Sir Ulmhar's eyelids from the site of the wound before gripping the splinter between my forefinger and thumb and beginning to tug. A bead of sweat trickled down my brow as the rough wood bit into the pads of my fingers. Clenching my teeth, I let the world fall away and applied firm upward pressure, careful not to complicate the injury. The splinter gave way slowly, rising bit by bit until it slipped free all at once, like the sudden arrival of a babe. Blood and viscous fluid coated its tip. I flung the splinter aside as a proud sort of elation flooded through me. Beneath my touch, Sir Ulmhar didn't so much as moan, lost to the sweet relief of the Black.

It wasn't long before the bright lord's men arrived. One stood beside Lenghan, looming over me as I continued tending to Sir Ulmhar. The others corralled the crowd and fetched a wagon to transport the war chief to his apartments at Castle Highdale, where his uncle kept court over Daorender.

While we waited, I lifted the war chief's swollen eyelid. Vitreous wept from the site of the wound, thick and bilious. I swallowed a sigh. Suturing ocular tissue was difficult at any time of day, let alone in the dark of night. Even Imbela's eye was none so fiery as to be of aid. The task would have to wait until we arrived at Castle Highdale, where the bright lord's court surgeon would no doubt usurp my role. I swallowed another sigh at the thought of Cannan Larmach administering the necessary stitches, then pulled a clean handkerchief from my sporran. Closing the lid of Sir Ulmhar's injured eye, I used the handkerchief to pad the wound, tearing a strip of cloth from the hem of my shift to use as binding.

As I cinched the fabric tight around Sir Ulmhar's head, something sharp stung the pad of my right forefinger. A tiny wooden sliver jutted from the calloused skin. I grasped it with the tips of my nails and tugged, frowning at the thick bead of blood that arose as it sprang free.

"Here," said Lenghan, pressing a handkerchief into my palm. A strange sensation danced across my skin as he made a show of dabbing at the blood. When he withdrew, only unmarred skin remained. My heart pounded with sudden intensity, stirred equally by fear and wonder. For the third time that night, Lenghan had demonstrated the unnatural power he possessed. There was no time for me to consider why before the bright lord's men returned.

"I could teach you," Lenghan said softly as I climbed into the wagon bed. Two men lifted the war chief into the wagon, settling his head in the cradle of my lap.

"Slow and steady, if you please," I said to the wagoner, feeling the heat of Lenghan's attention upon me. Then we were off, the night whirling around us as Imbela burned high above.

Shadows inked the corners of Sir Ulmhar's bedchamber at Castle Highdale, encroaching on the vast expanse of the richly furnished room. I asked the servants to stir the hearth and light candles as the bright lord's men carried the war chief to his bed.

A moment later, Cannan Larmach swept into the room like a cutting wind. He was gangly, all long, sinewy limbs and hawkish bones. And with him, he carried an air of such cold arrogance that I fought the urge to shrink back in his presence. Loath as I was to admit it, he was doubtless the finest healer the clan had produced in a generation. If it weren't for his responsibility as heir to Clan Larmach, he might have ascended to serve in courts far greater than could be found in Daorender. But Young Lord Larmach wasn't free to leave the highlands to seek glory in some grand and distant hall. Not as I was. Perhaps that was why he didn't so much as look at me as he hurried to the war chief's side.

Hanging a lantern from the bedpost, he assessed Sir Ulmhar's injured eye. "You removed the splinter in the courtyard?" he said with a voice like nails on stone.

"Aye, Young Lord," I replied evenly.

"Describe it to me."

"The injury? Or the splinter?"

"Both." Young Lord Larmach cut me a sharp look. "And your removal of the latter."

Quickly, I relayed the night's events. When I was through, the young lord made a small noise at the back of his throat that I understood to be a dismissal. Annoyance thrummed in my veins. Despite my efforts in the square,

Young Lord Larmach wasn't going to relinquish his role as the bright lord's chief surgeon so that I might stitch Sir Ulmhar's wound—not when I'd already seized the opportunity to remove the splinter myself.

Swallowing my disappointment, I strode from the war chief's bedchamber and allowed one of the bright lord's carriages to ferry me home.

I remember wishing I was alone that night.

It wasn't Lenghan's touch that reviled me—his arm curled around my waist, his rib cage pressed to the column of my spine—but rather the way he warmed my bed in the most literal of senses. The man's body was a Black-damned brazier. Even the wisps of cold air that trailed through the casement window couldn't quench the heat of his breath on the nape of my neck. Still, I lay silently in his embrace, welcoming the distraction. Better to be over-whelmed by his warmth than to dwell on the unsettling power he had worked earlier in the night.

Lenghan hadn't possessed the knowledge to use such power in the days of our youth. We'd spent our time as weans playing beside hearth fires and in the garden patches where our mothers worked, growing herbs and roots for use in healing. Lenghan had reveled in teasing me during those days. He made a game of plucking foul-tasting leaves from the garden beds, daring me to eat them if I couldn't name their source. Other times, he'd grip me by my ear or elbow and refuse to let go until I'd identified the bones that lay beneath his grasp. Soon, I learned to give as Lenghan gave—and my mind proved itself the cannier. Lenghan had bristled at this revelation. But then he had come of age to study in the guild, and our childish rivalry came to an end.

While Lenghan attended lectures, I helped my father in the grand archive and minded my wee sister, Ailis, as my mother worked. I saw even less of Lenghan when I began my own studies the next year. Never mind that we lived and learned within the same walls. Clan Larmach trained its students from dawn 'til dusk, eager to maintain the power and respect it had cultivated over hundreds of years of service. On occasion, Lenghan and I would greet each other in passing or share a few words as we broke our fast, but those times were brief. The bond between us had withered until the day when . . .

My blood ran cold as I thought of the body at the base of the stairs.

I shoved the vision from my mind, flooding its absence with thoughts of Lenghan. The jut of his jaw. The soothing brush of his knuckles. That wretchedly sweet voice of his that had once filled me with so much promise. And now? What had become of that promise? Once, I had clung to the comforts of his body and the company of his mind. But something between us had shifted. It wasn't just the growing boldness with which he practiced his power that unsettled me, nor even his gentle insistence that I should learn that power for myself.

Nay. It was something within *me* that was changing. Each day, I yearned a little more for the ghosts of years gone by and the road that lay ahead, for possibility and the voice that prompted me to be more. To be *great*. To be . . .

"Cliana?" The rasp of Lenghan's voice trailed me as I stumbled from the bed, desperate to relieve the grip that choked my lungs. The bedsheets rustled as he sat up.

"I cannot sleep," I said. Leaning against the windowsill, I drew in long sips of the frigid air that snaked through the crack in the shutters.

A sigh rumbled in Lenghan's chest. "All this restlessness, this sorrow. She wouldn't want it for you, lass."

"*She* wouldn't want to be *dead*," I snapped, glaring at him.

Lenghan scowled, his jaw tightening. His frustration softened the edges of my anger.

"Nor forgotten," I added softly.

Lenghan rubbed his hands along the bare length of his thighs. The fire within him seemed to fade as the silence stretched between us. I looked once more through the gap in the casement window. My apartment faced west, where the Lady of Fire had disappeared beneath the swell of distant mountains. The Imbelaine festivities would begin in earnest when She returned at dusk. Until then, there was work to be done.

Dressing, I donned my stays and woolen doublet, my overskirt dashed with the muted blues and grays that marked me as kin to Clan Larmach. I ignored the heavy weight of Lenghan's gaze on my back as I combed the tangles from my hair, careful to avoid catching my feathers in the tines.

"Take some rest," I said, settling my cloak around my shoulders. "There is an hour yet 'til dawn."

"My love is with you, Clìana."

The words stilled me at the threshold. I wasn't surprised by the proclamation. Lenghan had spoken of his love for me before, whispering it along the shell of my ear, sated in the wake of our coupling. Once, I had said the same in kind. But there was an edge to his voice now, a note of desperation. I inhaled as it cut through me. He'd caught scent of the ache growing within me, I realized. That was why he'd used his power so prolifically earlier in the night, and why he'd offered to teach me its use. He knew of my growing unease and what Imbela's arrival might mean for me. And he didn't want to let me go.

Glancing back, I offered him a small, sad smile before closing the door behind me.

# CHAPTER 3

I paced the length of the guildhall's courtyard until dawn, thinking of the feathers twined into my hair. Each one signified a healing art I had mastered. Though I bore one-and-twenty in total, there was one I yet lacked. This final feather kept me bound to Aversere, ever an apprentice until I earned the honor to wear it—and I *would* earn it. Some would say I already had, given the measure of my skill. But Erune had yet to deem me a master healer; and it was her right to withhold that title until my dying day if she saw fit.

I willed away the bitterness that rose within me. Erune had never been cruel or unjust. On the contrary, I suspected she was as sage and skilled a tutor as they came. Still, something led her to withhold my final feather. I'd thought long and hard about her reasoning over the last year. But try as I might, I couldn't understand it. Tamping down my irritation, I readied one of Lord Larmach's horses for the ride to Castle Tarne.

The stench of woodsmoke clouded my nose as the

mare and I made our way through the streets of Aversere, the heavy smell hanging like a canopy over the city after the night's bonfires. It was an early morning for most who had followed Imbela's arrival, and I passed through many empty streets. Disquieted by the stillness, I urged the horse into a trot until the avenues broadened. Townhouses and shop fronts gave way to storehouses and stables, then to small crofts and open fields. Soon, the turrets of Castle Tarne rose on the horizon. The keep stood at the mouth of the Serenault, where the river poured into the broad embrace of Loch Argan. Sunlight slid between the clouds as I rode, glistening on the distant peaks and painting the sky in broad swaths of red and gold, an echo of Imbela's fire.

Of the many Stars that hung watchful in the night sky, Imbela was of the highest order and the most sacred esteem. Astral tradition declared that Her dawning marked the arrival of warm earth and swift waters, bounty and new birth. Echoing the Bright Star as She burned away the burdens of a long winter, the Daor sacrificed their burdens to ceremonial bonfires during Imbelaine. The practice was said to ease the pains that plagued one's heart, and Stars knew I bore many. But rather than give them to the fires, I tended to them as one might a fragile seedling, allowing them to nourish my pursuit of greatness.

With a shaking breath, I pushed the thought from my mind and focused on the work to come. The people of Daorender celebrated Imbelaine with three long nights of revelry. The festivities drew to a close when the Lady of Fire rose above Niamhar, the steel gray planet that shone pale as a river pearl from the first frost until the last. Until then, a host of preparations needed to be made.

Imbela had long ago woven the blood of the highlands with the fire of Her blessing; and with that fire, the Daor had grown into a headstrong, brazen people. Thanks to their bold tempers and unchecked pride, there was no doubt that blood would flow as free as whisky in the nights to come. Bodies would be bruised and bones crushed, stomachs would roil and dignities would be tested. There was little anyone could do for the latter. But for the ailments of the flesh, Clan Larmach would serve as their oaths demanded.

But before the healing could begin, there was work to be done: herbs to harvest, instruments to sharpen, and bandages to cut and sew. In truth, the clan's preparations had begun weeks before. As had my own, for Imbelaine and beyond.


I hadn't known true, untempered anger since the day Ailis had died. As her body burned atop her pyre, I had raged against the cruelty of the Stars, shouting such ugly, heretical words that Lenghan had dragged me out of the Sanctuary at the luminaries' insistence. But as my sister's spirit had risen to the bosom of the Dark, the fire within me had given way to the unyielding grip of grief. I hadn't felt such rage again until I entered the surgery at Castle Tarne that day and was greeted by the sight of Erune standing over one of the Kelkevie lads, his shoulder clearly out of its socket.

As the story went, the brothers had decided to see which among them could land cleanly from the highest stair in the castle. The challenge had yielded several bumps and bruises, but one of the younger brothers had suffered the unluckiest fate. I tried not to think of Ailis, her body broken at the bottom of a staircase, as I popped the lad's shoulder back into its joint with an audible crack.

Were the brothers' injuries—always banal and never ceasing—not a monumental waste of my skill? Was this truly how I was to spend my life, seeing to wounds that a first-year student could just as easily mend? I fought the urge to rage at Erune, at the Kelkevie brothers, at the Stars themselves. I knew the inclination was mad. It wasn't my post that angered me. Rather, it was Erune's refusal to name me a master healer. I wanted to run as far from Daorender as I could, to make peace with my sister's loss somewhere I wouldn't see her ghost in every corner. But I could only make that peace if I sought the greatness Ailis had seen within me, and there was no greatness for me here in Daorender.

With a heavy sigh, I bound the Kelkevie lad's arm in a sling and urged him not to shirk the bandages the second he left the surgery. When he was gone, Erune appraised me. Whatever she saw made her eyebrows knit low with worry.

"You look tired, lass," she said.

I fought the urge to turn away from her appraisal. I didn't want to feel the concern in her touch; I wanted *freedom*. I wanted to earn my final feather so I could leave this Black-damned realm behind me and seek glory in Carastile.

"I suspect few slept long last night, my lady."

With a humph, Erune leaned back against the worktable and withdrew a folded piece of parchment from the pocket of her skirt. "'To the honorable Lady Erune of Clan Larmach,'" she read aloud from the missive. "'I extend an invitation to you and your apprentice, the mistress Clìana Goddan, to join me in celebrating Imbelaine at Castle Highdale this night in gratitude for services rendered on behalf of my nephew, Sir Ulmhar, war chief of Clan Dalmorie.'" Lowering the parchment, she pinned me with a hard look. "I've heard stories, you ken."

"None so mundane as the truth, I suspect."

Erune scoffed. "Pulling a sliver of wood from the lord protector's eye after a drunken brawl?"

"He's no lord protector yet." Turning, I collected a bundle of dried thyme that hung from the rafters. "And now he may never be so."

"Yet one would think your actions remain worthy of note," Erune replied. "Of *more* than note, perhaps?"

I stilled as I reached for a mortar and pestle. "Of more than note," I repeated, willing my tone not to betray the sudden pounding of my pulse.

"Do you ken why I withhold your final feather, lass?"

I drew a steadying breath as I turned to face her. "My skill is not yet worthy of the plume," I said carefully.

Erune gave a half-hearted laugh. "You ken I didn't think you fit when you first begged your apprenticeship of me? You were an understudent of little note, the true extent of your skill untapped. Yet your insistence spoke to your potential. With every feather you earned, you proved my assessment unfit. But the role of a master healer relies on more than skill alone." She took a step toward me. "Do you remember what you said to me, when you begged me to take you on as my apprentice?"

The memory struck me like a wicked blow. *I was a child, my lady,* I had said. *A soft-pated slip of a lass. But that lass is dead now. She burned to ash on my sister's pyre.*

"Your grief is an open wound." Erune's calloused fingers curled around my hands. "I would see you go out into this world, Clìana, in the full knowledge that you are *living* in it."

I fought the urge to recoil as bitterness rose within me. It had never been some deficiency in my skill that had led Erune to withhold my final feather, but rather my refusal to pretend that I was something other than what I was. To feign that so much needless death had left me unaffected.

"I ken this world, my lady," I said through gritted teeth. "And it is cruel."

"Aye," came Erune's soft reply. "But it can also be kind, if you let it." She gave my hands a gentle squeeze. "Come with me to Castle Highdale tonight, Clìana. Send forth your burdens. Give them to the fires."


I met Erune in the guildhall's courtyard at dusk. Though Imbela hadn't yet risen, a cacophony of celebratory sounds already rose above the resonant call of smallpipes that beckoned the city to the night's festivities.

"Ready, then?" Erune called from the dark confines of the Kelkevies' carriage.

Joining her on the plush velvet seat, I smoothed the wrinkles in my overskirt. The sage-green wool was finer than my typical blues and grays. Its matching bodice was offset by a stomacher embroidered with feathers. I tugged at the capelet that topped my attire, the silky black badger fur tickling the nape of my neck. Erune wore similar finery, as was appropriate for any guest at Bright Lord Dalmorie's court.

Erune and I said little as the carriage plodded up the

Great Road, slowing as it passed through several packed market squares. I fiddled with the edge of my knitted gauntlets as we journeyed north, rattling over Castle Bridge and the rush of the Serenault before drawing to a stop in Castle Highdale's outer bailey. As I alighted from the carriage, I glanced up. The sky was a wide swath of navy silk, pinned by silver Stars. With only the merest hint of sunlight in the west, Imbela would soon lift her head in greeting.

Tucking my hand in the crook of her arm, Erune led me through the gathering in the castle's inner courtyard, then up a flight of stairs to the keep. Bright Lord Dalmorie's hall rose around us, its walls lined with tapestries depicting battles of yore. Long tables capped with benches lined the center walkway, offering the bright lord's guests an opportunity for respite from the cold. At the far end of the room, the bright lord sat beside his husband and their young daughter, greeting his guests as they came to pay fealty.

"Lady Erune," said Bright Lord Dalmorie, nodding in greeting when we bowed before him. He was plain, his build and features almost entirely unremarkable. If he'd been common-born, few would have paid him mind. But a circlet of gold captured more attention than a striking face. "Mistress Clìana," he addressed me as I rose. "I heard tell of your deeds on my nephew's behalf. Clan Dalmorie is in your debt."

I bent my head in acknowledgment. "I trust Sir Ulmhar is recovering."

"Aye," said the bright lord. "Though regrettably, Young Lord Larmach tells me he will not regain use of his eye."

"I'm sorry to hear it," I replied, though I hadn't suspected otherwise.

Bright Lord Dalmorie made a soft noise of regret that both acknowledged my words and served as an end to our conversation.

I frowned as Erune led me back to the courtyard. She had been uncommonly quiet since our arrival; and though I couldn't say why, there was an edge to her silence that made me bristle. Blessedly, the call of greatpipes smothered the question that rose within me. We turned our heads in unison with the bright lord's guests, watching as Imbela rose in the east.

"Make merry, lass," she said when the moment's stillness devolved into drinking and dancing. "And make right what you can bear to make right, aye?"

After giving my arm a squeeze, she was gone, the crown of her gray-black hair disappearing into the throng of celebration.

Sighing, I set about finding a drink. Unlike most highlanders, I didn't care for spirits. I knew healers who claimed that downing a dram honed their focus as they took up a scalpel or bone saw, but whisky had only ever dulled my senses. But with the close crush of celebration and Erune's voice echoing in my ear, I decided that a wee nip of cider wouldn't be unwelcome.

After a second sip, the world seemed a little surer, a touch less in disarray. I appraised the courtyard, dissecting the chaos of celebration as I might the trauma of a broken, bleeding body: to better understand the battle into which I had stepped. To my left, a short flight of stairs descended to the castle gardens, where the music of tin whistles and bodhráns carried up to fill the courtyard. Ale cups clanked from the parapets while the bright lord's guests shouted greetings over the din, their heels clacking as they reeled. Beneath it all, Imbela's bonfires droned.

A sense of calm seeped into my bones as I observed the festivities from afar. Then a man broke from the crowd and spewed the contents of his wame against the wall near my boots.

I smothered a disgruntled sigh as I darted away from him. What I wouldn't have given for a surgery to call my own, a place where I could lose myself in the work of my trade. Better a battle against death than a celebration among the living. But there would be no surgery for me to call my own until Erune saw fit to name me a master healer.

*Send forth your burdens. Give them to the fires.*

The memory of Erune's words soured the cider on my tongue. Passing my cup to a servant, I weaved through the courtyard toward the bright blaze of a bonfire.

The flames sizzled and snapped at the dry parchment like a frog snatching flies from the still summer air. I stood near the blaze, watching as highfolk came, one by one, to write their pains on wee scraps of paper before feeding them to Imbela's fire.

Earlier that day, when Erune had asked me to attend the bright lord's festivities, I'd told her that I ached for renewal the same as anyone else did. Yet what words could I write in confidence on my own slip of parchment? If renewal was anything like freedom, then I yearned for it as desperately as I wished to remake my sister's fate. My desire for freedom, however, was no burden I wanted to cast aside. If I wished to become a master healer—if I wished to pursue the greatness Ailis had seen in me—then I would need to leave the high glens of Daorender. There was no glory for me here, within reach of those who held my heart.

Lenghan rose to my mind, a storm of passion and unholy power. Already, there was so much he wanted of me that I could not give. Then there was Erune, whose kind heart and open arms felt more like a prison than a sanctuary. I knew what it was to love another. I also knew the fierce, unrelenting ache of loss—the torment that chafed raw as any open wound. And I was no longer willing to pay the cost.

Crossing the courtyard to the small table that held parchment and ink, I wrote down the meager burden I had to offer, the only one I'd known for eight long years to be true:

*I ache for the pains I cannot heal.*

Folding the parchment in half, I fed it to the flames. The scrap caught on the edge of the brazier and tugged for a second, fluttering, before curling in slow demise.

# CHAPTER 4

When I turned away from the fire, I spotted Erune leaning against the castle wall nearby, watching me with keen eyes. As I drew near her, I noted the tiny emerald plume clutched between her fingertips. "Is it Carastile for you then, lass?" she asked.

I blinked at her in surprise. Erune had known of my desire to serve at the emperor's court, but it wasn't something we had openly discussed. I glanced at her, then once more at the feather between her fingers. My mind whirred as the reality of the moment sank into my bones. "My lady—"

"The emperor should consider himself honored," Erune said, regarding me with her steady gaze.

Before I could form a coherent response, a servant approached us, his wiry eyebrows raised in expectation. "Mistress Clìana?"

"Aye," I managed, feeling as though I was being jerked about by unseen hands.

"Sir Ulmhar wishes to speak with you."

Once more, I was taken by surprise. I glanced back at Erune.

"Go on, lass," she said, her gnarled fingers closing around mine as she pressed the feather into my palm. "We'll speak more on the morrow."

"If you'd follow me," said the servant, turning on his heel.

With one final, wide-eyed look at Erune, I followed, allowing the servant to lead me away from the thrum of celebration. The feather in my hand fluttered as we rounded the corner of Castle Highdale's hulking keep. An icy wind cut through the dark passageway between buildings. I tucked the feather into my sporran before the breeze could carry it away.

I had barely a breath to consider why Sir Ulmhar might wish to speak with me before the servant ushered me into a small courtyard. Spindly shrubbery hemmed a square of low stone benches that likely saw little use this time of year. A lone figure stood in the center of the square, one hand splayed against the trunk of a blackthorn tree.

"Sir Ulmhar?" I balked at the sight of him. He was standing—*standing*, damn him—as though he'd not been gravely injured the night before.

"Ah, so you're the lass, then." Sir Ulmhar's lazy smile was likely meant to charm me. But his body swayed as he tried to rise to his full height, and the smile bled into a grimace. "Mistress Clìana," he said, nodding in greeting.

I hastened to his side, ready to brace him should he stumble. "I thought I'd meet your summons in your bedchamber."

Sir Ulmhar snorted at the unintended insinuation in

my words, and my cheeks grew warm. "I've not broken a leg, mistress," he said. "I can walk."

"Can you?" Raising my brows in doubt, I directed him toward one of the stone benches. "Come. Let me have a look at it."

The war chief gave a heavy sigh. "Och. Go on, then."

Between the full moon and the braziers in the courtyard, there was enough light for me to make a simple assessment of the injury. Carefully, I unwrapped the layers of cloth that protected the wound, noting the swollen and bruised skin that surrounded Sir Ulmhar's eye. He winced as I peeled back his upper eyelid. Sympathetic to his pain, I assessed the wound as quickly as I could, pausing only long enough to gauge that Cannan Larmach had sutured the torn ocular tissue with masterful wee stitches. I let out a humph as I lowered the eyelid.

"Well, then. Will I live?" Sir Ulmhar asked as I rewrapped the bandages to bind his eye.

A quiet laugh escaped me. "Aye, though you'll do well not to heed the call of your feet toward yonder courtyard." I gestured toward the castle's inner bailey, where the bright lord's Imbelaine festivities were well underway.

"Would you believe me if I said I'd only wanted a bit of fresh air?" His expression was uncharacteristically sheepish.

I tucked in the end of the bandage to keep the binding snug. "Will it bode ill for me if I express my doubt?"

He smirked. "Let us say, for the sake of my pride, that the extent of my injury had not been fully impressed upon me." He threw a hand toward the blackthorn tree. "I'd been standing there like a dullard—dizzy, ken?—before you walked through that arch."

"Humble words for one such as yourself, sir."

"Oh? And what 'one such' would that be, mistress?"

"A *man*, Sir Ulmhar," I replied, biting back a smile.

The war chief barked with laughter as I helped him to his feet. We took the first steps toward his chamber slowly, his arm braced around my shoulders.

"You're a canny lass," he mused. I could tell from the weight of his arm that he was trying not to lean too heavily upon me. "Fair to have around."

"I'm no trinket, Sir Ulmhar."

"Nay," he said, then lapsed into silence as we mounted the stairs that led to Castle Highdale's apartment hall. I could feel his body trembling with each step. When we reached the landing, he levered himself back against the wall and met my eye. "You're a healer."

"So I am," I replied.

After a moment's pause, Sir Ulmhar motioned for me to once more help him to his feet. Together, we made our way down the hall until we reached his bedchamber, where I deposited him in a low-backed chaise near the hearth. Turning, I added several logs to the fire.

"Whether I have one good eye or both," he said, "my uncle plans to name me lord protector when I've healed."

"A worthy honor, from what I hear."

He acknowledged the compliment with a nod. "They say you didn't hesitate to take charge of my care last night, barking orders as the crowd closed in." His gaze took on a degree of sobriety I wouldn't have thought possible of one who had so recently been inebriated out of his wits. It took me a beat to recognize the look as one of respect. "'Tis the same initiative needed in times of battle. My companies could use a healer of such fortitude."

It was all I could do not to gape at him. "Are you offering me a commission?"

He draped a hand over the back of the chaise and quirked an eyebrow. "What say you, mistress?"

The offer whirled through my mind. To serve under the Lord Protector of Daorender would offer a wealth of renown among the highlands. Yet it would keep me tethered here, in this land I'd been yearning to escape for so long. I shook my head. "I'm already bound for Carastile," I said without thinking.

"Carastile?" Sir Ulmhar said curiously. "You seek a commission at the Court of Stars?"

I fought the urge to pinch the space between my brows. The future lord protector sat before me, offering me a commission that many would commit violence to secure—and I'd rejected it without a moment's hesitation. In favor of seeking an unsolicited commission at the highest court in the eight realms, no less.

"Aye," I said dumbly, my mind reeling.

"You've earned your wee feather, then?" Sir Ulmhar asked, flashing a wicked grin. "On account of my eye?"

Once more, I was taken by surprise. At some point during the evening, Sir Ulmhar must have noted that I lacked the bright emerald plume that denoted a master healer—and which any Daor physician would need before seeking a commission at imperial court.

When I nodded, the war chief's countenance shifted into something that seemed almost reverential. "Well, then, Lady Clìana," he began. Something bright and warm blossomed in my chest at his use of my new courtesy title. "Let it not be I who stands in your way."

When I found my way back to the main courtyard, Erune was waiting for me. She must have sensed that the evening's events had exhausted me. "Eager for home, lass?" she said with a knowing smile.

We rode through Aversere in silence. When the carriage stopped before the guildhall's gates, Erune bid me good night. "Take some rest, Lady Clìana," she said as I alighted from the carriage. Something about her use of my new title didn't warm as dearly as Sir Ulmhar's had.

Still, the title echoed in my mind as I cut through the guildhall's crowded courtyard toward my bedchamber. Only a few hours earlier, Erune had pressed the emerald plume into my hand. It seemed an almost unreal occurrence, made all the more surreal by the events that had followed. I tried to wrap my mind around the reality of it all: the feather in my sporran, Sir Ulmhar's commission, and the confession I'd made in refusal. *I'm already bound for Carastile*, I had told him. I'd longed to say as much aloud for years—and now, at long last, I had.

"Clìana."

I startled as Lenghan darted toward me from the shadows of the apartment hall. "Stars!" I cried, then frowned when I noted Lenghan's ashen pallor. "What is it?"

He drew me back into the shadows. "I've been to see a diviner," he said, raising a hand to silence me when my lips parted in reply. "Aye, I ken you think little of them. But their power is none so different from our own."

I nearly scoffed at the daft notion. Diviners were said to be blessed of the Stars, capable of discerning futures in the shape and pattern of the night sky and in the Lights that reigned upon one's name day. Their gifts were considered sacred throughout the Astral Empire's eight realms—while knowledge of Lenghan's unnatural power could see him killed.

Too weary for a fight, I swallowed my rising retort. "What did they portend?" I asked instead.

Lenghan shifted his weight from one foot to the other. "Loss. The diviner saw loss."

My brow furrowed. "We're healers. 'Tis our fate to see such things."

"He did not speak of death, Clìana."

Our parting that morning rose suddenly to my mind, weighted with the unspoken truth that had passed between us. "Lenghan—"

"There is something I wish to show you," he said, grabbing my wrist.

I hurried to match his pace as he led me up the nearest stairwell. When we entered my bedchamber, he tasked me with lighting every candle in the room as he shed his woolen overcoat and waistcoat, his kilt swaying as he tossed the garments aside.

"What are you doing?" I asked as he rolled one shirt-sleeve to his elbow.

"Watch," he replied, taking up one of the scalpels from my roll of surgical tools. I watched in horror as he drew the blade swift and deep across his bare forearm.

"By the Black!" I wrestled the scalpel from his grasp. It clattered as I tossed it to the floorboards. "Have you gone mad?"

When I grabbed his wrist to examine the wound,

Lenghan shook free of me. Undaunted, I reached for him again.

"Stars! Just watch, Cliana, would you?"

The fierce insistence in his voice stilled me. There was no sign of fever in his gaze, nor any touch of feral temper. Beyond the faint shadow of dark circles beneath his eyes, he looked as he always had: young and eager. Only the hard set of his mouth spoke to the imperiousness with which he was known, on occasion, to act.

"All right," I relented.

A drop of blood fell to the floor as Lenghan pinned me with his gaze. After a beat, his eyes fluttered shut. The air vibrated almost imperceptibly, as if a taut cord had been plucked by an unseen hand. Or was that only a fancy in my mind? A chill finger traipsed up my spine as Lenghan worked.

I'd seen him practice bloodcraft before. He'd trusted me with the knowledge of it some eight years earlier, the same year I had trusted him with my bed. In the time since then, I had seen him perform only a few small wonders. Healing cuts. Easing pain. But the power he'd worked had always been mild in consequence, and he had only ever used it upon himself. When he'd warmed me on the night of Imbela's dawning, it had been the first time he'd practiced bloodcraft to my benefit. But even then, he'd not worked with such wild abandon as he did now.

His brow furrowed. His jaw tightened. Sweat gleamed in the hollows of his temples. Slowly, the flow of blood that wept from his wound weakened. I watched in thrall as the edges of his skin drew closed, then smoothed as if unmade by a brushstroke. A bone-deep shudder rattled through me. Then Lenghan used a cloth from his sporran to wipe away the blood that marred his skin. Only the faintest scar trailed the width of his forearm.

I trailed a finger along the ghost of the wound. "This should not be."

"And yet it is." Lenghan gleamed with rapture. "Can you not see the possibility in such power, Clìana?"

I cut him a hard look. "You cannot think to heal this way. Not publicly."

"It need not be conspicuous."

"Need not—" I pinched the bridge of my nose, exhaling sharply. Before I could question my sanity, I seized a clean scalpel from the worktable and drew the blade along the pale expanse of my forearm, hissing against the searing pain. "Go on, then," I said, thrusting my injured arm toward Lenghan. "Work the power within your blood."

His glare turned blistering. "And if I cannot?"

"Can't you?"

"And if I won't?"

I fought the urge to snarl at him. "Then I suppose I'd best start stitching."

Fury rolled in waves from the hard lines of his body, so palpable I could almost see it. Yet when Lenghan spoke again, his voice was quiet. "You could heal yourself, you ken. I could teach you."

I knew at once that he spoke of bloodcraft. Instinctively, I stepped back, as if recoiling. "*No.*"

"Clìana—"

"Heal the Black-damned wound, Lenghan!" I shouted, holding my arm out toward him once more. "You've shown me enough of your power without first asking whether I wished to see it. Aren't you now glad for my interest?"

The hearth fire crackled as we stared at each other, seething. Drop by drop, my blood splattered on the floor. After a beat, Lenghan snatched up my arm, yanking me toward him. My skin prickled as he worked his craft.

"Can you not see?" I said when the wound had been unmade. "If you have the power to stem the flow of my blood, could you not also drain me dry? Bloodcraft is reviled for a reason, Lenghan."

"And could you not turn your scalpel into something wicked?" Lenghan's white teeth flashed in the chasm of his mouth. "Your bone saw? Your wee tinctures and drams? You have the blood of Gode in you, Clìana. Think of how this power could aid in your work."

*Gode.* The name made my blood run cold. The ancient conjurer was said to have been mad, a healer who had wielded unnatural power over the body as a weapon to seize the Daor throne. He'd ruled the clans through the threat of pain for decades before his daughter had used her inherited power to murder him. Fearful, the clans had seized Morowen in turn, drowning her alongside her father's kin in the dark of a river pool. The line of Gode was said to have ended with Morowen, the surname Goddan deriving from some other source. And yet . . .

"There is a reason mothers yet whisper to their children of a conjurer who feeds upon wicked bairns," I said.

A vein ticked in Lenghan's jaw. "You would not stay even to learn such power?"

"No."

"Nor for any reason?"

"You ken there is only the shadow of death for me here," I said softly.

A humorless smile twisted Lenghan's lips. "Am I nothing, then? Not even the smallest of lights in your life?"

A wave of exhaustion rolled through me. I was tired—of Lenghan, of this talk of power, of the great ache inside me that threatened to devour me. "You *are* a light to me, Lenghan."

"But none so bright as to hold near, aye?"

Shame flooded through me, its heat crawling up my neck. Lenghan was right. I didn't love him as a woman ought to love a man, especially one who had offered me such care and attention in the midst of grief. But then, it had never been love that had bound us, had it? It had been something darker, each of us seeking to fill some unspoken need.

Silence stretched between us before Lenghan said, "I would ken what you fear, Clìana. Such that you do not want this great power in your blood."

Suddenly I wished nothing more than for him to understand. Maybe if he did, I could leave the highlands behind me, free of the weight of one more pain I couldn't heal.

"The stories of minds twisted," I said, taking up his hand in mine. "Of the dark of a river pool."

Lenghan scoffed. "Old bard's tales?"

"Are they not true?"

"And what if they are?" He tore his hand from my grasp. "The day may come when even the great skill of your hands is not enough to save a man from dying, Clìana. May you not live to regret your unwanted power then."

# CHAPTER 5

The following week, as the sun bowed its head toward the western horizon, I stared at the tiny emerald plume lying upon the worktable in my bedchamber.

For eight long years, I'd yearned to earn that feather, my chest aching with the need for it. Now it had been in my possession for six days, and I still hadn't taken to wearing it in my hair. Something about the idea of donning it made my palms sweat and my heart race, as if I stood upon the precipice of a ben, the wind screaming at my back. But I couldn't keep the feather confined to the worktable any longer. Tonight, the chief of Clan Larmach planned to hold court in the guild's gathering hall, and though it might have been Erune's right to name me a master healer, it wasn't her permission I needed to seek a commission at the Court of Stars. That privilege belonged to Diarnan Larmach, and I couldn't plead my case before him without the wee feather in my hair.

I stared at the plume for a few moments longer, listening to the sounds that floated through my open window: the yawn of a passing guard, the creak of a gate swinging shut, a few strains of bawdy music chased by the unfettered laugh of a drunkard. Each noise was as familiar to me as the scrape of a mortar and pestle. Yet tension hung heavy in the air all the same, gnawing at the edges of my nerves.

Feeling suddenly foolish, I plucked up the tiny plume with a huff and bound it into my nest of curls. Then, to keep myself from going mad while awaiting the gathering hour, I did as I had always done when faced with the threat of unraveling like a well-worn hem: unfurl my role of surgical tools and arrange them one by one on the worktable. Lancets and clamps, a pair of suture scissors, half a dozen scalpels, needle threaders, a sharp-toothed bone saw. I'd been a lass of six-and-ten when I'd selected the set, the same year Ailis had died and Erune had named me her apprentice. It had been a good selection, a set of simple steel-bladed surgeon's tools, impeccable in their make. Thumbing my whetstone into my hand, I let the low growl of scraping metal fill the air.

*We've a smith for such things, you ken. . . .*

Lenghan's chiding rose to my mind as I worked. He'd never understood why I loathed the expediency of taking my tools to the blacksmith for sharpening, and I'd never understood his desire for such help. A surgeon's tools were their trade, nearly as valuable as their mastery of the craft. I shuddered at the thought of handing off my set to anyone else to maintain. In any case, I found myself endeared to the task. With every sharpened blade, I lost myself a little more to the chore's repetition, forgetting the world around me for a short while.

Blade by blade, an hour passed, then another. The

tension in my chest unwound as I worked, only to snap back into place when the call of smallpipes rang through the guildhall.

Setting aside the whetstone, I rose to my feet. The time had come for me to learn my fate.

The gathering hall was nestled deep in the heart of the guildhall, a massive, buttressed building of hewn gray stone and towering glass windows. The room was warmly lit. Fires murmured in the hearths, and candlelight flickered in the heavy iron chandeliers hanging high above. The room's center walkway was hemmed with tables laden with food and drink, the path itself leading up to the dais where the clan chief presided. I glanced around the room as I entered, seeking out the bright blond cap of Lenghan's head. I hadn't crossed paths with him since the night we'd argued, and each day that had passed without sight of him had tightened the unease that gathered in my chest. I knew he was angry with me for wanting to leave. But to the best of my knowledge, he'd yet to learn that Erune had named me a master healer, and I feared what emotion might overtake him when he did.

I weaved through the hall in search of Erune, my pulse calming when I failed to find Lenghan among the crowd. Instead, it was Young Lord Larmach who caught my eye. The heir to the clan sat at the long table atop the dais. The seat to his right remained empty, reserved for the chief, though the lady of the clan was already seated on the other side of her husband's chair. The young lord's attention alighted on me briefly before flitting away.

With lips pressed thin, I found my way to Erune's side.

"Ah, there you are, lass." She patted the empty bench to her left. "Come, sit."

A hush settled over the room as I nestled down beside her. Diarnan Larmach cut an imposing figure as he took his seat upon the dais, his graying hair smoothed back behind his ears to reveal the blunt lines of his face. His features were crude as rough-hewn granite, and he appraised the room with an iron gaze.

"May all those of Clan Larmach be welcome," he said, holding his wineglass aloft.

One by one, folk from our clan arose from their suppers to bring their concerns before the chief. Erune seemed content to bide her time, happily eating as the evening waned. For my part, I could stomach little, my gut roiling in anticipation of the moment when Erune would present me before Lord Larmach for his approval. I focused on him as I waited, as though mapping his face might reveal some way I could fix myself more firmly in his esteem.

At last, Erune took a long swallow from her glass and stood. My heart gave a heavy thump as I trailed her to the foot of the dais.

"Cousin," Lord Larmach said as we bowed before him.

Erune smiled warmly. "As you ken, I've dedicated myself to the training of an apprentice these last eight years. Today, I present to you Lady Clìana Goddan, having bestowed upon her the final feather of her learning."

"And so it is earned?" the clan chief inquired.

"And so it is earned," Erune replied.

Lord Larmach regarded me. "Lady Clìana, my cousin

has deemed you fit for commission. Have you a preference in your post?"

"I do," I said, swallowing against uncertainty. I thought of what Ailis had said to me only a few short days before she'd died: *There is a greatness in you, sister, as sure as the rising of the dawn.* The words bolstered me now. Raising my chin, I met the chief's eye. "I wish to lend my skill where I might best bring honor to Clan Larmach: at the Court of Stars in Carastile."

A tide of whispers rose behind me as Lord Larmach raised a thick eyebrow. "You wish to serve the emperor?"

"I do."

Lord Larmach considered this. "I do not make the decision to send healers to Edarigo's court lightly," he said, tapping a finger against the arm of his chair. "Cousin, I trust that you're as wise as you are skilled. Tell me, do you find Lady Clìana worthy of such a post?"

"Lady Clìana is one of the finest physicians I have known in all my long years at the guildhall," Erune replied. "'Twas she who spared the eye of the bright lord's nephew some eight days past—and possibly his life as well."

I glanced at Cannan Larmach. The only indication that Erune's words chafed at his pride was his hesitation as he raised his fork to his mouth. When I glanced back at Diarnan Larmach, the chief's discerning gaze was fixed upon me. He licked his lips, his tongue flicking out as if testing the air to see which way the winds of my fate would blow.

"So be it," he said at last. "To Carastile you may go to seek the emperor's commission. But if the Astral throne doesn't want you, Lady Clìana, it is to these halls you shall return."

Despite this unsettling condition, triumph surged through me. I was bound for Carastile in truth now. In a matter of days, I could leave the high glens of Daorender behind me in pursuit of the Court of Stars. I bowed before Lord Larmach in gratitude before turning to make my way back to my seat—only to catch sight of Lenghan in the crowd.

He was sitting beside his father near the back of the hall, among the other healers of the lesser lines of Larmach. Yet even at a distance, I could see the hard set of his jaw and the anger in his eyes. Rising, he strode through the hall and out into the night.

"Pardon me, my lady," I said to Erune, pasting on as best a smile as I could manage. "I find myself in need of air."

Slipping out of the gathering hall, I discovered Lenghan pacing the courtyard. When he saw me, he cut sharply in my direction. "So the diviner's portents prove true," he spat as he drew near. "Stars, Clìana. You hadn't even the courtesy to tell me to my face. Yet I *knew*. I knew, damn you."

"Lenghan—"

"When do you intend to leave? Hmm?"

A breeze whipped through the courtyard, pulling at my clothes and tangling my hair. I curled my fingers into the thick wool of my skirts. "Within the fortnight."

Lenghan flinched. "And so you'd leave me, just like that?"

"You ken I wish nothing but happiness for you."

"Happiness?" Grasping me by the arms, he shook me.

My mouth rounded on a gasp, but an unnatural vise constricted my lungs.

"If you wish me happy, you would stay!" Lenghan shouted.

Panic rose within me as I struggled to breathe. I fumbled at my throat with my fingertips, as if I could peel away the invisible hands that seemed to wrap around my neck. Silently, I mouthed Lenghan's name.

Confusion cut through the anger that twisted Lenghan's face, followed quickly by understanding. He stumbled back, releasing both my arms and his unnatural grip on my lungs.

"Stars, Clìana," he said as I gasped, my eyes watering. He caught my face between his palms and pressed a hard kiss to my brow. "Forgive me. I didn't mean to. I didn't—"

I wrenched myself from his grasp. "I will not stay in the highlands," I said, putting several paces between us. "Not for this man you've become. You frighten me, Lenghan."

Once more, his face darkened with anger. "Then why allow me into your bed all these years? Hmm?"

"You ken why," I said softly.

Lenghan gave a joyless laugh. "Aye, to take and take as you've always done. And ever the fool I was for it."

He retreated into the shadows of the guildhall as his words pummeled through me. Had we not gone to each other's beds in mutual understanding? In the wake of Ailis's death, I had longed to feel again—something, *anything*—and Lenghan had offered me that comfort. But now doubt niggled at the back of my mind. Had I been blind to the fact that he had found his light in me? Had I taken advantage of his desire for something more between us?

I don't know how long I stared into the dark where he'd disappeared, turning these questions over and over in my mind. But at some point, my sorrow hardened into something bitter. Had I not suffered enough in the flush of my youth? My mother and sister were dead, and my father had turned to the bottle rather than mourn the loss of his wife. I had raised Ailis on my own, a child rearing a child. Now that she was gone, was I to be responsible for Lenghan as well? For this man who cared more for his own whims than my ambitions and pain? Nay, that wouldn't be my fate. I wouldn't allow it.

Ailis had seen greatness in me, and now I had Diarnan Larmach's permission to seek a place within the Court of Stars. The time had come for me to leave Daorender, and I would do it with or without Lenghan's blessing. Tonight, perhaps, I would mourn him. But tomorrow, my life would begin anew.

# CHAPTER 6

The dregs of winter faded as morning dawned warm and bright. The day after Lenghan had nearly stolen the breath from my lungs, I had purchased a sturdy chestnut mare called Fraisie to bear me on my journey north. Now, less than a week later, I led her into the guildhall's courtyard as pink light filtered through the clouds, bloodying the puddles that pockmarked the muddy ground. Erune sidled up beside me, a basket of provisions in hand: bannocks and spring onions, a few lengths of spiced sausage, and the last of the withered winter apples.

"Ready, then?" she asked, tucking the food into my saddlebags.

I released one of the packhorse's hooves, satisfied that there weren't any stones or embedded bits that might pain her on the road. "Ready as I'll ever be," I replied.

I hadn't packed much for the journey, only a small trunk of medical supplies, two clean shifts, and other necessary bits of clothing. There was little sense in hauling an extensive store of medicines to a surgery I hadn't yet acquired, nor in ferrying the entirety of my small woolen wardrobe to a city renowned for its smothering heat. Nay, it was coin that would serve me well in Carastile. I'd tucked half a dozen silvers in my sporran and distributed twice as many between my saddlebags and the purses I'd sewed into the lining of my skirts. Mounted watches might patrol the roads that ran between the eight realms, but Erune had warned me that the best thieves were never brutes or brigands. Better to err on the side of caution when coin was involved.

"Have you written to your father?" Erune asked.

Her question doused the anticipation fluttering in my chest. "Nay."

"Lass—"

"I've not seen him in as many years as I've been your apprentice, my lady." My mother's death had broken my father's spirit, but it was the loss of Ailis that had led him to flee from Aversere in search of a commission in the lowland straths. Never mind the ache his absence had left behind in the midst of my mourning. "He doesn't write, nor does he come to call. He is gone, like all the others."

I inspected the rest of Fraisie's hooves, my jaw clenched tight against what I expected would be Erune's inevitable reproach. But when she spoke, her voice was soft, almost reverent. "She would be proud of you, lass," she said, grasping my hand as I reached to check the horse's girth strap.

I knew she was speaking of Ailis. My sister's words had been echoing through my mind all morning: *There is a greatness in you, sister. . . .*

Erune's thumb swept across my knuckles. "As am I," she added.

"Thank you, my lady."

She placed her palm against my cheek before withdrawing. "There'll be a rush of merchants headed over the pass now that the snows have broken. You should be safe enough if you join them, though the going will be slow if they've any wagons. Even so, travel with them as far as you can. Mind caution, and caution will mind you, aye? Now, up you go."

Erune may have treated me with maternal instincts from time to time, but she had always done so with imposing candor. The sheen that now glistened in her eyes startled me, and I found myself blinking back tears of my own.

"I promise to forget naught that you've taught me, my lady," I said, appraising Erune as I spoke, trying to commit her face to memory while she stood before me: the soft wrinkles lining her face, the low bend of her brow, the way she sucked in her cheeks as she practiced patience on the most trying of days and with the most trying of patients. Never mind with her own stubborn student.

"I'd never suspect you would, lass," she said, smiling softly. "Now, the time has come."

I knew Erune was right. The pass into the realm of Brenmere was half a day's journey when the weather was fair, and one could never speak to the weather in the highlands. It was best not to delay now that the sun had risen.

I placed one foot in a stirrup, ready to fit myself into the saddle, when someone called my name. Lenghan strode across the courtyard as I eased my foot back to the ground, frowning at the sight of him. His clothes were wrinkled, his face shadowed. When he drew near, I noted the faint stench of ill wash—and the small, dark object tucked beneath his arm.

"Clìana," he said hesitantly, as if testing the waters of my mood.

"Lenghan," I replied as evenly as I could manage.

Erune glanced briefly between us. "Until we meet again, lass," she said with a final nod of farewell. I watched as she mounted her horse, then rode through the guildhall's gates toward Castle Tarne.

When she was gone, Lenghan cleared his throat. "You should have this," he said, pressing the object he held into my hands. My brow furrowed as I appraised the small leather-bound book wrapped firmly in a strip of aging twine. "'Tis a grimoire," he explained. "A witch's personal book of learning."

Startled, I tried to press the book back into Lenghan's hands. "I do not want this."

"Please," he said, resisting me. "You needn't learn the craft, nor call upon the power in your blood. I only ask that you read it. There are things you should ken, Clìana. Things this book can teach you." When I continued to hesitate, he added, "If you are to leave, then let this be my parting gift to you."

I didn't want the book. I didn't want to feel some measure of affection for the man standing before me. But if the grimoire was Lenghan's version of a blessing, then I couldn't deny that the gift lifted a weight from my chest. With a thin smile, I tucked the book into one of my saddlebags.

"I have to go," I said as I met his eye. "Be well, Lenghan."

"Clìana," he said with a note of finality, as though in saying my name he had placed the final stone atop a cairn.

He retreated as swiftly as he'd arrived, stalking across the courtyard without so much as a hand held high in parting. In his wake, a quiet sort of loneliness seeped into my bones. It wasn't just Lenghan I was leaving behind. It was the healers of Clan Larmach, the patients I had tended, the familiarity of the only realm I'd ever known. . . . Still, the shades of tenderness and sorrow I felt were overshadowed by grief and ambition. I took one last glance at the guildhall before hauling myself onto Fraisie's back. From the saddle, I could make out the peaks of the snow-capped mountains in the west, beckoning me to the great beyond.

Of all I had imagined about the day I'd set forth for Carastile, I had never envisioned Ulmhar Dalmorie waiting for me at the base of the mountain pass, his ruined eye patched in tooled black leather. If his injuries pained him—and I had no doubt they did—then he hid his discomfort well. A lazy smile played on his lips as I approached.

"Lady Clìana," he said, doffing his bonnet as he bowed in greeting. "Would you allow me to escort you to the coast?"

I blinked at him, taken aback by his offer. The man plainly intended to travel. Beneath the faded kilt that trailed across one of his shoulders, he wore a riding coat and muddied boots, his woolen bonnet now set low upon one ear. His muscular bay was hobbled nearby, outfitted with two small saddlebags and a bedroll cinched high across its rump.

I could think of only one reason why Daorender's new lord protector might wish to journey with me beyond the highlands. "My lord, your uncle keeps the guild well-compensated. You've no need to repay my services in this way."

"Perhaps not. But I owe you a debt all the same."

"I'm afraid I do not understand."

Fraisie stamped beneath me, as if sensing my agitation. Catching the mare's harness, Lord Ulmhar ran a soothing hand down the length of muzzle. "If you'd been one of my soldiers and that wee sliver an enemy's blade, then I would owe you for the breath that yet swells my lungs, my lady. 'Tis no different now." His mouth quirked with amusement. "And seeing as you've no injury I might tend, I'd be grateful if you'd allow me to see you safely to your ship."

Despite the honor-bound nature of Lord Ulmhar's offer, I hesitated to accept. I hadn't anticipated carrying a piece of Daorender with me beyond the confines of its rocky crags, but then I supposed it would have been no different if I'd joined a party of merchants traveling between realms. I fought a grimace as I imagined the wagons that would no doubt sink into the muddied earth, slowing the pace of our journey west. Lord Ulmhar's gaze grew heavy with expectation as Erune's words of warning echoed in my ear: *Mind caution, and caution will mind you, aye?*

"Well, then, Lord Ulmhar." I recalled the words he'd spoken to me at Castle Highdale. "Let it not be I who stands in your way."

✦⋆

Together, Lord Ulmhar and I climbed the rocky pass that bridged the Daor highlands and the western realm of Brenmere. Any warmth I'd felt in the glen that morning had quickly faded into memory. A winter gale cut through the pass, tearing at our clothes and tangling my hair. With every passing minute, I retreated further into the woolen confines of my cowl.

"You're not one for talk, are you?" Lord Ulmhar said, as if it was impolite to remain silent even as one's teeth chattered.

"I'm not one for words that mean little," I replied, nearly shouting to be heard above the wind. I didn't know where to look. If I angled myself toward Lord Ulmhar, I feared I might lose my balance and tumble from the saddle. Yet to view the pass as it stretched on before us seemed as cruel as any form of torture. I settled for a spot in the road that fell between Fraisie's ears.

"Then I suppose we must find some words of meaning, my lady. What is it that calls you to Carastile?"

I swallowed a heavy sigh. "Must we speak just now, Lord Ulmhar?"

"It's a long road to Calas, my lady. Does it grieve you to leave the highlands behind?" Lord Ulmhar asked, changing tack.

Suddenly I wished I'd thought better of accepting his offer to escort me to the coast. The thought of bearing several days of his chatter set my nerves on edge. If only I could thumb my whetstone into hand. . . .

"Perhaps. In my own way," I replied.

"Perhaps? You've no great love for Daorender, then? For your homeland?"

There was a note of offense in the lord protector's

voice, but the look on his face was as mischievous as ever. The bloody man had taken to teasing me, damn him.

I decided to answer in truth. "'Tis the memories they keep for which I do not care, my lord."

His smirk faded. "Aye?"

"Are you to question me the entire way to Calas, Lord Ulmhar?"

"I've never been one for silence, my lady."

"Then I suppose it's well you didn't lose an ear," I muttered.

A torrent of wind shrieked through the pass, followed by Lord Ulmhar's bark of laughter. "May it never be said that the lady hasn't a strong wit." Several moments passed before he added gently, "Will you share these memories? Leave them behind before you travel north?"

Nothing I could say would excise the grief from my soul. Nevertheless, I found myself telling Lord Ulmhar about my pains, if only to ease the sudden tightness in my chest.

"My mother died of a fever when I was ten. Six years later, my sister fell to her death. She was only a few months shy of womanhood," I added. If Ailis had lived until autumn, she would have been five-and-ten. Instead, her ill health had taken her, her frail body failing her as she had descended a flight of stairs at the guildhall. I could still see the crude bend in her neck in my mind's eye, studded by the tiny white knobs of vertebrae jutting from her skin. I swallowed thickly. "Grief drove my father from the city, as it now drives me."

Over the years, I'd come to loathe the pity I had received in light of my grief. So I braced myself for Lord Ulmhar's inevitable words of consolation. Yet he merely nodded, his grim expression speaking to the unutterable pain of so much loss. "Surely you could find yourself a commission in the lowlands if you wished to leave the city?" he asked after a long silence.

"Perhaps. But I don't wish for a commission in the court of a lowland lord of little consequence, where nary a hint of glory might find me."

"Glory?" The surprise in Lord Ulmhar's voice should have eaten at my patience—I had little desire to suffer men who couldn't accept a woman's ambitions—but I suspected he wasn't of such a mind. He was simply curious, ever eager to poke and prod in the hope that all the world might reveal its secrets. On this, I didn't intend to disappoint him.

"I've a skill, Lord Ulmhar. There is greatness in me that I will not waste."

Surprise flickered across his face before he grinned wickedly. "Aye. You'll do just fine at court, my lady."

I couldn't help the swell of pride that flooded through me. In the wake of Ulmhar's words, even the relentless jolting of the road seemed distant. I was bound for Carastile, for the famed Celestial City and the hallowed halls of the Court of Stars, where I would find whatever glory might await me as one of the emperor's physicians. I was still reveling in that possibility when we crested the mountain pass at midday. With one last look at the highlands I'd called home since the day of my birth, I drew Fraisie around and journeyed into the great unknown.

# CHAPTER 7

That evening, Lord Ulmhar and I rested at an inn not far into Brennish lands. I fell into a seat near the main room's hearth, dumb with fatigue. The journey down the mountain pass had proven even more jolting than our ascent, and my body felt as though it had been pummeled to a pulp. I winced as I rolled my shoulders, then hissed as I dug my fingertips into the tight muscles at the back of my neck.

"Not a pleasant thing about the pass, is there?" said Lord Ulmhar. He sat opposite me, tending to his own pains while we awaited our suppers.

"The view from the peak wasn't so bad," I replied dryly. In truth, my first glimpse of Brenmere had been marvelous. A blanket of pale yellow grass had unfurled as far as the eye could see, awash in golden sunlight.

Lord Ulmhar snorted at my sorry attempt at humor. "Aye, well. 'Tis a bonny thing the road to Calas now lies flat as my nose."

"You've made the journey to Calas before?"

"Oh, aye. Once or twice. When I was newly knighted, my uncle bid me escort Lady Oirich to Calas for the same journey. She's his representative at Bright Council, ken?"

I hummed softly in acknowledgment. That meant Lady Oirich was the person I needed to seek upon my arrival in Carastile. Though Emperor Edarigo held ultimate authority over the affairs of the Radiant Astral Empire, each of the empire's eight realms was governed by a bright liege. If Lady Oirich served as Bright Lord Dalmorie's representative at Bright Council—the meeting of advisers who spoke with the emperor on their realm's behalf—then she would have Edarigo's ear. My chance at gaining an audience at court might very well rest in her hands.

The innkeeper delivered our suppers before I could give this revelation further thought. The meal was familiar, a heaping plate of roasted hare and parsnips. Only the flecks of fresh herbs distinguished the dish from Daor fare. Even in the summer, the high glens of Daorender were often too cool and rugged for such delicate herbs to survive. Those used in my healing work were often specially grown in the guildhall's greenhouses and rarely used for anything save medicines. I savored the first bite of the meal, its earthy, floral flavors bright on my tongue. Then my stomach gave a wicked rumble, awakened by the taste of hearty fare, and all other thoughts fled from my mind. I ate as though it were the first meal I'd had in weeks, as did Lord Ulmhar. The mountain had hollowed us, it seemed—and possibly pained the lord protector more than it had me. Already, he was reaching for his third cup of ale.

"My lord," I said pointedly.

He stilled, the tankard halfway to his lips. "Have pity, my lady. I've lost an eye."

"Was it not drink that lost you the eye in the first place?"

"Och, it was nothing of the sort," he insisted, though he set the tankard aside. Still, that didn't mean he wouldn't pick it up again.

I raised an eyebrow. "You owe me a debt, my lord."

"You doubt my capacity to repay it?"

"I will if you're too inebriated to walk in the morning."

With a long look and a short grunt, Lord Ulmhar pushed the tankard out of reach. "You're a cruel lass, ken?"

"You're not the first to say so, Lord Ulmhar."

"Aye?" he questioned. I was taken aback by the unexpected edge in his tone.

"Did you not just say so?"

"In jest, my lady. Tell me."

Even with one eye, the startling sincerity in his gaze unnerved me. "I had a lover," I confessed, failing to keep the note of bitterness from my voice. "At the guildhall. He wasn't happy to see me leave."

"He didn't want what was best for you?"

"He believed *himself* to be best for me, my lord."

"Och, the wee bastard."

I couldn't help but laugh. "I might have called him that myself a time or two."

"Ha! There's a lass." Lord Ulmhar rapped the tabletop with his knuckles, his grin as wicked as the Shadows. "Now, best yourself to bed. We've another long day in the saddle tomorrow."

Rising to his feet, he pulled the woolen bonnet from his head and scrubbed at the sheen of sweat glistening at his temples. With an abrupt bow, he hastened toward the stairs that led to our rented chambers. That seemed to be his way, all energy and excess. He held no notion that the world would pull its punches and so held nothing back in return, moderation long since left to the cradle. That was why it surprised me when he hesitated, with one hand upon the stair rail.

"This lover," he said, turning to face me. "Did you find your light in him?"

I understood his meaning well enough. According to the luminaries, the Bright Stars had created humanity against the will of the Dark. Despite that betrayal, the Dark had allowed humanity its life, leaving within each soul the small sliver of light that the Stars had granted them. To love another was to share that light, to find it reflected in the other's soul.

"If I had, I would have stayed," I answered.

The lord protector's face creased with doubt. "Aye?"

I didn't like the way the question curled in my gut as Lord Ulmhar nodded, then headed off to bed. When he was gone, I reached for the tankard he'd set aside and drank the ale greedily.

By midmorning the next day, I'd lost sight of the Daor mountains at my back. The forests of Brenmere rose around us, a canopy of rich yellow leaves that shielded us from the worst of the sun's heat and blinding light. Winter might yet linger in the highlands, but the same couldn't be said for its northwestern neighbor. We hadn't been long in the saddle before I tore the woolen cowl from my neck, sweat trickling down my spine. The grimoire Lenghan had gifted me pressed tight against my ribs beneath the laces of my stays.

The night before, I'd thought to read the book as Lenghan had requested, but the journey over the pass had exhausted me. Yet even though I'd eagerly crawled into my bed, sleep had eluded me. Lord Ulmhar's words on the stair had set my nerves on edge, and the longer I had lay awake, the more my chest tightened with unease. After a fitful night, the discomfort had morphed into paranoia. I didn't trust the grimoire to my saddlebags, not when anyone might stumble upon it and its contents might spell my death. I would carry it close to me, or not at all.

"Here's as good a place as any," said Lord Ulmhar when we happened upon a gurgling burn. I peeled myself from the saddle, thinking fondly of the meal we would eat while the horses drank their fill, then caught sight of Lord Ulmhar grimacing as he dismounted. I caught his eye when he turned.

"The wee sliver was none too kind, but neither was the damned ground I fell upon," he said by way of explanation.

"You've further injuries?"

He bent down to loosen his horse's girth strap. "Only a few bruises."

"Let me have a look."

"My lady, it's—"

"Humor me, Lord Ulmhar," I insisted.

With a half-smothered sigh, he pulled off his coat and

waistcoat before shucking his undershirt. A smattering of scrapes and scars lined his torso, no doubt marks of his life as a man who lived by the sword. Turning him about, I discovered a sickly yellow-brown bruise on the left side of his lower back. When I prodded the area, he hissed.

"Have you been vomiting? Any blood in your urine?"

"I've not hurled my supper yet, thank the Stars. Though that bastard Cannan Larmach might have mentioned something about bloody urine the night I was injured. I'm not sure." He tapped his brow. "Wasn't of sound mind then, ken?"

I bit back a smile at the memory of his drunken foray through the crowded market square, as well as our shared dislike of Young Lord Larmach. "No blood since, though?" I asked, gesturing to indicate that Lord Ulmhar was free to don his discarded clothing.

"Nay, lass."

"Good. You've likely a bruised kidney, though it should heal fair enough if you've not been pissing blood. But if you should, or if you feel at all unwell, then get yourself to a healer."

"That shouldn't be too difficult."

"*After* I'm gone."

Lord Ulmhar snorted. "You're sure I cannot hire you away from the emperor?"

"Not for all the gold in Daorender," I replied, not bothering to hide my smirk.


"Tell me about yourself, Lord Ulmhar," I said once we were back in the saddle. The forest had thickened, its dense overhang imparting a peculiar sense of intimacy that loosened my tongue.

Lord Ulmhar's reply was a road-weary "Hmm?"

"You've managed to prod to the heart of me on this journey. Will you not tell me something of yourself?"

"Somehow I doubt I've gotten to the heart of you, my lady. But aye. Fair's fair." The lord protector straightened up in his saddle. "What is it you'd like to know?"

"Will you be able to fight without the use of your eye?" I asked. Lord Ulmhar's skill as a warrior was renowned throughout the highlands. I couldn't imagine what role he might play if the loss of his eye spelled the end of his fighting days.

"It'll be an adjustment, to be sure. But never fear, my lady." He patted the hilt of the sword at his hip. "I wouldn't carry a blade if I thought I couldn't wield it."

"And the fighting. Is it naught but duty for you? Or. . ."

In addition to his new role as lord protector, Lord Ulmhar had long served as the shield of Clan Dalmorie, a customary role that entailed the safekeeping of his clan. In Daorender, the shield of a clan was commonly known as a war chief, but the former term was used more widely across the eight realms. In all likelihood, Lord Ulmhar had been trained to fulfill the role from the day of his birth.

"Oh, aye. It's duty," he replied, confirming my suspicions. Then he leaned toward me, a glint of mischief in his eye. "But I've a secret for you, lass. It's glory for me, too."

When he was sober, Lord Ulmhar was a storyteller. Perhaps he was when drunk as well, but I'd only seen him truly inebriated the first night of Imbelaine, and he'd not been telling stories then. But now, as our days on the road bled on, he regaled me with everything from the most recent gossip from his uncle's court to tales of youthful indiscretions and remembrances of battlefield glory. From time to time, he even spoke of the Shadows that were said to dwell in the deepest caves and darkest forests, feverish with hunger as they awaited the opportunity to steal the lights and lives of unsuspecting passersby. Lord Ulmhar claimed to have fought one such creature when patrolling Daorender's farthest reaches during his youth. Perhaps he had fought *something*, though I sincerely doubted he'd stabbed the Shadow-creature with its own bloody, razor-sharp tooth. I shook my head, unable to keep from smiling.

I didn't mind that Lord Ulmhar seemed unsure of what to do when handed silence and so chose to burn it in a fire of his own making. The chatter kept the worst of my anxious thoughts at bay, and the lord protector was far from a poor storyteller. Still, it wasn't lost on me that I was now over three days' ride from my homeland. The day before, we had crossed the border between Brenmere and Calas, the northernmost of the eight realms.

The further north we rode, the more populated the Calasian landscape became. The road before us was dotted with tiny hamlets that gave way to villages and larger towns. When we spotted the small city of Tengras wedged into the hillside, Lord Ulmhar declared that we were less than two days' ride from the port city of Marnos. It was there that I planned to book passage on a ship bound for Carastile, the capital of Istanel and the seat of the Radiant Astral Empire. In less than a week, I hoped I would find myself standing before Edarigo Vendegal.

Fear and elation flurried in my chest. I let Lord Ulmhar babble on, his meandering tales a welcome distraction from my fraying nerves. As we neared the coast, his stories took a turn beyond the highlands.

"Do you ken much of the Court of Stars, my lady?" he asked, dabbing at his brow with a neckerchief. He'd long ago abandoned his woolen bonnet and riding coat. Seeing him in naught but his undershirt and kilt seemed an impropriety, but I had never been one for decorum. I'd seen too much in the surgery to be offended by casual dress, which was why I'd sold my own woolen cloak, cowl, and gauntlets to an innkeeper two nights past. My unlaced doublet sleeves were also safely tucked in one of my saddlebags.

"Some," I replied, huffing at a damp curl that dangled in front of my face. "They say it's ruled by an emperor."

Lord Ulmhar humphed. "Aye, well, that's a start." He hesitated before continuing, rousing my curiosity. "My uncle had a message from Lady Oirich before we left Aversere, the first letter he'd received from Carastile since winter sank its teeth into the highlands. There's been some news of the happenings at court."

"Oh?" I said mildly, as if I weren't eager for each scrap of knowledge I could gain about the Court of Stars.

"You ken the emperor's offspring, aye? Gabrialo, Leomar, and Sastiona? Well, Lady Oirich wrote of a rift between the emperor and his children—or rather, between the emperor, the princess, and the bright prince." The latter title belonged to Gabrialo, the emperor's eldest son and heir. "Gabrialo remains at court, but it's said that his sister has traveled—rather suddenly, mind you—to Nyengun to study fine music at the khagan's palace. A sort of fanciful emissary position, if you will."

I didn't know enough about the court to judge how strange a princess's sudden departure might be, but I wasn't eager to admit so to Lord Ulmhar. "The cause of the rift?" I asked instead.

"Lady Oirich did not say, only that Prince Leomar seems to have naught to do with it. But then it's said that the shield of the House of Vendegal has never been on happy terms with his siblings. Quite the zealot, that one. Mad for the Stars."

Fraisie nickered as I mulled over Lord Ulmhar's words, curious about why he'd chosen to share such information with me. "I doubt Bright Lord Dalmorie would approve of your sharing the contents of Lady Oirich's message so freely."

Lord Ulmhar shrugged. "Perhaps. But a warrior minds their feet, aye? I'd hate to see you cast from court on account of not knowing the terrain," he said as though he was merely remarking upon the weather rather than sharing court secrets to help smooth my potential transition into palace life.

I looked at him with no small amount of gratitude. "You're more than making good on your debt, Lord Ulmhar. I'll tell you that."

"As anyone should."

"Remind me to buy you a pint when we reach Marnos."

The port of Marnos was as large a city as I'd ever seen, its colorful tiled roofs stretching for miles from east to west.

The city curled itself around the crystal waters of Iona Bay, which had been named for the last true queen to rule Calas before the end of the Thousand-Year Skirmish and the unification of the Radiant Astral Empire. I inhaled deeply, and the crisp, clean scent of the sea cleared the dust of the road from my nose.

We found the harbormaster, Enaz Octarin, shortly after noon. The portly, dark-skinned woman booked me passage on the *Harbinger*, which was scheduled to set sail for Carastile the following day.

"Harbinger of what, I wonder," I mused as I eyed the formidable tall ship the next morning.

Lord Ulmhar stood beside me, idly eating one of the pan-fried sweetbreads that were typical morning fare in Calas. "I imagine the captain wanted his ship to precede him," he said, his words muffled as he chewed. "Or perhaps he hastily dubbed her anew when he saw the name of one Lady Cliana Goddan on his manifest."

I gave him a hard look. "And what is it exactly that I signal the arrival of, my lord?"

"Only such glory as the Court of Stars has never seen!"

Though he spoke in jest, Lord Ulmhar's words dampened the thrill of excitement fluttering in my chest, reminding me of why I was seeking a commission in Carastile: *There is a greatness in you, sister* . . . I bit my lip to keep from shuddering. There would be no turning back once I'd set foot on the *Harbinger*. Perhaps there hadn't been since the moment I'd chosen to leave my life in the highlands behind. But what lay ahead was a duty, and a privilege. Since Ailis's death, my fate had been leading me ever on toward Carastile. I would not hesitate now.

A shout from the *Harbinger*'s purser returned my attention to the present. The time had come for lingering passengers to board, so I heaved the strap of my medical trunk over one shoulder. One of the ship's hands had already taken my saddlebags aboard, but I'd be damned if I allowed my precious instruments out of my sight.

The broad, flat lines of Lord Ulmhar's face turned grave. "I should tell you, my lady, that I shall ever miss my eye."

I frowned, taken aback by his sudden change of mood. "I expect you shall, my lord."

"Still, to have no eyes upon you, that will be the greatest shame of all."

I snorted. "And how long have you spent conjuring that line, Lord Ulmhar?"

"Well, you did give me a wee bit of time to think on the road."

"That I did, didn't I?"

In one easy motion, he caught my hand in his and brought my knuckles to his lips.

"Thank you for your kindness, Ulmhar," I said as he straightened. His good eye flashed with pleasure at my use of his given name. "I will not forget it."

"I'm glad to hear it, my lady. For neither will I forget what you've done for me. If ever you return to Daorender, if ever you find yourself in need . . ." He placed his palm flat over his heart and bowed. "May the Stars be with you, Lady Clìana."

"And with you, Lord Ulmhar."

Turning, I strode up the *Harbinger*'s gangplank. I had one foot on the ship's deck when a thought stilled me.

"Lord Ulmhar?" I called, meeting the lord protector's

gaze amid the busy quay below. "Try not to lose your other eye. 'Tis such a bonny shade of blue."

His eyebrows shot up in surprise. Then he laughed that full-belly laugh of his, rich and deep and rumbling; and I wondered what my life among his company might have been like if greatness did not bid me yon.

# CHAPTER 8

Shortly after the *Harbinger* left port, the churning in my wame began. Wave after wave of nausea roiled through me, driving me to the starboard rail, where I heaved the contents of my stomach into the sea. Someone snickered at my back. Dragging my hand roughly over my mouth, I sank to the deck, my spine flush against the side of the ship as I fought to keep my gorge from rising yet again. Trembling, I rummaged through my medical trunk in search of a piece of mallow bark to chew.

"What did the sea ever do to you?" someone said in Istanelan, the common tongue of Istanel that was also widely spoken at courts throughout the empire. Given that Clan Larmach's master healers were often commissioned by peers among the eight realms, Erune had begun teaching me the language in the early days of my apprenticeship. Now, eight years later, I had a strong command of the tongue—though, as ill as I currently felt, I had little desire to speak it.

Reluctantly, I dragged my gaze upward. A woman

leaned against the mizzenmast, her features hidden beneath the low-slung swoop of her hat. Her skin was a shade of sun-deepened brown that I'd come to recognize as commonplace among the northernmost of the eight realms. Ropes of thick black hair trailed over her shoulders; and her long, spidery limbs were clad in breeches and rough-spun linen. A long dagger sat at each hip. Though she stood with one foot flat against the mizzen and her arms banded across her chest, I had the strong sense that she could have the tip of one of those blades nestled firmly beneath my chin at a moment's notice.

I met her regard with grim determination and replied, "I rather wondered what I'd ever done to the sea."

"Haven't given her the time of day, I'd wager. One as temperamental as she does not take well to being ignored."

"Hard to set sail in a landlocked realm," I said, chewing on a chunk of mallow bark. Its mild, astringent syrup soothed the raw flesh of my throat and began to settle my gut.

The woman raised an eyebrow. "Daorender?"

"Aye."

A gull's cry pierced the air as the woman appraised me from beneath the brim of her hat. At last, she humphed. "If you have the need again," she said, gesturing vaguely at my stomach, "be sure to mind my boots."

With that, she pushed off the mizzen and climbed the stairs to the quarterdeck, the twin hilts of her daggers glinting in the bright Calasian sun.

As I fell into the crude comforts of my cabin's tiny cot, Lenghan's grimoire pressed tight against my chest. Sheer exhaustion had kept me from reading the book on the road, just as nausea now led me to fling a hand over my face in grave acceptance of my fate. The mallow bark had helped temper my sickness, but it seemed I wouldn't feel well again until I set foot on dry land.

Sleep came slow and troubled. The deeper its pull, the more vivid the memories that whirled through my mind. Lenghan came to me first, his features frenzied, his invisible hand gripped tight around my throat. When my palm flashed out to meet his face, the sound of the slap became the crash of a bottle. Shards of glass glinted in the firelight as a foul curse leaped from my father's drunken tongue. Broken blood vessels in his eyes painted him a thing of nightmare. When I turned my face away, the gray stone hearth dissolved into muddied ground, its fire now ablaze atop my mother's pyre. My eyes stung with tears as I watched my mother's body burn. The frail bones of Ailis's wee hand tightened around mine. When I looked down, I found her tucked into bed, her body cocooned in woolen blankets as I ran my hand over her hair.

*Mistress Georie says I am weak because I am unworked*, she said. *I do not mean to be idle, Clía. I am sorry. So sorry.*

My sister sobbed once, then again, until her tears became a great flood of weeping. Water rose around us, pulling at my hair and stealing the breath from my lungs. When Ailis slipped from my fingers, panic mounted in my chest. I tore through the water, desperate to reach her, but she only seemed to drift further away. Then the flood closed in around me, dragging me down into Shadow.

I landed in the mud beside my sister. Cold rain fell in sheets, obscuring the walls of the guildhall around us. Ailis was older now, not far from the first flush of womanhood and yet still very much a child. She lay sprawled on the ground, her limbs flung wide. Thin tendrils of hair clung to her face, and her skin had gone blue with chill. When I gathered her in my arms, her eyelids fluttered open. *I only wanted to feel the rain*, she murmured. *Only the rain.*

I carried her birdlike body up to our small bedchamber and stripped the sodden nightdress from her skin. A shiver racked Ailis's tiny frame as I laid her on the rug before the hearth fire. Turning, I collected the furs from my bed to warm her. But when I drew around, I found her body burning, her gaze wide and glassy with death. With a scream, I strived to reach her. But my skin bubbled and popped in the flames, and an anguished cry tore from the depth of me.

As if in answer, Ailis rose from her pyre. The fire behind her guttered and died, dousing the bedchamber in darkness. My sister now stood on sure legs, her skin flush with health. Her body was soft and full, no longer a breath away from crumbling. A wild, vibrant energy blazed across her face. With each step, she drew closer, expanding in size until she loomed unnaturally large before me. I shrank from her in confusion, then in terror as a booming voice reverberated from her lips.

*There is a greatness . . . a greatness . . . a greatness . . .*

Wrenching myself from sleep, I pulled the chamber pot beneath my cot and vomited. Dread coursed through me, feverish and suffocating. I held myself aloft with one hand on the floorboards as quick, gasping breaths racked my body. I could still see Ailis in my mind's eye, first the frail-boned lass she'd been in her youth—and then the dark-eyed terror from my dreams. Beneath my stays, Lenghan's grimoire cut into my ribs.

A strange sense of awareness prickled my skin. Glancing up, I startled. The woman I'd met earlier on the deck was standing in the cabin doorway, limned in the thin light of the sconces in the hall. Despite her low-slung hat, I had the distinct impression that her brow was furrowed. She gestured at me with the sharp point of her chin.

"You a healer?" she asked.

After a brief pause, I nodded.

"Good. Follow me."

With my medical trunk in hand, I trailed the woman through the belly of the ship, passing between rows of deckhands swaying in their hammocks as we made our way toward the stern. "If I'm to tend to you as a patient, I should like to know your name," I said.

"Who says you are to tend to me?" the woman replied, ushering me into a large cabin at the ship's stern before shutting the door behind us.

"Am I not?"

She cut me a hard look as she leaned back against the large wooden desk in the center of the room. "I am Anadis Ibidala. You may call me captain."

"Captain?" I said in surprise.

The captain's mouth twisted, her displeasure evident.

"I only—" I cut myself short. Captain Ibidala's rough appearance might be less dignified than I had expected of a ship's captain, but I wouldn't put it past her to draw her daggers on me should I say as much. I offered her a nod instead. "Captain."

After a beat, the captain pulled the hem of her shirt from her trousers, revealing a large strip of bandage wrapped around her torso. A quiet sound of displeasure escaped me.

"That bad?" The brim of Captain Ibidala's hat tilted back just far enough for me to catch sight of her wide-set eyes, so pale and verdant that they seemed nearly unreal.

I tore my gaze away with marked determination. "I'll need to remove the bandage."

"Is that a question?"

"Only if it needs to be."

She snorted. "Go on, then."

I unwound the long strip of linen carefully, taking care not to touch the captain's skin. She sucked in a short breath as I tugged at the last piece of cloth, which clung to the half-healed wound. Stepping back, I appraised the injury. A ragged gash curved around her side, just below her rib cage.

"You were stabbed?"

"Gutted, more like. It bled like a bitch, though it doesn't seem to have nicked anything serious."

Gently, I prodded the wound in search of pockets of pus or the telltale heat of infection. "You were lucky, Captain. It seems the blade caught naught but flesh." Though how her enemy had found enough meat on her scrawny frame to cause such an injury, I couldn't say.

"Is it healing cleanly?"

"For now." I drew a tin of salve from my medical trunk. "You'll have a scar that's like to scare your lovers, but you'll live—*should* you continue to keep the wound clean and well-dressed."

"I'm no fool."

"I didn't mean to imply you were."

Plucking the tin from my fingers, the captain smoothed

a glob of musky calendula salve over the mottled edges of her flesh. The wound had been neatly sutured with thin black gut, but the angle of the stitches seemed strange.

"Stars," I breathed. "You stitched the wound yourself."

"Damned surgeon died the day before the raid. Still, I knew what I was doing."

Her words confirmed my growing suspicions. "The *Harbinger* is no merchant vessel, is it?"

The captain raised an eyebrow. "It is."

"You might not be a fool, but neither am I."

"Is that so?" Her voice took on a mocking tone. Pressing the tin of salve back into my hands, she crossed the room to pull a fresh set of dressings from the trunk at the foot of her bed. "The *Harbinger* is a merchant ship, little highlander. We fly legal colors, same as any other."

"And do all merchant ships go raiding?"

"Perhaps we were the ones who were raided."

"Were you?" I spat back.

Captain Ibidala shoved her shirt back into her breeches without saying a word. When she finished, she leaned back against the desk, banded her arms across her chest, and stared at me. "On occasion, the *Harbinger* confiscates illegal cargo in the emperor's name—though never when we have passengers aboard," she added swiftly.

"And are you often injured?"

"What does it matter to you?"

I snapped the clasp on my medical trunk with more force than necessary. "'Tis clear you can take care of yourself. I will leave you."

"How much do I owe?" Captain Ibidala called before I could fling open the door.

"You'd no need of me. There is no debt."

Sighing, the captain tugged the brim of her hat ever lower. "You should learn to pay me no heed unless I am giving orders."

It was as near an apology as I was likely to get. "Truly, I did nothing."

"I would pay my debts, lady healer."

The words brought Lord Ulmhar to mind. "I've no need of money."

"What, then?" the captain asked.

I cocked my head to one side. "How well do you ken the Celestial City?"


While standing on the deck of the *Harbinger* the next morning, I watched as Carastile rose on the horizon, gleaming atop salt-spattered cliffs. The city was built of towering sandstone and hemmed by ancient curtain walls that hid all but the silver spires of Alamada Palace. My lungs swelled at the sight. Even the roiling in my gut couldn't sour the thrill of possibility that seemed to thrum in the air as the ship glided into port.

Sometime in the night, the *Harbinger* had sailed through the Strait of Jibrani and into the belly of the ocean that the deckhands called the Ifros. When I'd first boarded the ship in Marnos, I'd found the silvery waters of the Waking Sea to be a wonder. Little had I known just how expansive an ocean could be. I had appraised it that morning with no small amount of awe—and a faint sense of discomfort— until one of the rig hands caught sight of Carastile on the horizon. Then my attention had been captured by the Celestial City.

In payment for my meager services, Captain Ibidala

had agreed to serve as my guide through the city. My heart hammered in my chest as we passed through Carastile's western gate. The stench of salt thickened the air as the wild song and dance of the city swirled around us. Gulls cried, and hooves clattered. Merchants hawked goods in more languages than I could name as colorful palanquins wove through the streets. On occasion, an elegant arm would slip through the silken drapes to indicate some new bobble it favored, and a servant would break from the entourage with a small purse in hand. Then there were the urchins who darted through the crowds, slippery as fish. Never mind the barrage of scents that rose around us: spices, sweat, roasting meats, cloying perfumes. . . . If the city was a feast for the senses, then I quickly devoured more than I could chew. My pounding pulse only began to ease as we left Carastile's main thoroughfares behind us.

"You've a commission from the emperor," I'd told the captain the night before. "I travel to Carastile to seek the same."

Captain Ibidala had smirked. "Not *quite* the same, I imagine."

"A commission all the same."

"I don't have the emperor's ear, if that is what you are after."

"No matter. If you ken Carastile, then I'd be grateful for your guidance."

"Wary of foreign streets, are we? Wise girl." The captain's voice had slithered low with humor. "I am yours for an hour, no more. Now, where are we bound?"

The answer was the preeminent district of the city known as the Pearl. Among the manses of wealthy merchants and peers of the realm, the Pearl housed several ambassadorial offices, Lady Ilona Oirich's among them. It was there, before the doors of the Daor consulate, that Captain Ibidala deposited me with nary a hint of fanfare or parting sorrow. She did, however, grasp my forearm in a foreign gesture I'd come to recognize as an acknowledgment of respect. Her fingers lingered on my skin. When she tilted her head back to meet my eye, her eyebrows knit low.

"I had thought to say nothing," she said with quiet intensity, her pale gaze strange and somber. "And maybe it is nothing that I say, but I find that I must say it all the same. You will be a woman of no small renown, Clìana Goddan. Your legacy will be forged of blood and suffering. All that you desire will be yours, then none of it—and perhaps some of it yet again. It will be enough."

The heat of the day seemed to thicken around me, and sweat rose to bead my skin. "You speak in riddles."

"I speak prophecy, riddle though it may be."

I tugged my arm from her grasp. "I didn't take you for a diviner," I said, my distaste for Star-readers evident in my sour tone.

The captain bristled before shrugging indifferently. "The river gives what it gives, and I share what I feel I must."

"The river?"

"You will understand soon enough, little highlander."

"But—"

"I have said all that I will say. Now I must go." With a lingering look, she nodded. "May the Stars keep you, Lady Clìana."

Thin as a wraith, Captain Ibidala faded into the crush of the street before I could demand an explanation.

I raised a trembling hand to my chest, desperate to regain some measure of composure. After eight long years of striving to master my craft in pursuit of a commission in the Court of Stars, I had arrived in Carastile. My hour of greatness was upon me, and Captain Ibidala was a stranger. I wouldn't allow her parting words to toy with my resolve.

Turning, I strode with grim determination through Lady Oirich's door.

# CHAPTER 9

In Daorender, bearing the feathers of a Larmach healer afforded me a level of respect reserved for few among the highlands. So it came as no surprise that Lady Oirich happily took up my cause at the Court of Stars. Still, I had no misconceptions about the difficulty I'd find in gaining an audience with the emperor. Though Larmach healers were renowned throughout the eight realms, I was still a lady of relatively little consequence among the Radiant Astral Empire. It wasn't within my power to simply stride into the halls of Alamada Palace to seek a commission. Lady Oirich would have to bring my request to the attention of Edarigo advisers, who would, in turn, determine whether my entreaty was worthy of the emperor's ear.

During those days, I spent many long hours pacing the consulate's inner courtyard while Lady Oirich attempted to persuade the court on my behalf. There was little for me to do otherwise. After tending to what small pains ailed the consulate's servants, I took to sharpening my surgical instruments to as fine an edge as I could manage. I hadn't yet brought myself to read the grimoire Lenghan had gifted me. Every time I touched the worn leather cover, my lungs ached in remembrance of when Lenghan had stolen the breath from my lungs. Sickened by the memory, I fashioned a hidden compartment in the bottom drawer of my medical trunk and stashed the grimoire within it.

Fifteen days after I'd arrived in Carastile, Lady Oirich bade me join her in the courtyard for a glass of pale Brennish wine.

"I'm sorry, Lady Clìana," she said, brushing a stray strand of ruddy-gray hair from her brow. "I fear I've exhausted the goodwill of every last person at court, adviser or otherwise. The emperor simply has no need of another healer." With evident remorse, she explained that Edarigo's advisers were loath to so much as speak the word *physician* to the overzealous emperor. "Already he employs two-and-ten healers of varying skills and studies who are said to bicker over the emperor's health from dawn 'til dusk."

"So many?" I took a sip of the faintly floral wine, hoping to conceal my growing despair.

"'Tis the plague, you ken?" Lady Oirich didn't need to explain. I suspected everyone in the eight realms knew that the House of Vendegal had dwindled during the Plague of Great Sorrow. The loss of one's entire family was reason enough for anyone with deep pockets to keep an army of healers at hand. Still, my heart sank at the realization that there was no place for me at court.

"I suppose that's that, then," I said, my pulse throbbing at my temples. Would all my long years of training truly amount to such a disappointing end? "Stars."

Lady Oirich's face softened. "I *am* sorry."

I offered her a thin smile. "Please excuse me," I said, then fled from Lady Oirich's table.

Having failed to secure a commission at court, I needed to return to the highlands as Diarnan Larmach had commanded. Any other choice of action could result in being stripped of the feathers I had earned; and as reluctant as I was to set foot in Daorender again, my mood was none so grave that I was willing to relinquish so many years of effort. Even so, I slept fitfully that night before rising at dawn to depart for home. I'd only just hoisted the strap of my medical trunk onto my shoulder when a knock sounded at my chamber door. "Lady Oirich requests your presence in her offices, my lady," said the dark-haired servant who entered the room.

When I arrived, the ambassador's rooms were awash in soft morning light. "Ah, Lady Clìana," said Lady Oirich, waving me into her office. "There is someone here to see you."

With a knowing smile, she gestured to a figure I hadn't noted upon entering the room. A man of Istanelan descent stood in the shadows, clad in a livery of deep navy silk that marked him as a member of the royal Vendegal household.

"Lady Clìana." The man dipped his head in deference as my heart thundered in my chest. "I have come to escort you to Alamada Palace."

The famed Carastilan palace proved more glorious than any legend had rendered it in my imagination. Its towering spires seemed to pierce the sky, standing sentinel over a sprawling expanse of gleaming white stone. I trailed in the servant's wake, trying not to gawk as we wove through the palace's many halls and courtyards. Sunlight filtered through arched windows trimmed with intricate plasterwork. Gilt ceilings gleamed. Colorful tiles spun impossible mosaics beneath my feet, a swirling display of hand-painted artistry.

Despite the early hour, the dark amber silk of my gown couldn't keep the worst of the Istanelan heat at bay. Sweat gathered at the nape of my neck, and fine curls had slipped from the elegant confines of my hairpins. I ran a trembling hand over the cap of my head as we came to a halt in a courtyard hemmed by arcades and fragrant with orange trees. At our arrival, a second servant stepped from the shadows of the eastern colonnade.

"Lady Clìana," he said, dismissing the man who had escorted me with a small nod. "If you will follow me?"

Physically, the second servant was perhaps the most remarkable man I'd ever seen. Tall and thin, he had arresting gray eyes, a clean-shaven head, and deep black skin. His garb, though dyed the deep navy of the House of Vendegal, was like none I had yet seen among the eight realms. A long sheath of silk wrapped around his body in a complicated pattern I couldn't quite discern. I noted the array of gold earrings that lined the shells of his ears as I followed him deeper into the palace.

Soon, an unfamiliar scent began to tickle my nose. I inhaled deeply as we passed into yet another courtyard, where the fragrance grew richer and more enticing. I blinked against the glare of the sun to find Alamada's renowned spice gardens stretched out before me, the flowers and foliage carefully cultivated to produce a rare perfume. Even as studied as I was in herbalism, I didn't recognize many of the plants and trees blossoming around me. I had only a moment to survey the gardens' wonders before the servant ushered me up a wrought iron stair to the covered terrace above.

As the man turned toward me, I was once more struck by his unusual features. He was Ishmeni, I realized. That would explain the deep hue of his skin and his unfamiliar dress. I considered what I knew of the lands of Ishmen north of the Waking Sea. Though dotted with several powerful city-states, most of its peoples were nomadic, following the warmth of the winds that rustled through the grasslands. More notably, the Ishmeni were said to live without a concept of gender. Each person's role was influenced by their aptitude rather than their sex, and the nature of their clothing was delineated solely by the tribe or class to which they belonged. Still, I didn't know how to refer to the Ishmeni servant who stood before me. I'd been thinking of them as male, but I was unsure whether that was a term they would use for themselves.

"We will wait here, my lady," said the servant, their speech lightly accented with clipped vowels. "Do you wish anything to drink?"

"Nay, thank you." As parched as I was, I didn't think I could swallow against the knot of anticipation in my throat. "May I ask for whom we wait, master . . . ?" I used the masculine title before I could think better of it. "Or, rather—"

The Ishmeni servant smiled. "Forgive me, I have not introduced myself. I am Yadi-Rafin Kalla. You may call me Yadi-Rafin, or simply steward, for I am steward to the

Bright Prince Gabrialo of the House of Vendegal. It is he for whom we wait."

Just then, a man strode through the doors that connected the terrace to the second story of the palace. A silver coronet circled his head of rich brown hair. "Lady Clìana?"

I dipped in a hasty curtsy. "Yes, my prince."

"Please, rise," he said in a pleasant tone.

I appraised him as I straightened. Bright Prince Gabrialo was young, no more than several years my elder, with golden skin and long, elegant limbs. Though finely dressed in the colors of his house, his raiment wasn't nearly as ostentatious as one might expect of royalty. His clothing was modestly cut—almost practically so—and his crown was little more than a simple band of silver.

"I am aware of the great esteem with which healers of Clan Larmach are regarded," said Bright Prince Gabrialo. His words carried the serpentine cadence I'd come to recognize as common among Istanelan peers. "I trust that your skill is a testament to your clan, yes?"

It was all I could do to nod in affirmation.

"Good," he replied. "It has come to my attention that you traveled to Carastile to seek a commission in my father's court. This I cannot offer you. However, there is another commission I may put forth in its stead."

I exhaled softly in relief before remembering Lord Larmach's command. If this commission didn't secure me a place within the Court of Stars, I would have to return to Daorender.

"There is a woman of our court in the south," the bright prince continued. "At a royal holding called Granara. My father's physicians would see to her here at

Alamada Palace. But alas, her condition leaves her unable to travel. If it pleases you, I would engage your services on her behalf."

"It would be an honor, my prince," I said, knotting my fingers at my back. "One I would readily accept, were I not bound to the chief of my clan." The subtle tilt of Bright Prince Gabrialo's chin prompted me to explain. "Having failed to secure a commission here at imperial court, I am bound to return to Aversere. It was a condition of my journey."

The bright prince considered this for a beat. "Having come of age as heir apparent, I am entitled to form a court of my own. Should all go well at Granara, I see no reason why you should not have a place in that court, Lady Clìana. Would such a commission satisfy your lord's conditions?"

I smothered the rush of relief that coursed through me before it could make its way to my face. "I believe it would, my prince. You honor me."

"Then you accept the commission I propose and will travel at once to Granara?"

"I will."

The corners of the bright prince's lips curled slightly, the only indication that he was pleased with my acceptance. "Yadi-Rafin will see you prepared for the commission. Do not hesitate to ask them for anything you might need." I noted the way the bright prince referred to his personal steward. "You will leave on the morrow, at first light. One of my brightswords, Sir Casdar Belorán, will see you safely escorted."

He stepped aside, revealing the figure who lingered in the doorway. I'd only just noted the brightsword's rich brown skin and powerful build when his gaze met mine—and I nearly startled at its intensity. But when Bright Prince Gabrialo turned to face him, Sir Casdar's expression shifted to one of mild disinterest, and I wondered if I'd mistaken the hostility in his regard. Perhaps my brain was simply addled from how nearly I'd been forced to return to Daorender.

"At your service, Lady Clìana," said the brightsword, his tone devoid of emotion.

I managed a curt nod in reply.

After bidding me a safe journey, the bright prince retreated from the terrace, followed by his brightsword. With a gentle hand, Yadi-Rafin ushered me back through the winding maze of the palace. My mind reeled as I walked, turning over all that had come to pass that morning. It was only when Yadi-Rafin inquired about the provisions I would need for my post that I realized I hadn't asked after the condition of the woman I'd be treating.

That night, I cracked open the shutters in my chamber at the Daor consulate. Carastile was a city that didn't sleep. Late though it was, I could hear voices in the street below, accompanied by the thrum of a lyre and the bleating of a goat. Leaning against the sill, I looked at the rich canopy of Stars above.

Upon dying, those of the Astral faith were burned upon pyres to ensure the light within them could rise to the Stars above. Only those whose light had grown dim with guilt or grievance remained, fleeing to the dark places of the world. There, Shadows were said to torment them until no shred of light remained. Little though I believed in such tales, I found myself searching the dark smear of the night sky, hoping I might find something to give evidence to my sister's fate. Had her light returned to the Stars above? Or had she lingered here, lost to Shadow?

*I am here, sister,* I said silently to the sky above. *In Carastile. I've done as you have asked. I have not failed you.*

A bout of laughter rang up from the street below, its tone mocking. I imagined the sound breaking from my sister's lips—and the words that might have followed: *You've found no greatness yet, Clìana.*

A shiver prickled the hair on my arms. I remained at the windowsill that night, the words echoing in my mind until the deep black sky faded to the pale gray of morning. Only then did I rise and ready myself for the journey to come.

When I met Casdar Belorán in the consulate's courtyard at dawn, his appearance was once more black with loathing. For a moment, I merely stared at him, confounded. I'd known some folk to carry anger with them as they walked through the world, nurturing it as though it were a flame against the night. But something about the brightsword's ire felt more personal, as though it was my throat alone to which he wished to hold a blade.

Pushing the thought aside, I bade Lady Oirich farewell, thanking her in earnest for her efforts on my behalf at court. Then, after readying my saddlebags and inspecting the hooves of the packhorse I'd been provided, I fitted myself into the saddle.

"If we ride swiftly, we should reach Granara by noon," said Sir Casdar as we set out from the consulate.

Beyond the city's gates, the Istanelan moorland unfurled before us, an endless stretch of swaying grasses. I kept pace behind the brightsword, appraising him as we rode. The way Sir Casdar carried himself was in stark contrast to the quiet dignity of the bright prince he served. Each line of his body was honed to a hard edge, his bearing a coil poised to spring. Briefly, I considered what such a man might do if that coil sprang free, but it wasn't a thought on which I cared to dwell.

We stopped around midmorning to water the horses before crossing the Ségua, the river that meandered through the countryside before pouring into the Ifros to the west. A cool breeze licked up off the cliffside as we set out on the road once more. All around, the landscape was swathed in brilliant shades of green and gold.

"'Tis a bonny coastline," I found myself saying. "Yet there are so few villages."

Sir Casdar surprised me by answering my unspoken question.

"In high summer, this region is battered by wicked storms that few fortifications can withstand." Glancing back, he caught my eye. "Beautiful things can be deceiving, can they not?"

The note of implication in his voice unsettled me. I fixed my attention on the southern horizon—but not before noting that Casdar Belorán's expression twisted into a sneer.

# CHAPTER 10

Granara was a shimmering black pearl on the horizon. From afar, the small royal holding seemed to be built in much the same style as Alamada Palace. An array of sharp spires towered above sprawling keeps, and intricate stonework capped its crenellations. But if Alamada Palace was light and air, then Granara was the night itself. Its dark gates were a welcome sight amid the empty coastline.

Still, I couldn't shake the stirring of doubt that had wormed its way through my gut as Sir Casdar and I rode into the castle's outer bailey. Perhaps it was merely a touch of nerves. Part of me remained rattled by how close I'd come to returning to the highlands. Even now, my position at the Court of Stars wasn't yet secured. My fate hinged upon what would happen within these walls. And with nary a hint as to the work that awaited me, was it not natural that I should feel unsettled?

I squared my shoulders against my unease as we dismounted from our horses. A servant emerged from the castle to tend to my saddlebags and medical trunk, followed shortly by a groom who led my horse away to the stables. Sir Casdar dismissed a second groom who tried to offer him the same courtesy.

"Casdar Belorán, are you to be my sight for sore eyes?" The voice rang clear and sweet through the bailey. Turning, I found a lass standing beneath the archway that led toward Granara's inner courtyard. Her tan skin and dark hair marked her as native to Istanel, and she had a canny gaze that made her seem uncommonly self-assured. But most notable was the swell of her frame, which revealed her to be well into the latter days of pregnancy.

I bit back a snort. Unable to travel, indeed.

"Sósia," said Sir Casdar, inclining his head briefly. The edge in his voice softened when he spoke. "I have come to deliver your midwife."

The lass regarded me briefly before turning back to the brightsword, her eyebrows knitted in disapproval. "You know as well as I that the lady is no mere midwife, Casdar. One would think you would have learned a modicum of respect after so many years at court."

"Among that nest of vipers?" Sir Casdar huffed.

"Only a fool denies the adder its due regard. Now, will you introduce us, Sir Casdar? Or must the lady introduce herself?"

The brightsword's shoulders stiffened. I stepped forward before he could reply. "I am Lady Clìana Goddan of the clan of Larmach healers, mistress."

"A pleasure, my lady," the lass replied, nodding in deference to my station. "I am Sósia de Garzas, though I do hope you will call me Sósia. Six weeks is far too long a time to stand on formality in such circumstances, no?"

If the lass bore an ounce of timidity within her, she hid

it well. Unbidden, I found myself smiling. "So long as you will call me Clìana."

Sósia nodded, her face brightening in reply.

Sir Casdar cleared his throat. "If there is no message you should like me to bear to court, mistress, then I would away."

"So soon?" Sósia frowned.

"My place is at court, mistress."

"You do not even wish for a warm meal?" When Sir Casdar made no reply, Sósia sighed. "Very well, then. Off you go, Sir Casdar. May the Stars keep you."

"And you, mistress," said the brightsword with another quick incline of his head. He took to the saddle with equal haste, offering his horse one short pat on the neck before urging it through the palace gates.

When the dust in the bailey settled, Sósia's expression remained distant. "And still the stone remains untouched," she said. I knew the proverb she referenced. *The lush of the earth ever grows and gives way beneath the arc of Stars*, it began. I found a measure of comfort in the words, for if the stone remained untouched, then perhaps there was nothing personal in Sir Casdar's ill regard of me.

"Come," said Sósia, drawing my attention. "You must be starving—and in desperate wish of a bath, no? Stars, the dust this time of year! Let us see you settled."

Hooking her arm through mine, she led me through the small inner courtyard and into the heart of the palace. The grimoire pressed tight against my ribs as Granara's keep closed in around us.

✦

"I was told you're a woman of court, yet Sir Casdar called you mistress." There was an unmistakable question in my voice as Sósia and I walked along the cliffside that evening. The day was still warm and the winds soft. High above, the clouds were tinged pink with fading sunlight.

At supper, Sósia had introduced me to her lady's maid, a young Istanelan lass named Adalina who seemed ill at ease in the presence of new company. "A pleasure to meet you, my lady," she had said, the words rushing low and quick as she bobbed a hasty curtsy, her fingers fluttering in the folds of her skirts. She was dressed more finely than any servant I'd met, and she surprised me by taking a seat near Sósia at the supper table.

"Adalina is most pleasant company," Sósia had explained, taking note of my furrowed brow. "A learned linguist, and my only true friend here at Granara. Without her, I surely would have expired of boredom weeks ago."

Briefly, I'd wondered what sort of lady's maid spoke several languages. But then Sósia had begun talking of her desire to take an evening stroll after supper, fearing that summer storms would soon shutter them indoors, and the curious thought had fled from my mind. Despite Sósia's invitation, Adalina had elected to forgo the walk along the cliffside in favor of preparing Sósia's evening bath and bedclothes. And so Sósia and I now walked alone along the beaten cliffside path, the sheer drop to the Ifros only a stone's throw away.

"My father is no lord, and as nothing more than a doña, my mother could not confer titles upon her children," Sósia replied, her cheeks flushed from the mild exertion of our walk. "I am but Sósia de Garzas, and happy to be so."

Curious, I raised an eyebrow. "Is it not uncommon for an untitled woman to live at court?"

"Indeed." The lass bit her lip in hesitation. When she spoke again, her tone was careful. "I am, you might say, *beloved* of the bright prince."

It took me only a second to catch her meaning. From the moment Bright Prince Gabrialo had bidden me to ride south and attend a woman of court, I'd had some inkling of the significance of the charge. Now it was clear. The bright prince had sent his lover south to spare her the scrutinies of court—and me, in turn, to ensure the bairn was safely delivered. That Sósia had been the bright prince's lover also explained how she knew Casdar Belorán well enough to note that his demeanor had remained unchanged.

"You must think me a fool," said Sósia, startling me from my thoughts.

"Not at all," I said, surprised by her suggestion. "So long as this be a bairn you welcome."

The teasing glint faded from Sósia's eye. "It is."

Her sudden solemnity further roused my interest in Sósia's circumstances, but I held my tongue. I didn't need to know why the lass had chosen to bear the bright prince's illegitimate child rather than take the herbs that could easily have prevented such a pregnancy. I had come to tend to her birthing, and that was what I would do.

Sósia laid a hand upon my arm, stilling me. "Tell me, who are you?"

I blinked at her. "Forgive me, but I do not take your meaning."

"I know you are Lady Clìana Goddan of the clan of Larmach healers, which means you hail from Daorender.

And, I know the bright prince sent you to attend me. But if you are to be the woman who ushers my child into this world, then I should like to know a great deal more."

I huffed in amusement. "Is it not the skill of my hands that matters most?"

"Oh, to be sure," said Sósia, laughing a little as we turned to make our way back toward the palace. "But let us be honest with each other, yes? Lying in wait for a babe is dull work. Will you not humor me?"

With a nod, I acquiesced. "What is it you wish to ken?"

"Oh, anything shall do. Perhaps, did you always wish to be a healer?"

"I was born to it."

"Yes, but is it something more than duty for you now?"

Ailis's face rose to my mind, pale and slack with death. "Aye," I managed, swallowing against the unwelcome memory. For what was my life if not the work to which I had pledged myself? If not for the greatness I was seeking? "Aye, it is the air I breathe."

"Ah, that air is music for me," Sósia replied, mistaking my sincerity for passion. "The lyre, most often—and singing. I could sing every hour of the day and never grow weary of it, though I was no great admirer of the craft when I was first bid to learn."

"Did you sing for the bright prince?" When Sósia's fingers tensed around my arm, I shook my head. "I'm sorry. I should not have asked such a thing."

"No. No, it is all right." Sósia's voice grew wistful. "I did sing for him. He always loved to hear me sing."

Night crept over us as we walked, the sound of the ocean soothing as it crashed against the cliffside far below.

"Perhaps one day your bairn will do the same," I said quietly, hoping to offer Sósia some semblance of comfort.

The lass's face darkened. "No, that cannot be." She laid a hand atop the swell of her womb. "I fear that is all I desire now, Clìana. What cannot be. What I cannot have."

We ambled back to Granara in silence. All the while, I fought to find the words to apologize for the unhappy thoughts my carelessness had roused. But by the time we reached the palace's western colonnade, a glint of humor had returned to Sósia's eye. "You must think nothing of my storm clouds, Clìana," she said, patting my arm. "For even the darkest ones are only temporary. Now, we should both of us take our rest."

Soft linen sheets and fine pillows topped the plush feather bed in my chambers at Granara. Still, sleep eluded me. In only half a day, I'd come to know the resilience of Sósia's spirit—and it reminded me of Ailis. Even on the worst of my sister's days, when pain had crippled her joints so badly that she wept to wipe her brow, Ailis hadn't allowed suffering to dampen her good cheer.

"Do you think the rains will break tomorrow, sister?" she would whisper between gritted teeth. "For I should like to see the sun."

Suspicion niggled at the back of my mind as I lay awake, thinking of her. So much of what I had known of Ailis had faded. The gaunt lines of her face had softened in my memory, as had the shape of her hands and the sound of her breathy laughter. That was the way of grief, I had learned. Each day brought fresh loss as memory proved frail. Even then, as the cool Istanelan night stretched long around me, the images of my sister that rose most readily to my mind were those I had dreamed in fear upon the *Harbinger*: the thinness of her frame as she lay in the mud, the blazing heat of her pyre, her face flush with uncommon health as she grew ever larger and more menacing before me. The images drove me to my feet. I stoked the fire and gathered myself before the hearth.

Even before I opened the grimoire, I knew what I would find within its pages. Despite all reason, I knew why Lenghan had pressed this book into my hands. I unwound the leather thong and gently drew the cover open. Sure enough, Ailis's feeble script crawled across the page:

*I have seen something I should not have seen, though perhaps it was well for me to see it. 'Tis better to ken with certainty, I think, than to dwell in ignorance. I've found no bliss in that state of being. Only frustration, only a sense of loss. Nay, 'tis better to ken the rumors and legends to be true. For knowledge, they do say, is power—and I should like to find my power.*

My hands trembled as the words unfurled before me. I read the grimoire ravenously, arrested by fear and desperate for answers. Ailis had seen Lenghan, I soon learned. On one of the days when she had been sound of strength, my sister had risen from her sickbed in search of me and instead found Lenghan in his workroom. He was cursing, his hand red and swollen where boiling water had burned his skin. The wound should have festered for weeks. Instead, Lenghan had called upon his unnatural power to heal the angry skin—and Ailis had watched him do it. When she confronted him, wanting such power for herself, Lenghan had been all too eager to teach her.

And so Ailis had learned to use reviled magic to bring health to her feeble body.

Sickened as I was by this knowledge, I couldn't blame her. I had seen pain hollow Ailis in a way that hunger never could. I had seen her face darken with torment and her chest rattle with the desperate need for reprieve. Wielding bloodcraft had brought vitality back to her limbs and spared her the pain that had plagued her since the day of her birth. But it couldn't cure her.

In the face of immedicable illness, Ailis had realized that the effects of her unnatural power could only be temporary. Each day, she would awake to discover her body once more aflame with pain, then use her newfound power to abate it. But the use of bloodcraft didn't come without cost. Nay, to manipulate the body was to sacrifice the soul—or at least some small part of it, Lenghan had told her—until naught remained of hope or humanity. One must be careful, he'd insisted. One must be wise. But Ailis wouldn't listen.

With every page, my sister's words grew darker. She spoke of how Lenghan would come to see her, warning her time and again against such wanton use of power:

*"The soul might recover, given time," he said, as if some part of me were broken. But can he not see that I have never before been whole? This power has given me life such as I have never known. No longer do I fear. No longer do I cower. What a pitiable thing I had been upon my sick bed. How contemptibly weak, delicate, and craven. . . .*

Ailis's last words were scrawling and incomprehensible,

lost to the madness of her mind—the same madness that had driven her to her death.

My stomach turned, and I shuddered. Setting the book aside, I gave myself to the wild gale of emotion swirling within me. My horror was relentless, as was the grip of grief. But somewhere amid sorrow, there was also anger. Aye, I was angry at Lenghan for having introduced my sister to such dangerous and unforgivable power, but I was also angry at myself for not having seen it. Over several months, Ailis's demeanor had hardened and her words had grown biting. But children on the cusp of maturity were often known for their tumultuous moods, and Stars knew Ailis had more right than most to be angry with the world. How quickly I'd contented myself to the assumption that her darkening attitude was merely a matter of age. Even when I'd found her standing on the walls of the guildhall, her features wild with abandon, I hadn't understood. "There is a greatness in you, sister," she had said in the pale gloom of early morning.

All these years, I'd thought Ailis had spoken of my skill as a healer, but she'd never seen greatness in the medicine I practiced. She'd seen it in my blood. In *our* blood. The blood of Gode.

For eight long years, her words had driven me toward greater acclaim.

For eight long years, I had been a fool.

"Oh, Ailis," I whispered into the deep shadows of night. "Shall I never know the depths to which I have failed you?"

There was no rising from the sorrow that Ailis's grimoire had imparted, and so I buried my anger and grief in the work of my trade. Long days passed as I distilled tinctures and brewed tonics—harvesting, macerating, boiling, and grinding anything that resembled the most obscure medicines I'd once heard had been used during a birthing: a cooling salve for the brow, a dram intended to ease pain, a fiery brew that was said to induce labor should a babe prove stubborn in the womb.

As I worked, there was one truth above all others that gnawed at me. I wasn't angry only with myself, nor only with Lenghan. I was angry with my sister, too. Ailis had fallen victim to the lure of unnatural power, and this knowledge compounded the heavy weight of guilt and grief I bore. Was it not enough that I had failed her in the weakness of her body? Had I failed to save her from beguiling power as well? My anger made me want to retch with shame. I couldn't blame Ailis for what she had done. She'd been but a wean, and there had been no reprieve from the painful reality of her broken body. Nay, I could not blame her—but I could be angry with myself all the same.

"The hour is late for chopping herbs, is it not?" The bright call of Sósia's voice tore through Granara's quiet surgery one night.

Startled, I let my herb knife slip. It nicked the calloused skin of my thumb, and I sucked in a sudden breath.

"Stars, forgive me," Sósia said, surging into the room. "I should have known better than to disturb you with a knife in your hand."

"'Tis nothing," I assured her, tasting only the faintest hint of copper. "Don't worry yourself, lass." The crease between Sósia's eyebrows faded when I showed her the shallow cut. "What brings you to the surgery at such a late hour?"

Sósia smoothed a hand over the roundness of her belly. "He loves the Stars, this one. Keeps me awake every night, his little hands and feet beating against me as though he wishes nothing more than to be free."

"You believe you bear a son?"

"I do." Sósia laughed. "I cannot say why, only that it feels true."

Despite her easy cheer, dark shadows ringed Sósia's eyes. I drew her toward the balcony that overlooked the sea. "Come, sit. I'll brew something that should calm him."

"No, no," Sósia said, settling herself into a cushioned seat. The moon was full and bright, and a warm breeze stirred the loose tendrils of her hair. "Let him be. It comforts me to feel him move."

I was tempted to press the issue, knowing how important it was that Sósia rest. But when she turned to look up at the Stars, a look of such indelible peace overcame her that I found I couldn't argue with her. I took a seat beside her, and a comfortable silence settled between us. Somewhere far below, the sea broke against the cliffside in a lulling rhythm.

"Sósia," I said quietly, fearful of upsetting the serenity of the moment. "Would you sing for me?"

The lass's smile was an unexpected balm. And when she sang, her voice was as delicate and wondrous as dew upon gossamer in a glen.

# CHAPTER II

It was decidedly tedious, waiting upon the coming of a child.

Hours stretched as long as days, and days as long as weeks, as the bairn in Sósia's belly grew. There was little to be done until the lass's labors began. Though I encouraged her to rest, I saw no reason to confine her to a lying-in chamber, as was common practice among some courts in the eight realms. Larmach healing taught that it was good for a mother to take fresh air and mild exercise in the days leading up to her labor, so as to maintain a healthy flow of blood that would keep the unborn child in good strength. Sósia would often walk through the winding paths of Granara's gardens in the morning. Sometimes she strode arm in arm with Adalina, their heads bent close as they spoke in languages both foreign and familiar. Though the lady's maid was clearly the superior linguist, it surprised me that Sósia spoke several languages as well. Some I recognized as the ancestral tongues spoken among the empire's eight realms, while others seemed to belong to peoples across the seas.

"Do you speak the Daor tongue?" I asked her in my ancestral language as we journeyed once more along the cliffside one evening.

"Only a little," Sósia replied, the words heavily accented. "Adalina has a much heavier command of the language."

"I think you mean *stronger*," I said, correcting her Daor before switching to her native Istanelan. "Is it not strange for a lady's maid to speak so many languages?"

Sósia nodded in appreciation at my return to the empire's common tongue. "Yes. But Adalina has an uncommon interest in foreign tongues *and* the mind to learn them. A good thing she was raised in Telór," said Sósia, referencing one of the northern Istanelan port cities on the Waking Sea. "She had access to more spoken languages than most."

Aside from this brief interlude, Sósia and I rarely spoke during the time we spent together. Though her singing had offered a momentary consolation that night on the balcony, the discovery of Ailis's grimoire had cast a pall over my spirit. I moved through the long days with only half a mind for the world around me. The rest had rooted itself in Aversere, in the days leading up to my sister's death. The more I thought about it, the more I remembered. All the little tells I should have recognized as unnatural madness but had interpreted as nothing more than pained ramblings—or, worse, the temperamental sulking of a youth.

At one point, I recalled the morning I'd awoken to find Ailis missing from her bed. Frantically, I had searched for her. She had a habit of rising on her better days, desperate for a reprieve from the stale confines of our chamber, only to find herself too weak to return to bed. Often, I had found her trembling as she leaned upon whatever she could find to hold herself up. But there were also times when I'd found her in graver circumstances: a bruise blossoming on her head, or her clothing soaked through as an inescapable rain poured down upon her. That morning, however, I'd found her standing tall and proud upon the walls of the guildhall.

"Ailis," I breathed, a rush of relief washing over me. "You ken it isn't well for you to walk alone."

"Have I not grown stronger in recent days, sister?"

"Aye." I placed my hand over hers on the parapet. "But such spells rarely linger, lass."

Ailis cut me a hard look. "Can you not see that this is different?"

She undoubtedly was healthier in those days than she had been in years, but I knew that pain still plagued her. Each morning, she would awake with a hiss, her jaw ground tight as she would lever herself up to sit.

"I am glad to see you well, Ailis. Truly. But I would still ken your comings and goings."

"Are you to mind me as a wean forever, then?" she snapped.

I frowned at her petulant retort. "I only wish to ken that you're safe, lass."

"But I *am* safe." She spread her arms wide. "Do you not see me standing hale before you? I am a child no more, Clìana."

"That may be," I said, intending to chide her further. But then the bell atop the archival hall tolled, beckoning students to their morning lectures. "I only ask that you mind yourself, lass," I went on. "I'd rather find you abed after my classes than lying pained or panting in some dark corner of the guildhall, aye?"

Squeezing Ailis's arm, I turned to head toward the lecture hall.

"There is a greatness in you, sister," Ailis had said, drawing me around. Her pale skin seemed to glow gold as the sun crept over the horizon. "As sure as the rising of the dawn. Will you not seek it?"

All these years, I'd thought she had spoken of my potential as a healer. I had been no great student in those days, consumed by my care of Ailis. I'd assumed that she wished for those days to end, for me to stop mothering her and apply myself wholly to my trade. But I understood now that I'd been wrong. So very, very wrong.

Shame was a heavy-handed master. In the wake of its blow, I became a shell of myself, a specter who haunted the halls of the tiny palace upon the sea. Sósia should have come to loathe me, but she did not. Perhaps she failed to find my behavior unusual, given how little she knew of me. But she was a keen slip of a lass. She had noted the sudden change in my demeanor; I knew she had. Yet she said nothing, content to keep my company in silence. It was because of her kindness that I was taken aback when she leaned across the supper table one evening, a twinkle of perverse humor in her eye, and said, "My time is drawing near, as you well know. So tell me the truth of it, Clìana. Do you resent serving as my physician?"

The Brennish wine I'd been nursing threatened to catch in my throat. I coughed as Sósia smirked. "You are a woman of no mean skill," she continued. "And I know you to be troubled. There is, after all, so little in the way of opportunity for you here. Surely, you must be disappointed to be sent so far from court."

"'Tis an honor to serve the bright prince," I managed, speaking truthfully. In the five long weeks since arriving at Granara, I had indeed been troubled by the relative ease of my commission, but only insofar as such ease offered little escape from the sorrows I carried with me.

"I am glad to hear it. Gabrián is . . ." Sósia hesitated, glancing away from me as she swallowed. "It is time that Bright Prince Gabrialo formed his court. It has been his right for some five years now, since he first came of age to inherit. You are the first he has commissioned, save the occasional itinerant bard or poet—most of whom he took on for my sake, I suspect. But do not mistake me. It is not irresponsibility that stays the bright prince's hand. It is, I believe, a mindful hesitancy."

I shook my head, failing to follow her thoughts.

"It is a grave thing to be born heir," Sósia explained. "When the time comes for the bright prince to assume the throne, he will excel. He has the mind for leadership—the discipline and heart as well, tender though it may be at times. But that is what makes him acutely aware of what it is to rule. Bright Prince Gabrialo hesitates to form his court because to do so would be to turn the key on the collar about his neck, to make fully real the knowledge that his life is not his own. It has never been, of course. But to form a court, to serve it and be served by it in return . . ." She frowned. "It is a strange thing, how power can shackle as surely as it can liberate."

The words speared me with violent familiarity. *Can he not see that I have never before been whole?* Ailis had written. *This power has given me life such as I have never known. No longer do I fear. No longer do I cower.* And yet that same power had been her undoing, in more ways than I wished to contemplate. But Sósia wasn't speaking of unnatural power. She was speaking of leadership. Of the power to reshape realms.

"Would many not kill for such power?" I asked, the hint of a challenge in my words.

"They would indeed, and that very ambition would prove them unworthy of it. It is dangerous to covet power. There is a hunger in such desire that can never be filled. Perhaps that is why the emperor is determined by birthright, so that no one should ascend to power out of greed. Only duty." Sósia's gaze turned distant. "Only ever duty."

The assessment quelled the riotous energy rattling through me, and I found myself suddenly exhausted by the conversation. I was tired of ruminating upon power. Tired of considering the many ways it could twist and poison and corrupt. Blood, broken bones, and a desperate gasp for breath were all too fresh in my memory.

"I have upset you," Sósia said, mistaking my grief for disagreement. "Do not mistake me, Clìana. There is a time for ambition, and I do not think you wrong for seeking a commission at court. I know the skill of your people and the greatness you must possess to bear so many feathers. You will be a fine asset in the bright prince's court, I assure you." She leaned forward in her chair as best she could, given the swell of her belly. "But the desire for power is a perverse thing, a great and futile grappling for control. And that control, we are none of us afforded."

Sósia's words came to me as if through water, as though I'd lost myself to the vast embrace of the Ifros, never again to breach its surface and breathe freely. *I know the greatness you must possess,* she had said. The words were too familiar, the grimoire's revelations too raw a wound.

"Are you unwell, Clìana?" Sósia's voice was ripe with concern.

"Nay," I tried to assure her, but my skin felt too tight for my bones. I pressed a hand to my chest as Sósia appraised me, frowning. "I apologize. I thought something of our supper did not agree with me, but the moment has passed."

"I am glad to hear it," said Sósia, though she scrutinized me over the rim of her raised glass. Still, she didn't press the issue. "I meant only to say that I am sorry the bright prince has sent you here, to tend to a simple birthing, when you could be at the palace. But take heart. In commissioning you, it seems that Bright Prince Gabrialo has begun to form his court. Soon you will have many souls to tend to."

"It will be an honor," I replied.

Slowly, Sósia rose from her seat. "Come. Let us walk along the cliffside. I think it should do us both—" She stilled then, gasping.

I darted to my feet. "Your waters?"

"Yes."

I rounded the table, the turmoil within me receding as the call of my craft beckoned me to action. Despite the stain that darkened the carpet in the dining hall, I didn't fret when Sósia's labors stalled later that night. A delay wasn't uncommon after a woman's waters broke. Neither did I worry when Sósia spent the next day in frustrated anticipation, Adalina trying in vain to distract her with conversations in foreign tongues. But when the third day dawned and Sósia complained of an ache in her belly—an ache entirely unlike the pain of labor—I knew that this would be no simple birthing.

A fever took hold of Sósia by dusk, confirming the worst of my suspicions: an infection had taken root in her womb. Confining her to her bed, I plied her with tisanes, cup after cup intended to quell the infection and bring about her labor. The sooner the child could be born, the greater the likelihood that both mother and child would live.

It was another week before the first contraction gripped Sósia's body.

By the time my feet carried me to the bedchamber, a foul stench had clouded the air. Sósia glanced up as I drew near, her face pale and pained, her eyes wide with fear. I lifted the hem of her shift to find the bedsheets splotched with fluid, dark and foul with disease. A hard knot twisted in my gut.

"What is it?" Sósia's small fingers curled around my arm. "Tell me."

"The waters of your womb are ill. I—"

"Is he going to die?" she demanded. I knew she spoke of the bairn she believed to be a boy.

"There is little certainty in childbirth." I squeezed her hand. "But I assure you, Sósia de Garzas: I am well-trained in complication."

With that, I set about my work. As Adalina hung a pot of water to boil over the hearth, I gathered vials of white willow bark and raspberry from my surgical trunk. Sósia's palms were damp when I pressed a cup of the medicinal brew into her hands.

"You must save him, do you understand?" Her voice

was low with quiet insistence. "Promise me, Clìana. If the worst should come to pass and a choice must be made, you must save him. No matter the cost."

I didn't know the horror of violence. Not truly. I had never been assailed by brigands or borne witness to bloody feuds. But I knew the trauma of the body. I knew how to steel myself against its gore, how to cut through flesh and bone and slip my hands into the warm, dark chasm of a wound. How to harden myself against the unnerving animal cries of a patient in pain. Or so I'd thought.

I should never have opened my heart to Sósia. That I knew with certainty as the foul stench of infection clogged my nose. Gritting my teeth against rising panic, I guided the lass to her feet, urging the laws of nature to play their part in the child's birth. We paced the room until Sósia gripped the bedpost, her eyes screwed as she cried out in pain.

"Oh, Clìana," she whispered as her body eased.

Stars, there was so little control in childbirth. For such a wide array of ills, there was definitive work to be done. I could mend a broken leg as surely as I could soothe a racking cough or excise a bulging tumor. But for labor? I could brew tonics, replace compresses, and palpate the womb, urging the child down, down, down. But such tasks seemed woefully insufficient in the face of such grave danger.

Reaching for oil of lavender, I dabbed the soothing balm on Sósia's temples, encouraging her to breathe deeply as Adalina whispered prayers to the Stars above. But long hours passed, and still the child would not come.

Exhausted, Sósia fell into bed as the night deepened, snatching short bouts of sleep between her labors. Adalina sat vigil at her bedside, dabbing sweat from Sósia's brow and offering her a hand to clench. The lady's maid prayed in a quiet litany to the Stars as a steady rain began to fall.

"It will only get worse," Adalina whispered lest she wake Sósia from her slumber. "The storm, I mean. I should bar the shutters." It was only when she peeled back the curtains that I saw the thick, burnished slabs of metal, clearly intended to withstand uncommon weather. The shutters creaked on their hinges as Adalina drew them closed.

"We'll need candles," I said, a note of instruction in my voice.

With a nod, Adalina slipped from the room. Weary, I took up Adalina's seat at Sósia's bedside, watching the rise and fall of her chest as the metallic clang of storm shutters echoed through the castle.

The lass's eyes shot open, meeting mine with panic. "Is he coming?"

"The child?" I said, smoothing a damp strand of hair from Sósia's brow. Her skin was burning.

"My love. Does he ride to me? Does he hear my song?" The fevered words tumbled from her lips. "I would remake the world for him, if he wished it. I have told him such, as he has said in kind. I cannot forsake him now. I cannot—" She cried out as her body tightened.

"Shh, you must rest now." I needed to break Sósia's fever somehow. Perhaps cover her in blankets and warm cloths. A tincture of dreamwine might help, if only to stave off her panic.

"He said he would—"

"Rest, Sósia."

Her grasp on my hand tightened. "But it is time!"

Her back arched as another contraction gripped her. Hopeful, I sprang to my feet. But when I lifted the hem of Sósia's chemise, the spark of hope in my chest faded. The bairn wasn't ready. Damn the Black, why would he not come? There was only so much torment Sósia could endure.

As if on cue, the lass's eyes rolled back, and her breath became rapid and shallow.

"Light! I need light!" I called, shucking up Sósia's underdress. Adalina rushed into the room with several candelabras and a second attendant in tow. "See if you can calm her, aye? She's not herself."

Taking up a cloth that had been boiled in hot water, I cleansed the skin that stretched over Sósia's womb. It was no longer safe for the child to linger, and I had made Sósia a promise. *No matter the cost.*

Drawing a hard line within myself, I plucked a scalpel from my surgical roll, placed a hand on Sósia's abdomen, and brought the blade to a mere inch above her flesh.

*"Sósia!"* A resounding crash stilled my hand. The noise was too loud to be a set of storm shutters blowing free. Someone called for a footman to bar the palace doors as booted feet thundered up the stairs. *"Sósia!"* the voice called again.

Seconds later, Bright Prince Gabrialo burst into the room, his fine clothes soaked through with rain. Sir Casdar entered at his heels, spearing me with a suspicious look.

The bright prince took in Sósia's frail form and swore. "Stars, she is not well," he breathed, his appearance souring further when he noted the scalpel in my hand.

"She has taken to fever, and the bairn will not come," I said. "If I am to save the child, I must act."

Despite the warm flush of the room, the bright prince paled. "There is no hope for her?"

"She bade me favor the child, my prince."

"Can both of them not . . . ?"

When I shook my head, the bright prince grew unnaturally still. He stared at me, tension ripe in the long lines of his body as every last drop of imperial pretense drained from his face.

Sósia's voice jarred Gabrialo from his trance. "You came."

"Of course I came," he said, hastening to her side. After pressing a kiss to her brow, he took up her hand in his.

"It hurts," said Sósia.

"I know."

"The babe . . ."

"I know." Gabrialo pressed his lips to Sósia's knuckles before meeting my eye, his expression once more impassible. "Do as you must, Lady Clìana."

"There will be blood," I said softly.

"I will not leave her."

I turned toward Casdar Belorán, a question in my gaze.

"I know blood, my lady," said the brightsword, taking his place by the chamber door. His fingers curled around the hilt of his sword. There wasn't time for me to examine the chill that coursed up my spine in response.

Turning, I adjusted the scalpel in my grip. Just then, a contraction racked Sósia's body. With a sigh of relief, I set the scalpel aside. At last, the babe was crowning.

"Lady Clìana?"

The question pierced through the rushing in my ears. I paid it no mind. Not when the black-haired bairn in my arms wasn't breathing. I stuck my finger in its mouth and nose, clearing away the mucus of the womb. Even with its airways freed, the babe refused to breathe.

*"Lady Clìana?"*

I placed a palm over the wean's heart. His body was still beneath my touch. With a curse, I pumped my fingers against his chest. Swift compressions, a knuckle's width deep. Pausing, I felt for a heartbeat and listened for breath.

Nothing.

"Does he not breathe?" Gabrialo's words were thick and rough.

His question drew a strangled cry from Sósia. I could not hide this from her. From either of them. I turned toward the bed, the bairn slick and still as a river rock in my arms.

The bright prince cradled Sósia in his embrace, looking as though his own heart might stop beating. But it was Sósia's attention that seared through me, clear now despite her fever. I remembered with sudden clarity the promise I had made her. *No matter the cost.*

I knew at once what I must do.

As if scenting danger, I felt the hard press of Sir Casdar's scrutiny on my back, but I couldn't help his presence. Let the brightsword think what he would think. There was work to be done. Not as a Larmach healer, but as a daughter of Gode.

Uncertainty curled tight in my gut and fluttered in my chest. Pressing my fingertips to the child's skin, I reached for the unnatural power in my blood. I didn't know how to use it. I didn't even know if it was truly there. Maybe Lenghan had been wrong to believe I possessed the capacity to use bloodcraft. Perhaps there was learning I had to gain before I could successfully call upon its use. Still, for Sósia, I had to try.

Three Daor words rose instinctively within me. "Àil i blethìn."

It was a desperate prayer, a fierce invocation.

*Let him live.*

# CHAPTER 12

I didn't know what to expect when I called upon the power in my blood. I had thought that I'd feel some strange surge of energy within me, or perhaps the quiet numbing of the soul that Ailis had described in her grimoire. Then the child's cheeks would redden, his lungs would swell, and a cry would break from the soft curve of his lips. That seemed a reasonable expectation, given what I'd witnessed of Lenghan's power and Ailis's maddened writings. But why would there be anything of reason in the unholy power of Gode?

Magic, I learned, was a tide—a great roiling wave that drew me deep into the dark of night. My stomach clenched against its violent pull, and my flesh stretched so taut that I feared it might tear me from limb to limb. I cried out in agony, a guttural scream that resounded with a piercing echo in my ears. The slow tick of time meant nothing. There was neither up nor down. No earth. No sky. Just the wicked pull of power, raging and relentless. I lost myself to its might—until, all at once, it released its crushing hold.

I spilled suddenly into life, my body cocooned in water that dampened my hair and seeped through the thin linen of my dress. I drew a deep breath as the world around me came into focus. I wasn't in Granara anymore, nor any place I recognized. Instead, I was floating in a river with a low, dense fog clinging to its surface. I thought of the river pool from my dreams and flailed, panic fluttering in my chest. My heel struck something close to the water's surface—a riverbed, I realized—and found that I could sit. Dark water skimmed my hips, its current dragging gently at my skirts. I fought to catch my breath as my heartbeat thundered in my ears.

That was when I heard a soft cry cut through the fog. The bairn.

I scrambled to my knees, splashing through the current in search of him until my hands struck something soft and cool. A wee body was floating in the dark. "There!" I cried, pulling the child close. His hands flexed against my chest, as if seeking his mother's breast. A sense of triumph surged within me. I had promised Sósia that I would save her child no matter the cost, and I had kept my promise. I'd found her wee lad, here in this otherworld. And though I couldn't say how, I was going to bring him home.

Holding the bairn close, I rose to my feet, my head breaking through the fog as I straightened. That was when I saw it—the night sky. Teeming. Shivering. Shining. Awash with Stars. The great, endless cavern of the Dark surrounded me, studded by Lights that seemed as distant and yet near as they had ever been. My breath shallowed, and a wave of uncommon peace washed through me. I could lie down. I could give my body to the river, and it would carry me forth, folding me into the embrace of the Dark Between. I closed my eyes and gently sighed.

How pleasant it would be, to forsake the troubles of the world. . . .

The babe's wee fingers pressed suddenly against my sternum, drawing me from my reverie. *No matter the cost*, I had promised Sósia. I couldn't forsake her now.

Bundling the bairn close, I turned my attention inward and called again upon the power in my blood to bring me back to the realm of the living.

Almost at once, I pitched forward as I emerged from the otherworld, as if experiencing some strange rebirth. The walls of Sósia's bedchamber materialized around me, and the bairn's cry rent the air.

"Holy Stars!" Gabrialo exclaimed as I righted myself.

Terror should have pounded in my chest. I'd practiced foul magic to bring the babe back from death—and in front of the Bright Prince of the Radiant Astral Empire, no less. Instead, a strange sense of apathy flooded through me. Why should I be fearful when I'd wrought life from death with the power in my blood? What should ever tempt me into panic or alarm? Distantly, I remembered what Ailis had written in her grimoire. To exercise power over the body was to forfeit a measure of the soul, Lenghan had warned her. But if it was fear that I had forfeited, why should I not continue the use of such power? If Gabrialo condemned me for a witch, could I not defend myself against him?

I turned to face the bright prince with the bairn in my

arms, expecting to meet his contempt. But Gabrialo's gaze held only wonder, his attention flitting between me and the child I held. Surprised, I glanced in Sir Casdar's direction. He seemed no more suspicious of me than he had upon our first meeting. Was it possible that I had only been in the otherworld for the span of a breath? That I had never truly left my corporeal body behind?

"He lives!" said Gabrialo, drawing my focus.

Pride blossomed in my chest. "Aye, my prince. You have a son."

"A son." Gabrialo laughed in wonder. "Sósia, you have a son!"

It should have been a glorious moment, full of mirth. But when the bright prince shifted Sósia in his arms, her head slid from his shoulder and hung limply. He lifted her chin. Sósia looked back at him with empty eyes, her expression cloaked in death.

An hour later, the Bright Prince of the Radiant Astral Empire was sitting in a simple wooden chair, his eyes red with grief, his arms curled as though he yet held the babe the wet nurse had taken from his grasp. Water dripped like quiet bells of mourning as I wrung a damp cloth above a basin of fragrant water. Sósia's body lay on the worktable before me. Taking up her arm, I began to cleanse the grime of labor from her skin.

I had tried to save her, even as a strange sense of indifference had gripped me. I'd spoken the same Daor words over her body as I had over her bairn, pleading with the power that had swept me away to the otherworld only the minute before. But no matter what I'd said, Granara

Palace had remained firmly fixed around me, the Stars hanging somewhere high above. Gabrialo had wept openly when I'd declared that she was gone.

"Not here," he'd said when I had begun gathering materials to cleanse her body for burning. The hard edge in his voice had stilled me. A familiar hollow look had replaced his open grief—an echo of the reflection I'd so often seen in the mirror. Yet I didn't feel such deadened emotion for myself. Not in the wake of Sósia's death, nor even upon remembering the twin losses of my mother and sister. In truth, I felt nothing at all.

The realization chafed at the edges of my apathy. Was this the cost of employing the unholy power Ailis had written about in her grimoire? The more I considered my sister's scrawled words, the greater my unease became. The awareness of my indifference seemed to chase it from my mind, and a quiet sense of loss soon seeped into my bones.

"You loved her," Gabrialo said from the dark corner of the surgery's sickroom.

Tears burned in my eyes, I realized. Suddenly I felt as fragile as glass. "Aye."

"You knew her for so little a time."

My hand stilled on Sósia's brow. "To ken her a day was to ken her heart."

I felt the hot press of the bright prince's regard upon me. "Only if she allowed you to see it," he said. Rising from his seat, he took the damp cloth from my grasp. "I should like to be alone with her."

The room drew close around me, warm and sticky. "Of course," I said, then closed the sickroom door behind me.

It was Casdar Belorán who spared me from the dark pull of mourning. Shortly after I left the bright prince and returned to my chamber, a loud rap sounded at my door.

"My lady, Sir Casdar has taken ill," said the servant in the hall.

The brightsword's hard ride through the driving rain had given way to fever. He was now lying abed in the chamber that had been prepared for him, the broad lines of his bare chest damp with sweat. Delirious, his lips twitched as he mumbled.

I placed the back of my hand against Sir Casdar's brow and cursed. "How long has he been like this?" I asked the servant.

"No more than an hour," he replied. "The chamberlain sent me to serve as valet to the brightsword when he retired. Sir Casdar did not look well when he bade me fetch a bottle of spirits. By the time I returned, he was damp with fever."

"We need to get him to my surgery."

The valet sprang into action, setting out in search of other servants to assist him.

Returning to my surgery, I set a kettle over the open hearth and tried not to think of Gabrialo mourning his lover in the sickroom next door. As the water began to boil, several men carried Sir Casdar into the room, laying him on one of the cots that had been removed from the sickroom to prepare the small infirmary for Sósia's body. I fed the kettle a handful of bog myrtle leaves as the servants retreated, then perched on the edge of the cot to bathe the sweat from the brightsword's face. Even as he was lost to a feverish sleep, his eyebrows grew taut with anger. For a brief, mad moment, I considered smoothing the furrow with my thumb, as if I could ease his black temper with something as simple as a touch. But then Sir Casdar spoke, in a string of garbled words. One in particular caught my attention, making the breath hitch in my lungs.

"Witch."

Sir Casdar's fever broke late in the night, his body sinking into untroubled sleep. Still, I didn't leave his side. Never mind exhaustion and grief; I knew what the brightsword had said. I'd heard the word with perfect clarity—and I was terrified. Did he know what I had done to bring Sósia's babe back from death? Had he somehow learned of the grimoire hidden in my medical trunk, which sat just a few paces across the room? I stared at Sir Casdar for what must have been hours, my mind whirring with the implications of that one simple word.

"How is he?"

The question tore me from the grip of fear. I turned to find the bright prince standing in the open doorway, still dressed in his riding habit. His once-sodden clothing was now stiff and wrinkled with wear. His expression could have been described in much the same manner.

"His fever has broken," I said, rising to meet him at the door. "It won't be long now before he is recovered." Up close, I could see the dark circles that lined the bright prince's eyes. "Have you slept, my prince?"

He shook his head. "I do not think I can."

"I could prepare a dram, should you wish it."

"No, not yet. I—" He grimaced before shaking his head in firm resolve. "No."

"Tonight, then," I said, knowing he would need his rest for the long days to come.

"Tonight, then." He made to leave, then hesitated. "Thank you, my lady, for all you have done. For Casdar, as well as Sósia and her babe."

I stiffened, my heart pounding in my chest. I didn't deserve to be thanked, not when Sósia was dead. Not when I had failed the bright prince and his child. If I was worthy of anything, it was condemnation.

When I said nothing, the bright prince nodded. "Lady Clìana," he said before retreating, leaving me to bear the weight of my guilt alone.


Later, in my chamber, I stood on aching legs, feeling not so much as half the person I had been the day before. Despite the early hour, the storm shrouded the room in darkness. I took up a damp cloth and scrubbed at my skin until no trace of death remained. Still, Sósia's glassy gaze lingered in my mind.

Sometime afterward, a servant brought me a meal on a silver platter. Though the food tasted of ash, the weight of it seemed to settle me. No longer did I feel outside of myself, lost to fear or apathy or grief. I could feel the breath in my lungs and the pulse in my chest. I thought to take some rest then—the bright prince wasn't the only one who hadn't slept—but I feared what I might see should I close my eyes, waiting for sleep to take me. Instead, I went in search of the babe and found his wet nurse standing in the hall outside the nursery.

"Is something amiss?" I asked as the wet nurse curtsied.

Rising, she shook her head. "His lordship wished a moment alone with the child."

"His lordship?"

"I could see no harm in it, given that the babe was sleeping."

To my knowledge, there was no lordship in residence at Granara Palace. Either the bright prince had kept his identity from the palace servants, or the wet nurse wasn't sure whether his identity was being kept from me. I hazarded a peek through the open door, intending only to ensure that the so-called lord was indeed the bright prince. As I glanced into the room, Gabrialo's unerring gaze found mine.

"You wish to examine him," he said, his voice lilting in question. He sat in the gliding chair near the open hearth, rocking his newborn son in his arms.

I took a small step over the threshold. "I can wait."

Gabrialo's thumb stilled on the dark cap of the babe's head, and a measure of tension unwound from his shoulders. He offered me a nod that was as much a dismissal as it was an acknowledgment of the offer.

"Will you name him for his mother?" I asked softly.

Several weeks earlier, Sósia had told me that it was custom for Istanelan children to be named as such should the mother die in labor. Gabrialo seemed as surprised by the question as I was to find myself asking it. A pang of sorrow flashed across his face. "It is not my decision to make," he said.

# CHAPTER 13

Gabrialo didn't elaborate upon his meaning—not then, at least. Yet there was a strange weight to his words. I felt it lying heavily upon my chest and saw the truth of it lingering in his eyes. Desperate as I was to relieve the pressure, I didn't beg an explanation of him. His words on the threshold of my surgery had done more than remind me of how deeply I had failed him. They had pierced through the fog of my grief, reminding me of the gravity of his person. Gabrialo was no mere man. He was the bright prince. One day, when his father was gone, he would assume the role of emperor and the responsibility of safeguarding the eight realms of the Radiant Astral Empire. It was a role of unfathomable importance and prestige. Already, I had spoken with him too freely.

In the days that followed, I held my tongue in his presence. It wasn't difficult to do so. Our paths rarely crossed as we each made our way through the haunted halls of Granara Palace. Only at night, when I would bring the slim vial of dreamwine to his door, did I catch more than a glimpse of him. Even then, it was only the outline of his shoulders, limned in fading sunlight, as he sat on his private balcony, staring out at the sea. The storm that had shrouded Sósia's deathbed had passed, but the one clouding the bright prince's mind was another matter. One of the chambermaids would return the empty dreamwine vial to my surgery each morning.

Three days after Sósia's death, a retinue of mounted soldiers arrived to escort her body to Carastile, where she would presumably be given a court burning at Bright Prince Gabrialo's request. The night before we were to leave, I dreamed of a river pool black as night—and in the pool, a woman drowning. I hovered over her as she fought to keep her head above the surface. A thin sliver of moonlight broke through the heavy clouds above, illuminating the fine lines of Sósia's face as she thrashed about in the water. With a gasp, I tried desperately to reach her. But my body was airy and unreal, held back by some unseen force. Horror-struck and immobile, I watched as Sósia's heavy skirts dragged her down into Shadow. The surface of the water settled. My throat clogged with the weight of a sob that would not break from my lips.

The polished obsidian surface of the water suddenly fractured, but it wasn't Sósia who burst up from the depths of the pool. Instead, it was Ailis.

My sister's fragile features drew back in a gruesome caricature as she cackled, heedless of the water pouring into her mouth and consuming her. I fought in vain to break free of my nebulous form to aid her, but I was little more than a specter. There was nothing I could do but watch as the water swallowed Ailis whole. It was only when the water stilled once more that I found I could finally press closer. I hovered above the darkling pool as a swollen body rose slowly to its surface.

This time, its face was my own.

I awoke with a start and lay awake for some time, deeply shaken by the memory of the dream. The silence that permeated the palace closed in around me, heavy as a shroud. Unwilling to bear its weight a second longer, I rose and wrapped my shawl around me. I could still hear Ailis's laughter echoing in my ears, as surely as I could envision Sósia thrashing in the dark water. Worse yet was the memory of my own swollen body, putrid in death, my pale skin sloughing from my bones.

A shudder coursed down my spine. Nay, I wouldn't sleep, not when the deep shadows of my chamber mirrored the yawning chasm of the river pool. I needed light and air. Something to ease my panic and chase the vile vision from my mind.

Desperate, I padded barefoot down the chamber hall and out onto the terrace that overlooked the palace gardens. Beneath the Stars, the night was cool and bright. I drank of it greedily, my knuckles white around the chill stone railing. Slowly, my pulse began to calm. The river pool had been a night terror, and nothing more. A trick of the Shadows, scenting my sorrow and seeking purchase in my head. Never mind that I considered the Shadows as mythological as the deity of the Stars above. Imagining the creatures, exiled to Starless places for their sins, gave me somewhere to place my anger and stake my grief. I refused to give them leave to play their wicked games within my mind. When I glanced up, the Ifros stretched out before me, shimmering in the moonlight. I tried not to see the dark water I had dreamed of rippling in its place.

I'd been standing there for some time when I heard the sudden *wheet* of a sandpiper cut through the night. The sound startled me, so near and loud as it was. The first call was followed shortly by another. Only this time, the bird-song seemed distorted, the sound prolonged rather than sharp.

I leaned over the balustrade, hoping to catch a glimpse of the source of the sound. Sure enough, the call came again. Only this time, I recognized the sound for what it was: the fussing of a babe. *Sósia's babe.* Its cry came from below, followed by gentle shushing and faint footsteps as someone walked across the tiled portico beneath the terrace.

I fought the urge to lean farther over the balustrade, needing to know who had taken the babe from its nursery so late at night. A beat later, a figure emerged from the cover of the portico, cradling Sósia's babe as he strode along the footpath toward Granara's storm-battered gardens. I relaxed upon recognizing the long lines of the bright prince's frame.

I knew the bairn was safe with Bright Prince Gabrialo. The man cared for his son, as surely as he'd cared for Sósia. Still, I lingered on the terrace, curiosity bidding me watch as they wove their way through the gardens. Something about the sight of them soothed me far more than fresh air and an open sky. There was a peace to them—father and son—despite the unconscionable pain that had brought the bairn into the world. It was some comfort to know that the child would not be forsaken despite the loss of his mother, that his father cared to hold him close.

When the pair entered the garden's central courtyard, a second figure emerged from the shadows. At first, I thought it might have been Casdar Belorán, for the figure had the brightsword's broad, stocky build. But this man was much shorter, and when he stepped into the full light of the moon, I could see that his complexion was nearly as pale as my own—an uncommon sight in northern Istanel.

My pulse quickened. The man might be a danger to the child or the bright prince, but then Bright Prince Gabrialo didn't seem startled by his appearance. Rather, the two men began to talk. Their words didn't carry far enough for me to hear them, but I noticed when the bright prince's posture stiffened. He leaned forward to kiss the bairn's head, then passed the child into the stranger's arms. The men exchanged a few more words before the stranger turned and stalked into the night, taking Sósia's bairn with him.

Bright Prince Gabrialo made no move to cry out or give chase. He simply stood beneath one of the courtyard's trellised gateways, watching the mysterious man carry his son away into the dark. I couldn't say how long he stood there, nor how long I watched him for any sign that something was amiss. A minute, perhaps? Two? Three? At last, the bright prince drew a heaving breath, turned on his heel, and quickly walked back toward the palace.

Carefully, I eased myself away from the balustrade. I didn't understand what I'd just witnessed, but I knew I'd been privy to something I wasn't supposed to see. Shame warmed my cheeks when I considered how Bright Prince Gabrialo might feel should he look up and see me upon the terrace. I nestled back against the rough stone of the castle wall, thinking to stay there until the bright prince had returned to his private quarters. But the sound of his footsteps slowed in the hall as he neared the terrace doors.

My pulse quickened as he stepped onto the balcony and strode the few short steps to the balustrade, seemingly oblivious to my presence. His fingers curled around the rail as I frantically considered what I should do. Perhaps clear my throat and alert him to my presence? Or carefully slip back into the hall?

"It is late to be out of doors, is it not?" he said, startling me from my thoughts.

I stilled, the way a forest might grow silent in the presence of a predator. It was clear from his tone that he must have seen me watching, and I felt my cheeks grow even hotter. "Forgive me, my prince. I did not mean to pry."

"Even so," the bright prince said before turning. When he regarded me in the dark, I was surprised to find his expression soft. "It is likely well that you saw what you did tonight, if you are to serve within my court."

I blinked at him, dumbfounded. "You intend to commission me? Even after I failed so utterly to spare Sósia?"

Bright Prince Gabrialo frowned. "Renowned as the healers of Clan Larmach might be, I do not expect you to work miracles. I was there, Lady Clìana. I saw the blood and the skill with which you worked. I blame you for nothing."

My chest tightened with emotion. I hadn't realized until that moment how much fear I had been harboring, how certain I'd been that realization would soon pierce through the veil of the bright prince's grief and he would remember how deeply I had failed Sósia. I had tended to her child. I had called upon the power in my blood to bring him back from death. But at what cost? Sósia was dead. She had been alive, and the child had been gone—

and yet I had chosen to revive the bairn at her expense. What if I had accepted the child's death, rather than trying to do the impossible? What if I had minded Sósia's pains, rather than working bloodcraft? A bitter laugh rose within me. Gabrialo's lover was dead because I had neglected her care, and still he wanted me to serve in his court.

I wanted to deny the bright prince, to tell him how deeply undeserving I was of the role. But before I could speak, he said, "If you are to come to court, there is something you must know. Something you *deserve* to know, given what you have seen this night." My chest tightened in anticipation as the breeze rose around us, thick with salt. "Sósia trusted few," he went on, "and fewer still with her heart. But it seems she trusted you, and that is how I know that I may do the same.

"The man you saw tonight, the man who took Sósia's child . . . I cannot tell you his name. But I can assure you that he will keep the child safe." He turned toward me then, his gaze heavy. *"His* child, Lady Clìana."

The world slowed in the wake of his words. *"His child?"*

"Sósia was not my lover, Lady Clìana. She was Princess Sastiona of the House of Vendegal. My sister."

Acid rose in my throat. I imagined Sósia once more, thrashing in dark water until the Shadows swallowed her. This time, a glint of silver circled the crown of her head.

The night once more closed in around me, stealing the breath from my lungs. "Forgive me," I said, managing the briefest of bobs before fleeing into the haunted halls of Granara Palace.

✦

Dawn rose thin and gray over the palace's curtain wall. I stood beneath the stable's eaves, listening to the muddle of sounds that rose around me: the somber rustle of servants; horses stamping in the gravel; the long, high wail of the wind cutting along the cliffside. I felt weightless again, outside myself, as I had the night of Sósia's death. Only this time, there was nothing to ground me. My stomach roiled. My fingers floated through my hair. I drew the merest hints of breath through a throat thick with fear.

What had I done?

In a matter of days, the whole of the Radiant Astral Empire would know of the princess's death. Would they know that I had been the one to fail her? Nay, the world believed that Princess Sastiona had been living these past six months at the court of the khagan of Nyengun, the powerful northern kingdom across the Ifros. They would never know that a birthing had killed her, nor that I had not seen her safely through the ordeal. My knees threatened to buckle against the weight of my guilt—and I might have let them do so, had I not spotted Casdar Belorán striding toward me across the courtyard.

"The bright prince wishes to know whether you have all you need for the journey north," he said, his tone clipped with reluctance.

I thought of the word he had spoken when he was lost to fever—*witch*—and a shudder passed through me. Since recovering from his illness, Sir Casdar had given me no indication that he knew of the power in my blood. Still, that didn't mean he was ignorant of it, and I felt compelled to brace myself whenever he drew near.

"Thank you, sir," I said, nodding. "I am well-prepared."

With a grunt of acknowledgment, he stalked off to ready his mount. A groom led my horse from the stables shortly thereafter. As if sensing my discomfort, the mare blew a long cloud of warm, white breath.

Knights of the imperial guard had gathered in the bailey, aligning themselves in twin columns before Granara's gates. A low, enclosed wagon sat within their ranks, covered in the deep blue banner of the House of Vendegal. Its sigil was a rising sun bearing eight silver rays, one for each realm that pledged loyalty to the emperor's rule. Within the mourning carriage lay Princess Sastiona's body, prepared for the journey north. The mere sight of it made my skin prickle with shame.

Bright Prince Gabrialo emerged from the palace then, his fine features darkly drawn. He tugged on his riding gloves in two quick motions, his stride long and sure, before taking the reins the stable lad held outstretched. His shoulders rose and fell, as if he was drawing a fortifying breath, before he fitted one boot into a stirrup and mounted. With all the swiftness of an arrow, his gaze found mine, far softer than it ought to have been. I could make no sense of it. His sister was dead. My lack of attention had killed her, and yet the bright prince looked at me with kindness. It must have been a ploy; the bright prince had a canny mind. Perhaps he was toying with me, offering me false comfort before exacting whatever vengeance might satisfy him. Whatever it was, I deserved it. I'd let him flay me bare if that was what he desired. Yet somehow, I imagined that the slow ride north toward Carastile would prove more torturous. I resigned myself to my fate as the palace gates swung open for our departure.

As we set off across the battered Istanelan heaths, I found my place at the end of the retinue, content to follow the somber party. The miles bled on as the heat of the day rose. I said nothing, too weary and troubled to look beyond some vague point between my horse's ears.

At midday, we crossed a running burn, an offshoot of the Ségua, where we stopped to break our fast and let the horses drink. I ate a bit of bread to keep up my strength, the smell of yeast sharp and sour in my nose. I didn't care to eat, but I'd seen those who refused sustenance in their grief, their expressions hollow and distant as their bodies wasted away to bone. I refused to give myself that early grave. Not as I had with Sósia—and with Ailis. I swallowed bite after bite, trying not to think of Sastiona in her mourning carriage, nor of the quiet compassion in Bright Prince Gabrialo's regard. The latter proved vain when he drew beside me in the saddle a few minutes later.

"Ride ahead with me," he said before tucking his heels into his horse's flanks and cantering past the procession. Sir Casdar made to follow, but the bright prince waved him off. The brightsword's body stiffened when I trailed in Bright Prince Gabrialo's wake. Guiding my horse over the rocky plains, I tried to quell the anxious whirring of my mind.

"You must have questions," the bright prince said when the procession was some lengths behind us. We slowed our horses to a trot. "Will you ask them?"

"I have no right to question you, my prince."

He frowned. "You are angry with me."

His words caught me off guard. Not only because they

were unexpected, but because they were astute. I *was* angry with him—for keeping Sósia's true identity from me, for allowing the bairn's father to whisk him away without my approval, for not being angry with me. By the Black, his sister was *dead*. She was my responsibility, and she was *dead*.

Bright Prince Gabrialo sighed heavily, looking weary in a way that transcended the grief of loss. Just as quickly, his countenance became inscrutable. "I am the bright prince, my lady. Not the Dark Itself. Let us speak plainly."

His request snapped the last thread of my restraint. "I would never have tended to the child first if I had known."

"Why not?"

"Sastiona was a *princess*, third in line to your father's throne. Her death comes at too high a cost."

He glanced at me sharply. "A cost?"

"That bairn cannot so much as bear a family name."

My mount gave an anxious whinny as the bright prince drew his horse around. "Do not regret that boy's life," he said, his voice low and thin with warning.

"I regret *death*."

"Sastiona's death, perhaps—"

"Aye, death of such great consequence—"

"You think the child does not matter because he cannot bear a family name?"

"I think your sister mattered especially, given the family name she bore!"

The bright prince made a noise of disgust. "You dishonor her."

The words pummeled through me. The bright prince's features softened as heat suffused my face. "Which do you think Sósia loved more, my lady?" he went on. "Her child?

Or her crown? You swore to her that you would mind the babe first. Do not regret that promise now."

For the first time, I stared openly at the Bright Prince of the Radiant Astral Empire, and I saw in him something I should have seen plainly from the start: a deep, abiding love for his sister. It was affection that had nothing to do with her station and everything to do with *her*—her light, her joy, her passion for life. The bright prince's word would have superseded Sósia's in that birthing chamber, yet he did not command that I mind his sister's life before her child of nameless birth. He had honored her wish that I tend to the bairn first, allowing her that final act of motherly devotion, and now she was dead.

"You blame yourself," I whispered.

Bright Prince Gabrialo shook his head. "Perhaps that first night, when I sat in that gloomy chamber and watched you prepare her body for burning. But I realized soon enough that to blame myself would be to rob my sister of her dignity. She made a choice, and I will honor her by respecting that choice—no matter the grave sorrow of its consequence."

I looked at the bright prince, and he looked at me. It was as plainly as we had observed each other in all the brief encounters we had shared. I hadn't realized until then how vague an image of him I had built in my mind's eye. I knew the gold-brown hue of his skin—a common sight in the balmy northern realm—and his dark hair, warm and deep as the richest of teas. I knew the fleeting glances, the low-bent eyebrows, and the grief that sloped his shoulders. But we had danced around each other in the days that had followed his sister's death, as befit our stations; and I hadn't noticed the dimple in his chin, nor the freckles that dotted his cheeks. Then there was his brow, high and proud, which seemed worthy of nothing more than the brightest of crowns. One day, he would wear the diadem of the Radiant Astral Emperor. It was that crown I had not failed but *honored*, if I were to take him at his word. It was a difficult sentiment to swallow, and yet it tethered me to something buoyant—to something that felt like hope.

The sound of hooves filled the air as the royal procession drew near.

"I would ask but one thing," I said to Bright Prince Gabrialo before they were upon us. "Was she ever called Sósia?"

A small, sad smile tugged at the bright prince's lips. "Only by those she loved."

# CHAPTER 14

Carastile was cruel in its brilliance. Golden light gleamed through its streets and capped its towering shops and sanctuaries, so contrary to the pall of grief that gripped the city in the wake of Sósia's death. In the days leading up to her burning, I learned that she'd been favored among the common people, beloved for her support of music and the arts. She'd been known to commission bards to perform in the streets and make frequent appearances at the festivals she funded, occasionally offering a song in blessing. "She had the voice of a linnet," I overhead Adalina say at court one evening, dabbing at her eyes. The words called to mind the night Sósia had sung for me on the balcony at Granara, and I swallowed against the grief that threatened to consume me.

Rather than returning directly to Carastile, the funeral procession had traveled to a small port town south of the city, where the emperor's soldiers had tucked away their sigils and carried Sósia's coffin onto a small merchant ship. It was only later, when I found myself once more bent over a chamber pot in my cabin, heaving up the contents of my wame, that understanding struck. If Princess Sastiona was believed to be in Nyengun, as Lord Ulmhar had told me, then her funeral wagon couldn't be seen arriving in the city from the south. Such an occurrence would give rise to questions the Astral throne couldn't afford to answer. Instead, Bright Prince Gabrialo was ensuring that she arrived home to Carastile by way of the sea.

The following day, the city awoke to the low gong of mourning bells and the sobering knowledge that the princess was dead, killed by a fall from her horse while riding near the khagan's palace. Her burning would take place at dusk the next night, following a ceremony in the city's Grand Sanctuary.

As a member of the bright prince's court, I was expected to attend Sósia's burning rites. But in truth, I didn't want to mourn her loss. I wanted to lay claim to my new Carastilan surgery and lose myself in the work of my craft. To forget that I had ever met her and that the bright prince had seen fit to name me to his court despite how profoundly I had failed him. I was tired of grieving. Tired of feeling the deep ache of loss in my chest and the hollow chasm that followed, where some essential *feeling* ought to have been. But I had no choice.

Yadi-Rafin procured me one of the mourning veils customarily worn by Istanelan women on the day of a loved one's burning. I donned the dark lace in my new apartment at court, a fine two-room suite with a balcony looking south toward Granara. I tried to push that fact from my mind as I smoothed my hands down the length of my bodice, feeling as ill as I had been at sea.

As the royal procession wound its way through the city,

trailing in the wake of Sósia's funeral wagon, I took my place among the other titled servants. A sea of faces lined the streets. People cried out as we passed, offering laments and pleas for the princess's swift passage to the Stars. On occasion, the sound of wailing swelled around us, reminding me of the luminary who had keened for Ailis on the day of her burning. A shudder coursed down my spine as the procession continued deeper into the heart of Carastile, until the city's Grand Sanctuary rose before us.

Like all Astral houses of worship, the Grand Sanctuary was built of solid stone, its walls entirely windowless so that its interior might evoke the embrace of the Dark Between. My lips parted as I stepped into the round inner sanctum, surprised to find that the ceiling shimmered with precious jewels rather than simple crushed stone. The effect was striking, a wash of gems glimmering in mirror of the Stars above.

A band of brightswords eased Sósia's body down onto the raised altar at the center of the Sanctuary. I took a seat on one of the low stone benches circling the dais as the ceremony began.

The following hour passed in a blur of somber words and ancient songs, candlelight flickering as the fragrance of perfumed oils filled my nose. I paid little attention to what was said of Sósia. My focus settled on her face instead, as if to look away from her would be some mortal sin. Over and over, I traced the curve of her cheek and the slope of her nose, the dark sweep of her brow and the bow of her mouth. She should have been smiling. At Granara, she had often smiled—though not on the night she'd lain in her birthing bed, the twist of her lips grotesque around my name.

*Clìana!*

Her cry echoed in my ears, the memory of it so loud that my eyes pressed shut, as though I could excise the wound of it by closing myself off to the world around me. When I became conscious of myself once more, I was standing in the Grand Sanctuary's inner courtyard, where Sósia was lying atop her funeral pyre beneath a golden sun. The sight of her felt suddenly like a brand, a reminder of how deeply I had failed her. I tore my gaze away—only for it to alight upon Bright Prince Gabrialo. He stood at the head of his sister's pyre beside his father and brother, weeping openly.

The priestess known as the Most Luminous stepped forward then. She set Sósia's pyre ablaze with a torch, relinquishing her spirit to the Stars above.

I watched Bright Prince Gabrialo as his sister's body burned, unable to look away from him. His grief was too familiar, the ache of it too keen. Part of me wished to reach out to him. To offer him what comfort I could in kinship with his loss. But I was a healer, and he was the bright prince. It wasn't my place to offer him any consolation, save that which could be found in a bottle of dreamwine. The thought seemed to sever whatever spell had fixed my attention upon him. For the remainder of the burning, I focused on the flames that rose above Sósia's pyre, snapping at the encroaching dusk.

As the burning waned, a realization struck me, sharp and sudden as a spear. If bloodcraft had allowed me to bring Sósia's son back from death, perhaps it could have spared Ailis as well. Perhaps I could have met her in that otherworld all those years ago, taken her in my arms, and led her back into life. If only I had known of the power I possessed—

The power *Lenghan* possessed.

I cried out in anguish. Lenghan hadn't just taught Ailis about bloodcraft. He'd known how to wield it for himself. He'd had the power to save her from death as surely as I did, yet he hadn't. He'd been content to let her die. Content to let grief consume me as I'd held her broken body, sprawled at the base of the stairs leading to the guild's apartment hall.

For years, I'd wondered what had driven Ailis to leave our chamber on her own. It wasn't the first time she had done so, but she had been old enough to know how perilous such an undertaking was for her. As many times as she had injured herself, what had motivated her to descend that staircase? For years, I had wondered—and now I knew. I'd seen the desperation scrawled into the pages of Ailis's grimoire. I understood the fear and desire that had coursed through her in those final days of her life and knew the madness that had blinded her to a wealth of dangers. I was disgusted—not by Ailis, but by the power Lenghan had taught her.

The power that had stolen her spirit.

The power I'd used to save Sósia's babe.

Nausea swirled in my gut as I watched Sósia's body burn. It was too much—her death, my sister's fate, Lenghan's betrayal. The weight of it all untethered me as the funeral procession wound its way back through the streets of Carastile. I didn't follow the other courtiers into Alamada's grand hall, where a mourning feast was to be served in Sósia's honor. Instead, I slipped away to my new bedchamber and scrambled to unearth Ailis's grimoire from its hidden compartment in my medical trunk. A vial of something medicinal crashed to the floor, and the acerbic scent of alcohol filled the room. With the grimoire in my grasp, I rushed toward the sideboard and lit a taper. In one hand, I gripped the candle. In the other, I held the grimoire aloft.

And yet I stopped myself. Aye, the the power of Gode was a poison, a weed. But the grimoire was all I had of Ailis.

Setting the taper aside, I slid the book back into the dark confines of my medical trunk. I couldn't bring myself to burn it. I wasn't sure I ever could.

# CHAPTER 15

Ailis's grimoire might not have been a living thing, but I could feel the hard press of its gaze on my back as I moved about my apartment. Its presence filled the room, squeezing the air from my lungs. I tried putting it out of my mind by watching the Stars awaken through the window of my bedchamber, but They only made me think of Sósia. I tried to envision her spirit rising to the night sky but failed. Could she tell that I was watching? Would she have been disappointed that I wasn't mourning the loss of her with the rest of court? The question drove me to my feet.

Alamada's grand hall was a room so cavernous that, from its doorway, I had to squint to discern the imperial family upon the dais. The room's tiered ceiling was inlaid with gold, and light from the hall's braziers danced across the elaborate patterns on its surface. The floor, the walls, the columns—each surface brimmed with warm color and vibrant texture. Even the dining chairs were upholstered in brightly colored silks. It was a feast for the eyes that nearly sickened me, the room's opulence too vulgar for the pall of a mourning feast. Nevertheless, I took a seat among the commissioned courtiers, needing to feel closer to Sósia.

I ate in silence, nibbling at the small bites of food on my plate. It was only when someone's fork clattered on the table that I realized how uncommonly quiet the hall was for a room full of hundreds. Conversations were held in soft murmurs, heads bent close when someone wanted to speak. The room might have been distastefully opulent, but the atmosphere within it was suitably solemn. I took a quiet sip from my wineglass, grimacing at the drink's sour bite.

Several minutes passed before a flurry of motion near the dais caught my attention. A servant bent low to speak in the emperor's ear. Edarigo Vendegal then rose and hastened from the hall, several advisers close at his heels. The commotion had caught the attention of much of the room. Noting this, Bright Prince Gabrialo pushed himself to his feet. His face remained impassive as he raised his glass and addressed the court.

"My sister would have despised such silence on her behalf," he said, holding his glass aloft. "Let us honor her memory with music."

The tension that had rippled through the room seemed to ease as the musicians began to play, as if the hall had released a long-held breath. The murmur of conversation grew louder around me, marked by clinking glasses and even the occasional peal of laughter. It was too much.

Setting aside my napkin, I hurried from the hall, desperate for air untinged by the heat of the crowded room and the scent of richly spiced food. The arcade beyond the grand hall spilled into a garden. I hurried along its paths, the crushed stone hard beneath the delicate soles of my silk slippers. Walkways dipped into hidden alcoves before opening into small courtyards dotted with fountains and hemmed by hedges. The faint strain of music carried on the breeze as I pressed deeper into the heart of the garden, paying little heed to whether I might find my way out again. I could feel Sósia's spirit at my back —and Ailis's, too. Stars, I needed to breathe. I needed—

Leaning against a trellised archway, I sucked in gasps of air, my fingers tight around the iron whorls. I stood there for some time, trying to ease the tight grip on my lungs, before I heard the crunch of footsteps on the gravel behind me.

"Lady Cliana?"

Softly as the words were spoken, I knew the bright prince's voice at once. He stood only a few paces away, his silver coronet sparkling in the moonlight. His eyebrows furrowed with concern as he appraised me.

"Walk with me?" he asked, gesturing vaguely toward the nearest path.

Briefly, I considered refusing him. I knew his invitation was genuine—an offer rather than a command—but something about being near him unsettled me. His sister was dead, and I had failed to save her. Yet accepting the kindness of his invitation seemed the least that I could do.

Together, we ambled along one of the garden's serpentine paths. A brightsword I didn't recognize trailed in our wake. Beside me, Bright Prince Gabrialo kept his hands clasped behind him, his head tilted toward the sky above. Surprisingly, the silence that passed between us wasn't uncomfortable. Though I could make little sense of the garden's design, the bright prince seemed to know its secrets, leading me left and right with assurance. Soon, a musky floral scent blossomed on the breeze. I cast a furtive glance beside me and found the bright prince's fingers trailing through the flowered hedge. He inhaled deeply as we walked, as if awakening.

"Are the customs in Daorender much different?" he asked.

The question took me by surprise. "Have you never been to the highlands, my prince?"

"I am often bound to Carastile, that is true," he said. "But yes, I have visited your highlands. I know how the customs of the Daor differ from those of the Istanelan people and elsewhere in the empire. I meant to ask after how you honor your dead."

I frowned. "We burn our dead in Daorender, the same as anyone else in the empire. We give their spirits to the Stars."

"But you do not remain inside thereafter?"

I nearly stumbled on the uneven gravel. "My prince?"

Bright Prince Gabrialo glanced down at me. "In Istanel, it is custom to remain within doors on nights of mourning, so as not to attract the attention of the Stars as they seek the spirit that rises to meet them."

A flush of heat crawled up my neck. "Forgive me, my prince. I didn't ken."

"Be at ease, Lady Clìana," said the bright prince, offering me a light smile before continuing down the walkway. "Perhaps there is some truth in such a custom, but Carastile is a great city. I doubt every citizen will keep to their bed tonight, beloved as Sósia may have been." There was a beat in which he hesitated, and I thought I saw his lips quirk briefly in the dark. "She was the brightest light among us. If the Stars do not see her even amid a sea of shining faces, then perhaps they are not worthy of such reverence as we give them."

The words were blasphemous, especially so coming from the lips of the empire's bright prince. Yet even as their weight settled between us, it was Gabrialo's heart—not his heresy—that compelled me. Ever so briefly, I brushed my knuckles against the back of his hand.

"She will not be forgotten," I said softly.

Beside me, Gabrialo stilled. His expression was as unreadable as ever, though I might have seen some flicker of emotion cross his face.

"Thank you," he said at last.

With a nod, I resumed walking. "You are also out of doors," I said lightly.

Gabrialo must have noted the question in my voice. "I am rarely selfish, my lady. It would not suit one who will someday assume the Astral throne. But tonight, given the chance to see Sósia's spirit one last time. . . ." He shook his head, as if to clear away a foolish thought. "I had hoped. But it seems that she is gone."

Perhaps it was his vulnerability that loosened my tongue. Or maybe it was simply my long-held desire to be known in my grief. Regardless, I found myself saying, "I ken what it is to lose a sister."

Beside me, Gabrialo stilled once more. "How?"

I couldn't speak of Ailis while facing him. The words were too great a pain to bear under his scrutiny. I crossed to a nearby bench and sat, appraising the marble figure of a woman that rose from the courtyard's fountain. Water flowed through her fingers, slippery as the words that were about to spill from my tongue. Gabrialo took a seat beside me.

"She was born frail and bedbound," I said, my vision distant with memory. "And she remained so for most of her life. Even with all our great learning, no one among the clan knew how to treat the disease that plagued her. But she was bright, Ailis, and eager for freedom. She took every opportunity she could to escape the confines of her room. She was nearly a lass grown when one of the students found her body broken at the bottom of the stairs." With a trembling breath, I added, "That was eight years ago."

I'd been in a lecture hall when it happened. My sister's name had risen on the tide of conversation flowing through the room. As soon as the whispers had reached my ears, I had bolted, my muscles screaming as I tore from the hall and across the courtyard. A circle of dark plaids had gathered at the base of the stairwell leading up to the apartment hall. A halo of blood surrounded Ailis's head. I'd held her in my arms for what had seemed an interminable length of time, weeping and pleading until several men had hooked their arms around me, tearing me away from her—but not before I'd seen the pale chip of bone jutting from my sister's neck.

Gabrialo's touch drew me back to the present, the brush of his knuckles warm against mine. "How do you bear it?" he asked.

I stared at the back of his hand, now still against my skin. Something prickled in the air around us, and my heart pulsed at the base of my throat. Before I could think better of it, I turned my hand upward and let the bright prince's fingers trail along the deep lines of my palm.

"I live for her as best I can," I said, meeting his steady gaze without restraint. "And pray it is enough."

Gabrialo withdrew his hand with a ragged breath. I mourned the loss of his touch for only a second before he placed something in my open palm: a pale yellow flower, its petals streaked with hints of gold.

"Aathani," I said, recognizing the rare blossom from the hedge Gabrialo had run his fingers through. Though I'd never seen it in person, I'd read of the bloom's medicinal properties in Larmach texts. Dried and crushed, the petals could be stirred into wine to ease pain and flush poison, administered as a poultice to encourage skin and bone to knit, or taken as a tincture to cleanse the liver of ill use. When brewed as a tisane, it was even said to alleviate the ache of an unwell soul.

"A balm to heal all wounds," Gabrialo said, mournful as the grave.

# CHAPTER 16

*A balm to heal all wounds.*

It was those words, paired with the ghost of the bright prince's touch upon my skin, that brought me to his chamber door that night. I bore a bottle of dreamwine in hand, though Gabrialo hadn't asked for it. It seemed a decent explanation for my presence, should one be needed. Or, perhaps I simply wasn't ready to admit why I'd stalked through the halls of Alamada Palace that night. Either way, the door to the bright prince's chamber peeled back slowly on its hinges. I swallowed once, hard, before collecting the frayed edges of my nerves and stepping into the room. The door thudded shut behind me.

The first thing I noticed was the candles. Dozens were scattered about the room in small clusters. Twin sconces flanked the washstand. A candelabra stood sentinel on the bedside table. A chandelier hung high above, bathing the room in warm amber light—light that played with shadow, speaking of comfort and quiet. And I understood, quite suddenly, the room into which I had stepped. It wasn't so much a bedchamber as it was a private sanctuary, a place for solace and respite amid the chaos of court.

My heart pounded in my chest. What had I done?

To my left, a floorboard creaked. I spun around, dipping into a hasty curtsy. "Bright Prince."

"My lady," came Gabrialo's soft reply.

He stood beneath the arched doorway to his balcony, the light from the chandelier casting deep shadows across the planes and contours of his face. He'd removed the silk doublet he'd worn that evening, as well as his crown. Clad only in breeches and the soft cream linen of his undershirt, he seemed a different man entirely, unburdened by the constraints of his rank. Only the crease between his eyebrows remained, the merest hint of the impassivity he wore like armor at court.

"Forgive me," I said. "I shouldn't have come here."

The crease between Gabrialo's eyebrows deepened. "Why *have* you come?"

"'Tis of no consequence, truly."

"I hesitate to think you do anything that is not of consequence, Lady Clìana." He took a step toward me. "Tell me."

"I brought dreamwine. I thought you might wish for it tonight."

"Is that all?" His gaze seemed to hold a thousand questions . . . and perhaps something more. It was the *more* that emboldened me.

"If that is all you wish, aye."

Gabrialo appraised me with canny eyes, searching for something I couldn't name. Whatever it was, he seemed to find it. The tension drained from his body, and he became once more the Gabrialo I had known on the balcony at Granara, in the shadows of the Sanctuary, and amid the fragrance of the spice gardens. Not the stoic heir to the Astral throne, but a man—honest and unguarded. His expression shifted, revealing emotion that was at once dark and bright, the moon in orbit. "What do you want, Clìana?"

His frankness startled me. "My prince?"

A moment passed between us. The only movement in the room was the flickering of candlelight, stirred by some unseen draft. Then, with sudden impatience, Gabrialo came to me, his long legs closing the distance between us. I could smell the salt on him—and something darker: hearth fire and ink, the sweat of the day, the anticipation of the night.

"Tell me why it is that you have come," he whispered.

My fingers answered for me, tracing the proud lines of his face, feeling the warmth of his breath on my skin. I rose, half hesitant, savoring the widening of his pupils and the way his hands gravitated toward my body. There was a tether between us that drew us nearer. He tasted of warm citrus, sunshine, and salt—heady with wanting and with grief. I gave him what comfort I knew to give, as another had once done for me, exploring the expanse of his body, the skin that stretched taut over firm muscle beneath the linen of his shirt. The solid weight of him anchored me, casting away all fear.

"Clìana," he said, his teeth dragging at my lower lip.

Stars, to hear my name on his tongue. It was music—a sweet, rich rumble that stirred embers within me that I had long thought buried. A sound of quiet pleasure escaped me.

Gabrialo drew back then, his hands settling on my hips. "Tell me what you want."

"I want to touch you," I said instinctively.

So he drew his shirt over his head and let me press my hands against his skin.


Sated as I was, I knew it wouldn't be difficult to drift off to sleep. Still, I kept my attention fixed on the canopy above us. Shadow and light danced across the surface of the navy silk as our breathing calmed. Should I excuse myself from Gabrialo's chamber? Should I stay? Only minutes before, I had seen Gabrialo as the man he was beyond the influence of the Astral throne. But now, in the wake of our coupling, I was painfully aware that I had kept the bright prince's bed—and I hadn't the faintest notion of how to respond to that reality.

"Why did you come?" Gabrialo asked, the mattress dipping as he rolled to face me.

"Hmm?"

"Tonight. It was more than lust."

"Was I wrong to come to you?"

"Yes." Upon his answer, I snapped my head toward his. I was surprised to find that his gaze was light. "Though I am pleased that you did," he added.

I sighed in relief. I understood his meaning well enough. Little good could come of the scrutiny the bright prince and I had welcomed by choosing to lie together, especially given the many small intimacies we had shared since arriving in Carastile. Our interactions would not have gone unnoticed. At court, even the darkest corners had eyes. Still, Gabrialo hadn't yet asked me to return to my chamber.

"Why do you let me see you?" I asked, turning to face him.

"What do you mean?"

"At court, you keep yourself guarded. Restrained. Yet when we speak in private . . ." The scent of his skin tickled my nose. "You let me see you, I think. The man beneath the crown."

"I am always the crown."

"Forgive me." I looked away. "I meant no offense."

My words seemed to chasten Gabrialo. When he spoke again, his voice was soft. "When the people of this court look at me, they see only what I represent: the Astral throne, and all that it has to offer. But you are different, Cliana. Perhaps I am a fool to trust you, but that morning at Granara, when you let me hold the babe a little longer—"

"I sought only to serve you."

Gabrialo shook his head. "That was not service. It was *kindness*. You are kind, Cliana, in ways I am not often afforded. I let you see me because you have shown me that I will be seen." My skin prickled as he trailed a lazy thumb across my cheek. "Will you tell me why you came to me tonight?"

The question doused the warmth that had blossomed in my chest. Turning onto my back, I returned my attention to the canopy above us. "Because we are alone," I said quietly.

"Alone?"

"Aye. Here, in this place, and in our lives. . . ."

"Is that so?"

"Is it not?" I turned to him once more, an eyebrow raised in challenge. "I am bound to body and blood," I said, fingering the rigid scar between my forefinger and thumb, the injury inflicted long ago by a scalpel and my own inexperience. "From the womb, I was bound to it—by nature, by name. I chose to leave my homeland and my people, to live without close kin in service of my oath. But what choice had you, my prince? Only a moment ago, you said that the people of this court see you solely for what you represent. Is that not how your life is to be?" Raising a hand to his jaw, I felt his pulse beneath my touch. "For our oaths, we are alone. Do we not deserve some consolation?"

The corners of Gabrialo's mouth drew taut. "That is why you have come, then? To seek your consolation from me?"

"I seek nothing that does not please you, my prince."

He caught my wrist as I withdrew, bending to press his lips to the map of lines that crossed my palm. "It would please me if you were to call me by my name," he said.

"My prince?" Somehow, it had been the last request I'd expected.

"My name, Clìana. Would you not give me that consolation?"

"Would that not be . . . inappropriate?"

"More inappropriate than what we have already done? It brings me pleasure to call you Clìana. Does my doing so not please you in return?" He appraised me as an unmistakable shiver chased up my spine. "Will you say it, Clìana? Will you give me my name?"

My nerves thrummed with anxiety. Our coupling had already been an unexpected intimacy, complicating our relationship as bright prince and physician. The thought of calling Gabrialo by his given name made me feel even more exposed, naked as I already was in his bed. Still, I couldn't deny the thrill that sparked in my chest when he said my name—nor my desire to give him the same pleasure.

Meeting his eye, I said softly, "Gabrialo."

The bright prince blanched. "Dear Stars, woman! Not that name."

"My prince?"

"*Gabrialo*," he said, mimicking the singsong lilt of my voice. Mirth colored his cheeks. "Oh, and the way you say it in that brogue of yours."

An uncomfortable heat worked its way up my neck. Gabrialo must have noticed my distress, for he ran his hand over my hair. "Forgive me. Gabrialo *is* my given name. You are not wrong. Still, you know what they call me, do you not? The ones I hold dear?"

The warmth of the night thickened around us. A beat passed, and then another, before the bright prince realized his slip of the tongue—the unintended insinuation behind his words. A different kind of color suffused his face.

I severed his growing unease with a word, recalling the name Sósia had once spoken in haste at Granara. "Gabrián."

He loosed a shuddering breath. "Again?"

"Gabrián," I said. Taken by a sudden urge, I cupped his face in my hands. "Gabrián."

The bright prince crushed me to him then, as if he could meld our lonely souls—as if he could purge us, for one night, of the unbreakable oaths that bound us. Again, we found each other in the dark, both of us needing more than what the world had offered us. More than the oaths to which we'd been born. I curled my fingers in his hair and drew him nearer still. His breath was warm on my collarbone, my name an exaltation on his tongue. "Clìana."

# CHAPTER 17

When I awoke, the bedchamber was dim with the gray light of a coming dawn, the sun tucked beneath the swell of the horizon. I had always relished this time of day. It was a sacred moment before the world crept in and awareness sprang into sharp relief, and I breathed deeply as Gabrialo's chest rose and fell beside me.

Nay, not Gabrialo. *Gabrián.*

Panic fluttered in my chest when I considered what had come to pass between us. It was nothing more than need, I told myself. Evening's dark embrace often encouraged intimacy, as I'd come to know while still in Aversere. But clarity always came with the dawn.

*You know what they call me, do you not? The ones I hold dear?*

The soft timbre of Gabrián's voice rumbled through my mind. I cast the words aside. They had been nothing more than a slip of the tongue. We had known each other for too short a time to grow near, and Gabrián was too wise to allow himself to consider me with any true intimacy. I certainly would not allow myself to do the same.

Beside me, Gabrián stirred. I felt the second he came into sudden awareness, his body jolting when his fingertips brushed against my bare forearm. When his gaze found mine, his body softened, melting into the soft down of the mattress.

"You're awake," I said, unsettled by his easy attention.

His brows furrowed. "I have not slept so well since . . ."

I heard the words he left unspoken. Not since Granara. Not since Sósia had died. Yet he had slept well at my side. Nay, he had slept well because of what we had done. Because he'd poured all his restless, raging sorrow into the momentary gratification of the body, and it had been enough to help him forget. For one night, it had been enough. But he was thinking of his sister now. I could see her memory etched in the curves and contours of his face.

Reaching out, I ran a finger along his brow as though I could smooth away sorrow as easily as wrinkles in a length of cloth. "Shall I leave you?" I asked quietly.

Hesitantly, he nodded. "For now."

"I understand, Gabrián," I said, pulling back to catch his eye.

He smiled softly. "Thank you."

Only a brief knock sounded at Gabrián's door before Casdar Belorán swept into the room, frowning even more so than usual. "Gabrián, there is something you must—"

He stopped short at the sight of our bodies tangled on the bed. His scowl hardened into something darker, but not before the briefest flash of fear crossed his face. It happened so quickly, I wasn't sure I saw it.

"Leave us," he said as I clutched the silken bedsheets to my chest.

*"Casdar."* There was a note of warning in Gabrián's voice that the brightsword pointedly ignored.

"What is this?" Sir Casdar demanded, one hand moving as if on instinct to the hilt of his sword. "You know it is unwise to give this woman a place in your court. But a place in your bed? It is more than foolishness. It is—"

"It is none of your concern who keeps my bed," said Gabrián, speaking with the same imperial command he used at court. He drew a tunic over his head as he rose. "Nor will I stand idle while you denigrate those who work within my court."

"Need I remind you that you are heir?" Sir Casdar replied, seemingly undaunted by Gabrián's station. "No concern is yours alone, least of all with whom you share your bed."

Gabrián's expression shuttered. When he spoke again, his voice was low and measured. "What is it you have come to tell me?"

Sir Casdar glanced at me briefly before pinning Gabrián with a pointed look.

Reaching to the floor, I snatched up my chemise and slipped it over my head. "I'll leave you to the business of your day, Gabrián."

Sir Casdar bristled so fiercely at my use of Gabrián's name that his contempt was nearly palpable. It occurred to me then that he had called Gabrián by his chosen name as well, upon first entering the bedchamber. But I didn't have time to consider what that might mean.

With a sigh, Gabrián nodded regretfully before pulling the cord that hung beside his bed. A few seconds later, Yadi-Rafin appeared through a side door, taking in the tableau of Gabrián's chamber with careful impassivity.

"Please escort Lady Clìana to her surgery once she is dressed, Yadi-Rafin," said Gabrián.

The steward nodded. "Of course, my prince."

Gathering up my clothing, I followed Yadi-Rafin from the room, feeling the full weight of Casdar Belorán's anger upon my back.


Sunlight crept through the surgery's tall windows, illuminating motes of dust as they danced through the muggy summer air. Filthy. Everything was so damned filthy. I flung open the shutters, desperate for a bit of breeze to blow it all away.

"The bright prince apologizes for the state of the room, my lady," said Yadi-Rafin. "It was rarely used before you came to court. Will it suit your needs once it has been scoured?"

"It will, aye." Dirty as it was, the room was larger than any surgery I'd seen in Daorender, including that which Bright Lord Dalmorie kept at Castle Highdale. Only the guildhall's surgery wards were larger, but those were used to treat upward of twenty patients at a time.

With a bow, Yadi-Rafin withdrew from the room to speak with a passing servant. Shortly thereafter, a menagerie of maids appeared to scrub away the filth.

"If you would come with me, my lady," said Yadi-Rafin, ushering me toward the door. "We shall speak elsewhere of Bright Prince Gabrialo's health and the duties expected of you now that you serve within his court."

Together, we walked the length of the spice gardens, where only the night before I'd trailed by Gabrián's side. As expected, the bright prince was in good health. He'd been a strong lad, his childhood free of any notable injury or illness, receiving only the best care the Radiant Astral Empire had to offer. Accompanied by frequent exercise and a mindful diet, that care had transformed him into a young man of health and vigor. There was little I might do for him now beyond soothing aches or settling the occasional upset stomach.

In my new role, I was also expected to tend to the bright prince's court, which consisted largely of young noblemen who served as Gabrián's companions. Some had wives who would need tending on their childbeds—a thought that sobered me, considering the last child I'd delivered. Others were known to be wild in their exploits, prone to hunting accidents or bouts of drunkenness. Only a few were fettered by chronic concerns in need of minding, though none were beyond my skill to treat.

My discussion with Yadi-Rafin proved long, though not unpleasant, as we passed beneath the fragrant boughs of sweet pepper trees and mock anise. Due to my lack of familiarity with the palace, the steward escorted me back to my surgery, the room now polished to a high shine. I took a minute to breathe in the crisp scent of the place, the air lightly perfumed with incense. The room boasted two wide hearths and towering windows, which allowed bright light to spill generously upon the tiled floor. It was a room well-suited to surgery, carefully selected and expertly arranged. A large worktable stood between the hearths, sideboards and shelving arranged with a variety of ingredients Yadi-Rafin had determined I might need for my work. With the commission came a large sum of coin with which I could purchase additional materials I deemed necessary. Yadi-Rafin tasked me with compiling a list of these supplies at my earliest convenience, which they assured me they would see procured.

I began by taking stock of the items that already lined the shelves. No sooner had I surrounded myself with an array of dried herbs, carefully jarred and labeled, than a man appeared at my door, knocking lightly as if to not startle me.

"I beg your pardon, my lady," he said. "Are you perhaps the new royal surgeon?"

The man was a swordsman if ever I'd seen one, his body at once broad and lean. From the proud set of his jaw to the soles of his squared feet, everything about him commanded respect. Never mind that he was barely a man grown. Something about him seemed vaguely familiar. I realized suddenly that I had seen him before: at Gabrián's side during Sósia's burning.

"Prince Leomar," I said, dipping my head in deference. The shield of the House of Vendegal carried the same easy air of importance as his brother, though there was something about his tight smile that unsettled me. "I am Lady Clìana Goddan. How might I be of service?"

"You knew me?" said Prince Leomar, a hint of surprise in his voice.

I offered him a tight smile of my own. "Does something trouble you, my prince, such that you've come to see me?"

"My wrist," he said, holding his right hand aloft. "It has pained me for some weeks now. I thought to test your prowess, to see how the great healers of Clan Larmach work."

"Of course," I replied, though I knew of several elder Larmach healers who served as Edarigo's physicians and found it unlikely that none had ever treated Prince Leomar. Nevertheless, I invited him to sit at the small worktable near the southwest window, where the light was strongest. When I took up his hand, his tanned skin was cool beneath my touch. "Is the pain sharp? Or more so an ache, my prince?"

"An ache, I would say."

Gently, I probed the joint for signs of inflammation or fracture. "And is the ache constant? Or felt only in use?"

"It pains me most often after a bout in the armyard, my lady."

Satisfied with my assessment, I released my grip on the prince's wrist. He rolled the joint as he withdrew.

"So far as I can tell, you haven't fractured the joint, my prince. I suspect you've merely strained the ligaments." Rising, I strode across the room to fetch a roll of bandages. "Avoiding the armyard for a few days should give the injury time enough to heal. Though if you must take a turn in the yard, I recommend binding the wrist to steady the joint and prevent further injury."

"Ah, but a swordsman needs his mobility, my lady."

"Certainly, my prince," I said, wrapping the cloth around his wrist. Prince Leomar kept his gaze fixed upon my face as I worked. Something about being the object of his attention made my chest tighten with apprehension. It took effort to keep my voice calm and measured. "But if you persist as you are now during training, without binding the wrist, I can only foresee future injury."

"I see," said Prince Leomar, rolling his wrist again after I tucked in the edge of the bandage. If the motion pained him, he hid the discomfort well. "Tell me, my lady. Are you aware of what happened to my family?"

I blinked, taken aback by the sudden shift in conversation. "You speak of the Great Sorrow?"

"The plague killed my great-aunt Lira first," he said by way of confirmation. For the first time, I noticed the tiny white scar that cut through his upper lip. "Then my grandmother, Queen Carmena. Next came the rest of my father's siblings: Juaran, Endro, little Ilín. Then it took my grandfather—the emperor—followed by my cousins, who were no more than babes." He spoke with startling detachment, his hands still upon the tabletop. "When at last only my father emerged unscathed—not yet a man, but neither so a child—it was said that the House of Vendegal must surely be ill-favored by the Dark. Why else would such a tragedy befall the imperial family?"

His lips pulled back into a humorless smile. I fought the urge to recoil as he leaned forward in his chair. "Every day, my father strives to ensure that our house is no longer perceived as weak. My brother follows in his footsteps."

"And you, my prince?" I asked, loathing how I felt as though I'd walked into a trap.

"My father and my brother act as though the threat of weakness is an enemy they must defeat, as though there is credence to what is said of the House of Vendegal." Prince Leomar shook his head lightly. "I operate on no such assumption, Lady Clìana. I say what must be said, and I do what must be done—and I do not doubt the Stars' holy favor or strength of my blood."

With this, he rose, towering above me, the hilt of his sword gleaming at his hip. He regarded me for a long moment before saying, "You will not keep my brother's bed again."

The words startled me to my feet. "I beg your pardon?"

"As shield of this house, it is my duty to see to matters that threaten the strength of the Vendegal throne. The bright prince is due to marry. My father's efforts to secure him a suitable match must not be hindered by passing fancies."

It was all I could do not to gape at Prince Leomar in astonishment.

He gave a cruel laugh as he rounded the corner of the worktable. "Do not flatter yourself, Lady Clìana. You are not the first mistress I have asked to leave my brother's bedchamber. I trust you will recognize my asking to be a mere formality."

Hot anger flushed through me. Biting back a string of foul words, I pasted a vague smile on my face. "In this matter, I will defer to the will of your brother, my prince."

The white scar on Prince Leomar's lip flashed like the flick of a whip. I expected him to step closer to intimidate me with the breadth of his stature and the depth of his fury. But when many men might have raved, Prince Leomar only smiled. "You are new to court, my lady. Freshly arrived from a realm of little consequence. Perhaps that is some excuse for your lack of sense, though I will not suffer it all the same. Resign yourself to your role as royal physician, or I will see that you are removed from this court."

A chill overtook me as Leomar Vendegal stalked out of the room.

✦

That night, I woke suddenly in my bed, certain that someone had been standing at its foot only seconds before. That the door to my chamber had been carefully, quietly shut. With this certainty came the niggling fear that, had I woken but a moment earlier, I might have seen many unwelcome things in the dark.

The harsh line of lips pressed thin.

The flicker of malice in a man's gaze.

The glint of moonlight on a dagger.

# CHAPTER 18

I awoke the next morning bathed in sweat, the bedsheets tangled around my limbs. There had been no dagger, I'd told myself during the night. It had been nothing more than a phantom threat conjured by a rattled mind. But an anxious energy had thrummed through my veins, and my eyes had darted from shadow to shadow, searching for nefarious figures in the dark. I'd had to light a candle to calm myself—and even then, I'd slept fitfully. Beating back the remnants of my unease, I focused on readying myself for the day to come, cleansing the sweat from my skin and carefully twining my feathers into my hair.

The day before, I'd asked Yadi-Rafin if someone might procure for me a collection of garments suited for court, for I had precious little in the way of Istanelan clothing. By evening, my wardrobe had held a dozen overdresses. Many were practical garments for surgical work, but among them hung an immaculate gown of deep navy silk, painstakingly embroidered with Stars. I nearly laughed when I saw it, striving and failing to imagine myself in such finery. I trailed my fingers over the cool silk that morning before donning a simple linen kirtle. As I stepped through the door that connected my private chamber and the surgery, I tried not to dwell on the memory of Gabrián's hands beneath my chemise—nor on the knowledge that he'd not invited me to join him in his chamber the night before.

With a steadying breath, I appraised the large workroom before me. Early morning light streamed through the tall windows, illuminating rows of shelves intended for medicines. Parcels of newly acquired goods sat atop gleaming worktables, and fresh candles had been placed in the room's iron chandeliers. Yet any elation I might have felt at the sight of my own Carastilan surgery seemed miles away. Memories danced through my thoughts: the brush of Gabrián's fingers along my sternum, the cruel bite of Prince Leomar's words, the ire in Sir Casdar's regard. I imagined the dagger arcing toward me in the dark, and a chill finger traipsed up my spine.

I shook my head to clear my mind. I had come to Carastile in search of glory, and I'd found the makings of it in the Court of Stars. Continuing its pursuit needed to be my focus. Yet the greatness I believed myself to possess had been a misconception. Ailis hadn't been enamored by my healing skill. She'd wanted me to seize the power of Gode that flowed through our veins, as she had done. Never mind that it had maddened her. A fresh pang of sorrow gripped me at the thought.

Discomforted by such ruminations, I threw myself into the work of my trade. Harvesting herbs and spices from the kitchen gardens, I labored to process them in my surgery—boiling, brewing, mashing, and macerating until

I had a fresh stock of many of the essential medicines I used in my craft. Yet even as I worked, I kept one eye on the surgery's open door, fearing who might appear there. Would Prince Leomar return to volley more threats? Would I feel the searing press of Sir Casdar's gaze on my back?

Despite my worries, no one entered the surgery until Yadi-Rafin appeared at dusk to relay an invitation: Gabrián wished for me to dine with him on his private terrace.

Anxious energy washed through me once more. Would the bright prince wish for me to keep his bed again? Did I hope that he might extend such an offer? And what would it mean for us both if I accepted it?

Yadi-Rafin cleared their throat. "My lady?"

"It would be an honor," I said, pretending to feel at ease. "Please, lead the way."

Gabrián's private terrace was the same gallery on which we'd met weeks earlier, when I'd first arrived in Carastile. The pungent fragrance of the spice gardens filled my nose as I climbed the wrought iron steps that led to the patio. He was waiting for me when I arrived, dressed in rich linen, his countenance kind but composed.

"Lady Clìana," he said, greeting me formally.

I bowed in deference. "Bright Prince."

After we were seated, Gabrián dismissed Yadi-Rafin and the servants who had been present to serve our meal, pouring me a glass of pale Brennish wine himself. The table between us was laden with an array of fragrant dishes, many of which I didn't recognize. There was some form of roasted poultry encrusted in fresh herbs, as well as filets of seared fish topped with a brightly colored sauce.

Dates and cashews were arranged on an elegant platter, accompanied by sticky slivers of dried apricots and fat red cherries.

"Thank you for coming," he said after sipping from his glass.

"'Tis an honor to dine with you, Gabrián," I said, hesitating briefly before adding his name.

Setting down his glass, Gabrián met my eye. "I must apologize to you for what happened yesterday morning. Casdar's behavior was unconscionable. It will not happen again."

The words took me by surprise. "I appreciate your concern, but you needn't apologize for another man's actions."

"On the contrary. Casdar is my brightsword. There is every need."

We picked at the food on the table, neither of us seeming to have much of an appetite.

"Do you ken why he seems to despise me?" I asked, feeling uncommonly shy. "I can think of nothing I've done to offend him."

"He has said nothing to me of any personal offense. As for his attitude toward you . . ." Gabrián leaned back in his chair, his gaze briefly distant. "Casdar's moods have always been black."

Over occasional bites of our meal, Gabrián explained that Sir Casdar was the second-born son of Janasta Belorán, heir to the Duchy of Aredo. Headed by Casdar's grandsire, Idário, the House of Belorán was one of the most prominent families in Istanel. Should the House of Vendegal one day fade to naught, a Belorán would likely be chosen to rule as Radiant Astral Emperor. Regardless, the House of Belorán was a formidable force in Istanelan politics, wielding significant sway over decisions made in regard to the realm.

Tradition held that the shields of the House of Belorán squired at Alamada Palace, and Casdar had been no exception. Life within the Court of Stars had sharpened his mind to history, politics, language, and geography. "But his favorite role was always that of the shield of his house," said Gabrián, idly rolling a dried fig between his forefinger and thumb. He went on to tell of how Casdar had trained relentlessly with sword, shield, war hammer, and spear, rising earlier than most and sparring longer. He'd been full of fire as a warrior, and he'd exhibited that enthusiasm proudly during exercises in the training yard. It had been during one of those drills that Gabrián and Casdar had first met.

"Not one of the squires would raise their sword to me," Gabrián said, a ghost of a smile on his lips. "They dared not risk injuring the heir to the Radiant Astral Empire. But Casdar strode into the armyard, took one look at me, and proclaimed, 'What good is an emperor if he cannot defend his people? I will spar with the bright prince.'"

"And did he best you?" I asked.

Gabrián snorted. "Bested me, bruised me, and likely would have bled me like a stuck pig had the master of arms not raised his sword. The old man swore he would punish Casdar for his insolence, but I would not allow it. I came back to spar with him every day."

"Glutton." I chuckled. "And did *you* ever best *him*?"

Gabrián let out a sharp laugh. "Not once. Truly, he is one of the greatest swordfighters I have ever seen."

Given his earlier declaration about Casdar's moods, it surprised me to see Gabrián speak so fondly of his brightsword. "He seems a good friend to you," I said.

"He is," Gabrián replied before sobering. "His grand-sire, Idário, rules Aredo with an iron will. His words have teeth, they say, and his blades are keen. His mother, Janasta, exhibits a similar temperament." He took a long sip from his wineglass, then sighed. "There is no kindness in that family. No joy."

"And so you offered him a way out?"

"He forsook his family when he pledged himself to my service," Gabrián confirmed. "But one does not escape the House of Belorán unscathed. I suspect his temperament is forever altered by his upbringing."

This explanation offered me some measure of under-standing, even if it didn't fully explain the loathing Casdar bore for me. Perhaps he saw a threat in the intimacy I shared with Gabrián, though that didn't account for the way Casdar had treated me the first time I'd set foot upon this terrace. I tried to puzzle out the mystery of him, but further consideration only gave rise to more questions.

Setting my curiosity aside, I focused my attention on Gabrián and noted the dark circles that shadowed his eyes. I placed a hand over his on the tabletop. "Shall I bring you dreamwine tonight?" I asked.

Gabrián shook his head. "I do not care for its effects."

I understood his reticence. Potent as it was, dreamwine often left a patient groggy upon waking.

Turning his wrist, Gabrián captured my hand in his. "I slept better with you beside me, Clìana."

My pulse began to race. "You wish for me to keep your bed again?"

"Yes."

Though Gabrián spoke without hesitation, I found myself unsure. "That night, you said I shouldn't have come."

"A relationship between us would stir gossip. But there is always talk at court. It can be weathered." I heard the unspoken challenge in his words: *Are you willing to weather it?* When I didn't reply, he added, "No matter your decision, please know that it will not affect your position here at court. I have no interest in forcing your hand."

"Of course. Nay, it is only . . ." Irritated by my stammering, I met Gabrián's eye. "Your brother came to see me yesterday."

Gabrián frowned. "Leomar?"

I nodded. "He warned me against keeping your bed again. He said that I am a distraction to you."

With a huff, Gabrián ran a hand down his face. "Leomar has never enjoyed being the shield of the House of Vendegal. He covets influence. No doubt he saw a threat in that which you possess."

"Because I kept your bed but once?"

"Because I wish you to keep my bed again," said Gabrián, pressing forward in his seat. "You *have* influenced me, Clìana. You must know this. But what you may not realize is that influence is currency at court—currency that many are desperate to possess."

That I had such an effect on Gabrián was a heady realization. Still, I hadn't come to court seeking threats and intimidation. The sense that an unwelcome stranger had stolen into my bedchamber last night was still fresh in my mind. I took a long sip of wine to conceal my hesitation, but Gabrián must have seen the action for what it was.

"I ask for nothing that you do not wish to give, Clìana. Surely, you must know that."

I did, and that knowledge endeared me to him. As bright prince, Gabrián possessed more influence than nearly anyone at court. It would have been easy for him to use that influence in reckless pursuit of pleasure, as was the wont of many a person in power. But he didn't see people as pawns for the fulfillment of his whims. If I were to join him in his bed once more, the decision would be entirely my own. Still, it wasn't a decision I felt ready to make.

"May I speak freely with you?" I asked instead.

"You know you can," he replied, though he appeared somewhat hesitant.

I took a fortifying breath. "Prince Leomar spoke of marriage. *Your* marriage. He said that you've not wed because a suitable match had yet to be found. But as the bright prince, are you not as desirable a political match as any in the world?"

This time, it was Gabrián who sipped his wine. "Once, the name Vendegal would have sent a thousand ships bearing daughters to court. But circumstances have changed."

"Because of the plague?" I prompted.

Gabrián nodded. "My father was the last of our name until my birth. We have no other relatives save those too distant to lay claim to the throne. And so there is nothing more important to this house than the children I will one day sire. But the House of Vendegal is weak, and the wolves are circling. It has been difficult to secure a suitable match given the threat of usurpation."

Startled, I set aside my wineglass. "No one has offered?"

"Many of the lower houses, yes. But to wed so far below my station would only give evidence to claims of Vendegal fear and desperation. Our hope has long lain with the khagan of Nyengun. Some years ago, he offered the hand of his youngest daughter, a girl who is now no more than ten. I have refused to marry one so young, of course. My father seeks to secure a match with the khagan's sister instead. Though she is of lesser esteem in the Nyengul court, she is at least of an age with myself. The marriage has been in the works for some years now, but there is a disagreement over the dominion of trade routes between our countries, I am told. Something to do with the import of timber, though it stands to reason that the khagan is simply waiting to see if the House of Vendegal lives or dies."

His words were rife with frustration and tinged by a bitterness I'd never before heard in his voice. Reaching out, I covered his hand with mine once more. "I'm sorry," I said softly.

Gabrián managed a thin smile and shrugged. "We are both of us bound to our oaths."

The words thundered through me, a reminder of all we had shared two nights before. With them came a striking realization: Gabrián might make himself vulnerable to me because he knew he would be seen, but he saw me as well. He listened closely to my words and understood the pains I shared with him. He did not try to change me. Nor did he chide me for my grief. Instead, he held space for my sorrows and offered me the same comfort I sought to give to him.

"I'm willing to weather it, Gabrián," I said, the words

driven by some deep, human need I'd long fought to suppress.

Gabrián's confusion gave way to a flash of longing, then something like relief. His imploring gaze met mine, as if seeking confirmation of my meaning. He must have found it there, for he pushed back from his seat and held his hand outstretched.

We left what remained on our plates untouched.

# CHAPTER 19

In the following weeks, Gabrián and I came to know each other in intimate detail—every sigh, each brush of skin. We spent long nights and lazy predawn mornings mapping this strange new territory, saying little but learning much. Admittedly, some awkwardness remained between us. Gabrián was still the bright prince, and I his royal physician. There was much he couldn't say about the politics that filled his days, just as there were many things I didn't wish to share about my sister and the unnatural power that often consumed my thoughts. Still, our bodies bridged the divide, drawing us near each time unease grew between us.

Soon, my days at Alamada Palace took on a familiar rhythm. I would linger in Gabrián's bed until dawn before rising to work in my surgery. Given the relative youth and good health of Gabrián's court, my work was often dull. I brewed tonics for wine sickness, administered treatments for venereal diseases, and distributed bitter herbs to women who did not wish to bear their lovers' children. There was little glory or challenge in such work, but I strove to push that thought from my mind as I prepared tinctures for pounding heads and roiling wames.

Some days, I'd cross paths with Casdar or Prince Leomar as I made my way through the palace. Gabrián must have exerted some influence over their behavior, given that their contempt never boiled over into confrontation. For my part, I was content to let their resentment simmer as I continued with my work, trying not to think of the dagger I'd once imagined in the dark.

Such worries faded away when I stepped through Gabrián's door each evening. Often, we'd sit upon his balcony as the sun set over the Ifros and Stars gave chase to the last thin tendrils of light. I wasn't one to speak freely, yet the more nights I spent on Gabrián's balcony, the more I felt myself crack open. "Tell me of Aversere," he would say, and I would speak of everything he wished to know. "Tell me of your clan," he would inquire, and I'd hold nothing back.

From the balcony, we'd make our way to his bed. Some nights, we'd simply hold each other close, sorrow a heavy weight between us. But most nights, we'd reach for each other as lovers, and the world would grow at once soft and sharp, fleeting and eternal.

"Tell me about this muscle here," he said one night. His hand floated down the length of my thigh before cupping the back of my knee. "Or of this joint."

"It is a hinge," I said, hooking that leg around his hip.

Gabrián's features quirked with mischief. "Is that so?"

"It is," I insisted, holding back a laugh. "What else would you like to know, my prince?"

Though I had asked playfully, the gaiety faded from Gabrián's face.

"What is it?" I asked, pulling back from him.

"Would you tell me why you came to court?" He spoke tentatively, as though his words might shatter something delicate between us.

"I came to court because I am skilled. Because it is my privilege to serve the empire."

"Is that all?" Gabrián prodded.

I knew what he was asking. Had something more than the pursuit of glory driven me to Carastile? Something more personal than professional acclaim? A twinge of shame shot through me as I replied, "Is it not what one does when they possess a particular skill? To offer their services at high court?"

Disappointment flickered across Gabrián's face. "I could not say. I have no particular skill to offer."

My brow furrowed. "Do not say you have no skill. It takes great fortitude to comport yourself as you do—with such kindness and dignity and strength. The empire is made blessed for your skill."

"Is it?" he replied, pulling away from me until he lay flush against the bedsheets. "I have dedicated my life to the Astral throne. All I do is to serve the empire. Still, people whisper that the House of Vendegal is ill-favored by the Dark."

Despite the lingering heat of the day, a shiver danced across my skin. I understood the power of such whispers, the way they could gather momentum before spilling over into something more dangerous. Already, Gabrián had mentioned the potential for usurpation. To think of him in harm's way, the object of some enemy's ill will, was chilling.

Unbidden, Ailis's grimoire rose to my mind. My skill as

a physician had much to offer Gabrián should danger befall him, but even the work of a master healer was not infallible. Yet I was not a healer alone. I was a woman of Gode, with the power of bloodcraft flowing through my veins. Already, I had brought Sósia's bairn back from the dead. Could I not keep Gabrián and his family safe as well? The thought both empowered and unnerved me.

Placing a hand on Gabrián's chest, I leveled my gaze upon him. "If the Dark finds ill favor in a man of your quality, then It is no master I wish to serve." The words bordered on heresy, but they weren't the first blasphemous words spoken between us. "Do not doubt yourself now. Your worries do naught but give evidence to your worth."

With a sigh, Gabrián drew me closer, draping my body over his until his lips brushed my mouth. "You are no mere consolation, Clìana," he whispered.


So it was that Gabrián and I grew closer than we ought to have been. In his bedchamber, the thick heat of the Istanelan summer curled around us like a womb, shielding us from the worries and dangers that lay beyond. Neither of us spoke of the intimacy of spirit we had found in each other, unwilling to acknowledge the inevitable impossibilities of that nearness. Still, we both knew that such willful ignorance would one day end.

Soon, rumors spread through the city like a sickness, poisoning the sorrow felt in the wake of Sósia's death. It came to me in spurts and starts, through the whispers of passing servants and the high-pitched squeals of courtiers who didn't care to shield their gossip. Soon, I pieced it all together. The stories claimed that Princess Sastiona had never traveled to Nyengun to study music while serving as an emissary of the House of Vendegal. Instead, she had been hidden away in the south to bear a child sired by Joriun Vitander, the Bright Lord of Geldegat—a man notoriously disdained by Sastiona's father, the emperor.

It was a scandal of the highest degree, made only more illicit by the belief that Bright Lord Vitander had wished to wed the princess. Supposedly, he'd offered Edarigo 10,000 goldens as a bride price, which would have significantly offset the taxes that the House of Vendegal found necessary to levy upon the Istanelan people. But Edarigo had refused the offer out of pride, unwilling to accept what he considered to be a bribe from the wealthy bright lord.

It was an ugly, sorrowful business. As scandalous details mounted, hushed whispers turned into sneers and grumblings of discontent. During this time, Edarigo neither confirmed nor denied the story, even as foul words began to stain the glow of Sósia's legacy.

"I am sorry for what is being said at court," I said to Gabrián while we lay together one night, my body neatly tucked against his. "It is cruel. All of it."

Behind me, Gabrián sighed. "When I gave Vitander the child, I thought I might be repairing something between our houses."

Startled, I turned toward him. "So the bright lord *did* sire the bairn."

Gabrián nodded grimly. "My father believes that Vitander lured Sósia to his bed, wishing to further weaken our family name by associating its only daughter with an unfavored house. But Sósia was not so naive. If anything, it was likely she who did the charming. In any case, there was love between them. I saw that much with my own eyes."

"Yet you believe Vitander has spread these rumors?"

Gabrián shrugged. "As I said, there was love between them. When I met with Vitander that night, he was devastated to learn of Sósia's death. I imagine he now wishes to punish my father for refusing the marriage—and perhaps for Sósia's death as well."

"For her death?"

"My sister expressed loathing for our father after he refused Vitander's marriage proposal. Is it possible that her grief led to the aggravation she experienced during childbirth?"

"Perhaps," I said carefully. "But childbirth is always a danger, regardless of the spirit of the mother. I'm sorry I did not do more for her."

Frowning, Gabrián ran a thumb along my cheek. "When you saved Sósia's son, you gave her the most wonderful gift. Do not regret that choice."

It wasn't the first time Gabrián had bade me not to blame myself for Sósia's death. Each time he reminded me, I felt a little surer of the decisions I had made that night. Sósia might have been gone, but the bloodcraft I'd practiced had given her son life—and that was a remarkable thing.

"I won't," I promised as I snuggled back against him. With a contented sigh, Gabrián gathered me in his arms. Together, we drifted off to sleep, allowing the cocoon of intimacy to once more shield us from the world beyond.

Each morning that I awoke in Gabrián's bed, I chased down a pinch of contraceptive herbs with the dark liquor he kept at his bedside. It took me several weeks to realize that Gabrián looked away each time I swallowed the bitter brew.

"Do they upset you?" I asked, wary of his silent disapproval.

He glanced up from the far side of the bed, one eyebrow raised as pale morning light sifted through the wayward strands of his hair.

"The herbs," I clarified.

Gabrián frowned. "Should they?"

"Some disapprove of such measures, viewing them as defiant of the will of the Stars."

Gabrián shook his head. "We were not given good sense to dash upon the rocks of fate," he replied.

"Then why avert your eyes?" I cinched the ties on the small pouch that held the herbs. "I thought perhaps you viewed some shame in it, but—"

"No. If there is any shame here, it is my own."

My heart stuttered at his words. For a moment, I thought Gabrián regretted allowing me to keep his bed. But then I saw the truth etched plainly in the lines of his face and the warm intensity of his gaze, and my breath shallowed.

"I fear I want what I cannot have," he said softly.

My thoughts washed white at his words. I opened my mouth to reply, but what was there to say? Too much— and yet nothing at all.

After a beat, Gabrián rose, the bed ropes creaking. "Forgive me," he said, retreating toward his bathing chamber.

"You imagine a life with me?" I asked, and Gabrián stilled. "One where I might freely bear your children?"

He turned to face me. "Yes."

"That's not what you want."

"It is," Gabrián insisted.

Vehemently, I shook my head, my pulse racing in my throat. "'Tis the freedom you crave. The freedom of what we do here in the night, when all the world fades away. But it is an illusion, Gabrián. Nothing more."

I could see at once that my words had gutted him. I tried to take them back, to swallow them down alongside the taste of the herbs still biting at my tongue. "Gabrián—"

He silenced me with a single, pointed look. "You may lie to yourself as you please, Clìana. But do not lie to me."

With that, he strode into his bathing chamber and shut the door behind him with a thud.

I cannot say how long I sat on the edge of his bed, my body and mind growing numb. I only know that Gabrián's confession unnerved me deeply. He'd all but admitted that he'd found his light in me—and, in doing so, he'd prompted me to consider whether I'd found my light in him. And for me, that was an intimacy far more dangerous than mere friendship or physical delight.

Rising, I fled from Gabrián's chamber before he could return.

# CHAPTER 20

As I worked in my surgery that day, I couldn't help but think of all the men I'd come to care for throughout my life.

My father had been the first one. In the time that I knew him, his mind had been as sharp as a well-honed dirk, and his skill as a medical scholar had made him renowned among the academic circles in the highlands. But he had been kind as well, an attentive father in the days of my youth. I remembered bouncing on his hip as a wean as he ushered me down the many aisles of the guild-hall's grand archive, introducing me to a wealth of texts I'd not yet learned how to read. But then my mother had gone to her pyre, and the light in my father's face had faded. A shell of the man he'd once been, he had remained in Aversere until Ailis's passing. Each day, he had withdrawn further into his academic work, leaving me to my grief and the primary care of my sister. I'd been a lass of ten at the time, shortly to come into my womanhood but still very much a child.

Then there had been Lenghan, all fire and ice, doling passion and cool displeasure in fickle doses. Anger rose within me to think of the nights I'd spent in his bed, never knowing how deeply he had betrayed me with the same power he had used to charm and entice my interest.

Lord Ulmhar, thank the Stars, had been a kinder creature. I thought fondly of the time we'd spent together on the road. Though his rambling stories had been grating at first, they had soon become a source of gaiety I hadn't felt in years. Looking back, I suspected that Ulmhar had known how those stories would disarm my defenses. From the moment I had confessed my desire to leave the highlands behind, he'd seen me in a way that few ever had.

But as much as I was grateful for Lord Ulmhar, I'd never considered him with anything more than simple fondness. Nay, there was only one man who had truly captured my heart—and I was desperate to deny the reality of his affection.

*You may lie to yourself as you please, Clìana. But do not lie to me.*

Gabrián's words echoed in my mind, stirring a flutter of panic in my chest. Unwilling to examine this unease, I threw myself into my work—just as my father had done in the wake of my mother's death. As long days passed, I wondered whether I didn't understand him better now, for it was a terrible thing to have found your light in someone you could not have.

The hour had grown late one night the following week, though not so late that all was quiet. I could hear voices rising from the courtyard beyond the surgery window and the occasional patter of soft slippers in the hall. The surgery itself was bright with candlelight and hearth fire. I should have been asleep, but my mind wouldn't settle. Gabrián's words from our last parting were still ringing in my ears. So I took to analyzing the state of my medicinal stores: the vials, tins, pots, and jars all neatly aligned on the shelves flanking both sides of the hearth. One by one, I examined the contents of each shelf, noting which stores had grown low and which would soon spoil. It was in the midst of this work that a finger of awareness crept up my spine. I didn't have to turn to know who was standing at the surgery door.

"Clìana." The low timbre of Gabrián's voice filled the room.

A vial of willow bark slipped through my fingers, shattering on the floor at my feet. Cursing, I bent to collect the shards, then hissed as a piece of glass bit into my palm.

Gabrián crossed the room and crouched at my side. Unsettled by his nearness, I felt myself stiffen. His long, slim fingers deftly plucked up bits of broken glass.

"I could not let it lie," he said, meeting my gaze with grave intensity. "Not as we had left it."

Opening my mouth to speak, I found I had nothing to say. An awkward silence stretched between us, punctuated only by distant sounds from elsewhere in the palace.

Gabrián shifted uneasily on his feet. "Do you wish to leave, Clìana?"

The question startled me from my stupor. "I beg your pardon?"

"It might be easier for us both. I would see you well-commissioned. You need not worry."

Something in me hardened at the words. "Do I have a choice in the matter?"

Gabrián frowned. "Of course you have a choice. I would not take that from you."

"And if I wish to remain your physician?"

"Then you will remain my physician," he said assuredly, then hesitated. "Would that be enough?"

Would it? I wished to tell him that I would make it so, but the words wouldn't come. I rose suddenly, needing to put space between us. Needing to feel as though I could breathe.

"Clìana." Gabrián caught my hand as I retreated. I hissed as his fingers curled around my palm. "Stars, you're hurt," he said, his fingertips stained red with blood. I'd all but forgotten about the shard of glass that had pierced my skin.

Setting the bits of broken glass on the worktable, Gabrián nodded toward the cut on my palm. "How may I help?"

"Gabrián," I said, a note of resistance in my voice.

"Clìana," came his insistent reply.

Perhaps it would have been wise to refuse him. Perhaps I could have ended things then and there. Yet despite my misgivings, despite my daft desire and the wretched aching of my heart, I found that I couldn't deny him.

With a nod, I let Gabrián take me under his care.

"You will need to instruct me," Gabrián said as he stood before the hearth fire, waiting for a cauldron of water to boil. It should have seemed strange, the Bright Prince of the Radiant Astral Empire performing such a domestic task. But he'd come to me that night without his courtly demeanor, all the strictures of his title forsaken at the door. Here with me now, he was simply Gabrián—or so I allowed myself to believe.

At my instruction, he dropped a finger's length of white willow bark into the water and waited for it to steep. An uncomfortable silence once more yawned between us as it brewed.

It would have been easy enough for me to tend to the wound on my palm. The cut wasn't deep enough to require suturing. Yet it seemed cruel to deny Gabrián the opportunity to care for me. It wasn't his admission of love that swayed me, but rather the knowledge that he was permitted to do few menial tasks for himself. His clothing was arranged by his master of wardrobe, his beard trimmed for him by the steward of his toilette. He had never taken a bite of a meal that hadn't first been tested by another, nor stepped into a room outside the palace that hadn't first been swept for dangers. In so many ways, his life was not his own. So I let him take my injured hand and dip it into the basin of warm, astringent water he'd boiled.

"Apologies," he said as I bit back a hiss, the cut stinging as water met open skin.

I tucked my bottom lip between my teeth and waited for the cutting wave of pain to settle into something milder. A small, pink cloud of blood blossomed in the basin.

"Have you often played the part of patient?" Gabrián asked as he lifted my hand, holding it gently as water dripped from my fingers.

I shook my head. "Rarely."

Setting my open palm in the cup of his hand, Gabrián

gently mopped the ruddied water from my skin. "This scar here?" he said, noting the thick white line between my forefinger and thumb.

I snorted. "A fool's error from one of my earliest surgeries, I'm afraid." When Gabrián raised an eyebrow in curiosity, I continued. "One of the wee Kelkevie lads I served had a terrible pain in his stomach. Nothing we offered seemed to aid him, and his pain soon became excruciating. So we strapped him to our table and opened him up. He'd had an abscess nigh on the biggest I'd ever seen, very much in need of draining."

Gabrián wrinkled his nose in feigned disgust. "And the scar?"

"Ooh, I nearly cut my hand to ribbons in my haste to see the deed done. Grabbed the wrong end of the scalpel and—*thwick!* 'Twas more than the wee lad in need of stitches that day."

Gabrián chuckled. "I do not think you will need stitches now."

"Nay, I think not."

Setting the basin aside, Gabrián fetched a tin of healing salve. "*We*, you said?"

"Myself and Lady Erune," I said softly as a pang of longing shot through me. "She was my tutor, a master healer in her own right."

"I imagine she must be a formidable healer," Gabrián said, massaging the salve into my broken skin. The sweet, resinlike smell of calendula filled the air. "To have trained a woman so brilliant as yourself."

"Flattery doesn't become you," I teased.

"Not flattery. Honesty. For that is what I desire between us, Clìana." With a sigh, he stopped rubbing the salve into my skin and held my hand in his. "I understand the pain I have caused you, and I am sorry for it. But I am weary of pretending that I transcend all it is to be a man. I want you, in all the ways a man should want a woman. And I understand this desire is fruitless, even should you reciprocate it. But is honesty not some consolation? Can it not be enough to share what we have for now? For as long as we might?"

The look in Gabrián's eye was naked—and not a small bit desperate. His soul seemed to yearn for something it had never been allowed to know; and now that he had tasted it, it was all he wanted. Could I not say the same for my own longing?

The thought blazed along my skin, setting my nerves alight. I wanted Gabrián, I realized—not in body alone, but in whole. The stark realization scraped at the edges of my composure. Was it not merely an invitation for grief to hold another dear? And yet . . .

"I do not ken," I replied at last. It was all I could do to whisper the words, knowing each syllable would be a barb.

Gabrián's eyes fluttered shut, confirming my worry. Already, his love for me had incited sorrow. Would it not be best to end this thing between us now, before it could grow any greater? I thought I knew the answer to that question. But when Gabrián's gaze once more found mine, he was no longer the man who had entered my surgery. In his place was Bright Prince Gabrialo, heir to the throne of the Radiant Astral Emperor. And already I yearned for the man he'd left behind.

"Gabrián—"

"I understand," he said as he rose, leaving me to tend to my pains alone.

# CHAPTER 21

The pale dome of Carastile's Grand Sanctuary towered above me, offering a moment's respite from the midsummer sun.

There was perhaps some irony in wishing a reprieve from the Bright Star Omarin on the feast day held in His honor, but I couldn't help sighing as I stepped into the shade. Slick drops of sweat gathered at my nape and made the fine silk of my gown cling to my body. As I smoothed my hands against my bodice, I tried not to think of the last festival I had celebrated. Still, thoughts of Imbelaine crept into my mind. When the Lady of Fire had first appeared east of Aversere, she'd set in motion the series of events that had led me here, to Carastile—and to the impossible decision Gabrián had given me.

I'd slept little in the days since our encounter in the surgery. Fear and longing gripped me in equal measure as I went about my work, Gabrián's words ever echoing in my ear. The brief glimpses I'd catch of him only deepened my wanting. But I knew enough of intimacy to recognize that it rarely ended in anything but grief—and I'd had my fill of grief long ago. So I kept to my surgery as best I could and tried not to think of Gabrián. But with the whole of the Court of Stars gathering for Omarin's rites, I knew there would be no avoiding him that day.

With a tremulous breath, I stepped into the dark embrace of the Grand Sanctuary. Unlike the day of Sósia's burning, the air was free of perfumed oils. Tall braziers lined the rows of curved benches that encircled the dais, and the inner sanctum's bejeweled ceiling glimmered with firelight. I took a seat among the other lesser members of court and tried to keep my gaze from alighting on Gabrián, who sat with his father and his brother in the front row. I spotted Casdar seated beside Gabrián and several other brightswords hemming the imperial family. Despite my reservations, my fingers itched to reach for Gabrián, recalling the last time we had gathered in the cool dark of the Grand Sanctuary. Had it truly been only a few short weeks since Sósia's death? A pang of grief shot through me, a mere echo of what Gabrián must have surely been feeling.

A haze of incense wafted through the air as luminaries gathered around the dais, chanting of how Omarin had come to be favored of the Dark. Low and melodic, they spoke of how the Bright Star had been captivated by the newly formed people of the earth. Seeing them shiver against the cold of their dark world, He had drawn closer, forsaking His kin to offer humans the gift of His warmth and light. Pleased by this selfless act, the Dark Between had named Omarin chief among the Bright and Lesser

Stars and allowed him to keep His new place among the Black.

Something about the luminaries' steady intonation quieted the restless energy within me. By the time the chanting waned, my breath had slowed and my mind had settled. A sense of calm washed through the inner sanctum as the luminaries turned their attention toward lighting the sacred candles that ringed the dais.

As the Most Luminous keened in worship from the center of the room, a tiny movement caught my eye. Several rows ahead, a man leaned forward in his seat. I thought at first that he was merely adjusting his posture, but he continued stretching forward until he was near enough to whisper into the ear of the man in front of him: Casdar Belorán. The brightsword's shoulders stiffened as the other man spoke. Then the stranger rose to his feet, pulled a small dagger from somewhere on his person, and drove it deep into the meat of Gabrián's chest.

Chaos erupted in the heartbeat that followed. Twisting, Casdar grabbed the assassin's wrist and used his own dagger to slit the man's throat. Someone screamed as blood sprayed across the brightsword's face and Gabrián's back, marring the gleaming silver gowns of the nearest luminaries. A series of shrieks and shouts followed as other daggers appeared, gleaming in the candlelight. Courtiers rushed from their seats, pushing and trampling one another in retreat as a single word beat a steady rhythm in my mind.

*No, no, no, no, no . . .*

The desperate need to reach Gabrián broke through the dam of my fear. I clambered forward, climbing over benches and shoving my way through the fleeing throng.

Rough hands pushed me aside, and I fell, a bolt of pain shooting through me as someone's boot clipped my shoulder. With a gasp, I rolled beneath the nearest bench before scrambling to my feet. Spotting the dais to my left, I turned, seeking Gabrián amid the fray—and stopped short when I found the tip of a sword pointed at my belly.

"Fires above!" Casdar cursed when he realized it was me. He angled his sword away—but not before I cried out in terror.

"Cliana," said the figure leaning heavily on his shoulder. A dark red stain inked the left side of Gabrián's chest.

"Gabrián!" Surging forward, I flung his free arm around my shoulders. Together, Casdar and I helped him stumbled away from the dais and the crowd, toward one of the halls beyond the Grand Sanctuary's inner sanctum.

"The prayer room," Casdar growled, nodding toward one of the closed doors that lined the hall.

Springing forward, I threw open the door, then bolted it shut with a vicious clang once the two men were inside. Turning toward them, I cursed.

There was no light in the prayer room. Not even the faintest sliver of torchlight snuck beneath the hem of the door. And why would it? Prayer rooms were designed for communion with the Dark Between. To bring so much as a candle into this place was sacrilege. Still, I understood why Casdar had brought us here. Prayer rooms were the only chambers in a Sanctuary that could be secured from within.

The two men shuffled in the dark. A second later, Gabrián hissed in pain.

"Tend to him," Casdar said. "Tend to him *now*."

"In the dark? The best I can do is—" I grunted as I

collided with Casdar's chest. "Stanch the bleeding," I finished, taking a step back.

"Then do it." A shrill, metallic sound—what I could only assume was Casdar's sword scraping against the far wall of the prayer room—pierced through the dark. "Shit," he spat.

"We cannot stay here," Gabrián said as I tentatively made my way toward him. My hands found his shoulders at waist height. Casdar must have lowered him onto the bench at the back of the room.

"This is the safest place for you," Casdar replied.

I probed for the wound in Gabrián's chest. When my fingers were slick with blood, I tore the fichu from my neck and pressed it hard against the injury, cursing when I felt blood weep through the delicate lace.

"There is only one exit," Gabrián said through gritted teeth as I abandoned the fichu and fumbled with the cravat at his neck.

"The city guard will secure the Sanctuary before anyone breaks through that door," Casdar replied.

"But if the . . ." Gabrián's voice trailed off as blood continued to pool through his crumpled cravat.

"He's bleeding out," I exclaimed.

"He is *not* dying," said Casdar. "Gabrián, by the Black, you are not—"

"That's . . ." Gabrián inhaled sharply. "Blasphemy."

A mad cackle threatened to tear from my chest. I drew a sobering breath before I lost my wits and tried to think. For the wound to bleed so profusely, the assassin's blade must have struck the subclavian vein or artery in his chest, but both were neatly tucked behind his collarbone. To sever them without piercing the heart would require an extraordinary stroke of fate—or perhaps the dagger had been curved. That was a more likely explanation. But how Gabrián came to be injured was of little consequence at the moment given that I felt his pulse slowing beneath my touch.

"By the Black, Clìana! Speak to me," Casdar demanded.

"Quiet," I hissed, an idea taking root in my mind.

"Clìana, so help me—"

"I said *quiet.*"

When Casdar fell silent, I swiftly took stock of what I knew. An assassin had driven a blade into Gabrián's chest. I didn't have my surgical tools. There was no light in the room, nor any way of procuring it without risk. We had no way of knowing how long it would take for the city guard to secure the Grand Sanctuary, though it wouldn't matter regardless. In minutes, Gabrián would be dead—and there was nothing I could do to stop it.

Not without calling upon the power in my blood.

I don't remember coming to a conscious decision. I only recall how the darkness of the prayer room surrounded me in one second, and the next I was no longer trapped within the confines of my body. Instead, I was tumbling forward—not into the distant foggy night as I had weeks ago at Granara, but into a new body. Into *Gabrián's* body. I could feel his flesh and bone around me. I could hear the loud, uneven thud of his heart and see the ragged edges of his flesh.

But this vision had nothing to do with sight. It was *power.* Delicious, all-consuming power.

In that moment, I was everyone and no one at all. Each heartbeat in the room was my own. Each twitch of movement. Each breath. I could hear Casdar's pulse thundering in his ears and feel the sting where Gabrián had bitten the inside of his cheek. But most palpable of all was the searing pain of the wound that tore deep into Gabrián's chest.

Reaching out, I used my power to see the wound in detail. The assassin's blade had cut through skin and muscle cleanly, nicking Gabrián's clavicle before slicing through the artery beneath. Blood flowed from the laceration, leaking into the cavity of his chest—a mortal wound, if not tended quickly. I flung forth my power again to catch the frayed edges of the severed artery, stitching them together as a seamstress might mend a rent in a length of cloth. It took only the span of a breath for my power to heal it.

I stared at the now-whole artery, awe awakening in my chest. Could it truly be so easy to heal the impossible?

Gabrián's heart recovered its rhythm as I withdrew my power from his body, his lungs expanding on a gasping inhale. The darkness of the prayer room surrounded me once more, and a bead of sweat dripped down my brow. *The use of bloodcraft comes at a cost,* Ailis had written in her grimoire, the words rising unbidden in my mind. *To wield unnatural power over the body, you must forfeit a piece of your soul.*

A wave of fear rolled through me. Aye, I had saved Gabrián—but at what cost?

"Clìana?" Gabrián's voice was clear and bright, casting all fear from my mind. What did the cost matter when Gabrián yet breathed?

"You're alive," I said, the words coming on a breathy laugh.

"I feel different."

"What happened?" Casdar demanded from across the room.

I felt Gabrián begin to stand and placed a hand on his shoulder. "Stay still. You're still wounded."

"Clìana?" Casdar's voice was sharp.

Gabrián answered for me. "I thought I was . . ." He paused, swallowing. "I thought I was dying. I could feel my mind slipping from me. And then . . ."

"Then what?" Casdar prompted.

"I cannot say. I felt suddenly better."

"The bleeding has slowed," I said. Only the tiny capillaries in Gabrián's chest yet wept.

"Just like that?" Casdar asked.

I shrugged in the dark. "Aye."

"What did you do?" Suspicion edged the brightsword's voice.

"I don't know," I said, fumbling for some explanation that might satisfy him. "I suppose I just . . . prayed."

A long silence punctuated my words.

"Are you saying that you *prayed?*" Casdar spat. "And now he is no longer dying?"

"We are in communion with the Dark Between, are we not? Why should such a thing be impossible?"

Casdar loosed a hard laugh. But before he could speak, a fist thundered against the prayer room door.

"Is the emperor within?" someone shouted, the voice muffled but familiar.

A low scrape of metal sounded as Casdar drew back the bolt. I blinked against the bright light that spilled into the room. As my vision adjusted, I caught sight of Prince Leomar over Casdar's shoulder. He had a shallow cut on his cheek and a small band of city guards at his back.

"I have Bright Prince Gabrialo and his physician," said Casdar. "Is the Sanctuary secured?"

Prince Leomar gave a curt nod. "If Gabrialo is within, then so is the emperor." He caught his brother's eye in the dark. "Our father is dead. Long may you reign."

# CHAPTER 22

There is a weariness one can only know in the face of loss, at once bone-deep and brittle. It burrows deep in your sinew, feeding upon your vigor until the thought of lifting a finger seems as if you mean to move a mountain. It bends time and dulls sound. It can blur sight into a wash of gray-brown hues. Or, it can burn too bright and leave all the world feeling somehow wrong, somehow broken. It is this brokenness that you fear—that one touch might shatter you, that your weariness might implode into a sort of catatonia from which there is no resurrection or release. Only sorrow. Only the slow, unyielding march of grief.

It was a weariness I knew well in the wake of Ailis's death, which was why I saw it plainly on Gabrián's face the evening of his father's assassination. It was in the wanness of his skin, in the glaze of his attention, in how he seemed to draw upon every fiber of his will to keep his eyelids open. He was exhausted, and the blood he'd lost could not be discounted. Still, this was no mere exhaustion of the body, even in the wake of his grievous injury. This was grief itself, compounded by the reality that he would not be left alone to mourn. Not that night, at least. Not when his father had been killed only hours earlier.

"What do we know?" asked Emperor Gabrialo of the House of Vendegal, Defender of the Eight Realms and Bright Lord of Istanel, whose charge was the keeping of the Radiant Astral Empire. His voice held the full authority of his station.

Rather than answering their new emperor, the roomful of imperial advisers shifted toward where I sat at Gabrián's bedside, ready to tend to him at a moment's notice.

Gabrián took note of their hesitant glances and frowned. "I had only just begun to form my court as bright prince before this wretched day," he said, eyeing his councilors one by one. "Even so, I brought few into my trust and esteem. Lady Clìana is foremost among them, for far more than the company she is known to keep in my bed. You are the members of my father's council, and now my father is dead—murdered by assassins granted access to the Grand Sanctuary by means that are yet unknown. Make no mistake, I hold each of you in suspicion until the time comes when my father's faith in your fealty becomes my own. Do not give me reason to disfavor you this night."

He paused, and the air itself seemed to hold its breath. "Now, tell me."

"The assassins are dead, Your Radiance," said Lady Var of the House of Dumarza, a viscountess grandee who was well-known at court as Edarigo's Minister of Intelligence. Her appearance was as severe as one might expect of her station, all sharp bones and a sharper gaze.

The corner of Gabrián's mouth twitched with displeasure. "How?"

"Your father's brightswords dispatched two in the fray," she replied. "No bloody scratch seemed to alter their determination to fulfill their mission. Their bodies are now kept under guard in the jail, for it seemed unseemly to house them in the Sanctuary. The third known assassin was captured and imprisoned but gave chase to death in his cell."

"He killed himself?"

"Yes, Your Radiance."

"How was this allowed? Was he not searched for arms?"

Lady Var inclined her head. "Stripped and searched, Your Radiance. He possessed no weapon, save the fortitude to bash his skull upon the stones of his cell. By the time he was reached, there was no possibility of his survival."

If the assassin had been another man, I might have pitied him over the gruesome death. But I held no compassion for anyone who dared raise a hand against Gabrián and his family.

Rubbing at his brow, Gabrián asked, "Were they Vitander's men?"

"No." Rather than Lady Var, it was Casdar who responded from his post near Gabrián's chamber door. The councilors' regard swung in his direction. "No, it was not."

I recalled the assassin who had whispered in Casdar's ear before plunging his dagger into Gabrián's chest, and a shiver ran up my spine. Gabrián raised an eyebrow in question.

"Before his knife fell, I felt the assassin's hot breath upon my ear," Casdar explained. "'Idário wishes you well,' he said. My grandfather did this."

Silence settled over the room. If the air had been still moments before, it was now seized by a viselike grip. No one so much as moved the smallest muscle.

"He wishes to usurp me," Gabrián spat, unable to keep the bitterness from his voice.

"No," said Lady Var. "It was your father whom Idário Belorán wished to usurp. You were merely an obstacle, and now you are a greater one still."

"You are certain that Lord Belorán sent the assassins?" Gabrián pressed.

Lady Var nodded.

"He wanted me to watch you die," said Casdar. I didn't pretend to understand the bond he and Gabrián shared, but any doubts I held for the earnestness of his affections dissolved with the unmistakable anguish in his voice.

"Why?" Gabrián's fingers curled into a fist. "Why attempt to usurp the throne?"

"You know him to be a man of no mean pride," Casdar replied, the tension in his shoulders slowly unwinding. Something in the motion seemed to release the pressure that bound us all in silence. Fabric rustled as Gabrián's advisers shifted on their feet. "Your father refused to sanction the marriage that Idário proposed between you and Teolina," Casdar continued. "Just as he rejected the idea that Sastiona and my brother might wed. If he could not have his claws in the Astral throne by marriage, then it seems he wishes to claim it by blood."

I remembered then that Gabrián had once spoken of

Casdar's sister, Lady Teolina. She had been but four-and-ten when her grandfather had proposed that she and Gabrián wed. Edarigo had refused the match outright. A third-born child was no match for a bright prince, he had said. Never mind the wealth and esteem of her family. In truth, Edarigo simply hadn't wanted to give the House of Belorán a foothold in the imperial family. Not when Idário was known to be ruthless in his quest for power.

"What an interesting supposition, Sir Casdar," said a new voice, sharp and nasal. Lord Mateno Iscar—the wiry, middle-aged marquis grandee who served as Minister of Law—turned his hawkish eyes upon the brightsword. "Tell me, why should we accept your word as truth, when you are of the House of Belorán? How can we be assured of what the assassin whispered in your ear?"

Casdar's jaw ground tight. "How can we be assured that you did not allow the assassin to commit suicide in your dungeon, Lord Iscar?"

"*Sir,*" Lord Iscar blustered, his face reddening. "How dare—"

Across the room, Bright Prince Leomar cleared his throat. "Is there not merit in the Minister of Law's concern?" he said, leaning against the far wall of Gabrián's bedchamber. The new bright prince spoke so casually—so indifferently—that he might as well have been discussing the state of the stone that lined the gardens' pathways. "Your brightsword is a Belorán, is he not, Your Radiance?"

Casdar's nostrils flared, his mouth widening in retort.

"Bright prince," Gabrián interrupted, one hand raised in admonition. "Lord Iscar, your concerns are noted, as are those of Sir Casdar. For now, let us proceed on the assumption that the brightsword speaks in truth, given that he did not skewer me in his grandfather's name while we sheltered in the Sanctuary's prayer room. To that, my flesh can attest. Yes?"

"His flesh, and my eyes."

I spoke before I could think better of my words. Once more, the councilors glanced my way. Near the doorway, Casdar stiffened. Surprise flashed across his face before returning to a look of grim disapproval. Still, I'd spoken in truth. Casdar might have loathed me for reasons I couldn't discern, but I'd seen his fear before the prayer room door had swung shut behind us. I'd seen the panic he'd beaten back, replaced by his fierce determination to protect Gabrián from further harm. "The brightsword was prepared to protect the bright prince with his life," I said simply.

From across the room, I thought I noted a flush of warmth suffusing Casdar's dark skin before he cleared his throat, drawing the attention of Gabrián's advisers once more. "I may share blood with Idário Belorán, but I bear him no loyalty. No mercy. If you wish to burn the House of Belorán to the ground for what my grandfather has done, know that I will be the first to wield the flame."

When the last of Gabrián's advisers left his bedchamber, Casdar closed the door with a soft thud. Leaning back against the burnished wood, he pinched the bridge of his nose and let his eyes flutter shut. I took the moment to observe him from my seat at Gabrián's bedside. The brightsword's frame, ever proud and tense, seemed to slacken, as though he could no longer bear to carry the weight of the day's troubles.

"I would have dreamwine," Gabrián said, drawing my attention. "I will need rest for what lies ahead."

"Aye," I said, rising to fetch the vial from my medical trunk across the room.

It was strange to now think of Gabrián as emperor, to know that the lives of millions fell under his dominion. He had the strength for such a charge. His mind and manner were well-honed to the task of ruling. Yet he was still a man—a man whose flaws and pains I knew nearly as well as my own. It grieved me to think of the immense responsibility that now weighed upon his shoulders, and with such sudden and unexpected force. His father was dead, and now Gabrián was thrust into a role for which no one could ever truly be prepared.

Returning to his bedside, I pressed the vial of dreamwine into Gabrián's hands. His throat bobbed as he swallowed its contents before easing himself down to lie in bed. When he settled his hands on his stomach, I shuddered, the sight too akin to the way a body would be arranged upon a funeral pyre.

"Clìana?" Gabrián rasped as I made to turn away. "Stay?"

Taking up my seat once more, I captured one of his hands in mine. It wasn't long before he fell into a deep and dreamless sleep.

I cannot say how long I sat vigil at Gabrián's bedside, watching the rise and fall of his chest, before Casdar pushed away from the door and crossed to the sideboard to pour himself a dram. A moment later, he appeared at my side, holding a second glass of amber liquor in my direction. When I eyed the glass, surprised by the brightsword's sudden generosity, he snorted. With a sardonic smile, he took a swig and swallowed.

"I did not think it poisoned," I told him, accepting the glass with a grateful nod.

Casdar leaned against the nearest bedpost. "He will mend?"

"Aye."

"He should have died today," he said, tapping a fingernail against the side of his glass.

My heart stuttered. I stared deep into my drink. It wasn't hard to imagine where this conversation might lead, but I had no answers for the questions Casdar might ask— or rather, no answers I could reasonably confess.

Casdar continued to tap his glass, his pace slowing as he thought. "I did not know the man who whispered in my ear. Nor the blade he carried. But I know where that dagger sank. I saw the blood on Gabrián's doublet. On your *hands*." There was a note of accusation in his voice as he regarded me. But any disdain I thought to find in his expression had vanished by the time I met his eye, replaced by the firm grip of resolve. "You should leave, Clìana."

"I would prefer to stay a while."

"Not here. Carastile."

"Carastile?" I blanched.

"I do not know what you did today, whether the Dark Between heard your plea or whether something more fell came to pass within that prayer room." A chill finger coursed down my spine as Casdar continued. "I do not know, and I cannot bring myself to care. He would have died if not for you. Despite my attentions, despite my—"

He scrubbed roughly at his jaw. "Stars, he should have died today."

"But he did not," I said.

"You are a Larmach healer. A *master* healer. Any court in the eight realms would commission you, as I suspect would many a foreign court. You have your pick."

Surprisingly, Casdar's words held little venom. Still, I couldn't help the bitterness that rose within me. "I didn't think you held me in such high esteem, sir."

"Do not make this difficult, Cliana. For your sake, as well as his."

"And what do you think it would do to him? Hmm? To lose what comfort I have offered him since the loss of his sister? And here and now, in the wake of his father's death? How much torment do you wish him to suffer?"

Casdar frowned. We were near then, nearer than we'd ever been. I could see the scruff of his jaw and feel the warmth of his breath upon my cheek. His nose was slightly off-center, as though it had once been broken and well set; and there was a fine rim of amber that circled the deep brown of his irises. When his gaze raked over me in return, I wondered what he saw in my face, even as I came to a sudden realization.

"I'm no threat to you," I said softly. "He speaks fondly of you, you ken. Always fondly. And though it may be that I've known Gabrián only a short time, that time has been true. I cannot believe he would esteem anyone who trades so readily in small cruelties." I swallowed against the knot of tension in my throat. "You harden yourself to me, Casdar Belorán, to intimidate and rebuff that which I can only imagine you see as a threat. But I do not wish to stand between you and Gabrián, as surely as I do not wish to see him harmed."

Candlelight flickered as Casdar appraised me, and a warm breeze snaked through the open balcony doors. Somewhere in the dark beyond, a gull cried in alarm. Then the brightsword twitched, and his chest puffed on an abrupt exhale that landed somewhere between a scoff and a peal of laughter.

Setting his glass on the floor, he leaned forward to scrub both hands over his face. "By the Black," he muttered. "If there is anything I fear of you, it is the power you hold over him. Do you not know that you wield it?" When I stared at him in confusion, he huffed. "You say you do not wish to see him harmed, yet you will certainly do the harming."

"I do not understand," I said.

"You protest ignorance of it?"

I thought of the fever that had taken hold of Casdar at Granara, of the chilling word he'd spoken as he slept. *Witch.* My pulse hammered in my chest. "Sir, I assure you—"

"Do you truly not see that you hold his heart?"

I recoiled as if slapped, stunned by this revelation. Stars, it wasn't the power of Gode that Casdar feared, nor even that I intended to usurp his place in Gabrián's esteem. It was for Gabrián alone that he saw a threat in my presence at court.

"Aye, so I ken," I replied on a heavy exhale.

Casdar leaned close once more. "The duty he now bears is unfathomable. There is a war to come, make no mistake. And if he is to win it and claim his throne without further contestation, then he cannot afford distraction."

I swallowed the bile that rose in my throat. "He cannot afford me."

Firelight danced across the lines of Casdar's face. There was pity in his appraisal that stripped me to my core. "Let him go, Lady Clìana. Leave this place, and let him be."

In the deep black of night, I sat before the hearth in my bedchamber, contemplating all that had been said in Gabrián's bedchamber hours earlier. I considered Idário Belorán and the war he sought to wage against the sovereignty of the House of Vendegal. I considered Gabrián's commitment to the Astral throne, his determination to extinguish the rumors that plagued his household and restore the legacy of his family's rule. I considered the stark reality that Casdar Belorán had laid at my feet: the love that Gabrián bore me, and the dangers it posed to his sovereignty. I pondered all of this as the deep black of night faded gray. By the time a pale and hazy sun had risen in the east, I'd come to three conclusions.

First, as surely as Gabrián had made his heart known to me, I could no longer deny the love I bore for him, great and terrible as it was.

Second, I feared for all this love might ask of me— and, in turn, what it might take.

Finally, I had no intention of heeding Casdar's words and leaving Carastile, not when the power in my blood alone could ensure the rise and fall of Gabrián's breath each morning. Damn the consequences of its use. I had suffered my fill of grief, and so had Gabrián. If it was within my power to keep him safe, then I would do so. No matter the cost.

Reaching into my medical trunk, I eased Ailis's grimoire out from its hidden compartment. For weeks, I had reviled the power in its pages. Now, the time had come to learn the art of that power.

# CHAPTER 23

Gabrián's coronation day dawned cold and bitter. A distant storm smothered the sky in dense gray clouds, riling the waves that crashed upon the cliffside and conjuring a southerly wind that shrieked through the serpentine halls of the palace. It seemed fitting weather for the day. As I stood amid the throng of courtiers in the throne room, I remembered the night before, when the last of the sun's rays had bathed Gabrián's balcony in crimson light and I'd held the emperor in my arms as he'd wept for all that he'd lost. I could still feel the ghost of him in my embrace, at once tense and soft with need. Trembling, he had said, "If I were but a man, I do not know who I would be."

Gently, I'd lifted his face so we could look upon each other. "Ask me again if this could be enough," I whispered. "Let me prove myself to you."

His eyes had searched mine. Then, finding what he'd sought, he had breathed my name in exaltation, and I had opened for him—my lips, my arms, my heart. I'd made myself a sanctuary, offering him the consolation of "but a man," if only for one night.

Later, when the dark had drawn close around us, I'd lifted a hand to Gabrián's temple and let the power of Gode flow through me until the drum of his pulse had eased and his breath had grown long and even. It was the unnatural peace of his easy sleep that I remembered as the Most Luminous, clad in silver robes, placed the diadem of the Radiant Astral Empire upon Gabrián's head.

I prayed it would remain there, Stars willing, for many long years to come.

At dawn the following morning, I found a candle outside my surgery door. Its tiny flame burned bright in the dark chasm of the hall. A finger of unease traipsed up my spine at the sight of it. Candles were often lit in offering to ward against Shadows or give evidence to holy blessing. But I could see no reason why one should be left outside my door. Perhaps it had been placed there by mistake, forgotten by some passing servant in the night. Whatever the reason, I snuffed the flame and added the taper to my surgery's stock. Still, the tightness in my chest remained.

It wasn't long before the whispers began, before I took note of the lingering looks and the wondrous words spoken behind cupped hands as I passed. I slept fitfully in my chamber that night, tossing and turning, unable to keep the whispers from my mind. It was clear that I had captured the court's attention. But why?

Sometime in the early hours of the next morning, I rose from my bed, needing to dispel the anxious energy coursing through me. I encountered no one save the palace guards on duty as I paced through the palace. There was only the soft sound of my footsteps on the tile and the silver glow of the moon where it streamed through the mullioned windows. When night began to give way to morning, I returned to my surgery, stopping short at the threshold.

Three candles flickered before my surgery door.

My growing suspicions were confirmed later that day, when a servant fell prostrate at my feet in the bustling eastern colonnade. "Blessed Lady," he said again and again, his fingertips brushing the toes of my silk slippers.

I stared down at him as a dozen pairs of eyes pressed upon me. "Please," I said, desperate to dispel the unwanted attention. "You must rise."

"Blessed of the Dark!" the servant cried as he scrambled to his feet. "Salvation of the emperor!"

The event was none so singular as I had hoped. It was as if his public display of worship had burst the dam on some great cataract of praise. The words of courtiers and servants alike began to trail me through the halls of the palace.

*Blessed Lady!*

*May the Stars keep you!*

*Honor to you, savior of the throne!*

When more candles littered the entrance to my surgery, I knew I only had myself to blame.

"It is true what they say?" Gabrián asked as we sat upon his balcony one evening. Through the navy silk of his tunic, he thumbed the edge of the bandage that bound his chest. "That you communed with the Dark Between to spare my life?"

My pulse thundered in my throat. I didn't wish to lie to

Gabrián, yet neither could I imagine revealing to him the full truth of what had happened in that prayer room. "The assassin's blade sank true," I said, scrambling for some explanation that might quell his curiosity. "There was nothing I could have done within my skill to save you."

Gabrián seemed to consider this for a long moment, his attention fixed upon the sun as it dipped below the horizon. "If you are favored by the Dark, then perhaps I am as well." He met my eye, firm with resolve. "It is time I defended my throne."

His words heightened the anxiety coiling in my chest. I reached out to him, needing to feel his skin, as though I could tether him to me with something as simple as a touch. "Then I bid you call upon the aid of Clan Larmach. If war is upon us, you will need healers by your side."

A fortnight after I encouraged Gabrián to call for help from my clan, he received a missive from Bright Lord Dalmorie. Diarnan Larmach had agreed to send three dozen healers to aid in Gabrián's war efforts. The knot of tension in my chest drew tighter at the thought of so many Larmach healers here in Carastile. I didn't want to be reminded of the world I'd left behind when leaving Daorender—of Lenghan, Erune, and Ailis. But Gabrián had already signed the healers' commissions; and as his chief physician, I had inked them with my seal. If my own journey had been any indication, it wouldn't be long before my kin arrived in Carastile.

I saw little of Gabrián in the days that followed our discussion on the balcony. His time was often spent deep in conversation with his council, and my own was consumed with preparations for the war to come. I would labor in my surgery from dawn to dusk, an eerie echo of the days I'd spent preparing for Imbelaine at Erune's side.

It was on one of these mornings, as I snaked through the palace's winding pathways toward the herb gardens, that the fight began.

The garden plots that served Alamada's kitchens and surgeries lay just beyond the palace armyards, where the highborn at court often trained with steel, bow, and spear. As I drew near one of the training yards, the rumble of a familiar voice carried to me on the breeze, low and laced with violence.

"You mean to cleave to him, then."

"I do," said another man whose voice I recognized. Then a long, metallic scrape filled the air.

As I rounded the verge, I saw Casdar Belorán sitting on a low bench, his broadsword carefully balanced against his thigh. With a whetstone in hand, he sharpened the blade with determined focus while Bright Prince Leomar looked down upon him.

The bright prince's face was flushed with anger. "Despite the stain of your name?" he spat.

A veined ticked in Casdar's jaw, but he made no reply. A beat passed before Bright Prince Leomar drew his sword.

Casdar stilled, then his gaze flicked up. "Take my name, if that is what you wish." Setting aside the whetstone, he rose to his feet. "Stars know I bear no love for it."

Bright Prince Leomar huffed a derisive laugh. "Your family betrays the House of Vendegal, and still you will not renounce your charge?"

"I am sworn to the emperor, not the bright prince. If I am to be disjointed from my duty, it will be at Gabrialo's behest."

"Or on the end of a blade."

My lips parted at the bright prince's words, but Casdar's face remained unmoved.

"I impugn your honor, yet still you issue no challenge?" said the bright prince, stepping closer to Casdar.

"No."

"Then I challenge *you*, Sir Casdar. Will you rise to it?"

"I will not, for there is no honor in your challenge," the brightsword replied. "And your words are marked by more than I."

I drew a shuddering breath as Casdar locked eyes with me over the bright prince's shoulder. Hesitantly, as if sensing some ruse, Bright Prince Leomar raised his sword to Casdar's chest before glancing in my direction. "All the better," he said upon noting me. "My brother's mistress may bear witness to this reckoning."

"I see no reckoning in this," I replied, moving into the armyard.

Casdar raised a hand in warning, stilling me.

"Never mind the healer," said the bright prince. "Will you not meet my challenge?"

"No," Casdar repeated.

A long silence passed before the bright prince shrugged. "All the same," he said.

Then he lunged with sudden ferocity, his sword gleaming as it arced toward Casdar's chest. But the brightsword was already stepping aside, twisting so that Leomar's blade struck the gravel. The bright prince rallied, launching another attack, but Casdar was quick. Time and again, he evaded Leomar's advances without so much as raising his sword, moving with all the swiftness of a cat. Still, he lost ground with every step. Once he was backed into the shadow of the hedge, he had no choice but to engage with Leomar's offenses. Steel clattered as he parried the bright prince's blow.

Leomar was a skilled swordsman. That much was evident as I watched the duel unfold. Not once did he hesitate, nor did he falter as the fight progressed. Even so, he seemed surprised by the vicious grace with which Casdar drove him back across the armyard. When his boots skidded in the gravel, a hint of fear flickered across his face. He grunted as he took the full weight of Casdar's attack against the edge of his blade.

The sound jostled me from my stupor. "Guard!" I shouted as the men clashed behind me. "Guard!"

Footsteps thundered up the walkway, and a red-faced soldier soon appeared.

"Call for the emperor," I commanded.

"My lady?" said the soldier, his eyebrows knit low in confusion.

I seized him by the arm. "Call for the emperor!"

"There is no need," said Gabrián, appearing as suddenly as an apparition behind me. But there was nothing immaterial about the anger that blazed through him as he took in the scene in the armyard. "Enough!" he bellowed as he brushed past me.

Leomar fell to one knee in the gravel, crumpling like a puppet upon a string. At Gabrián's command, Casdar reined in his attack—but not quickly enough. The edge of his blade sliced through silk and skin, painting the bright prince's chest a vivid red.

Leomar cried out as Casdar tossed his blade aside and knelt, his nostrils flaring as he buried his gaze in the earth. "Forgive me, Your Radiance," he said, his voice deathly earnest.

The bright prince raised a hand to his chest, cradling the weeping wound. I rushed toward him, my instincts as a healer overriding the disdain I felt for him.

When I drew near, Leomar grabbed me roughly by the arm. "How near was his blade?"

"Leomar," Gabrián warned.

"How near?" the bright prince insisted. When I said nothing, he released me, diverting his attention to his brother. "Your brightsword tried to kill me today, as surely as his grandsire's assassins attacked in the Grand Sanctuary. They are traitors, brother. One and all."

I rolled back on my heels, recoiling in sudden understanding. Leomar wished to force his brother's hand, to ensure that Gabrián must strip Casdar of his duties as brightsword—or worse. But why? For the same reason he'd visited me in my surgery earlier that summer? Because he'd seen a threat in Casdar's influence?

I rose to my feet, too disgusted to stanch the bleeding that Leomar had so carefully orchestrated. He may have been the bright prince, and his care might have been my keeping, but I could see little princely merit in him then.

"You would have me name my own brightsword a traitor?" Gabrián said, cold fury in his voice.

Leomar clambered to his feet. "Did he not raise his sword against me?"

Time stretched thin as Gabrián stared at his brother. The hard lines of his face spoke to the anger he fought to restrain. At last, he turned to Casdar. "'Forgive me,' you said. Why?"

Casdar kept his head bowed as he spoke. "I injured the bright prince."

"And would you beg his forgiveness as well?"

"I would not."

"Rise, damn you," Gabrián commanded with a huff of exasperation. As Casdar pressed to his feet, Gabrián speared him with a hard look. "Why not?"

"Because it was he who issued the challenge."

"And did you meet it?"

"No."

Gabrián raised an eyebrow. "You rejected his challenge?"

"Yes."

"And still he raised his sword against you?"

"Yes."

"You were witness to this affair?" Gabrián said, turning toward me now.

I nodded, feeling the full weight of Leomar's attention as I spoke. "The bright prince raised his sword in unlawful challenge against your brightsword."

Gabrián didn't acknowledge my words. Instead, he surveyed each of us in turn—his brother, his lover, and his friend. His expression was so imperious that I fought the urge to wither beneath his inspection. This was the man he must be, I knew. The emperor, the keeper of the Astral faith. Even still, I yearned for the man I knew from the dark halls of Granara Palace, from the spice gardens and the private sanctuary of his bedchamber. I wanted Gabrián. Perhaps it was that desire that led me to note the slight furrow between his eyebrows, the one he couldn't hide even when he wore his cool countenance at court. The one that spoke of his sorrows and the longing of his heart.

"You are all late for council," he said. "We speak of war."

# CHAPTER 24

The Bright Council chamber was set high above the palace. Beyond its lofty windows, red-shingled houses and arrow-straight streets sprawled to the south and east, the vast expanse of the Ifros glittering in the west. Within the chamber walls, Gabrián's advisers had arranged themselves around a long table, facing Gabrián at its head. As the emperor's chief physician, I had also been afforded a seat for the discussion. But my duty that day wasn't limited to providing council. Instead, I sat with my back to Gabrián, carefully suturing the cut on Leomar's chest.

Silence shrouded the room as I worked.

"Have you finished?" said Leomar as I tied off the last suture.

"I need to coat the wound in salve if—"

"Fuck the salve."

*"Leomar."*

I jumped as Gabrián slammed a hand against the table, his voice laced with warning.

Beside me, the bright prince's knuckles whitened

around the arm of his chair. "We are here to speak of war, are we not?" he said coolly. "Let us get on with it."

Gabrián matched his brother's gaze with calculated calm. "I will decide when this council commences. The salve, if you please, Lady Clìana."

The room fell silent again as I finished tending to the wound, smothering the suture in ointment before binding Leomar's chest with a lengthy bandage. Only when I took my seat on the opposite side of the table did Gabrián look away from his brother, appraising each of the advisers seated around the room.

"In the wake of the attack in the Grand Sanctuary, we can no longer deny that the threat of usurpation lurks in the shadows," he said, his voice hard as stone. "Lady Var assures me that each of you who is present here today remains loyal to the House of Vendegal. Do not give me reason to distrust this. As for Idário Belorán, today I strip him of all titles and holdings—and I will do the same to anyone who might aid him with coin, council, or arms. The Duchy of Aredo will fall under the governance of the House of Vendegal until the time comes when one can be entrusted with its care."

I glanced at Casdar, who stood sentinel by the chamber door. If he was disturbed by the systematic dismantling of his family's legacy, he was hiding it well.

"Idário Belorán now mounts his forces in the south, intent upon bringing siege to Carastile. Today, I call upon the banners of the House of Vendegal to meet them in the field."

A sense of resignation settled over the room with Gabrián's pronouncement. From the moment Idário Belorán's assassins had struck, war had been inevitable.

But then Gabrián leaned forward in his seat and said, "But first, we will take Aredo Castle for ourselves."

The room erupted in outrage, advisers shouting one over another.

"It is unlike the Astral throne to play the role of aggressor, Your Radiance!"

"Truly, Lady Amanar? It is aggression to forgo flinging oneself on the enemy's sword?"

"To seize Aredo Castle would require an unnecessary expenditure of resources, Your Radiance."

"There is no precedent for the Astral throne to seize property in such a manner. To do so would risk ill favor among the—"

"Enough!" Gabrián pushed himself to his feet, the legs of his chair scraping across the tiled floor. "I will not permit Idário Belorán the possession of a fortress in which to conspire against me. We *will* take Aredo Castle."

Lowering himself into his seat, he folded his hands in his lap and leveled the room with an iron gaze. "Now, let us concern ourselves with the seizing of it."

Over the coming hour, I learned a great deal about Aredo Castle. It sat perched atop a rocky tor in the southern Istanelan heathlands, a full day's ride from Carastile. Built at the height of the family's wealth and prestige, the fortress had long been considered the House of Belorán's crown jewel, as beautiful as it was capable of withstanding an army who might wish to besiege it.

"We cannot attack the castle in force if we are to defend Carastile," said General Lord Tévarez, who—as befit his roles as General of the Imperial Army and Lord

Protector of Istanel—had a nose like a battle-ax. "A successful siege would require an army of thousands. Never mind that Idário has positioned his forces in our path. We simply do not have the numbers."

"Could we sail?" Gabrián inquired.

"An army of thousands?" Leomar raised an eyebrow in incredulity.

Gabrián ignored his skepticism. "Yes."

"It could be done," said Young Lady Férez, Captain General of the Armada. "But such a large force at sea would surely draw Idário's attention. He could turn south and rout us."

"Even disregarding such a risk, we do not have the numbers, Your Radiance," General Lord Tévarez insisted.

"How many would it take to defend Carastile?" asked Gabrián.

"Three thousand at minimum."

Gabrián balked. "Three *thousand?* Surely Idário has no more than a thousand soldiers in retainer."

To my left, Lord Peóncio—the Minister of Coin—drew an audible breath.

General Lord Tévarez leaned forward in his seat. "Your Radiance, Idário Belorán has gained the fealty of half your banners. Marqueza is lost, as is Dunvares, Apolista, Rodaña. . . ."

A vein ticked in Gabrián's temple. "He has rallied the south against me."

"Yes."

"And what of the north?"

"Teliz is yours. Vendara. Juaréncia. Everything north of Carastile, certainly. If you call your greater banners—"

"No," said Gabrián.

General Lord Tévarez drew back in his seat. "You will not call for aid from other realms?"

"This war is an Istanelan matter, and an Istanelan matter alone."

"Idário aims to usurp the Astral throne," said Leomar, his voice edged with disdain. "Surely, this is a matter that concerns the empire's greater banners."

Gabrián pinned his brother with a stare. "I will decide what matters concern the eight realms."

"If you do not call the greater banners, that is a privilege you may soon no longer possess," Leomar shot back.

Fury seared along the lines of Gabrián's face, threatening to shatter his careful composure. I knew how badly he must have been fighting to keep himself in check. I could see it in the way his mouth pursed and his nostrils flared, the hard set of his shoulders tightening. He would loathe himself if he lost his temper, I knew.

Reaching out, I wrapped my power around his heart and willed his pounding pulse to ease. Was it necessary that I calm every weak-minded man?

The thought knifed through me, sudden and unexpected. A wave of shame followed, and my pulse quickened in reply. Still, my unnatural efforts seemed to work. Gabrián drew a long breath before addressing his brother with steady insistence.

"Let us not pretend, Bright Prince, that we are anything but the dregs of a dying line. The House of Belorán acts upon the doubt that has plagued many a mind since the Great Sorrow laid us low: Is the House of Vendegal ill-favored by the Stars? Is the rapid dwindling of our line evidence that the time for change has come? If we are to put these questions to rest, we must defeat Idário Belorán for ourselves."

A long moment passed before Leomar bent his head in deference. "May the Stars favor us in this endeavor, then."

Gabrián acknowledged his brother's words with a nod. "Now, General Lord Tévarez," he said, shifting his attention. "How great are Idário's numbers?"

"Lady Var informs me that Idário commands three thousand strong, Your Radiance," the general replied, one hand scratching at his graying temple.

"Idário keeps himself at Aredo Castle," Lady Var corrected. She'd been sitting quietly at Gabrián's right, observing the council as it had unfolded. "It is his daughter Janasta who commands the forces."

"And how many to our name?" Gabrián prompted, glancing at Casdar.

"Two thousand six hundred," said General Lord Tévarez. "More if we rally the city guard, though they have been trained to fight in force only to quell riots."

"Could we defeat Idário in the field with such numbers?"

"It could be done. But only if we did not divide our forces to storm Aredo Castle."

Gabrián scrubbed absently at his jaw. "And there are no more banners to call? No houses left to add to our numbers?"

"I have not yet confirmed the allegiance of the House of Réntaz, Your Radiance," said Lady Var. "If Lady Réntaz remains true, her companies would add another three hundred soldiers to your numbers."

"Even so, that would not be enough to take Aredo Castle."

"No, Your Radiance," Lady Var replied. "But then, you might not need numbers to take Idário's seat."

Curiosity flickered across Gabrián's face. "No?"

"There is the option of a spy."

"A spy?"

Lady Var nodded. "A more covert course of action might—"

"No," Casdar interrupted from his station near the door. "Not a spy. An ally."

"Within the castle grounds?" Gabrián asked.

"Yes."

A long silence punctuated Casdar's answer before Gabrián shifted. "You cannot mean—"

"Teolin," Casdar confirmed.

Gabrián's laugh was humorless. "And why would she betray her family?"

"Why would she not?" Casdar parried. "Idário sold her to the highest bidder after Edarigo—Stars keep him—refused to sanction your marriage. She was wed to a viscount of little youth and ill health. I heard that she refused the marriage bed, prompting the viscount to will her nothing but the meanest sum required by law when he died. In any case, she now resides at Aredo Castle. I have no doubt that Idário will wish to see her wed again once her bereavement is through."

"She will want freedom from it all?" said Gabrián. "You're sure of this?"

"She bears no more love for the House of Belorán than I do."

"And she has the lion's heart to betray them?"

Casdar smirked. "I have heard many colorful tales of

the threats my sister made should the viscount so much as touch her. She has the lion's heart."

Gabrián considered this for a moment before turning to Lady Var. "Could a message find its way to Lady Teolina?"

"It could," Lady Var confirmed.

"And the spy you mentioned?"

"If Lady Teolina proves uncooperative, an alternative course of action could be arranged."

"Your Radiance," General Lord Tévarez interjected. "Even if Lady Teolina delivered Aredo Castle into Vendegal hands, Janasta Belorán could easily round her forces to retake it."

"At the expense of Carastile? I think not," Gabrián replied.

"You think any Belorán would suffer the indignity of losing their seat?"

"Janasta may be proud, but I doubt she is a fool."

General Lord Tévarez's jaw tightened. "And if you are wrong, Your Radiance? How many soldiers are you willing to risk for the sake of your pride?"

Color rose swiftly in Gabrián's cheeks, but it was Leomar who shot to his feet. "You are mistaken if you believe the House of Vendegal will suffer such insult, my lord."

General Lord Tévarez rose to meet his challenge. "I am here to advise the emperor, am I not? Would you rather I allow him to lead our people to needless deaths?"

Leomar opened his mouth to retort, but the woman seated beside General Lord Tévarez spoke first. "My prince." She addressed Leomar as she stood, then turned her attention toward Gabrián. "Your Radiance. I beg forgiveness on my father's behalf, as surely as I beg his forgiveness for what I am about to say."

"Catanín." There was a warning in the general's voice that his daughter pointedly ignored.

"My father's legacy is long," she said. "In the waning years of his life, I suspect he does not wish to see that legacy marred and so warns you against any action that he cannot be assured will end in victory."

Red heat flashed across the general's cheeks. "*Catanín*," he blustered.

"But here is what I know to be true," she continued. "Aredo Castle can be held by as few as sixty guards, and its stores can last upward of a year in times of siege. Even if Janasta were to round her army to retake the castle, our forces at Carastile could engage her. She would have no choice but to fight or flee farther south. In either case, Aredo would remain lost to her."

Several seconds passed while Gabrián appraised the general's daughter. She was roughly half of General Lord Tévarez's age, with her father's deeply tanned skin and broad build. She wore her dark hair woven tight against her scalp, revealing a hard-boned face and glittering obsidian eyes.

"You are the shield of your house, are you not, Lady Catanín?" asked Gabrián.

"I am, Your Radiance."

"You spent your youth in the saddle at your father's side?"

"In the saddle, the armyard, the council chamber," she replied. "I will not claim my father's experience, nor his depth of knowledge. But of this, I am certain: Aredo Castle can be held."

"So long as there is someone to provide us a way in?"

Lady Catanín nodded. "So long as there is someone to provide us a way in."

Gabrián swung his focus toward Catanín's father. "Would you speak against your daughter in this matter, General Lord Tévarez?"

Lowering himself into his seat, the aging general scrubbed his hand over his brow. "My daughter speaks true, Your Radiance. I beg you allow me to lead you in this war to come. Then, when your throne is secure—and with your holy permission—I will retire from service to the empire."

"In favor of your daughter?"

"Should she prove herself in your esteem, Your Radiance."

After a beat, Gabrián extended his palm. "So may it be done, General Lord Tévarez."

Rising, the general clasped Gabrián's wrist. "So may it be done, Your Radiance."

The vow settled over the room with a note of finality.

"And what will be done with your brightsword?" Leomar asked, his voice piercing through the silence.

Gabrián rounded on his brother. "Why should anything be done with him?"

"He has assaulted me, no? Such an action is punishable by death."

Cold fury blazed across Gabrián's face. "Is that what you call that dishonorable challenge you instigated in the armyard? An assault?"

Leomar gestured toward his bandaged wound. "He met it, did he not?"

Gabrián scoffed. "You are right, of course. I saw him

cut you with my own eyes. And for that, he must be punished." Straightening, he addressed the room. "Let it be known that I strip Sir Casdar of his brightsword's cloak."

Near the door, Casdar paled.

"Do you yet wish to serve the Astral throne, Sir Casdar?" Gabrián asked.

"You know I do, Your Radiance," he said, swallowing once before replying.

"Good. Then I bid you take to the field. You will marshal the companies that seize Aredo Castle."

Casdar blinked before a wicked smile curled his lips. "As it pleases you, Your Radiance."

"You would give him the captaincy?" A bright flush suffused Leomar's face. "When I am the shield of the House of Vendegal?"

"It is because you are the shield that you will command a brigade in defense of Carastile," Gabrián countered. "You will have more soldiers, more prestige. You won't be skulking in the night."

Leomar scoffed. "You favor *him*, brother. It does not become the Astral throne."

"Nor does it become you to question your emperor," Gabrián replied. "Sir Casdar has proven that he knows when to stay his sword and when to use it. You would be wise to learn such a thing should you wish to be savior to Carastile."

"Savior to Carastile?"

"You want the glory, do you not?"

Leomar frowned. "Do you not intend to ride out with your army?"

"How can I, when I will be at Aredo Castle?"

"*Aredo Castle?*" I nearly shouted, my concern echoed in the faces of many advisers around the room.

"Your Radiance," General Lord Tévarez began while the Minister of Coin shot to his feet.

Gabrián stayed us all with a raised hand. "Idário Belorán killed my father," he said, his tone brooking no argument. "I intend to be there when he dies."

# CHAPTER 25

My head ached despite the willow bark tisane I was drinking, overwrought from so many long hours spent huddled over bubbling cauldrons, fragrant mortars, and bloody gashes.

I'd made camp among Gabrián's army on the golden heaths south of Carastile's moorlands some two weeks past. Each day had brought new banners as forces loyal to the House of Vendegal rallied to Gabrián's side. With each influx of soldiers, my duties to the Astral throne had multiplied. General Lord Tévarez's chief field surgeon, Idgar Antaral, was responsible for coordinating all healing work in the field, but my role as the emperor's chief physician meant that Idgar's efforts were ultimately subject to my approval—at least while I traveled with the army.

"My lady, I have your morning report," he said as he ducked into my surgical tent, stooping to accommodate his wiry frame. This wasn't an unexpected occurrence. Idgar appeared at all hours of the day with reports on the more than one hundred field surgeons and physician's assistants within my care, including the dozens of Larmach healers who had arrived in Carastile three days past. I'd assigned the eight master healers to battalions without field surgeons and given Idgar leave to distribute the rest among the companies where they would prove most useful.

"That time already?" I said, only half jesting. As I reached across the worktable for the report, I leaned into the slice of sunlight that cut through the tent flap. The shock of light sent a searing pain along the inside of my skull.

"Are you unwell, my lady?" Idgar said, noting my grimace.

"Only a headache," I replied. With one glance at the morning report, the painful throbbing in my skull seemed to double. I pressed my eyes shut, tamping down the panic that threatened to crawl up my throat.

By the Black, I was unprepared for this. When I'd longed to secure a position within the Court of Stars, I'd never imagined bearing responsibility for such an immense force of healers, let alone the soldiers they tended to. If any surgeon was ill-equipped to serve their company—if they didn't have an adequate number of assistants or supplies—there would be blood on my hands. Never mind the weight of the guilt I'd feel should I fail to keep Gabrián safe. I took another long sip of the astringent tisane.

Idgar frowned. "Have you been sleeping, my lady?"

"Well enough." I'd slept for two or three hours before dawn that morning. It had been more than the night before.

His brow creased in doubt. "You are no good to us without your health, my lady."

"I don't need to be mothered, Idgar," I snapped,

regretting the words the moment they left my mouth. Leaning back, I rubbed at my temple. "Forgive me. I'm not myself."

"An hour of sleep would do you good, Lady Clìana. I will see that you are not disturbed."

"Nay," I said, rising slowly to my feet. The air was thick inside the tent, and the heady scent of the mudgrass that hung drying for use as plasters wasn't helping. "At least not yet. I need a nip of fresh air."

"Of course."

Idgar held the tent flap open as I passed through, stepping out into the balmy heat of the Istanelan sun. The morning sky was cloudless, and the blaze of light made my head feel as though it were caught between an anvil and a blacksmith's hammer. For a moment, I considered easing the pain with bloodcraft. I had used the power to spare Gabrián's life. Why not use it to relieve the pounding in my head? But I still felt the hollow ache behind my ribs where the bright warmth of my humanity had briefly faded, and that particular consequence of power left me shaken. If I was going to use bloodcraft again, it would be to spare Gabrián's life—and Gabrián's life alone.

My boots smacked in the muck as I wove through tents and training yards. The camp was loud that morning. Captains shouted orders as soldiers drilled in formation. Loud clangs pierced the air as blacksmiths mended armor and tack. A young messenger shouted, "On your left!" before darting past me, ferrying news between the army's generals and commanders. Each sound heightened the ache in my head. I was about to return to my surgical tent to rest when a pair of soldiers brushed past me.

"The emperor? Fighting?" one remarked.

"That is what I heard," said the other. "Olivar said he is to duel with Sir Casdar in the armyard any moment."

The two men hastened toward one of the small training grounds near Gabrián's tent, where dozens of soldiers had gathered. My feet followed them on instinct, panic fluttering in my chest. All I could see was the tip of Casdar's sword tearing through Leomar's chest. Had something brought the good friends to blows? I elbowed my way through the crowd until I caught sight of them.

Gabrián held his sword aloft, a wicked smile on his face as Casdar lunged toward him in attack.

"How long has it been since you last raised your sword, Your Radiance?" said Casdar, his tone mocking. "Can you recall?"

"Surely, an emperor must be forgiven some laxity, weighted as he is with such immense"—Gabrián grunted as Casdar redirected his strike—"responsibility."

I sighed in relief. If the men were jesting, this was surely a friendly bout. The shrill scrape of metal filled the air as they clashed.

"Surely, the emperor will need to forgive himself. No?" Casdar deflected another blow with his shield, flinging Gabrián's sword arm wide—and leaving his torso open to attack. Raising one booted heel, he kicked Gabrián in the stomach.

The crowd gasped as the emperor fell back-first into the dirt. Gabrián took the blow in stride, rolling with his body's momentum to rise to his feet.

"Always the dirty fighter," he said, his amusement dispelling the tension that had gripped the spectators.

"Better to fight dirty than to be dead," came Casdar's swift reply.

The gathered soldiers seemed to hold a collective breath as Casdar renewed his attack. Gabrián met him blow for blow.

They were glorious in their violence. Muscles taut. Lips curled. Blades flashing bright before retreating. They fought with single-minded focus; and the crowd watched, enraptured, as the duel played out over several long minutes. But in the end, Gabrián proved himself correct; there was no swordsman as brilliant in his mastery of the blade as Casdar Belorán. Steel sang against steel in a flurry of maneuvers before Gabrián stumbled back and Casdar's blade came to rest near the apex of his throat.

A hush fell over the crowd. Even sure as I was of Casdar's loyalties, my breath grew shallow. No matter how many years Casdar had served as brightsword to the House of Vendegal, he still bore a traitor's name. The silence that followed was tense, the air itself seeming to still in anticipation. Then Gabrián chuckled, and Casdar grunted in amusement.

Lowering his blade, Casdar grasped Gabrián's forearm and drew him to his feet. The two men gripped each other in an embrace, both beaming bright as spoiled lads.

Unbidden, a smile rose to my lips. I'd never seen Gabrián so alive. He was more than capable as a swordsman, his parries quick and sure. Yet it was Casdar who had caught my attention. There was a grace to his movements that I'd first noticed when he had fought Leomar. Aye, his tactics may have lacked honor, but there was an elegance to them all the same. His movements had been as fluid as silk, each a natural extension of the last.

"Cunning as ever," said Gabrián, sheathing his sword.

"And you forever slow on the offensive," came Casdar's reply.

Stepping into the yard, I caught Gabrián's eye. "You were right when you said you'd never best him," I said. "Still, you were magnificent. Both of you."

A flush of pride colored Gabrián's cheeks as Casdar's face darkened.

"I did not know you would be here," Gabrián said, pressing a kiss to the back of my hand.

"I was taking some air," I explained. "Imagine my surprise upon hearing that the two of you were dueling."

"Ah, well. You will have plenty of fresh air tomorrow," said Gabrián. "We board at first light."

"The time has come, then?" I replied.

A message from Teolina Belorán had arrived one week earlier. Casdar had rightly assumed that his sister would be eager to help deliver the family's ancestral seat into Vendegal hands. As soon as the mission could be organized, Gabrián would sail south alongside Casdar and three companies of knights to seize Aredo Castle. Gabrián had wanted me to stay among General Lord Tévarez's army when he left, but I'd refused. "I was there when the Dark Between spared your life in that prayer room," I'd said. "If you're sailing south, then I'll be sailing with you."

That memory faded now, as a horn sounded on the breeze.

Beside me, Gabrián stilled. An uncommon silence settled over the camp, everyone straining to hear how many times the horn would blow.

A second call cut through the thick Istanelan heat. I placed a hand on Gabrián's arm, half in comfort and half in anticipation.

The horn cried a third time, followed by a long silence. Gabrián's muscles twitched convulsively beneath my touch.

If the alarm proved true, the enemy had arrived by sea.

Not long afterward, I stood beside Gabrián in his privy tent. A bead of sweat traced down his brow, but he made no move to wipe it away as his councilors filed inside. Indeed, he barely seemed to move at all, as though his composure was as fragile as glass. The war was weighing on him. I could see it in the paleness of his skin and the weary look in his eye.

"What do we know?" he said when the last of his advisers took their seats.

"Six ships arrived in the harbor less than an hour ago," said Lady Var, her eyes sharp as daggers in the dark confines of her face. "Cutters built for swift warfare. We believe they belong to Bright Lord Dajnek of the West-mead." When Gabrián raised an eyebrow in question, Lady Var added, "The ships bear no colors or banners, Your Radiance."

"Yet you believe they belong to Dajnek. Why?"

"A man rowed ashore. He called himself Dmirian Onja, Lord of Moslen and captain of the *South Wind*. He claimed to have been tasked by Bright Lord Dajnek to carry his daughter north to Carastile. Onja relays that Lady Alyene, second of her house, has been sent to treat in her father's name."

"To treat?"

Lady Var nodded. "He would say nothing more, save

that he would wait on his ship for your reply."

"If Dajnek wishes to treat, then he may be under duress," said one adviser.

"Or he senses an opportunity," countered another.

"I cannot see how he might be under duress," said a third. "Idário Belorán could benefit from his aid, certainly. But he does not have the strength to threaten a bright lord."

Gabrián turned toward Lady Var. "Do you have any idea why Dajnek might wish to treat?"

"There has been activity in the south," she said, folding her fingers in her lap. "Stirrings among the Gelds."

"Stars," Gabrián cursed, rubbing his brow.

General Lord Tévarez frowned. "Your Radiance?"

"Call the banners, Tévarez. Calas. Brenmere. Any who might arrive before winter."

"Your Radiance?" another adviser echoed.

Gabrián drew a long breath. "This is Vitander's doing. He may have attached himself to Idário's cause and pressured Dajnek to join him."

I thought of the figure I'd seen in the dark of Granara's gardens, holding Sósia's bairn in his arms—now conspiring with traitors to usurp the throne from the man who had given him his son.

"How can you know?" General Lord Tévarez asked.

"It seems that my father's habit of refusing betrothals is what haunts us," Gabrián said with a sigh. "He would not grant Joriun Vitander my sister's hand in marriage, so now Vitander seizes a new opportunity to gain power."

"You are sure of this?" said Lady Var.

"Get me an audience with Lady Alyene, and we will see if I am wrong."

Gabrián called me to his chamber that night as the sun sank into the sea. The ships in the harbor had brought with them a sense of fear and urgency. Though it had barely begun, the tide of war was already shifting—and Gabrián's meeting with Lady Alyene that afternoon had no doubt stirred new currents. I stood beside him on his balcony as cool air drifted up from the sea below, making the skin on my arms prickle. Though he'd yet to speak, I could feel my heartbeat pounding in my chest.

"Matten Dajnek is dying," Gabrián said, his gaze far out to sea.

"The bright lord?"

"Yes." He turned his head a little, his expression shuttered. "Do you know of their ways there? Of the great inequities in the southern realms?"

Frowning, I shook my head.

"In the Westmead, a woman is rarely seen as anything but her father's daughter or her husband's wife," Gabrián explained. "She is permitted to inherit only when her father has no male heir, and sometimes even then she is overlooked entirely in favor of an uncle or nephew."

It was an unconscionable thought, but my mind was elsewhere. "Why tell me this?"

Gabrián forced a long breath through his nose. "Matten Dajnek has no sons. His eldest daughter, Evesa, will inherit his estate, but the Westmead will never recognize her as bright lady. Leadership of the Westmead will fall to her husband, and Lady Alyene tells me that Evesa is soon to be wed to Joriun Vitander."

"Vitander?" I balked. "Can a bright lord hold dominion over more than one realm?"

"He can if he remakes the world to his liking," Gabrián said, his knuckles going white around the balcony rail. "I was wrong to underestimate him. His armies are vast, his coffers recovering quickly from the days of his father's foolish rule—and he offers both to Idário Belorán in exchange for the right to rule two realms. Lady Alyene said that Idário has forced her father's hand, promising to have his house deposed entirely in favor of Vitander should Dajnek refuse to sanction the marriage. The might of the south—Geldegat, the Westmead . . ." Gabrián gave another long sigh. "The Astral throne could not have fought such a force. Not without the aid of Arivis and Olska, whose armies would not reach Carastile until spring."

*Could not have fought*, Gabrián had said. Dajnek didn't wish to wed his daughter to Joriun Vitander, then. He'd sent Lady Alyene north in the hope of negotiating an alternative alliance. I understood at once what this meant.

"Which sister are you to marry?" I asked, the words little more than a whisper.

Gabrián glanced at me, looking as though he was being dragged to his pyre. "Alyene," he confirmed. "Leomar is to marry Evesa."

"When?"

"As soon as the war is won."

If you'd asked me who I was in that moment, I couldn't have told you. I felt outside myself, untethered to the tangible world around me. I had known that I would never marry Gabrián, that we would never build the kind of life together that he desired. That *we* desired. He would always be emperor, and I his royal physician. But to think of him building that life with another, of taking that woman into his confidence and his bed . . .

It was too much. Turning on my heel, I stalked toward the door.

"Clìana." Gabrián's footsteps padded across the floor behind me.

"This was foolish," I said, rounding on him. "Foolish from the start!"

He stopped short before me, his expression crumbling; and a wave of hot anger rolled through me. How dare he lay claim to suffering, as if the consequences of his choices weren't carving through me like a knife. He was forsaking *me*, as I'd always known he would—and he could drown for it, for all I cared.

The thought flashed through me like the strike of an adder, followed by a revulsion that cooled the anger burning hot within me. Where had such a thought come from? Could I truly have wanted such a thing? *To exercise power over the body is to forfeit a measure of the soul*, Ailis had written in her grimoire. Was this the consequence of working bloodcraft to save Gabrián in the dark of that prayer room? Uncommon anger? The lick of cruelty? A wave of nausea swirled in my gut.

"Forgive me," I said, stumbling away from him. "Forgive me."

Then I was gone, my feet carrying me over cool tile and plush carpet, my hand reaching out to wrench open Gabrián's chamber door. I was all breath—all racing pulse and searing shame. I'd taken only a few steps down the hall when someone else's fingers closed tight on my forearm, drawing me around.

"Do you see now how this hurts him?" Casdar said, his face smug with condescension.

I took a step toward him. "If I had not stayed, he would not have lived."

"Would you like for me to leave an offering at your door?"

"I would like for you to leave me alone," I said, tearing my arm from his grasp.

"I only wish that I could!" The words seemed to bubble up from Casdar's chest unbidden. I blinked up at him, unsure of what to say as he continued. "If I proclaimed that you would be his death, would you leave him?"

Incredulous, I shook my head. "What are you saying?"

Casdar stared at me for a moment, as if teetering on the edge of some grave decision. I tried to parse the meaning of his question, but my mind was already too troubled to make sense of it. The air in the hall was stifling, and shame weighed heavy on my chest.

"Sir Casdar?" I prompted, needing to get away, to go somewhere where I could clear my head and breathe.

"Nothing," he said at last, his face impassive. "Nothing at all."

If Casdar was playing some kind of game, I was too weary to play along. Turning, I retreated to my surgery, where I watched through the window as the Stars wheeled cold and distant through the sky above.

# CHAPTER 26

Salt was thick on the air as I made my way down the quay three days later. I moved slowly, no more familiar with Carastile's harbor than I'd been on the day I'd arrived in the city; and this time, I didn't have Captain Ibidala to guide me. As I skirted around dock hands and idling travelers, I wondered how many of the people on the quay belonged to Casdar's company. Idário Belorán undoubtedly had spies in the city, so we'd been instructed to dress plainly, boarding under the guise of a lowly mercenary crew rather than an imperial company.

I lifted a hand to tug at the rough linen wrap that bound my curls and feathers as a warm breeze licked up off the water. *Third ship from the end of the quay,* I'd been told. I nearly snorted when I came upon the familiar sight of the *Harbinger.*

"If you are feeling green, mistress, you would best walk on." Captain Ibidala leaned against the mizzenmast, the low swoop of her hat obscuring her gaze. "My boots do not deserve it."

"Captain," I said by way of greeting, smirking as I stepped aboard. My gaiety dimmed as the ship swayed beneath me. Swallowing against a rush of bile, I set down my surgical trunk and drew beside her. Together, we watched the bustle of the quay, Captain Ibidala nodding now and then as one of Casdar's soldiers found their way aboard.

"You found your place at court, then, healer?"

"Aye, I did."

"I have heard tell of your great deeds, Blessed Lady. Have you found all that you desire?"

Despite the heat of the day, I shivered. The captain's parting words on the day of my arrival in Carastile still unsettled me. *All that you desire will be yours, then none of it—and perhaps some of it yet again*, she had said. *It will be enough.* When she'd spoken the divination outside Lady Oirich's door, I had desired only one thing: a commission within the Court of Stars, where I might gain glory as one of the empire's most renowned physicians. Now I was called Blessed of the Dark, but at what cost? My renown had come not through the skill of my hands but the unnatural power I had practiced—the same power that had driven Ailis to madness and, ultimately, her doom.

Shaking the unwelcome thought from my mind, I remembered something else that Captain Ibidala had said before we'd last parted. "You told me that the river gives what it gives. Was it the river of the dead you spoke of, beneath a blanket of Stars?"

I felt the sudden press of the captain's attention. "Are you a seer?"

I shook my head.

"Then what are you?" she demanded, shifting on her feet as if sensing danger.

I met her steady gaze and swallowed. "I cannot say."

The captain opened her mouth to reply but paused when several men journeyed up the gangway. Though they were dressed in simple leather jerkins and cheap linen, I nevertheless recognized Gabrián and his brightswords.

"Emperor," the captain said quietly as Gabrián stepped aboard.

He grasped her forearm in greeting. "Captain Ibidala, the House of Vendegal is in your debt."

"My fealty comes at no cost, Your Radiance."

He offered her a nod in gratitude. "Lady Clìana, if you would join me on the quarterdeck?"

Surprised by Gabrián's sudden attention, I allowed him to lead me up the short flight of stairs. Together, we walked toward the far side of the empty deck. When he turned to face me, his countenance was carefully composed. "There is no need for you to join us, if you do not wish," he said.

"I am your physician. If you're injured—"

"If I am injured, there will be other surgeons to tend to me," he replied. "I would have you happy, Clìana."

He spoke so softly that I barely heard his final words above the crashing tide and the noise of the quay. I swallowed against the sour thought that rose to my mind: *I do not ken how to be happy.* "We are both of us bound to oaths," I said instead, echoing the words I'd spoken on the night we'd first coupled.

Gabrián grimaced. "That night, you said that I am to give you nothing that does not please me. It brings me no pleasure to hold you to an oath that brings such grief. If you wish to be free of it, you are free."

"And if I do not wish to be free of it?"

"You will always have a place in my court, Clìana, should you wish it."

With a sigh, I turned toward the Ifros, grasping the ship's railing as I watched whitecapped waves rise and fall in the distance. "I must beg your forgiveness again for my words the other night."

Gabrián's hands settled beside mine on the railing. "We are none of us immune to anger, no?"

I loosed a long breath as the absolution in his words washed through me. The tense set of Gabrián's shoulders softened when I placed my hand over his.

"When I am wed, I might yet take a lover," he said quietly.

My pulse raced at the implication. It was a tempting offer, to be sure. I wanted nothing more than to shield Gabrián from any suffering, including the loss of what we now shared. But I knew Gabrián—and I knew that such an unjust affair would eat at him all the same.

"That is not the kind of man you wish to be," I said.

"Perhaps Lady Alyene might wish to do the same."

It was wishful thinking. "Lady Alyene would not risk the legitimacy of her children. And you would not dishonor her by taking for yourself what she cannot hope to seek."

Gabrián sighed. "Some days I wonder if honor does not come at too high a cost."

Surprised by this sullen response, I turned toward him. "Do you wish to be Leomar, then? Or Idário? You act honorably because you see those around you as more than mere obstacles or pawns. Do not treat Alyene in such a way."

Gabrián drew his hand from mine to rub at his brow. "You are right, of course. Forgive me."

"You may yet come to care for her. As the mother of your children, if nothing else."

"And what will become of you?"

"What do you mean?" I raised an eyebrow.

"When I am wed, could you yet live at court?"

My mouth bobbed open, then shut. "Gabrián."

"No, no," he said quickly. "That was foolish of me, to ask you to bear witness to what might have been between us in another life. To ask that you usher my children into this world, given birth by another." He shook his head. "I will see you safely commissioned elsewhere, at any court you wish."

"Thank you," I replied, unsure of what else to say. If I had allowed myself a sullen moment, I might have admitted that I didn't want another commission. But Gabrián was right. I didn't wish to see him build a life with another woman at his side.

Silence stretched between us until a shout carried on the breeze, followed by a flurry of motion on the deck below. We turned as Casdar strode toward us across the quarterdeck.

"We are ready to make way," he said, addressing Gabrián.

"All are accounted for?" Gabrián inquired.

Casdar nodded in reply.

"To Aredo Castle, then," Gabrián said as the *Harbinger* set forth from its port.

What awkwardness remained between me and Gabrián faded as the day grew dark, as did the last remnants of my ailing stomach. I wasn't just a woman among a company of knights. Nor even the courtier who kept the emperor's silks. I was the Blessed Lady, the one who had pleaded with the Dark Between to spare Gabrián's life. Company and crew alike tracked me across the ship with curious eyes. To show them anything but strength was to risk their morale as we headed south toward danger. Which is why, when the sea rose and my stomach roiled, I called upon blood-craft to calm the storm within.

It was an ongoing effort to quell the churning of my wame, and I could feel the toll that such a persistent use of power was exacting upon my soul. My fears and worries flattened to something harder, a sort of cool invincibility that didn't falter even as the Ifros rolled beneath us.

At one point, Captain Ibidala called for a spyglass. Looking out to sea, she cursed.

"Tell me," said Gabrián, his voice gruff with concern I couldn't feel.

"There is a storm on the horizon. Southwest." Captain Ibidala pressed the spyglass into his hands. "Do you see it?"

After a moment, Gabrián nodded. "Can we escape it?"

"Such storms are wicked this time of year, Your Radiance. It would be safest to row ashore."

Gabrián shook his head. "No, I will not risk falling into Idário's hands. What chance have we on the sea?"

"I could tell you with greater certainty in an hour, Your Radiance."

"There is a possibility, then?"

"That we might outrun it?" Captain Ibidala's lips pressed thin. "Such storms are often deadly, and the rolling sea will hinder our flight. But such a feat is possible, Your Radiance. And for the sake of your sovereignty, I should dearly like to outrun her."

"An hour, then, Captain," Gabrián replied.

The Ifros kept time by the rise and fall of its waters, each moment stretching longer and more harrowing as the thick wall of storm clouds approached. The wind began to howl. The sky darkened. Soon, the *Harbinger* seemed to hang weightlessly upon frothy crests before plunging into the dark valleys of the sea.

"Reel in the sails!" the captain shouted as rain pounded down. Her quartermaster, a man called Nafa, echoed the command to the rig hands, who scrambled to their tasks.

"Captain?" Gabrián shouted just before a clap of thunder, his hair now plastered to his face and neck. I curled my fingers around the rail of the quarterdeck, riveted by the black abyss of the encroaching storm.

"We may yet have a chance of escaping her," Captain Ibidala replied, taking command of the helm. "But the time has come to take cover, Your Radiance. It is no longer safe to remain above deck."

As if to prove the captain's point, a gust of wind caught abruptly in the half-reeled sails, causing the ship to list wildly. I cried out as the deck tilted, my grasp on the starboard railing the only thing that was keeping me aright. Gabrián was not so fortunate. Without a firm handhold, the listing ship sent him tumbling, his body sliding across the deck before crashing against the portside railing.

Sudden terror pierced through my hardened spirit as the deck tilted even further, peeling away from Gabrián until he seemed to be floating in midair. My scream cut through the wind like an arrow.

Then Casdar was there, hauling Gabrián against him with one arm as his other arm wrapped tight around the ship's rail. The helm spun furiously as Captain Ibidala fought to correct course, and soon the ship righted itself in the water.

It was only when the harsh pounding of my pulse eased that I realized the crew was shouting. Below, one of the rig hands lay splayed upon the main deck, blood pooling around his head.

"Is he alive?" Captain Ibidala shouted over the din.

Reaching out with bloodcraft, I wrapped invisible fingers around the rig hand's heart. One of the deckhands confirmed what I already knew to be true. The man was dead.

The realization hung over the deck like a shroud. I could see the weight of it pressing upon the crew, in their tightly wound stillness and the wild whites of their eyes. Fighting the storm had once been a welcome challenge. Now, it was futility. The crew had decided, then and there, that death would soon be upon them—and they were terrified.

It could not stand.

As the sea rolled and the sky raged, Gabrián stretched a hand toward me. "We must get below deck," he shouted.

I shook my head, and his eyebrows furrowed in confusion. "If the crew is not heartened, they will not fight," I said. "And they *must* fight."

"What would you have me do?"

"Speak to them! You're the Radiant Astral Emperor. You have the ear of the Stars and the favor of the Dark Between. If you rouse them, they *will* fight."

The ship shuddered against the power of the sea as Gabrián stared at me, blinking away the rain that pounded upon us.

"Emperor, you must seek refuge below deck," Captain Ibidala shouted from the helm.

Casdar tugged at Gabrián's arm. "The captain is right."

Still, Gabrián appraised me, as if seeking an answer to a question he could not voice. Then, all at once, he shirked Casdar's arm and called to the quartermaster. "Nafa, I need you to lash me to the main mast."

"What?" I spluttered as Casdar and the quartermaster protested.

"The whole of the deck cannot hear my words, but they can witness my strength," said Gabrián. "Nafa, a length a rope, if you please. Casdar, take Lady Clìana below deck and ensure she remains safe."

Thunder boomed overhead, jogging me long enough from my haze of fear to recognize the wisdom in his words. Casdar began to protest, but Gabrián silenced him with a look. After a beat, Casdar wrapped his hand around my arm and dragged me below deck, hurrying me down the hall to the quarters that Captain Ibidala had gifted Gabrián for the journey south.

"Was this your idea?" he demanded once he had flung me inside and barred the door shut.

"Nay, but—"

The bow of the ship plunged suddenly, and I tumbled toward the cabin door. Catching me by the arms, Casdar swung me around until my back was flush against the wall, his body large and heavy around me. His breath was hot against my cheek.

"We may die this day," I said. "Would you have him cower? He who is blessed of the Stars?"

Casdar's glare was as searing as a brand. He grunted as he stepped away, putting space between us. "You will be the death of him," he said.

When I said nothing in reply, Casdar turned away, stalking as far away from me as he could in the small space. I sank to the floorboards, bracing myself against the pitching of the sea. Reaching out with bloodcraft, I curled invisible fingers around Gabrián's heart and felt it beat.

And beat.

And beat.

The storm raged on.

# CHAPTER 27

I don't remember losing consciousness during the storm. One second, the sea had been tossing the *Harbinger* like a rag doll in the arms of an ill-tempered child. The next, there had been nothing at all until I'd awakened with a start, bolting upright on the bed in Gabrián's cabin. Instinctively, I reached out with bloodcraft in search of his pulse. I found his heart beating steadily just a hair's breadth away, where Gabrián was sitting in a straight-backed chair at my bedside.

"At last," he said, my relief echoed in his sigh. He was alive, thank the Stars. His dark hair was sticking out wildly, a few damp tendrils clinging to his temples and the nape of his neck. "Are you well? Casdar says you struck your head quite soundly against the floorboards."

The words beat back the last remnants of my alarm, though a throbbing ache rushed in to take its place. Probing the tender cap of my skull, I winced.

"Is there anything I can get you for the pain?" Gabrián asked.

I shook my head, then regretted the action when my vision flashed white. "I'll be all right in a moment. Tell me what has happened."

"Captain Ibidala navigated into the cover of a small inlet. We scraped up against a rocky outcrop, and the ship listed. Casdar says that is when you struck your head."

"The other ships?" I asked, using a small measure of bloodcraft to ease the pounding in my skull.

"The *Falcon's Bright Wing* ran aground half a league south. Its crew and company are accounted for, though they lost several horses to broken limbs. The *White Spire,* however . . ."

"It's not been spotted?"

"Not yet. We fear it may be lost to the sea." The tight purse of Gabrián's mouth betrayed his worry. If the Ifros had swallowed a third of his company, his aim to take Aredo Castle was at risk. Never mind what the loss might mean for his sovereignty.

I covered his hand with mine. "*The White Spire* may be lost, but you're still with us. Is that not evidence that the Dark Between yet favors you?" Little though I believed in Astral teachings, I knew such words would comfort him.

"Of course, you are right." The harsh line between his eyebrows softened. "I sent several scouts ashore to ascertain our location. The captain believes we have landed south of Aredo, but I wish to be sure. Until then, I have instructed the company to remain aboard. The crew is working to see if the ship cannot take to deeper waters, in case there is need for us to flee."

"And the storm?"

"Heading inland now, no doubt ravaging the country-side. With any luck, it will conceal our arrival from unfriendly eyes. Now, enough talk of our sorry state. Tell me what I can do for your head."

I smiled, grateful for his concern. "In my medical trunk, there should be a tincture of willow bark I can take to ease the pain."

"Of course," Gabrián replied. He'd only just risen to his feet when a knock sounded at the door. "Yes?"

Casdar appeared, glancing at me before meeting Gabrián's eye. "One of the crew spotted a man in the water, perhaps from the *White Spire*. He may yet be alive."


We hurried to the deck, Gabrián with my medical trunk in hand. The sky was gray with storm clouds, and we were soaked to the skin by the time the crew hauled the man aboard. Seeing his empty eyes, one of the deckhands pronounced him dead, but I barely registered his words. My focus had narrowed to the figure lying prone on the deck. Even several lengths away, I recognized the broad build of his body and the battered feathers twined into his hair.

*Lenghan.*

I flung myself to his side and felt for a pulse at his wrist and neck. Finding only stillness, I held the back of my hand above his mouth. Not even the shallowest breath slipped from his lips. With a growl, I ripped open his waterlogged shirt and pumped his chest with my hands. Hesitant as I was to use bloodcraft upon him, death remained too kind a fate for the man who had possessed the power to save my sister yet done nothing. Nay, he deserved far worse—and I would not let him die until he'd suffered it.

"Clìana," Gabrián said, placing a gentle hand upon my shoulder.

"No!" I cried, shirking from his touch. "He will wake up, damn him. Wake up!"

As if in answer, Lenghan's chest rose with a sudden gasp. I fell back as he rolled to his side, coughing and spluttering before spitting up half the sea. Any pride I might have taken in reviving him was razed by the anger burning in my chest.

Glancing up, Lenghan balked. "Clìana?"

I spat on the deck beside him. "I should have let you die."


Lenghan confirmed that the *White Spire* had been lost to the sea, overtaken by a rogue wave that seemed to swallow it whole. Gabrián gave him the captain's quarters in which to rest while the company awaited the return of the scouts. No one dared question me about the incident on the deck; even Gabrián had given me a wide berth after ensuring I was well. But I caught enough furtive glances and close-bent heads to know that company and crew alike were exchanging their fair share of whispers. I paid them no mind. My thoughts were consumed by Lenghan.

He was the only survivor we'd found from the *White Spire*. Naturally, I suspected that he'd used bloodcraft to survive the Ifros as long as he had. I envisioned him forcing his lungs to expel the water he swallowed over and over, compelling his heart to keep beating even as his body screamed for breath. But in the end, he hadn't survived because of the power in his blood. He'd survived because of *me*. Because I had hated him enough to wish him further suffering—and because I had questions.

"We need to speak," I said, slipping into the cabin where he lay resting.

Startled, Lenghan sat up on the bed. He looked haggard, and not only from the time he'd spent in the sea. The stocky lines of his frame had thinned since last I'd seen him, the bones in his face now standing out in sharp relief. His initial surprise bled into a sneer. "I must congratulate you on your commission, my lady."

I clenched my jaw against the fire that burned within me. "You taught Ailis how to wield bloodcraft."

"Aye, I did."

"You let her die."

His eyebrows rose in surprise. "Her body was broken, Clìana."

"Too broken for the power in your blood?"

"In *our* blood, aye."

"Aye, in our blood," I snarled, surging toward him. "I have read that book from cover to cover. I ken you had the power to save her."

"She was gone when I found her, Clìana," he said, pushing to his feet.

"And what of it? You had the power to bring her back, did you not?"

"To bring her back? Such a thing is reckless, dangerous in its asking."

"And was Ailis's life not worth the cost?"

"Nay, it wasn't," Lenghan replied, his eyebrows rising even higher.

His sheer astonishment at my question—as though he could not imagine that I'd consider my sister's life worth saving—pushed the growing tide of my anger over its banks. Lunging forward, I beat my fists against his chest over and over, cursing aloud the day that he'd been born.

"Enough," he said as he resisted me, his hands grappling for purchase until he managed to catch my wrists. "Enough, Clìana!"

We stared at each other in silence, our chests heaving.

At last, I wrenched my hands from his grasp. "Do not speak to me again. Do not touch me. Do not look upon my face. You are nothing to me now. Do you understand? You bear no right to speak my name."

Turning on my heel, I stalked toward the cabin door.

"Clìana," said Lenghan plaintively as he followed me across the room. I had half a mind to round on him, to bleed my vengeance from him drop by drop. But my hand was already peeling back the cabin door—

And revealing Gabrián on the other side.

From his expression, I could only surmise that he'd overheard nearly all that Lenghan and I had said. Heat suffused my face as Lenghan drew near behind me.

"Your Radiance," I said, dipping in a hasty curtsy.

"My lady," came Gabrián's cool reply.

I hurried past him, desperate to breathe air untainted by the consequences of unnatural power, by the shadow of Ailis's legacy and the blood on Lenghan's hands. I took the stairs to the deck two at a time, my footfalls heavy— though not so heavy that I didn't hear the hint of suspicion in Lenghan's voice as he acknowledged Gabrián, saying simply, "Emperor."

Gabrián found me sometime later on the quarterdeck, leaning heavily against the ship's rail. A warm drizzle plastered my hair to my skin. He said nothing as he drew beside me, both of us looking out over the shoreline.

"His name is Lenghan Goddan," I said. "He was my lover at Aversere."

Gabrián drew a measured breath. "Did he have your heart?"

"For a time. But I was young, ignorant of far too much when he first came to my bed." I swallowed against the knot of tension in my throat. "Do I have your heart, Gabrián?"

"You know you do," he replied, though he kept himself guarded.

Pressing away from the rail, I withdrew Ailis's grimoire from the safety of my cloak. "Then it is time you know the truth of me."

Gabrián noted the book in my hands. "What is this?"

"Power," I replied, passing the grimoire to him. Gabrián began to thumb through its pages, his back now turned to the rain. "Power that drove my sister to her grave," I went on. "It runs through our blood—the blood of Gode."

Gabrián closed the grimoire with a snap. "This is Shadowcraft. Have you—" He hesitated, as if unwilling to even ask the question. "Have you used this?"

I forced myself to meet his gaze.

He stepped back as though I'd struck him. "This is what saved Sósia's babe. This is what saved *me.*"

"Yes."

"Stars, Clìana," he said, pressing the grimoire to my

chest. It was now his turn to lean upon the rail, his head hung low.

"I couldn't watch you die," I said softly.

His shoulders stiffened, but he made no reply. A long silence stretched between us.

"You said this power drove your sister to her grave," he said at last, a clear question in his voice.

"To manipulate the body exacts a cost upon the soul. The greater the power one works, the less . . . *human* one becomes," I explained. "The spirit can recover in the wake of its use, given time. But Ailis was so ill, her body always pained . . ."

"She forfeited too much," said Gabrián.

"Aye," I managed.

"And you knew none of this? That she had wielded such power?"

I shook my head. "Not until Granara. That was where I first read the book. Lenghan only gave it to me the day I left Aversere."

"Lenghan gave this to you?" he questioned, glancing up at me swiftly.

"He was the one who taught Ailis how to use blood-craft. I only learned of it existence years later."

A beat of silence stretched between us. "Granara," Gabrián said, returning his attention to the shoreline. "That was where you first practiced this power."

This time, there was no question in Gabrián's voice. He had a canny mind, and now he was using it to piece together the truth that hung between us.

"The babe was dead. And you . . ." I found myself desperate to explain, to make him understand. "You were the bright prince."

"You practiced this craft because I offered you a position at court?"

"No!" Hot shame heated my face. "No. I believed the bairn to be your son—and because I loved Sósia. Because I had the power to spare you both the pain of grief."

Gabrián's regard turned pensive. "You thought to spare us the pain of grief, but Lenghan did not do the same for you. That is why you told him that you should have let him die."

Something about hearing those words spoken by another filled me with such emotion that tears stung my eyes. When I nodded, Gabrián's gaze darkened with anger. Not for me, I knew, but for Lenghan. And that gave me hope. For if he loathed Lenghan for failing to save my sister, could he then hate me for calling upon that same power to spare his nephew? To spare him?

"Did he lose your heart when you learned the truth?" Gabrián asked.

I shook my head. "Before. Long before."

Without another word, Gabrián began to retreat across the quarterdeck. My heart suddenly pounded in my throat. "What are you going to do to him?" I called.

Gabrián turned toward me. "Do you believe him to be a danger to you? Or to this company?"

"Nay, I do not think so."

"Then I will do nothing for now, so as not to betray myself should I not do the same to you."

My lips parted in surprise as he stalked down the quarterdeck stairs and out of sight. It was only when I turned numbly back to the rail that I noticed the rider racing toward the ship.

# CHAPTER 28

The scout confirmed what Captain Ibidala had suspected. The raging sea had carried the ship south of Aredo. Now that the storm had rolled inland, its harsh winds and heavy rains had driven the people of southern Istanel into the relative safety of their homes. Still, the storm was moving swiftly. In the hours that followed, the company made haste to offload the horses and supplies, preparing for the flight north to Aredo Castle. I spent those hours among the soldiers on the rocky shoreline, tending to those who had sustained wounds during the night.

Despite minor injuries and little sleep, the company was in good spirits. Never mind that the *White Spire* had not survived the storm. Such a close brush with death had imbued the soldiers with uncommon zeal. Many spoke in praise of the emperor's holy favor, which had spared them the depths of the sea. Though I understood their good cheer, I couldn't help but think of the thirty-some soldiers and shipmates lost to the sea—all save one.

Lenghan cared for other soldiers nearby as the

company made its final preparations. Though I tried to put him out of my mind as I worked, I remained keenly aware of his presence, as one might feel the stare of a predator press upon them in the wild.

Before leaving Carastile, I'd instructed Idgar to assign two Larmach healers each to the *White Spire* and the *Falcon's Bright Wing*, four in all to serve Casdar's companies alongside me. Who had been the other healer aboard the *White Spire*, then? Had they been of the line of Gode? And if so, could they have used bloodcraft to survive if only they had known they possessed it? I imagined the depths of the sea, so very like a river pool, and an array of feathers slowly drifting down into Shadow. Still, I didn't speak with Lenghan, fearful that my anger might turn to violence at the sound of his voice.

Neither had I spoken with Gabrián since our conversation on the ship's deck. After arriving ashore, he had taken to a hastily erected tent with Casdar and his seconds-in-command to discuss strategy for our flight north. I saw him again only when he emerged at dusk. He glanced at me briefly from across the rocky stretch of beach before turning away. I had only just begun to consider what his disregard might mean when word reached my ears. The company was to mount at once to journey north under the cover of darkness.

We rode through the night amid driving rain, slowing on occasion when sudden gales buffeted our steps. Hours passed before the storm abated. Here and there, thin slivers of moonlight broke through the clouds, offering us a better view of the terrain we covered. Still, it wasn't until the wee hours of the morning that we came upon our destination.

Inaza Tower stood atop the high ground to the west of Ininaza, the city that curled itself in subjugation before the hulking keeps of Aredo Castle. The tower itself was a crumbling remnant of the fortress held by Ridalgo Melián in the days of the Thousand-Year Skirmish, before the warrior king had declared himself emperor and united the kingdoms of Istanel, Brenmere, and Calas under his banner. In time, the Radiant Astral Empire would spread until it held near-total dominion over the expanse of the continent.

I climbed the steps of the ancient keep on tired legs, trailing after the man who now held the title Ridalgo had forged some 800 years earlier. Gabrián neither acknowledged nor rebuffed me as I joined him and Casdar in the small chamber at the crown of the keep. Its roof had long since deteriorated, leaving only a blanket of Stars above, and the sole remaining window faced east toward the dark outline of Ininaza. Aredo Castle sat atop a slope at the southern end of the city. The light from its parapets flickered in the distance, as though taunting our company to besiege the castle. But Gabrián didn't intend to starve Idário Belorán into submission. He wanted to sneak into the castle itself, seizing the Duchy of Aredo swiftly and without notice.

"It is time," Gabrián said, nodding toward Casdar.

Kneeling, Casdar produced a small bundle of tinder and flint from a dry box, lighting it on the sill of the small window. Wind whistled through the aging walls of the keep as we waited, still as stone.

"There," Casdar said at last. "Atop the southern keep."

Between the shoulders of the two men, I glimpsed the tiny candle burning bright in the window of the castle's tallest turret. The small pinprick of light disappeared before returning once more, then flickering again.

"She has secured the gate," said Gabrián, his relief evident.

Casdar's hand shot out, smothering our small flame. "Shall we proceed?" he asked.

When Gabrián nodded, Casdar wasted no time retreating down the stairs, his footsteps echoing through the hollow tower before he strode across the ragged remains of the castle's bailey. Mounting, his company retreated down the high ground, only faintly visible in the thin moonlight before they disappeared into the small copse southwest of the city.

It was all that Gabrián and I could do to wait as long minutes passed. We couldn't see the two knights who had been tasked to break from Casdar's company without their horses, their faces caked in mud to provide them greater stealth as they crossed the dark landscape. The rocky southern slope below Aredo Castle was rightly considered impenetrable by force in times of siege, but that wouldn't stop two skilled men from climbing its crags and slipping through an unlocked gate—if they weren't first spotted and slain.

The wait was unbearable, as was the silence that stretched between us. I tried to weather it for a time, focusing on the light from Aredo Castle and the wild pulse beating in my throat. But the more time that passed, the greater my discomfort grew.

"You're angry with me," I said, the words barely louder than a whisper.

I sensed Gabrián tense beside me. "I am not angry. I am . . ." He shook his head with a huff of displeasure.

"'Tis all right," I said. "I deserve whatever it is you feel for me."

"No, I—" Gabrián began, but the distant cry of a horn interrupted him.

We turned as one toward the window, where we watched as Casdar led his cavalry from the copse. The company raced across the short stretch of the plain before disappearing into the city, then charging up the north-western slope of the castle grounds. Squinting, we could just make out their movements as they tore through Aredo Castle's main gate, which meant that the two Vendegal soldiers who'd climbed the crags must have succeeded in seizing the castle's gatehouse.

Heedless of the tension between us, I placed my hand over Gabrián's on the windowsill, squeezing gently to offer him what strength I might. I knew the fear that plagued him, even if he held it firmly in check. To lose Aredo Castle would not cost him the war, but it would risk the claim to Vendegal strength he sought to bolster by seizing the traitor's seat. We looked out upon Ininaza with bated breath, noting on occasion an anguished cry upon the breeze.

The attack seemed to rouse the city from sleep. Candlelight began to dot the darkened landscape, accompanied by further shouts and the muffled clang of warning bells. Gabrián's hand stiffened beneath mine, his fingers digging into the stone beneath. For a moment, I thought I could make out shadows racing across the castle's parapets, though that might have been a trick of my mind. All the while, the air seemed to grow thinner, time stretching more interminably—until, at last, the clear call of a horn carried once more across the city.

Footsteps thundered up the crumbling steps of Inaza Tower. One of Gabrián's brightswords appeared, the hilt of his sword flashing in the moonlight. "Your Radiance," he said, "Aredo Castle is yours."

Dawn painted the inner bailey of Aredo Castle a gruesome shade of red, glimmering off the blood that pooled upon the hard-packed earth. I took small, shallow breaths as I surveyed the courtyard strewn with soldiers. Most were castle guards—and most were dead. Those who yet lived were now beyond my care. Casdar paced from guard to guard, his face grim as he eased his sword into the hearts of the dying. I wondered briefly whether he knew any of the guards from the days of his youth, before he'd been sent to squire at Alamada Palace. If he did, no flicker of recognition crossed his face. When his work was through, he looked past me and nodded.

Turning, I found Gabrián silhouetted in the archway that bridged the inner and outer baileys. He was near enough for me to see the pallor of his face, the only sign of his unease.

"A few soldiers for the sake of your sovereignty," I said softly.

"And many more in the days to come," he replied.

Casdar drew near, his blood-spattered face slick with sweat.

"Your grandfather?" Gabrián inquired. When Casdar shook his head, Gabrián frowned. "He must be found."

"At once," Casdar replied.

"There will be no need for a search," called a woman, her voice low and rich.

We turned to find Lady Teolina Belorán standing atop the landing that led into the nearest keep. She was a striking lass, tall and thin as her brother was broad, with deep umber skin and canny gray eyes. Despite the early hour, she wore a fine silk gown, her cloud of dark Ishmeni hair arranged in an elaborate array of plaits woven with glimmering jewels and stones.

"Idário lies bloody in his keep," she said. "Slain by his own hand. Such is the way of the House of Belorán, is it not? 'Death Before Indignity.'" Her mocking tone gave evidence to her opinion of the Belorán family motto.

Striding forward, Gabrián acknowledged Lady Teolina with a slight incline of his head. "My lady."

"Your Radiance," Lady Teolina replied, bowing deeply.

Casdar addressed her when she rose. "Sister, you are a child no more."

"Were we ever, in this place?" she questioned.

Climbing the short flight of stairs, Casdar pressed his lips to the back of her hand. "It is good to see you well, Teolina. We are in your debt."

"Your company? Or the House of Vendegal?"

Her brother's voice took on a note of warning. "Teolina."

"The House of Vendegal is indeed in your debt, Lady Teolina," Gabrián interceded. "Perhaps we can discuss how your fealty might be rewarded somewhere beyond this bloodied yard."

Lady Teolina smiled artfully. "As it pleases the emperor," she said before leading us into the heart of Aredo Castle, the House of Vendegal's banners now fluttering atop its keeps.

# CHAPTER 29

Lying upon the floor of the castle's grand hall, Idário Belorán didn't seem like someone who had been feared in life. Short in stature, with deeply wrinkled skin and a thick shock of gray hair, he appeared to be little more than an elderly man—one who seemed too soft and fragile to be anything but benign. Still, I knew that a plain face could disguise a shrewd mind and a cruel heart. Unremarkable as Idário's body might have seemed, it was nevertheless what remained of the man who had sold his granddaughter to the highest bidder, ordered the assassination of the imperial family, and ultimately driven a lengthy dagger between his ribs to pierce his heart.

"What will you do with him, Emperor?" asked Lady Teolina, the hem of her gown trailing just outside the pool of her grandsire's blood.

"Do you wish to plead mercy on behalf of his soul?" Gabrián inquired.

"I do not," came Lady Teolina's quick reply.

"Casdar?" Gabrián prompted.

The captain shook his head.

"Then I shall see his body transported to Carastile, where it shall be bound and tossed into the sea."

"I will have my trusted servants prepare the body," said Lady Teolina.

And so it was that Idário Belorán came to be dragged, unceremoniously, from the hall in which he'd once ruled.


Two hours later, Idário's blood had been scrubbed from the tile, and his body was replaced by a finely wrought table upon which a meal had been served. I ate impassionately, as did those around me, neither reveling in the meal nor refusing it. It was good for us all to keep our strength, even if we had little in the way of appetite. The night's violence was only the beginning of the war to come, and it was the importance of discussing the company's next steps that had led Gabrián to gather me and Casdar at Teolina's table.

"I thank you, Lady Teolina, for your aid in delivering Aredo Castle into Vendegal hands," Gabrián said after setting aside his plate. "I also offer a formal apology on behalf of the House of Vendegal for the way my father denigrated you when your grandfather sought a union between us. Though it may be within the purview of the emperor to deny suits of marriage, it is not the Astral way to offer a refusal in so unkind a fashion. I wish to right that wrong as best as I can now that I have assumed my father's seat."

"Thank you, Your Radiance," Lady Teolina replied, her face a mask of courtly composure as she nodded in deference.

"As it is, I cannot offer you my hand in marriage, as it is promised to another," said Gabrián.

Lady Teolina glanced briefly in my direction, and I was once more struck by her cunning. In the short span of the morning's interactions, it seemed that she had perceived the intimacy I shared with Gabrián despite the tension between us. Whether she assumed me to be Gabrián's intended bride, however, I could not say.

Gabrián must have noted her attentions as well, for he cleared his throat. "What I would offer is the rule of the Duchy of Aredo, should you wish it."

Lady Teolina's eyebrows rose swiftly in surprise. For the first time since I had met her that morning, she seemed something other than wholly self-possessed. "I am not the eldest of my house, Your Radiance. Nor even the eldest of my siblings."

"Is it not true that your sire is unfit to rule?"

Gabrián had once mentioned that Dar-Ir Naja—the Ishmeni half-heir who had given their children their dark coloring—was a person of ill mind, often kept confined to their bedchamber for their own safety.

"Yes, that is so," Lady Teolina replied.

"And your uncles and your eldest brother ride alongside your mother in open rebellion against the Astral throne, do they not?"

"Yes, but Casdar—"

"Has sworn his sword in service to the House of Vendegal," Casdar interjected, waving his hand in dismissal. "Better upon your head than mine, sister. We both know that you were born to it."

"And so, my lady," said Gabrián, his head inclined in Lady Teolina's direction. "It appears that you are the only recognized peer of the House of Belorán who is fit to rule. If you wish your family name to live on, the Duchy of Aredo is yours."

Lady Teolina considered Gabrián's words for a moment, her expression inscrutable. Then something within her seemed to shift, settling into place. Squaring her shoulders, she raised her chin and nodded. "And the repercussions upon the House of Belorán, when the war is through?"

"None beyond those which are necessary," Gabrián assured her, his hands folded neatly in his lap. "Monetary reparations must be made unto the realm and empire for damages caused by the rebellion of your house. Those terms may be negotiated. The execution of your immediate household not slain in battle, however, may not."

Lady Teolina shifted in her chair. "My mother? My uncles and my brother?"

"Yes," Gabrián replied without hesitation.

The words seemed to weigh upon Lady Teolina for only a moment before she nodded.

Satisfied, Gabrián forged ahead. "These are the only repercussions I propose on one condition: the ongoing fealty of the House of Belorán, sealed, when this war is through, by an alliance between our houses. I care not for the details: a trade agreement, a marriage between our children—"

"A seat at Bright Council," Lady Teolina interrupted.

Gabrián blinked in surprise as I gasped.

"Stars, Téa," Casdar groaned, one hand rubbing his brow.

"Do not patronize me, Casdar. We are here to discuss the future, are we not? These are my terms." She turned her attention back toward Gabrián. "What say you, Your Radiance?"

To his credit, Gabrián didn't balk. "The Radiant Astral Emperor has always served as the Bright Lord of Istanel."

"Yes," Lady Teolina acknowledged. "And the Houses of Aredo and Vendegal have always lived in contention with each other. Surely, something must change if there is to be peace between our families? As emperor, you have dominion over the whole of the eight realms. It is more power than the world has ever known—and certainly enough responsibility to keep one busy, I would imagine. Would it not be well for another to speak on behalf of the Istanelan people at council? To give full attention to their needs and ensure the emperor makes the wisest decisions on behalf of all his peoples?" Lady Teolina leaned forward in her seat. "Cede your place at Bright Council, and the House of Belorán will stand firm at your side for as long as I have the honor to rule it."

"And if I do not wish to cede so powerful a position?" Gabrián inquired.

"Do not mistake my request for an ultimatum on the assurance of my fealty, Your Radiance," Lady Teolina said tactfully. "The Astral throne shall have the loyalty of my house from the moment I assume the title. But it has been brought to my attention that the House of Vendegal is in need of more than mere fealty."

"Oh?" Gabrián raised an eyebrow in curiosity.

"If you will permit me to speak frankly?"

"Have you not already done so?"

Casdar loosed a hard laugh. Lady Teolina shot him another reproachful glare before continuing.

"It has been said by more than just my grandfather that the power of the House of Vendegal wanes." Sorrow softened the lines of her face, washing away her shrewd expression. "I know what it is to be diminished, Your Radiance. To rise in power from such a place, one needs more than fealty. One needs friends—allies who can be trusted beyond doubt and fear."

"And the House of Vendegal can buy such friendship at the cost of its Bright Council seat?"

"Trust requires action, Your Radiance," said Lady Teolina, holding to her convictions. "Trust on so grand a scale . . ."

She let the words hang heavy in the air, waiting patiently as Gabrián considered her offer. A fire had been lit in the grand hall's hearth to chase away the chill of the summer storm. Its snap and rustle filled the air as silence permeated the room.

"The Astral throne will retain its claim on the Bright Lordship of Istanel," Gabrián said at last. "Though it would be proud to commission its new ally, the Duchess of Aredo, to serve as steward of the realm, to speak on behalf of the Istanelan people at Bright Council. It will be an act of trust in which both our houses must partake, do you not agree?"

A slow smile spread across Lady Teolina's face. "I do indeed, Your Radiance. The House of Belorán will gladly accept these terms."

"Good," Gabrián replied, echoing Lady Teolina's satisfaction. "Now, my lady. What can you tell us of Janasta's armies?"

✦

Lady Teolina hadn't known that Matten Dajnek had broken faith with her grandfather and Joriun Vitander. The Bright Lord of the Westmead was to have sent 10,000 soldiers to fight alongside the House of Belorán, joining the 12,000 that Bright Lord Vitander had pledged in aid. The breadth of the armies under Janasta Belorán's command was staggering, even without Dajnek's soldiers, though it was known that Vitander's forces were still traveling north from Geldegat. Still, a large army alone couldn't fell Carastile—especially without taking the harbor, a feat that would have required Dajnek's ships.

"In addition to her cavalry and spears, my mother commands three siege engines," Lady Teolina explained.

Gabrián waved a dismissive hand. "Carastile's walls are ten lengths thick. They will not fall so easily."

"They will not," Lady Teolina agreed. "Which is why the siege engines were not built to fell the walls but rather to catapult fire and refuse over them."

"She intends to terrorize the city?" Casdar inquired, frowning.

Lady Teolina nodded. "Forcing a battle for it on the field."

"I would meet her there regardless," said Gabrián. "I will not have the people of Carastile suffer a siege."

"Have you the strength to meet her?" Lady Teolina inquired.

"We have two thousand infantry and eight hundred cavalry from Istanelan houses. Another eight thousand travel from Calas and Brenmere. Then there are Dajnek's soldiers and ships, should they arrive before the battle is waged. And your mother's?"

"She has at least three thousand, I am told. They

should reach the Plains of Anzales any day," she said, referring to the moorlands south of Carastile's gates. "I was not made privy to many of my grandfather's strategies, but I heard him say not two days past that Vitander's forces should arrive within a fortnight."

"Stars," Gabrián cursed, the muscles in his jaw grinding tight. "They will have left Geldegat weeks ago."

"Will the Brennish and Calasian forces arrive in time to greet them?"

"Some, to be sure. But those from the farther reaches of Calas and Brenmere . . ." Gabrián shook his head, uncertain. Then his eyes glinted with possibility. "If Vitander's forces are traveling north from Geldegat, could Brennish and Westmeadian forces not engage them on the road, hemming them in from east and west?"

"It is a possibility," Casdar replied, brightening with intrigue. "But would Vitander continue north if he knew our forces had already destroyed Janasta's army?"

Gabrián considered this for a moment before addressing Lady Teolina. "You say Vitander sends twelve thousand?"

"That is what I heard, yes."

Gabrián looked to Casdar. "Send a messenger to Lady Var. See if she can confirm that number and the location of Vitander's forces." When Casdar nodded, Gabrián continued. "I do not think Vitander would contend with us if Janasta was no longer a threat. Already, our numbers are too great, given Dajnek's support. When Vitander discovers how badly his forces are outnumbered, he will turn back."

"Even knowing that you ken him to be a traitor?" I inquired.

A shiver of unease ran up my spine as Gabrián looked my way. "As it stands, we have no proof of his treason. Merely speculation. If his forces return south and have caused no harm, I could not force him from his seat."

"But you are emperor," I said.

"Yes." Gabrián's tone grew terse. "And if I am to command respect in that role, then I cannot rule on whim and speculation."

"Even if a bright lord threatens your sovereignty?"

A vein in Gabrián's jaw ticked. "If I strip Vitander of his title and holdings, then Sós—" He clamped his mouth shut, his chest heaving.

I realized suddenly what he was loath to say, given Lady Teolina's presence. If he made Vitander a pauper, then Sósia's child would be as well. I thought of suggesting that Gabrián take the child, but I held my tongue for the time being.

"Joriun Vitander is a powerful man," Gabrián continued, his voice low and measured. "His house is among the most ancient in the eight realms. Even if I were to strip him of his title and holdings and stick him in a prison cell, there is still much he could do to harm my reign. Better his grudging fealty than to give him nothing more to lose."

"Of course," I said, reaching for my wineglass. Its brightness tasted like acid on my tongue.

"And what about my mother?" Lady Teolina's voice cut through the tension that had threaded through the air. "Your Istanelan forces may be nearly equal in strength, but you will not have time to wait upon Brenmere and Calas before her armies reach Carastile."

"Could we hem her in?" Gabrián asked Casdar. "Surprise her from the south?"

Casdar shook his head. "You would need to cross the Ségua to reach her. Our forces would be bottlenecked at any bridge we cross. Given the opportunity, she would flay us alive."

Gabrián's brow furrowed. "Could we not burn the bridges to delay her?"

"We already have."

"Idário anticipated that you would burn the bridges," Lady Teolina interjected. "Each company marches north with the materials to build what they need to cross the river."

Gabrián loosed a long breath through his nose. The muscles in his face twitched beneath his skin, as though he was fighting to maintain his composure. "We will have to meet her in the field then. Head-on."

Casdar shifted in his seat. "The numbers—"

"Will have to be what they will be," said Gabrián. "Already, she nears the city. We cannot tarry here any longer."

"But if her might proves greater?" asked Casdar.

"We have nearly as many soldiers."

"You would have more if you waited for the first of the Brennish and—"

"I will not delay." The edge in Gabrián's voice was sharp. "Your sister is right. More than the House of Belorán doubt the strength of the Vendegal name. I will not give the city more reason to suspect that I cannot protect them."

"You don't have to," I said, swallowing convulsively as each head in the room turned toward me. I met them each in turn: Lady Teolina's curious gaze, Gabrián's confusion, and Casdar's disdain. "I have poured many drams and tinctures in my work, almost as many as I have made. I ken well that water can flow both ways."

Gabrián's mouth pursed in frustration. "What are you saying, Clìana?"

"If your strength would be bottlenecked at the river, could the same not be true if Janasta's armies were forced to retreat?"

"They have the superior force," said Casdar gruffly.

"So play into that hand. Belorán is a proud house, is it not?" I said, arching an eyebrow. "Let Janasta think that you are weak. That is where you will find your strength."

"In pretense?" Light glinted in Gabrián's eye.

"Yes."

"We could attack when she believes us weakened, creating chaos—"

"Forcing a retreat," I added.

Casdar shook his head. "It is too great a risk. Janasta cannot be baited."

"Can she not?" Lady Teolina interjected. "Our mother has a keen mind for battle, but Lady Clìana is right. She *is* proud."

"Our mother is not a fool," said Casdar.

"Is she not? When I was wed against my will to that lecherous old man, our mother dragged me by the arm to my wedding chamber," Lady Teolina spat, each word laced with hatred. "He would have raped me, you know. My new husband. So I did the only thing I could do. I threw myself at our mother, screaming and clawing, trying to break free of her. In but a moment, she had me pinned against the wall with a dagger at my throat." Lady Teolina swallowed audibly. "She made her threats, but they did not matter. I'd already gotten what I'd wanted: a chance to slip the twin dagger from its sheath at her hip."

The air in the room had grown tense once more, each of us riveted by Teolina's story.

"What did you do with it?" Casdar asked, his voice taut with emotion.

"There is a reason my husband never touched me," Lady Teolina said simply. Her fingers drummed against the side of her wineglass as she let her insinuation settle in our minds.

Casdar leaned forward in his seat. "Téa—"

"So you see," Lady Teolina interrupted, taking a long sip of wine before settling the glass on the table with a clink. "Janasta can be lured."

Gabrián met her gaze with nary a hint of pity. "And we can do the luring."

# CHAPTER 30

Gabrián sent four messengers north from Aredo Castle. Two were tasked with delivering word to his brother, Bright Prince Leomar, commanding him to drive his army south to meet Janasta Belorán in the field three days hence. The other two he sent in search of General Lord Tévarez, instructing that a force of 500 mounted knights should circumvent Janasta's army to meet our small band of soldiers south of the Ségua. On the morrow, we would ride north to meet them.

The night before we left Aredo Castle, I left my bedchamber and journeyed through the dark apartment hall, determined to speak with Gabrián about the discord between us. As I reached his chamber, a stir of motion caught my attention. Farther down the hall, Lenghan stepped onto the landing at the top of the stairs. Catching sight of me, he stilled, his attention raking over me before flitting toward the door to Gabrián's chamber, where a brightsword was standing guard. "Clìana," he said snidely before retreating down the stairs.

I took a moment to shake off the discomfort of Lenghan's presence, then rapped on Gabrián's door.

"Enter," he called wearily from within.

I found him sitting in a simple wooden chair on the far side of the room near a window that overlooked Ininaza. He seemed smaller to me somehow. His posture was soft, and dark circles ringed his eyes. But whether it was the strain of war or the revelation of my power that diminished him, I could not say.

"I won't stay if you do not wish to speak with me," I said, seeing how dearly he needed rest.

He scrubbed at the hard line of his brow before answering. "No. Come."

Tentatively, I strode across the room and stopped in front of him, feeling for all the world like a prisoner facing judgment.

"From the moment you handed me that grimoire, I have turned the issue of your power over and over in my mind," he said, the words slow and careful. "I understand why you chose to use it. To pretend otherwise would be to make myself a liar. But it is *heresy*, Clìana. Each time you wield this bloodcraft, you unmake the will of the Stars—and you cannot persist in doing so."

I licked my lips before replying. "I won't."

"You won't?" Gabrián blinked at me.

Kneeling before him, I placed my hands upon his knees. "I will not apologize for saving you. Nor for sparing Sósia's bairn from death. But you must ken that I would promise you anything, Gabrián—that you hold my heart in your hands."

For weeks, I had longed to say those words. Yet even as they left my tongue, doubt niggled at the back of my mind.

Could I truly watch Gabrián die while knowing I had the power to save him? Could I stand by while his lifeblood spilled from his body and his breath fled from his lungs? He was asking me to forsake perhaps the only power that could spare his life—and spare me the grief of losing him. Could I truly promise him that?

Could I truly break his heart anew by acting otherwise?

It was an impossible decision, one I wasn't sure I knew how to make. All I could say with certainty was that the thought of his body cold with death carved a hollow in my chest. Frantic, I shook the thought from my mind as Gabrián leaned down to kiss my brow.

"Thank you," he whispered as he drew me onto his lap.

I burrowed into him, savoring the steady beat of his heart beneath my hand. An anchor against fear.

"We'll be no small force in the countryside," I said later, trailing my fingers through the hair on Gabrián's chest. "Will Janasta's scouts not spot us?"

"Lady Teolina has given us Belorán banners to fly as we ride north," Gabrián replied, his breath tickling the top of my head. "We shall be soldiers from Aredo. Nothing more."

A thought occurred to me suddenly. "And what will they make of me? There are no Larmach healers among Idário's court."

Gabrián's eyes darkened with understanding. "I will not ask such a thing of you," he said, one hand passing idly over the feathers twined into my hair.

"Come now. They are none so sacred as that." Sitting up, I reached back to remove the first of the feathers.

"May I?" Gabrían said, rising behind me.

The offer blossomed bright and warm in my chest. Though the feathers weren't sacred, allowing another to touch them was an intimate act typically shared between a tutor and student—or a healer and their lover. From time to time, I'd given Lenghan permission to remove them, aiding me in the task of cleansing and combing the dense curls that crowned my head. But those memories now twisted cold and sour in my gut. I grasped Gabrían at his nape and drew him near, seeking to burn those memories from my mind with the heat of his kiss. His gasp sent a shiver of pleasure up my spine.

"Please," I whispered against his mouth, the word breathy with need. Turning, I let him sink his fingers into my hair.


We set out the next morning at dawn, stealing our way north as crimson light bled over the horizon. Belorán banners flanked our lines, twin fields of gray embroidered with two golden hawks, their talons each straining for the head of the other. We traveled simply, Gabrían and his soldiers attired in modest garb, and kept to the well-worn roads and fields that Janasta's companies would travel. All attempts at stealth were abandoned in favor of pretense, lest some farmer suspected that we were anything other than a company of Aredo soldiers.

Before we left Aredo Castle, Casdar tried to convince Gabrían to stay behind.

"You are no shield," I overheard him say, using the

breadth of his body to block Gabrián from the view of the knights gathered in the courtyard. "What if you are slain?"

Gabrián cinched the gauntlet that covered his wrist, seemingly unbothered by Casdar's concerns. "Then Leomar will be emperor," he said.

Casdar scoffed. "And you think that is the best future for the empire?"

"Better than the future your mother has to offer, yes."

"Leomar isn't fit to sit on the Astral throne."

"And neither are you," said Gabrián, his voice now edged with irritation. "I will not barricade myself inside a tower while good people wage war in my name. My decision is made. I will flee in the face of mortal danger. Nothing less."

"One cannot always see the fell blow before it falls," Casdar warned.

"Then such will be my fate."

"And the empire?"

"It is all we can do to live with dignity, Casdar—and to die with it. I will trust in the will of the Dark. Perhaps you should do the same."

After a moment's silence, Gabrián stalked off to mount his horse, his boots smacking in the mud.

With a sigh, Casdar leaned against the rough stone of the keep. "Would he listen to you if you spoke sense to him?"

I startled, unaware that Casdar had known I was standing in the shadows of the nearby doorway. Sheepishly, I stepped into the courtyard. "He would listen, but he wouldn't obey. I do not think he could live with himself if he did."

Casdar scowled. "His foolishness will see him killed."

Once more, a vision of Gabrián's body cold with death flashed through my mind's eye. "It won't if I can help it," I promised.

Sometime around midmorning, Lenghan drew near to ride beside me. He'd removed the feathers from his hair as well, and I saw him note that I had done the same.

"Did he remove them for you?" he asked, his tone mocking.

I fixed my jaw against the sudden rush of anger that rose within me. Reining in my mount, I waited for the tail end of the company to pass, leaving me and Lenghan alone. "What do you want?" I spat.

"You've called upon it, haven't you? The bloodcraft. I can see it in your eyes."

"You see nothing."

"Nay, you're different—and not just because you've bedded in the emperor's silks."

I rounded on him, drawing my horse to a halt. "What I am is none of your concern."

"Even when what you are could mean the difference between life and death? I've heard what they say of you, you ken. The great feats you performed in the Grand Sanctuary through your piety and prayer." Lenghan scoffed. "Did keeping the emperor's bed make a saint of you?"

"You dare speak to me of life and death when you have my sister's blood on your hands?"

All traces of humor fled from his face. "Forgive me for thinking Ailis wiser than to fling herself at the very madness I warned her against."

"You saw what was happening. You could have stopped her."

"Oh, aye? And how could I have done that?"

"You could have spoken to her!"

"You think I didn't try?"

"You could have told me!"

Lenghan laughed in incredulity. "And what good would that have done? Hmm? You never saw her as anything more than a child. Kept her locked up in that dark bedchamber lest she dare see the light of day."

"She was *ill*, Lenghan. Weak since birth. What was I supposed to do?" My mount stamped beneath me. "Expose her to sickness and fatigue? To the cruelty of witnessing a thousand lives she would never lead? I kept her in comfort—"

"You kept her caged!" he shouted, his face flushed red. "I offered her a better life."

A sharp noise of disbelief tore from my chest. "That was your idea of a better life? An introduction to unholy power? To madness and a fatal fall down a long stair?"

"Do not pin her madness on me!" Spittle flew from Lenghan's mouth. "Time and again, I warned her of the consequences. Perhaps if you hadn't tempered her every desire in life—"

"*Me?* My only shame is that I didn't see the vile nature of your influence sooner."

"You cast all blame at my feet while absolving yourself of your complicity? *I* am the one who made things right, Clìana."

His speech struck hard like a blow to the gut. I didn't know why at first, but as my mind whirred in search of his meaning, a growing sense of horror crawled along my skin. "What did you do, Lenghan?"

He stared at me, his lips pressed thin in grim resignation. It was all the confirmation I needed.

"You put her down," I whispered, the words more breath than sound.

"She had become rabid. An animal, and nothing more."

I blinked at him. "And you are not?"

"You've read Ailis's grimoire. Do you truly think I share her madness?"

"You *killed her*, Lenghan."

"Aye," he replied, as though I'd merely asked him for the hour. "An act of mercy."

"Why?"

Lenghan raised an eyebrow. "Why was it mercy?"

"Why did you bother with bloodcraft at all? What use is there in power that chips away at the soul until naught remains but an empty, aching chasm where once there was *life*?"

His glare turned searing, pinning me in place. "On the day I arrived in Carastile, do you ken what I heard said in the streets? What I saw? Blessings offered in the name of the healer who had communed with the Dark Between. Altars ringed with feathers in reverence of the woman whose holy favor had spared the bright prince made emperor. So you tell me, Clìana. What use is there in such power?"

I could hardly breathe in the wake of his words. They were a mirror, reflecting back to me an uglier truth than I could bear to witness.

With an animal cry, I flung my power forth, squeezing invisible fingers around Lenghan's heart until it stuttered.

"Do it," he spat, forcing the words through gritted teeth. "You ken I could overcome you with flesh. But with power? You were always quicker than I to excel at such things. So go on, then. *Do it*."

Rage pounded in my veins as I stared at him, my anger at war with the disgust curling low and slick in my gut. It would only take the tiniest bit of pressure—more will than might—and I could kill him in a thousand unseen ways. I could crush his heart or rend his lungs. Break his neck as he had done to Ailis. But if I killed him, would I not become him? The mere thought made me want to retch with shame.

"You deserve far worse than death," I said at last, releasing my grip on his heart.

Lenghan drew in great, gasping breaths as I rounded my horse, intending to rejoin Gabrián's companies. But then a distant scream shattered the quiet of the still summer day.

"Aredo!" someone shouted. "Aredo is upon us! Rally to the emperor!"

# CHAPTER 31

The world washed white around me. Time thickened as I
dug my heels into my horse's flanks, desperate to reach
Gabrián's side as the enemy poured over a distant tor,
reining terror upon Casdar's company. Metal clanged.
Sharp cries sounded on the breeze. My pulse beat low and
ominous in my ears. Desperately, I sought some sign of
Gabrián in the fray, but all I could see was a writhing
tempest of horses and soldiers and steel.

"Rally!" someone shouted.

I recognized the deep rumble of Casdar's voice before
I caught sight of him in the skirmish—all grace forgotten
as he hacked through the band of enemy soldiers. His cry
was echoed by another, the bellow of a name that sounded
dearly like my own.

*"Clìana!"*

I spotted Gabrián's face in the fray, red with exertion
and twisted with fear. His gaze was pinned upon me as he
shouted my name.

In my periphery, I caught sight of a mounted soldier bearing down upon me.

Startled, I reined my horse in hard, rounding on the soldier as he raised his blade. The sudden attack tore a wicked whinny from my mount as it reared, throwing me from the saddle. Too late, I thought to roll with the impact. Pain seared along my shoulder blade as I tumbled across the hard, dry ground. Gasping, I scrambled to my feet just in time to see the flash of metal arcing toward me. A cry of terror ripped from my lungs.

Then the soldier's neck bent crudely, and his sword tumbled to the ground.

His body followed shortly, sliding limply from the saddle.

For what seemed like an immeasurable moment, I simply stared at the man's body, struggling to reconcile the sight before me. His neck lay broken at an impossible angle. Two tiny vertebrae jutted from his skin, reminding me of another body. Another broken neck. Bile rose in my throat as Lenghan crouched down beside me.

"You could have done the same as I," he said.


The company took one Belorán soldier captive, eager for any information he might provide. The rest lay dead or dying, mortally wounded by Vendegal swords. Pushing the horror of it all from my mind, I surveyed the remains of the skirmish and found Gabrián firmly fixed upon his destrier. Relief washed over him when he caught sight of me, followed by something darker when he saw that I sat fitted in front of Lenghan in the saddle.

Once on the ground, Lenghan offered a hand to help

me down. I disregarded him as both Gabrián and I dismounted, then strode to meet each other amid the mud and muck of the bloodied field.

"Are you well?" Gabrián asked, appraising me as I drew near.

"My horse fled."

"I saw you fall. The soldier—"

"Lenghan killed him. And you? Are you well?" I asked, though I could tell that the blood that flecked his skin belonged to another.

"I'm fine." Gabrián squeezed my hands in reassurance. "Can you heal?"

I swallowed against the tang of bile in my throat. "Aye."

"Good. He needs your aid."

It was only when Gabrián stepped aside that I saw Casdar Belorán sitting atop his horse some thirty paces away. A thick arrow was jutting from the meat of his thigh.


Stubborn as a boar, Casdar brushed aside the hands of those who sought to help him, swung a leg over his horse's rump, and promptly fell to the muddy ground below. In vain, he fought to find his footing, barking at any knight who ventured within arm's reach, even as his injured leg refused to bear his weight. I darted forward in time to catch him as his eyes rolled back, the two of us tumbling into the mud. He came awake nearly as quickly as he'd fainted, as if his very being was revolted by my touch.

"By the Black." Gabrián slung one of Casdar's arms over his shoulder as I scrambled to my feet. "Stay with me, Cas."

"Leave me be," Casdar replied, his gaze glassy with shock.

Gabrián huffed. "You've a Black-damned arrow in your leg, you bastard."

"And you're losing a lot of blood," I added. It soaked the linen of his breeks and trailed down his calf, so thick it was nearly black. No wonder lucidity had abandoned him. The arrow must have severed one of the arteries in his leg. "Quickly. Help me get him into the shade."

I slung Casdar's free arm around my neck just before his legs buckled. He was losing more blood than he could spare.

Perhaps if Casdar had been a different man, I would have acted differently. But he was no mere face in a sea of hard-worn soldiers. He was as dear to Gabrián as a brother, and Gabrián had already suffered enough. So as we hauled him toward the shadows of a scrawny, scraggly tree, I reached out with bloodcraft and yanked together the severed scraps of Casdar's femoral artery, suturing them as I would the ragged edges of a gash. With his blood stanched, I drew back into the confines of my body and helped Gabrián ease Casdar down to lie on the muddy earth.

Casdar glanced at me, then turned his attention on Gabrían. "Are there no others?"

The words grated on me more harshly than they should have. Grasping Casdar's chin, I forced him to look at me. "You do not need another. I am going to get this arrow out of your leg. You are going to lie still while I do it. And when I am through, you are going to thank me for it. Do you understand?"

Casdar blinked up at me, eyebrows raised in surprise.

"Do you?" I insisted.

He nodded once, slowly.

"Good." I smiled. "Someone fetch me a scrap of leather."

While one of Casdar's knights removed his baldric, I ripped through the fabric of his breeks to better inspect the wound. I couldn't say whether the archer's aim had been true, but the mark was no glancing blow. The arrowhead was lodged deep in the bone of Casdar's thigh, the surrounding muscle and tissue torn to shreds.

I cursed. This was a wound that would not heal cleanly. "I'll need men to hold him down," I said as I mopped the excess blood from Casdar's thigh.

Casdar rose onto his elbows. "I do not need to be—"

"Aye, you do," I retorted, pressing him back to the ground. "And you need the leather, too, unless you wish to have a leg full of shredded muscle and a mouth to match."

With evident loathing, Casdar acquiesced. I placed the edge of the baldric between his teeth with no small amount of relish as several knights knelt to pin him to the earth. A growl tore from Casdar's throat as I sank my scalpel into the mangled flesh of his thigh.

It was a simple surgery, all things considered. I needed to prevent further shredding of the muscle by opening the wound, then snap the shaft as near the arrowhead as possible and use forceps to pry the damned thing from the bone along the path of the incisions. Yet simplicity was not ease, nor lack of torment. Throughout the surgery, Casdar's neck flushed red with strain as he snarled, his eyes clamped tight in pain. Gabrián knelt above him, making soft noises one might use to mollify a wary horse. I strove to pay neither of them any mind as I worked. With my forceps clamped on the arrowhead, I wrenched, my muscles shaking with the force of the task.

Slowly, gruesomely, the arrowhead gave way. Then, all at once, it sprang free, its sudden release rocking me back onto my heels.

I tossed the arrowhead aside as Casdar spat the leather from between his lips. "Fuck," he said simply, his brow slick with sweat.

Threading my needle with gut, I met Casdar's stare. "Let's be done with it, aye?"

The company made camp not far from the site of the attack, sending out scouts to watch for further movement in the field while I tended to the wounded alongside Lenghan and the other Larmach healers in our party. I recognized one of them, an older man named Fargas, from the guildhall as a skilled bonesetter. The other was several years younger than me and Lenghan, a proficient student called Mhira who had not yet sought a commission within the guildhall or a highland court. The last one, a lad named Rab, had taken a Belorán sword to the belly during the skirmish, dying alongside five Vendegal soldiers.

We prepared all six bodies for burning before dusk, placing them in the bed of a wagon we would bear north toward Carastile. If our company had been attacked by Belorán soldiers while bearing their banners, then our safety was less certain than we'd assumed. There would be no proper burning held until camp could be made alongside a larger Vendegal force, lest the smoke from the fires give evidence to our position.

"Has the Aredo man said anything?" I asked Gabrián

when he found me scrubbing the day's blood from my hands. Light was fading swiftly in the west.

Gabrián shook his head. "It is likely to be some time before he breaks."

"And if he doesn't?"

"A quarter of the company will be on watch at all times throughout the night. We are well guarded."

Though Gabrián spoke surely, I knew from the look on his face that the skirmish had shaken him. We had flown Belorán banners, and yet we had been attacked. If our deception was evident, was it also known that the emperor was among us? Had the attack been an attempt to capture him—or worse? A chill finger coursed down my spine.

"Will he be all right?" Gabrián asked then.

I knew at once that he was speaking of Casdar. "There is a chance that the wound may fester," I said, drying my hands on the linen of my split skirts. "But I used clean bandages, and the wound's through with its bleeding. He's as well as he can be for now."

"And will he walk again? Will he fight?"

"If all goes well, he'll regain the use of his leg. But the wound was deep and ragged. That use may be . . . troubled."

"A limp, you mean?"

"Possibly. The damage to the muscle was extensive."

"Stars," he cursed, pinching the bridge of his nose. "It is all he has."

The fighting, he meant. Casdar's skill with a blade.

"He will bear his sword again, Gabrián. Do not doubt it."

"I do not doubt the strength of his arm. But his leg?"

"Have you ever known Casdar to have anything but a fighting spirit?"

I thought the words would comfort him, but Gabrián only frowned. "It is not a fighting spirit he possesses. It is anger, dark and barely tempered. For years, he has borne it for his family at my side. His position as brightsword was an affront to his house. But without that duty, without the capacity to fight as he has . . . I am loath to think of how that anger might manifest."

The thought slid like a knife into my chest. Did I not know of the fate he spoke about? Was the skill of my hands not my only tether to purpose? It was a terrible thing to be powerless, a poison that warped judgment and stole hope. Some chose to fill the chasm with drink, others with violence. But when faced with injuries I could not treat, I had chosen the unholy power in my blood—and it had stolen more than good sense each time I'd used it. It was chipping away at my humanity. My soul.

Still, had it not strengthened my purpose? Was it not equally unholy to watch life slip from my fingers when I possessed the power to save it? To save an empire? A people? I had lost Ailis. Lenghan had murdered her in the name of madness when all she had wanted was relief from her pain. Perhaps that would be my fate as well. Perhaps Lenghan would have to put me down as a rabid dog—or perhaps I would kill him first. Either way, Gabrián's life would be worth the cost.

In the gray light before dawn, I slipped from the dark enclosure of my tent. Picking my way through bedrolls and sleeping bodies, I made my way toward the scraggly tree at the edge of the camp and the captured soldier who was bound there. I could feel him scrutinizing me as I approached. The guard interrogating him turned swiftly, a tentative hand on the hilt of his sword. He relaxed when he caught sight of me.

"I'm told he is injured," I said, nodding in the captive's direction. I was speaking of the injury the man had suffered during the skirmish, not the bounty of bruises that now marred his face as evidence of Vendegal interrogation.

"Only a flesh wound, my lady," the guard answered. "May it trouble him."

"He'll be of no use to us should a fever take him. The emperor wishes his wound to be cleaned."

It was a convincing lie. The guard nodded, stepping aside.

"Why don't you go break your fast while I work?" I suggested.

He shook his head. "I am posted here until dawn, my lady."

"Of course," I said, smothering my irritation with a curt smile. Then I reached out with the power in my blood and stole the guard's consciousness. The captive gasped as I caught the guard's body before lowered him to the soft earth.

"What are you, then? A witch?" the enemy soldier said as I turned to face him. "Does the emperor keep company with sorceresses now, so weak has he grown in his own power?"

I appraised the man as I stooped before him. He was a soldier of middling age, his face wrinkled and his dark hair graying at the temples. One side of his shirt was stained red, some of the blood now crusted and flaked.

"Only one sorceress," I replied.

"Is he dead?" the man said, nodding toward the guard.

"Why would I kill a man of my own company?"

The captive blinked up at me. "You have come to torture me, then."

I swallowed a grimace. The soldier wasn't wrong. I had indeed come to torture him—if an unnatural torture was necessary to keep Gabrián safe. Still, to cause harm so intentionally went against my very instincts as a healer. It was not a task I relished.

"What is your name, man of Aredo?" I asked him.

"I would not give my name to a witch."

"You would—and you will."

Hardening myself, I reached out and closed invisible hands around his windpipe, as Lenghan had once done to me in the guildhall's courtyard many moons ago. The captive's eyes widened in terror, his body fighting against the ropes that bound him.

"Tell me," I said, releasing my grip.

"I am named for my liege lord, Idário," he replied through gritted teeth. "Many more will bear that name once the House of Belorán takes the Astral throne."

"Idário Belorán is dead."

"Ah, but his daughter is not. You would not like to meet her when she is unhappy."

"Then perhaps Janasta Belorán and I share something in common." Reaching out with my power, I tore through the delicate flesh at the captive's side. He hissed as his stanched wound broke open, blood beginning to weep down his torso. "This is but a taste of my unhappiness,

Master Idário. If you do not wish me to break every bone in your body one by one, you will tell me how your company knew to ambush ours."

The captive spat at my feet. "They will bury you deep in the earth, where you will know the pain of Shadow."

"That may be," I said, drawing so near that I could smell his sour breath. "But first I will have the truth."

With the mere will of my mind, I shattered the captive's femur. His mouth widened in a silent scream as I stole the air from his lungs. "Tell me, and I will not take the other leg."

The captive gave a pained laugh as I eased my unnatural grip on his lungs. "You may have seized the castle, but the people of Aredo hold no love for weak Vendegal rule. It wasn't even dawn before a messenger brought word to the general."

"And our company? How did you know us for the enemy? We flew Belorán banners."

"Do you believe the people of Aredo to be so foolish that we would not recognize one of our own sons, traitor though he may be?"

The tight coil of tension in my chest loosened at his words. If it was Casdar that the Belorán company had recognized, then perhaps they didn't know the emperor was among us.

"She will be happy to greet her son again, yes?" the captive continued. "Happy to meet him with steel—and your fumbling emperor, too. Perhaps even before dawn."

Panic surged within me. "What did you say?" I demanded.

The captive only laughed, his yellow teeth flashing in the weak predawn light.

"*Tell me*," I insisted, wrapping my power loosely around his throat once more.

"We know who Casdar Belorán whored himself to. We sent Janasta word."

In a rage, I made to shatter the captive's ribs. But the call of a horn stilled the flow of my power.

"Here already," said the captive. "Better run, little witch."

With a feral cry, I stitched his bones back together with bloodcraft. "May you never know peace," I said, then sent a flame of pain coursing along each nerve in his body. His scream was smothered by another cry of the horn, followed by shouts and the scrape of steel as the Vendegal camp prepared for battle.

I turned to find a wave of mounted cavalry bearing down upon us—at least several hundred knights, their suits of armor gleaming as the sun broke over the horizon. With our small company heavily outnumbered, there was naught to do but rally to Gabrián's side.

Lifting my skirts, I ran.

# CHAPTER 32

My pulse pounded in my throat as I tore through the camp, though it wasn't fear that rattled me. Rather, it was the dark beat of unnatural anger that drove me forward. Gabrián wasn't in the tent where I had left him. Nor was he nearby out of doors, damn him. Forget his reservations about my power. Forget the promise I had made him. If Janasta Belorán's soldiers intended to capture or kill him, he would need me by his side. I pressed on in search of him, shoving aside any knight who dared cross my path as they scrambled from their bedroll.

My nostrils flared in disbelief when I found Gabrián at the edge of the camp, facing down the mounted force that rode our way. Did the Black-damned man wish to get himself killed? I called his name as I raced toward him. He must have mistaken my anger for fear, for when he turned toward me, his expression was consolatory.

"It is only Tévarez," he said as I drew near, running his hands up and down my arms.

Confused, I turned back toward the approaching

cavalry. Sure enough, I spotted the aging general at its head, flanked by banners emblazoned with the eight-speared sun of the House of Vendegal.

Noting my relief, Gabrián offered me a reassuring smile. "We will not be so easily ambushed now."

"That might not stop Janasta if she knows you are among us."

Gabrián frowned at the hard edge in my tone, but General Lord Tévarez and his force reached camp before he could reply.

"Emperor," General Lord Tévarez called out as he dismounted.

"You received my message," said Gabrián.

"Yes, Your Radiance." The general bowed his head in deference to Gabrián. "And I congratulate you on taking Aredo Castle. It is good to know we have allies within the traitor's house, for I come bearing ill news. Janasta has besieged Carastile."

Gabrián ushered us through the camp and into the small confines of his tent. There we found Casdar sitting upright on Gabrián's cot, looking grim. "I will rest when my mother is dead," he said, taking in my disapproval.

Turning, I noted the same displeasure on Gabrián's face. Still, Gabrián did not argue with Casdar, not when there were such pressing matters to discuss.

"How has this been allowed to happen?" he asked General Lord Tévarez. "Leomar was to drive his compa-nies south to meet Janasta and create a wedge between her forces and the city."

"And so he did," the general confirmed. "Only he rode

too swiftly, thinking to ambush Janasta by the light of the Stars."

"To *ambush* her?" Gabrián balked.

"A show of Vendegal force, he said," General Lord Tévarez explained. "Lady Catanín reports that his brightswords had to drag him from the fray in swift retreat. He returned to Carastile with half his numbers, forcing Lady Catanín to withdraw their companies to within the city walls. Janasta's army now sits outside Carastile, her war machines besieging the city."

No strength of will could keep the anger from Gabrián's face. He loosed a foul curse, one hand scrubbing at his brow. "And our own war machines?"

"Those atop the city's battlements now harry the enemy. The rest of them, Lady Catanín was forced to burn in the field."

"Stars," said Gabrián. "He has buried us."

Casdar muttered something vulgar under his breath. Given his tone, my thoughts likely echoed the same sentiment. It would have been better for us all had Casdar's sword pierced Leomar's chest a bit deeper on the day of their duel.

"The bright prince's behavior was foolish, to be sure," General Lord Tévarez agreed. "Yet not all hope is lost. When your enemy is proud, a display of weakness can be played to one's advantage."

"You think to trick her into some unexpected defeat?" Gabrián questioned.

"It is possible—unless you wish to wait upon the arrival of forces from Brenmere or Calas."

"Are they near?"

The general shook his head. "They remain some days' ride from the city."

"And already Carastile burns?"

"Yes, Your Radiance."

"Then let us speak of this ploy you conjure."

General Lord Tévarez unfurled a map of Istanel between us, using small markers to indicate the known locations of enemy and ally forces. I let their conversation play out, listening intently to the strategies that the general outlined for luring Janasta's forces to their doom. It was a brilliant plan—or, at the very least, one brave enough to be lauded for its brilliance should the House of Vendegal prove victorious. But its risk was made greater by the knowledge only I possessed: that Janasta knew the emperor rode among the small Vendegal force in the south.

Gabrián needed to know this, yet the words caught in my throat. I'd been too hasty in my decision to interrogate the captive. I now had information too precious to keep and no good explanation for having it—no explanation save the truth, that was. It was knowledge that Gabrián would abhor, a betrayal far more intimate than any ill-advised rebellion. But only because he insisted that I not call upon bloodcraft to aid him, the daft fool. Still, a heavy weight pressed upon my chest when I considered confessing what I knew.

"There is perhaps but one impediment to this plan, save the risk it already bears," General Lord Tévarez said. "Yesterday, my outriders captured a Belorán scout. He was riding north to warn Janasta of the failure of her company to capture you, Your Radiance."

Once more, Gabrián cursed. "Were we that close to ruin?"

I loosed a long breath. I couldn't help but think how close I had been to the same.

The general nodded. "Janasta will have an eye upon the south. Yet the Stars surely favor you, Your Radiance. Your victories give evidence to this, as will your victory at Carastile."

"Indeed, General." Gabrián smiled thinly, as if reluctant to agree.

There was no time to consider what his hesitancy might mean. General Lord Tévarez launched back into the discussion of his strategies, their talk continuing until the Stars shone high above.


We were in the saddle at dawn, driving north toward the Ségua and Janasta Belorán's army. Despite my protestations, Casdar had elected to ride as well, grimacing as he fitted the foot of his injured leg into its stirrup.

"What would you have me do? Walk?" he asked when I raised an eyebrow.

"I'd send you back to your sister in a wagon bed if I thought you'd obey."

Though Casdar glared at me as he heaved himself into the saddle, I could see the pain that he was fighting to hide. Damn him, it would do no good if he snapped his sutures. Blood was likely staining the bandage beneath his breeches as it was. Reaching out with bloodcraft, I knit the rent muscle and tissue in his thigh, finding a balance between strengthening the wound for a day in the saddle and healing it altogether. I couldn't have Casdar bleeding all over his horse, but neither could he later discover his wound had miraculously healed. He might not have known of my bloodcraft, but word would surely spread. And then it wouldn't take long for Gabrián to hear—and for his suspicions to mount.

If Casdar felt my invisible touch, he said nothing. He only rode ahead to join Gabrián and General Lord Tévarez at the head of the cavalry. Lenghan led his mount forward to fill Casdar's absence at my side. Glancing over, I saw his mouth open as though he made to speak, but there was nothing he could say that I wished to hear. Urging my horse into a canter, I left him and his unuttered words behind me.

By midday, our scouts had sighted the river less than an hour's ride north. Hastily, we made camp among the lowlands, the last of the south's rolling hills rising before us, shielding our force from view. *A sea of steel.* That was what the scouts had reported beyond the waters of the Ségua—and beyond, smoke rising from within the walls of Carastile. The report tore through the camp like wildfire, yet the news did little to dim the soldiers' spirits. If anything, it emboldened them, rousing them to the defense of their holy city. Their fervor reminded me of home, of the fighting spirit of my people. *Long ago, Imbela gifted the Daor with the fire of her blood,* the legend said. Could I not see that same fire in the Istanelan soldiers around me?

Tonight, those soldiers would tell tales of glory, chasing the same prickle of possibility that had driven me to Carastile. And tomorrow? They would fight in the name of that glory—and in the name of the House of Vendegal.

Sometime later, when the moon was high, Gabrián found his way into my tent. I wasn't surprised by his arrival, but his bleak expression caused my brow to furrow. "What is it?" I said, reaching for him.

He kissed me deeply, almost desperately. When he pulled back, I noted fear in his eyes.

"The Stars will reveal Their will upon the morrow," he said.

My worry melted into sympathy. Gathering Gabrián's hands, I pressed my lips to his knuckles. When he winced, I drew back to find his fist mottled with bruises.

"Who did you hit?" I asked, astounded that Gabrián would raise his hand in violence against anyone save an enemy.

A faint blush crept up his neck. "Casdar."

"*Casdar?* Why?"

"I asked if he would care for you tomorrow, should the need arise."

"I don't understand."

"Should I fall, Clìana. Injured as Casdar is, he will not be on the battlefield. He could see you safely home to Daorender."

The words left me breathless. "Surely you do not mean to fight?"

"I do."

I balked at him. "Gabrián, 'tis one thing to ride north with your company, believing your identity to be safe. But to take to the field, knowing that Janasta will be looking for you?"

"Thousands of soldiers will fight in my name tomorrow, to secure my throne. My sovereignty. I will not have them defend my seat alone."

"And they will not," I said, pulling back. "Leomar will lead them into battle."

"You think my armies will take heart in my brother's leadership?"

"He may be a fool, but he remains the shield of the House of Vendegal."

"And I am the Radiant Astral Emperor."

"Have you considered who will be emperor should you fall?" I said pointedly, the words harsher than I intended. "Gabrián, you ken he is not ready to lead—just as you know your soldiers do not expect you to fight."

"Custom may dictate that the shield takes to the battlefield, but custom fails to account for circumstance. This is no skirmish over land or coin. Janasta intends to usurp the Astral throne because the dominion of the House of Vendegal grows weaker by the day. If I do not lead with strength tomorrow, then a Vendegal victory will mean nothing. Others would only follow in the Beloráns' footsteps, Clìana. I must fight."

"Then let me fight beside you tomorrow," I said, my heart thundering in my chest. "Let me keep you safe."

Gabrián must have known that I was speaking of using bloodcraft, for his expression shuttered. *"No."*

"You ken I have the power to ensure your survival. Your victory, even. Let me do this. Let me stand by your side."

"And have me win my sovereignty by such unholy power? It is heresy, Clìana! No, I will not allow it."

"Gabrián—"

He grasped me by the forearms. "Do you not understand what you have done? Every day, I worry that I am scorned by the Stars above. Every day, I wonder if I was meant to die in the dark of that Sanctuary. Because of *you*." His chest heaved as he spoke. "I cannot have my victory be in doubt as well. I will not. Do you understand? I will not allow it."

If Gabrián's intention to fight had been a shocking blow, then this speech was my undoing. I blinked at him, sobered by the knowledge that my use of bloodcraft had cast such doubt upon his every action. Even upon his conviction that the Astral throne was his to claim.

"Stars, Gabrián. I didn't ken. I didn't—" Shaking, I rested my head upon his chest. "Forgive me."

With a gentle touch, he urged me to look at him. "Tell me you will keep your promise. Tell me you will forsake this power."

The plea curled behind my ribs, twisting and writhing. I had sworn to myself that I would protect him. I had sworn that I would not let him fall. But what good was his life if such troubling doubts plagued him? If Shadow nipped ever at his heels?

Crossing the tent, I retrieved Ailis's grimoire from its hidden compartment in my surgical trunk. The immensity of what I held unnerved me. Was the power contained in this book not Ailis's downfall? Did her story not serve as a warning I should heed—for Gabrián's sake, if not my own?

"You have my word," I said, and tossed the book of power into the brazier.

With a sigh of relief, Gabrián drew me into his embrace. Together, we watched the pages burn.


"Why did you hit him?" I asked again later, as Gabrián had never truly given me a reason for why he'd felt compelled to harm Casdar. I held his hand aloft, appraising his bruised knuckles in the waning light of the brazier.

"You do not wish to know," Gabrián replied.

It occurred to me then that Gabrián must have hit Casdar for my sake. My eyebrows rose in surprise. "Why now? He has said plenty about me in the short time I've known him, but his words have never truly led to harm."

Gabrián gave a heavy sigh. "When I asked him to protect you should I fall, he said that I should send you from my sight. That if I were to die, it would be your doing."

My heart stuttered in my chest. I raised myself on one arm to meet his eye. "He thinks I mean to harm you? After all I have done to keep you safe?"

"That is what he implied. He begged me to forsake you, to send you away. We argued for some time until it became clear that he would not be swayed."

"And so you hit him?"

"It is the only language Casdar speaks. I love him as a brother, but I cannot abide his opinion of you. Nor do I pretend to understand it. He speaks of you in riddles, as if there is something he loathes to say plainly."

"Is it possible that he kens of the bloodcraft?" I asked, lowering myself once more to Gabrián's side. "I can't see how. He has seen a threat in me from the moment of my arrival."

"I cannot say. Given the house in which he was raised, it is no wonder he is stricken with Shadow," Gabrián said, his gaze fixed on the low ceiling of the tent. "At times, I think he is naught but angry. Still, I have never known him to be cruel—not until he met you."

I lay silent for a moment, considering all that Gabrián had said. "Could it be so simple a thing as jealousy that spoils him?" I asked.

Gabrián scoffed. "I should think not. Casdar might enjoy bedding men as well as women, but he has long viewed me as something of a brother. And he has never been one for attachment. Even if he were attracted to me as a man, I do not think he would covet the time that you and I share."

"I'm sorry you felt the need to hit him. I ken it not to be your wont."

Gabrián gathered me in his embrace. "It will always be my wont to protect you. Even when the time comes for us to part."

I ran my fingers down the long line of his jaw, memorizing the shape and feel of him. "I will carry you with me, Gabrián. Even unto the Black."

Later, as Gabrián lay sleeping, I rose from my pallet and stepped out into the night. The camp was eerily dark, barren of any bonfires that might betray our position. Only a sliver of moonlight snaked between thin clouds, lighting my way to Casdar's tent. I wasn't surprised to find him sitting solemnly in the faint glow of a brazier, kneading the muscle that surrounded his wounded leg. He raised his head as I entered, revealing a mottled red bruise upon his cheek.

"Gabrián throws a fair fist," I said, letting the tent flap fall closed behind me.

With a snort, Casdar returned to studying the dark embers in the brazier.

Faced with his silence, I cut to the heart of the reason I'd sought him. "Why do you think me his downfall?" I asked. When he made no reply, I pressed him further. "You must ken that I do not wish to see him harmed, that I want only to see him safely into his sovereignty."

"Then you should leave his side, as I have long encouraged you to do," Casdar said, still kneading his muscles.

"But why? What has so convinced you that I'm bound to be the cause of his suffering?"

"Not his suffering," said Casdar, glancing up at me abruptly. "His *death.*"

Slowly, he rose to his feet, so near me in the tiny space that I could smell the musk of his body, heady spice and leather and sweat. "All my life, I have seen portents in dreams. Grave horrors that have not yet come to pass, and yet always do." There was urgency in his voice—and something akin to fear. "I have seen you knelt beside him, Cliana. I have seen the paleness of his face."

My name on Casdar's tongue unnerved me, but it was his words that seemed to carve a hollow in my chest. "You've seen his death?"

"Yes."

"Have you told him?"

When Casdar said nothing, I knew that he had not.

"How does he die?"

"An arrow." Casdar swallowed. "It is an arrow."

I shook my head. "I am no archer."

"No, but I have seen him laid out in death all the same. Bloodied and glassy-eyed, with *you* at his side."

"You've had this vision from the start," I said, piecing together the long history of Casdar's anger and suspicion. "Since before I arrived in Carastile."

He nodded. "It came to me in the last days of winter."

"When Imbela first shone high above," I said, more to myself than him. "You must ken I would not hurt him."

"Does it matter? What I have seen cannot come to pass if you are *gone*."

"Has there ever been a time when these portents have not come to pass?"

Once more, his silence confirmed my fears. "Many a time, I have tried to alter the tide of my foresight," he said at last. "My efforts have always been in vain. But perhaps yours need not."

The weak light of the brazier danced across Casdar's cheekbone, highlighting the bruise Gabrián's fist had left behind. I seized upon it, desperate for something to ground in the tumult of this revelation.

"Stars, let me tend to your jaw," I said, catching his chin between my fingers to better appraise the injury.

Casdar flinched at my touch. "What are you—"

His words caught in his throat as I glanced up at him. We were close—too close. His breath was hot against my cheek, and awareness ripened along the lines of my body. He, too, felt the intimacy of the moment. I could see it in his eyes, even as his gaze hardened.

"Will you do it?" he said, stepping as far away from me as the small space allowed. "Will you leave him, if doing so might give him the chance to live?"

For all the disdain he bore me, it would have been easy to dismiss Casdar's speech as some type of ploy, a clever ruse to oust me from Gabrián's inner circle. But I had no reason to doubt that Casdar had the power of foresight. Did I not possess a strange and unholy power myself? And did the unwelcome nature of his omen not better explain why he had resented my presence the moment he first saw me?

As horrifying as it was, perhaps Casdar's admission was

more blessing than terror. With the battle for Vendegal sovereignty swiftly approaching, the time for consolation was coming to an end. To know that my absence might ensure Gabrián's survival was no small comfort to carry with me, warm as stone beneath the clear Istanelan sky.

"I'll leave at dawn," I replied.

For the first time since we'd met, Casdar Belorán did not look upon me with anger.

# CHAPTER 33

If ever the promise of glory hung on the air, it blanketed the Plains of Anzales that morning, thrumming with anticipation even before the first tendrils of light painted the horizon.

I woke Gabrián in the wee hours before dawn. He had been troubled in sleep, the muscles in his face twitching and tensing. Gently, I trailed my fingers through his hair until he awakened. "It is time," I said.

The look in his eye, at first disquieted, settled into firm resolve. We dressed in silence before parting. "May we meet once more when this is through," he said, reaching for the tent flap.

I offered Gabrián as warm a smile as I could muster. There was no need for him to know that I planned to leave him now, before the fighting began. Such knowledge would only distract him upon the battlefield. Still, my heart ached with the awareness that these final moments were the last that we would share.

"Lay your doubts to rest today, Your Radiance," I said,

placing my hands upon his chest. "The Stars are with you, as the Astral Empire is yours to keep."

With a sigh, he rested his head against mine, as if drawing strength for the day to come. "My love," he said softly before tearing himself away. I watched from the tent flap as the long lines of his body disappeared into the early morning gloom.


I was surprised to find Casdar waiting for me, sitting grimly atop his sable mount on the eastern outskirts of the camp. "I made a promise," he said as I drew near.

"Did you?" I retorted.

We rode our horses east in silence, seeking a bridge over the Ségua that had not been burned. After crossing the river, we set out for Telór, where I might board a ship to Marnos—or wherever I wished to go. In truth, I didn't know. Could I step foot within the walls of the guildhall once more, knowing the depth of the horrors that had taken place there? Or would I seek a commission in a new court? Perhaps in one of the eastern realms? Or overseas? I tried to imagine myself content within the walls of another palace, at another ruler's side. But my thoughts were consumed by visions of Gabrián—though not for long.

As our horses climbed the rocky tors east of Carastile, the dawn arose to illuminate the plains that unfurled from the city's gates, now occupied by an enemy force in rank. Row after row of foot soldiers stood behind fierce companies of mounted knights, dotted here and there by the mighty siege engines Teolina Belorán had described.

"Stars," I breathed, appalled by the immensity of Janasta Belorán's army.

Casdar had opened his mouth to speak when a horn sounded on the breeze. We drew our horses around sharply, both of us watching as Lady Catanín's companies rode out from Carastile's southern gate. They amassed themselves in swift formation before charging, their numbers less than a third of the Belorán vanguard they faced. In a matter of moments, they had crossed the thin stretch of empty plains before breaking upon the fierce wall of Janasta's cavalry, a clash of shrieks and steel that we could hear even from our distance on the tors. Given the disparity in their numbers, it was soon evident that the Vendegal force surely faced defeat. One by one, knights and horses fell, cut down by an assault of Belorán blades.

"Will it work?" I asked, more a prayer than a question. "Will she follow?"

As planned, a horn called twice upon the breeze, signaling a retreat. Vendegal cavalry broke from the battle-lines, riding in disorder toward the city gate. A moment passed in which my breath grew shallow and my pulse pounded, time stretching interminably in the way it so often does in the face of torment. Then, at last, Janasta's army began to move.

Three thousand Belorán soldiers marched on Carastile, Janasta's cavalry giving chase to the Vendegal knights in retreat. To the unwitting eye, it seemed an opportune time for Belorán forces to take the city, with Vendegal knights fleeing the battlefield and Carastile's southern gate wide open. But what Janasta Belorán did not realize was that Lady Catanín's cavalry did not comprise what remained of the northern Vendegal forces. While several hundred knights rode hard toward the city, drawing the Belorán army near, another 500 spilled from the eastern and western gates in twin columns, flanking Janasta's forces. Another call of a horn, and Lady Catanín's cavalry rounded, forming lines before the city walls as Carastile's southern gate swung closed. And so the second attack began, an inferior Vendegal army barraging Belorán soldiers on three fronts.

Together, Casdar and I watched the violent tableau unfold.

By noon that day, the story of the siege and defeat would be retold a thousand times by victorious Vendegal soldiers and the relieved citizens of Carastile. They would speak of Janasta Belorán hacking her way through Lady Catanín's initial offense, too blinded by blood to see that her enemy's eyes did not hold fear. They would sing of Bright Prince Leomar riding forth with a company of only 100 knights at his side, scattering Belorán soldiers like ants. The legends spoke of an enemy army in chaos and retreat, and of the emperor who laid waste to their ranks as they crawled their way across the Ségua. Some accounts even claimed that Janasta's brightsword son later rode from the battlefield with his mother's head upon his pommel. But legends and songs so rarely speak the truth.

As it was, the Belorán army rallied swiftly in the face of this unexpected assault. Janasta was a fierce general, and her captains were no cowards. Companies of Belorán soldiers fought viciously against the onslaught, gaining ground in the west where they had the rising sun at their back. And while Bright Prince Leomar did lead a force into the belly of the Belorán army, he was soon badly wounded and ushered from the battlefield by a band of brightswords, three of whom died during the retreat. The lieutenant general who took command of Leomar's forces found more success, forcing the eastern flank of the Belorán army back toward the river.

Upon re-forming ranks, Lady Catanín's cavalry drove deep into the heart of the fray, where Janasta Belorán fought viciously in the midst of the bedlam. Historical records would later note that she died when her horse took a spear to the belly, her neck broken upon impact when she fell from the saddle. Later, her trampled body would only be identified by the signet ring she wore upon her finger: a coronet encircling the twin hawks of the House of Belorán. Contrary to legend, Casdar never set foot upon the battlefield. Instead, he sat atop his horse at my side, watching the battle unfold with hawkish scrutiny.

Though the second assault was perhaps less efficient than planned, the whole of Janasta's army was at last pushed back toward the river. There, to the south, we spotted General Lord Tévarez's companies gathering atop the crest of the hill, too distant to note Gabrián among their ranks. What we could discern were the longbow archers who advanced before the mounted cavalry, raining volleys of arrows over the Ségua to further hinder the Belorán retreat. Still, many of Janasta's mounted knights did safely cross the river to launch a last-ditch uphill assault on the southern Vendegal force. Casdar and I watched with bated breath as General Lord Tévarez's companies bore down the hillside to meet them—and Belorán soldiers began to fall.

I should have been wholly riveted by this fighting. Gabrián was there, somewhere amid the skirmish. Yet something across the river caught my eye. A coordinated movement among the chaos of retreat. A company of Belorán archers had formed ranks and drawn their bows. Their first volley of arrows arced through the sky toward General Lord Tévarez's forces—and fear cut through the heart of me.

"He's out there," I said.

And then I was gone, galloping with my horse down the tor, heedless of the words Casdar shouted behind me. All I could see was Gabrián, pale with death, struck by a fated arrow. But he did not need to die. Not when I possessed the power to save him. Never mind my promises and Casdar's visions. Never mind that the use of blood-craft had driven Ailis to madness and an early pyre. Would I not have risked far more to spare her such a fate? Would I not do the same for Gabrián? Even if it was his love I chanced, the reward would be worth the cost.

As the horrors of the battlefield unfolded before me, I became ever more certain of my convictions. But then a heavy weight slammed into me, wresting me from the saddle. I landed with a bone-snapping crunch that wrenched a cry from my lungs. Casdar appeared above me, his hands pinning my wrists to the ground.

"You cannot do this!" he shouted, spittle flying from his lips. "Do you hear me? His *death* will be on your hands."

I fought in vain against his grasp. "Let me go!"

"Clìana—"

"I can save him!"

"You know what I have seen!"

"Let me go!" I said once more, using bloodcraft to weaken Casdar's muscles before pushing him away. Rolling to my feet, I called upon my power to stitch the jagged edges of my collarbone.

"I could make no sense of it," said Casdar, staring up at me in horror. "You, speaking over him in some fell tongue in my dreams. What *are* you?"

"Let me go," I insisted as he clambered to his feet.

"If you go to him, he will die."

"I spared him in that prayer room. I can do it again."

Understanding struck him suddenly. "This is Shadow-craft," he said, drawing his sword from its hilt.

"It is power that can keep him safe."

Emotion warred in Casdar's expression, a battle between the fear his visions invoked and the tempting promise of my power. "I saw his death," he said at last. "I saw you at his side."

I raised my hands as if in plea. "I don't want to hurt you, Casdar."

"You are a witch," he said, and drove his blade toward my heart—

But his sword fell from his fingers as I flooded his body with pain. Casdar crumpled in anguish, his screams ringing in my ears as I mounted my horse once more to ride to Gabrián's side.

# CHAPTER 34

The Ségua raged behind me as I tore south into the remnants of our camp. Quickly, I searched through the knights who had withdrawn from the battlefield, their armor stained with blood from their wounds. Gabrián's brightswords would have ferried him from the field if he had been injured, but I could find him nowhere. Was he bleeding out on the battlefield? Had his brightswords fallen by his side? Fear should have fluttered through my chest at the thought. But in the wake of my use of bloodcraft, something darker curled behind my ribs.

Something like *rage*.

Had Gabrián's brightswords even tried to see him safely from the field? Or were they all so inept that they lay bloodied beside him on that muddy Istanelan hill? Damn the will of the Stars. If I found Gabrián slain upon the battlefield, I swore upon all the Shadows that I would resurrect his brightswords just to make them suffer for their incompetence. They would know no peace until my body lay at the bottom of a river pool—and even then, I would rise from its depths to haunt them.

"Where in the Black have you been?"

The words dragged me from my violent reverie. I found Lenghan standing a few paces away, suturing a gaping gash in a soldier's forearm. "I am but one man, Clìana. I cannot stitch every damned—"

"Where is he?" I demanded.

Lenghan blinked at me. "Who?"

"The emperor! Have they pulled him from the field?"

"How would I know?"

With a cry of irritation, I ran toward the swift rise of the hill, climbing and climbing until the battlefield stretched out before me like a scene in some gruesome court tapestry. Arrows arced through the air as sword met sword and horses reared, their whinnies piercing through the anguished cries of soldiers cut down by brutal blows. I looked upon it all with a blinding rage. It was asinine—all this bloodshed for the sake of one daft family grasping for power, the very act proving them unworthy of the throne. Gabrián didn't care for power. He cared for his people, and *that* was why he must live.

The hard knot in my chest eased as three riders broke from the fray, their horses swiftly climbing the sharp slope of the earth. In the middle rode a knight in full armor, his helm rimmed with a silver coronet. Then I caught sight of the arrow jutting from the metal of his breastplate, and my heart stuttered in my chest.

*Gabrián.*

I must have screamed his name, for suddenly he threw back his visor, revealing eyes gone wide and bright. He reined in his horse as he drew near, dismounting in one fluid motion.

"All is well," he said as I raced to meet him. As if to prove his point, he grasped the shaft of the arrow and pulled it free, revealing an arrowhead unmarred by blood or gore. "The Stars are with me. It did not pierce my skin."

A rush of air fled from my lungs. He was fine. The Belorán arrow had found its mark, as Casdar had predicted. Yet still he lived. A sense of triumph surged through me, soon echoed by the deafening cry of a horn.

"Victory!" someone shouted. "Victory in the name of Vendegal!"

We turned our heads toward the battlefield. Together, we watched as Janasta Belorán's army surrendered.

I tended to the wounded soldiers of General Lord Tévarez's company in a haze, employing no power save the skill of my hands. There were few injuries, considering the scope of the battle. More than 500 soldiers had ridden toward the Ségua, and nearly 400 of them had returned unscathed, the only blood upon them the marks of the enemies they had slain. Another hundred had not returned, their broken bodies now gathered from the muddied riverbank in preparation for their burnings. Of the wounded, most had been cut by blades or pierced by arrows, their wounds a grisly rending of flesh. By the time all had been attended to, the heat of the day had come and gone, the sun now chasing the western horizon.

The emperor's victory had been assured by midmorning. Soon thereafter, Carastile's bells had sounded on the breeze, celebrating the victory of the House of Vendegal. But by midday, the bloodlust of battle had given way to the grim aftermath of war. Soldiers roamed among the fallen, seeking signs of life—and delivering swift mercy to those with wounds too grievous for natural skill to heal. Others rounded up the Belorán soldiers who had survived the battle, herding them into temporary jail cells until their fates could be decided.

Among the knights and foot soldiers, two high-ranking members of the House of Belorán had been captured. The first was Casdar's elder brother, Viego. The second was their uncle Gavro, Janasta's heir and the person most likely to have assumed the Astral throne should the Beloráns' rebellion have been successful. Both were taken to Alamada Palace and confined in the keep of Galmora, the tower reserved for prisoners of noble birth. Many city folk wandered onto the battlefield, picking through the wreckage like carrion crows in search of valuables to keep or sell. Behind them, the Belorán siege engines burned.

After washing the muck from my skin, I found Gabrián stationed in his tent. The deep tenor of his voice carried through the tent flaps, low and troubled. I caught sight of the familiar destrier cobbled nearby, and a pang of anxiety spasmed in my chest. As I entered the tent, two men turned toward me, their faces dark with anger.

"What have you done to him?" Gabrián demanded, one hand outstretched toward Casdar, who lay pained and panting on his bedroll. "What have you done?"

"He was trying to—"

"I do not care what he was trying to do! *Fix him.*"

Unmoving, I stared at Gabrián. I had never seen him so angry, let alone angry with *me*. Did he really think I had *wanted* to hurt Casdar? That I had taken some sick pleasure in crippling him with pain? I had done this for *his* benefit —to keep *him* safe—and now he dared chastise me for it as though I were a child?

"Was I to have let you die?" My mouth twisted around the words, thick with bitterness.

"Clìana—"

"He saw your death, this *brother* of yours. He saw the life drain from your eyes in a vision. But you didn't ken he had such power, did you? Poor Gabrián, too desperate for the blessing of the Stars to see the Shadows growing around him."

Something like a growl tore from Gabrián's throat. Lunging, he grabbed me roughly by the arm, his breath hot against my face. "You have gone mad with it. Have you not?"

"He sought to keep me from you—"

"Just like your sister—"

"He blames me for your death—"

"Perhaps he speaks in truth!" Gabrián shouted.

Stunned, I lowered my voice to an angry hiss. "Everything I do is to keep you safe."

"Then you serve your own desire."

I stared at him. "Do you not wish to live?"

"I wish the will of the Stars!"

I laughed, harsh with disbelief. "Then you will die a fool!"

Gabrián glared at me, his chest heaving. When he spoke again, his voice was low and even. "Better a fool than mad with power."

"Better mad than to see you pale with death," I replied.

His lips parted on an unspoken retort. Something in my words had struck him deeply. I could see it in his eyes, in the way they went distant for a second before settling back into focus.

"Can you heal him?" he said, releasing his grasp on me.

With barely a moment's effort, I quenched the fire in Casdar's veins. He sat up as the pain left him, his back arched as he drew several gulping breaths. Then, all at once, he lunged for me. I stepped back instinctively, preparing to call upon my power, but Gabrián was quicker. He planted himself in front of Casdar, placing a hand against his chest to still him.

"Leave her," he commanded.

Casdar looked at him incredulously. "But she—"

"Need I remind you that I am emperor here?"

"And you trust her not to harm you? After all she has done?"

"Did you see her harm me, in this vision of yours?"

"No," Casdar spat, his jaw clenched tight.

"Then go," said Gabrián. "And leave her to me."

Jerking himself from Gabrián's grasp, Casdar stalked out of the tent, never so much as glancing my way. When he was gone, Gabrián turned slowly to face me.

"Do you intend to harm me?" he asked simply, using the careful tone he employed at court.

"Must you truly ask such a thing?" I replied.

With a long-suffering sigh, he sank onto a cushioned stool, scrubbing one hand roughly down his face. His expression crumbled in its wake, like earth suddenly breaking from a cliffside. "What has happened to us?" he said, his voice thick with sorrow.

The words pierced through the dark haze of my anger. I knelt before him, placing my hands upon his knees as if in worship. "Could you watch the lifeblood leave my body, knowing you had the power to stop it?" I asked him.

He grimaced, as though I'd dealt him a stinging blow. "I cannot do this. I cannot answer you in truth and yet preserve the sanctity of my throne."

I sank back on my heels. "And so it is the throne you love more."

"I have a duty."

"As do I," I replied.

Gabrián shook his head. "Your duty is to heal, not to harm."

"And it is harm to keep you safe?"

"You know that it is, when you use this power in your blood to do so."

I frowned. "Is it that foul to use this skill for your protection? Could it not be a gift from the Stars?"

"It is eating away at your soul, Clìana. How can that be an Astral gift?"

"Perhaps not a gift, then, but a charge. To give my soul for your survival."

"No," he said, rising suddenly from his seat. My hands fell from his knees as he stalked across the tent.

"And why not?" I said, scrambling to my feet.

Gabrián turned toward me abruptly. "Because I could not forgive Them for it! Because I would tear earth and sky apart to punish Them for such a charge! And I cannot forsake Them, Clìana. Everything I am is defined by my service to Them."

The words thundered through me, stirring longing and grief in equal measure. There was nothing I could say in reply. Were we not bound to our oaths, as I had told him on the night we'd first coupled? To refute him now would only give him more cause for sorrow.

"They yet echo your name in the city," he said. "They will want to see you by my side when we parade tomorrow. But after that, you must leave, Clìana. If you bear me any love at all, you must go."

The wretched emotion in his voice was my undoing. I swallowed against a rising sob as I curled myself into his embrace. "I cannot bear to think of you on your pyre."

"It would not be the end," he said, his fingers idly trailing down my back. "The Dark will bind us, always."

"I do not want to leave you."

Gabrián nuzzled his head against mine. "Even so, you will always hold my heart."

The thought comforted me, if only in some small part. For too long I had ached for the loss of Ailis, and still I didn't know how to let her go. To think of suffering that same fate once more, of losing Gabrián. . . . It was too terrible a possibility to consider. But to know that I would always hold his heart was some consolation. And was that not what we had always offered each other? Consolation? *Could that ever be enough?* he had once asked me. The circumstances had been different, but my answer remained the same: *I will make it so.*

Gabrián held me in his arms that night, tracing the length of me in soft caresses, as a blind man might strive to memorize his lover's face. I looked back at him only once, meeting his soft regard in the dark. "Can you ever forgive me?" I asked.

With a gentle hand, he drew me around to face him. "If I were but a man, I would stride even unto Shadow to save you. The darkest cave, the deepest pool—all the Lights in the night sky could not stop me. How could I ever blame you for doing the same?"

I knew he would never have permitted himself to speak such words in the light of day. Nor beneath a blanket of Stars. Only here, enclosed in the dark, could he give voice to such thoughts. Even then, I suspected they would haunt him on the morrow. Still, they curled soft and warm within me. I pressed my lips to his in the dark, tender and full of meaning that words could not express. Then I settled back against him and let him hold me close, fighting to believe that this fleeting moment could ever be enough.

Eventually, a fitful sleep overtook me, studded with panicked dreams and the unconscious twitching of my limbs. Each time a fit gripped me, Gabrián brushed the hair from my sticky skin and soothed me with gentle words. At last, exhaustion drew me down into an unbothered sleep. I awoke suddenly at dawn, my chest heaving with the same terror that had shaken me hours before.

"The morn has come," said Gabrián, crouching low beside the bedroll. A thin shaft of morning light streamed into the tent, limning his figure in radiant shades of gold.

"You will make a fine emperor," I said, offering him a nod in deference.

"And you the finest of physicians," he replied. "No matter the court in which you serve."

Guiding me to my feet, he pressed a firm kiss to my brow, a thousand unspoken words in his touch. When he pulled back, his eyes had clouded with emotion. He ran a thumb along the curve of my cheekbone—a slow, lingering caress—and then he was gone.

I dressed in haste, my body trembling. The thick stench of carnage yet lingered on the breeze when I emerged from the tent, blinking against the bright Istanelan sun. We gathered east of the battlefield, General Lord Tévarez's companies forming ranks behind their general, who sat atop a massive destrier at Gabrián's side.

"Lady Clìana," said Gabrián with a courtly nod as I drew near.

"Your Radiance," I managed to reply.

The formality of our greeting weighed upon me, heavy as a shroud. It seemed to affect Gabrián similarly, for we both turned our gazes north. A beat later, Casdar appeared beside us, seated atop his sable warhorse. His face upon seeing me at Gabrián's side spoke of sorrow beyond sorrow, an unfathomable ache that burrowed into me with stunning force. But I knew that beneath it was the eternal ire that drove him, burning hotter than the sun.


Carastile rejoiced as the Radiant Astral Emperor passed victorious through its gates, leading his army into the people's embrace. The city's main boulevard was lined with a crowd dozens thick, a blur of revelry that stretched all the way from the southern gates to the Grand Sanctuary, where the Most Luminous waited to pronounce Gabrialo of the House of Vendegal the one true sovereign of the Radiant Astral Empire.

We made our way toward the Sanctuary slowly, Gabrián's brightswords clearing a path through the throng of celebration. Behind us, Lady Catanín and Bright Prince

Leomar led their companies in pursuit. Hooves clattered like rain upon the cobbles, mingling with the cries of the people of Carastile.

"Long live Gabrialo, chosen of the Stars!"

"May peace now be upon your reign, Emperor!"

The people's praise echoed through the city, marked here and there with words I did not wish to hear.

"Blessed Lady, look upon me! Hear my cry, Blessed Lady!"

"May the Stars keep you, favored Lady of the Dark!"

I swallowed against the shame that rose within me. If those who called out for me only knew of the power I had wielded, they would surely revile me. But I would not dim the glory of Gabrián's victory, nor bring new rumor upon him by behaving grimly. With a dignified expression upon my face, I paraded through the city at Gabrián's side.

At times, the journey to the Grand Sanctuary seemed interminable. I withdrew into myself as we rode, the weight of the day pressing ever more heavily upon me. What I remember of those moments now comes to me in flashes: the crest of the Grand Sanctuary's dome glinting silver between the rise of shops and manses, the dark mouths of open windows high above the city streets, the sense of unease that trickled alongside sweat down my spine—

And something whistling through the air near my head.

Startled, my horse began to stamp and bray, nearly unseating me in its panic. With the reins clenched tight in my grip, I fought to draw the palfrey around, away from the shrieks and alarm that now rose from the crowds gathered along the streets. Amid the chaos, I caught sight of a small child seated atop a man's shoulders, her face a mask of horror. A bolt of fear coursed through me. Then my horse circled toward the parade at my back, and the world narrowed to a single, all-consuming point: Gabrián.

His body splayed against the length of his horse, his head lolling. The long column of his throat lay bare, pierced through by an arrow that jutted from the ragged edges of his skin.

# CHAPTER 35

I don't remember screaming, though later I would know the excruciating pain of a throat made raw. What I do remember is the bright blood that welled and gurgled from the gash in Gabrián's throat, dribbling down to paint his horse's flanks. Perhaps it was that stark contrast—vivid red against a sea of flawless white—that pierced through the slow, disjointed movement of time.

Suddenly everything was frantic once again. The crowd dissolved into chaos, pushing and scattering in fear as soldiers shouted and brightswords flanked Gabrián's side. I slid from the saddle as Casdar, already dismounted, drew Gabrián's body from the back of his horse. I followed him as he carried Gabrián up the Sanctuary steps, brightswords brandishing their blades to protect our retreat.

"Surround the Sanctuary," Casdar shouted to the knights he'd once stood alongside in service of the emperor. "Defend it at all costs."

The captain of the brightswords nodded before giving

his own commands. Blood spurted from Gabrián's throat as he choked, coughing as Casdar draped his body on the cold stone floor. One of the Sanctuary's luminaries closed the doors behind us. An array of priests and priestesses stood farther inside the cavernous room, their features wide with shock and fear. The Most Luminous stood among them, her skin gone pale.

"Secure the Most Luminous!" Casdar shouted in their direction. "All of you! Lock yourselves in the prayer rooms until we can be sure the Sanctuary is not under threat."

"Gabrián?" I pleaded, cradling the emperor's face between my trembling palms.

Robes swished as the luminaries sprang into motion, scurrying in retreat to the long hall of prayer rooms. "We will beseech the Dark Between," intoned the Most Luminous.

The sound of footsteps faded, and soon we were alone.

"Gabrián," I said again. "Can you hear me?"

Slowly, painfully, Gabrián's eyes dragged up to meet my gaze. The motion awakened a fire within me. He was not gone. Not yet. Perhaps he needn't be at all. The thought coursed through me like a bolt of lightning. *I would stride even unto Shadow to save you,* he had whispered in the dark the night before. *How could I ever blame you for doing the same?*

Vaguely, I registered that Casdar was speaking, his words anguished. But already the world was fading around me as I reached forth with bloodcraft to assess the chaos and destruction of Gabrián's body.

The arrow had pierced the center of his throat. It nicked the anterior jugular vein and rent his trachea and esophagus before embedding in his spine, severing the long fibers that connected brain to body. The surge of energy that should have coursed through his nerves had vanished. This realization sobered me. Even if he hadn't been bleeding out, his body was irreparably broken. In a matter of moments, the severe hemorrhaging would steal the last shred of life that remained within him. It was an unthinkable fate.

A fate I could not allow.

I flung my power forth, weaving together the severed edges of the jugular vein to still the river of his blood. Its surface knitted and smoothed itself, made whole in only a few seconds. Still, his ruptured trachea leaked blood, much of which he aspirated. Pierced through as it was, I couldn't heal the windpipe until I'd removed the arrow from his throat. But could I do such a thing? Certainly not with bloodcraft. And could a surgery even be performed? I couldn't simply slice into Gabrián's throat as I had with Casdar's thigh, creating the fissures needed to safely draw the arrow from the bone. Or could I? Any damage I might cause could surely be healed with the power in my blood— but *only* if I worked quickly enough to heal him before his heart stilled or his lungs failed him.

Cursing, I drew myself from the confines of Gabrián's body. "I need to remove the arrow," I said, frantically reaching for the wooden shaft that jutted from his throat. But as I curled my fingers around the base of the arrow, a shuddering breath slipped from Gabrián's mouth.

"Cliana," he said, his lips stained red with blood. And then he said no more.

I waited for his chest to rise on another labored breath. For his eyes to blink. For the next bloody cough that would rack his body. But there was only his flat-eyed gaze, and stillness. A violent whine filled my ears, growing louder with each passing breath.

He was dead.

And strangely, I couldn't recall why I should care.

Aye, he had been my lover—this Gabrián, this bright prince made emperor. I still remembered the long nights I had spent in his bed, the many hours I'd devoted to his service at court and in the field. I remembered fretting over his survival, over Casdar's vision of his death and the power in my blood that might save him. But why?

I looked down at the body before me and felt nothing. Nary a hint of fondness or love. Was this truly the man I had fought to save, so anxious in my desperation? Had I not been wild with terror moments before? And for what? To save one person among millions, when all would soon be ash and dust? How foolish! How naive! A laugh bubbled up in my throat, vicious and mocking—but it never made it past my lips.

Instead, someone's fingers curled around my neck and slammed my skull against the floor.

Emotion once more flooded my body—not horror or grief, but *rage*. The dark, unholy anger of the monstrous. It coursed through me as Casdar pinned me to the floor, his hands squeezing my throat. "You Black-damned bitch," he roared. "Demon from the Shadows! I should have slain you where you slept!"

A beam of light sliced across Casdar's face, illuminating a countenance gone black with Shadow. Later, I would remember it as the light of day slipping into the Sanctuary as someone passed through its doors. But in that moment, I thought it was nothing more than a trick of the mind. My lungs ached. My vision had blurred. None of it mattered. All I could think as Casdar's grip tightened around my neck was how dare he accuse me. This man thought he knew pain? This bitter, tempestuous boy? Nay, he knew nothing of suffering. Suffering was the dark of a river pool. Suffering was power reviled.

For too long, I had rejected that power, too fearful to seize its possibility. But fearful of what? Of whom? Of men like Casdar Belorán, who considered themselves so assured in their knowledge of what was good and right? No more. If it was suffering that Casdar claimed, then it was suffering he would know.

With a wicked smile, I made to use my bloodcraft upon him. But before I could act, he let out an anguished cry, his grasp on my throat releasing as he fell back over Gabrián's body.

"*Do not touch her,*" came a voice as cold as steel at my back.

I pushed myself up, gasping for air. Before me, Casdar cradled his sword hand against his chest, now a broken, mangled mass of flesh. If it weren't for the desperate ache in my lungs, I would have sneered. Aye, let him suffer the loss of his power.

"Clìana?" said Lenghan, appearing at my side.

At his arrival, something in my anger shifted. I looked up at the man I'd once called lover and friend and remembered the lass I'd once been. The lass who had suffered and wanted and *needed* with such abandon—who, in time, had chosen unnatural power to spare herself yet another lash of grief. All my great and terrible deeds became evident to me, stark as blood on snow, in the shadows of Lenghan's face. And in that understanding, my rage and disgust turned inward. No longer did I point the finger of blame at the world around me. It was toward me now, as it had always been.

I had failed my sister.

I had failed Sósia.

I had failed Gabrián.

No more.

I might have heard Gabrián's last breath flee from his body, but I was through with failure. Bloodcraft might have made a husk of me, but there was still one good thing I could do with my life.

Dragging myself to Gabrián's side, I wrapped my hands around his face. "Àil i blethìn," I said desperately, knowing full well the cost of my actions.

Every last shred of my spirit for his life.

So be it.

My body melded into the Dark.


For a second, I was weightless, floating as a soul without its home. Then I lurched forward through the darkness and found myself once more in my body, stumbling into the night.

"Gabrián!" I cried, my skin chilled with sweat. When no response followed, I called out again. Shallow water swirled around my feet; and a low, dense fog clouded my vision. I waded through the bodies of the lost in search of him. Vendegal knights floated in their bloodied mail, as did Belorán soldiers singed by fire. Their chorus of pain rose around me, as surely as I'd once heard the cry of Sósia's babe in this place. But I could only save one of them: the man whose keeping was the Radiant Astral Empire. The one who held my heart in his hands and carried it with him even in the dark.

"Gabrián!" I called once more. Stumbling, I caught myself, my hands wrist-deep in the icy water.

And that was when I heard it, the shuddering sigh of breath.

"Clìana . . ."

He was there when I glanced up, not a few steps away from me. *Gabrián.*

He appeared in death as he had in life, ashen and glassy-eyed, the long line of his neck pierced by the assassin's bolt. He caught sight of me, his expression flickering with recognition—and with pain.

A sob escaped me then, one after another, an endless tide of emotion that threatened to swallow me whole. *I would stride even unto Shadow to save you*, he had said. This place was no Starless depth, but it had surely cost me my soul to reach it.

It was a price I was willing to pay.

Gathering Gabrián in my arms, I dragged him back from the great and endless night.

# CHAPTER 36

Life.

The stirrings of breath, the thrum of a heartbeat. The warmth of skin against skin. I felt it all as I pitched into the warm, familiar world I'd left behind. Hope fluttered within me as I felt the stickiness of the summer air once more, and the gentle ebb and flow of Gabrián's chest beneath my palms. He was breathing. He was alive.

A quiet sob escaped me. What strange power it was to save someone from death. I'd done it a dozen times before with surgeon's tools in hand, but this was different. This power was life itself, heady and unrelenting. For one single, indefectible moment, the world was bright—

And then came the wretched gurgling of something thick and wet, a rasping horror, sobering the thrill that was coursing through my veins. Blood bubbled up in Gabrián's mouth, spurting from his lips in fits and coughs.

I cried out his name as a foul voice swore behind me, cutting through the rush of blood pounding in my ears.

Lenghan's hand clamped around my shoulder, jerking me away. "What in all fires have you—"

I leaned into the momentum of his grasp, rolled to my feet, and struck him across the face. The blow left him cradling his cheek, the skin an angry red.

Once more I flung myself down at Gabrián's side. His body was blood and bone and ragged breath, even more gruesome now as panic coursed through him. Where others might have balked in the face of such horror, I hardened to it—like iron, like steel. It was the purpose for which I'd been forged.

Wrapping my fingers around its shaft, I wrenched the arrow from Gabrián's throat. A feral noise tore from deep within Casdar as Lenghan swore and blood sprayed across my hands.

"I have you," I told Gabrián as he groaned, an animalistic sound that echoed in my ears, searing itself into my memory. Desperate, I flung my power forth and held his broken, bleeding body in my unnatural grasp. His trachea was ruptured, his brain stem severed. Aspirated blood gurgled in his lungs. It was a hellish landscape, a surgeon's battlefield. I drew together the ragged edges of his windpipe, needing to stanch the flow of his blood before I could tend to any other part of him.

But before I could finish sealing the fractured cartilage, I was pulled back into corporeal form. I hit the ground as if thrown, my body sliding against the cold stone floor.

"Tell me you've not gone mad with it," Lenghan said as he stalked toward me. "Tell me I do not have to put you down."

I clambered to my feet, anger roiling through me. "Put me down if you must, but first I will heal him."

Lenghan grabbed my arm as I tried to move past him, drawing me around so that his gaze could bore into mine. "Have you not lost enough of yourself?"

"He is dying!"

"And you are losing yourself to power!"

"I would gladly give my soul for his."

I thought I heard Casdar speak behind me, but his words were lost to Lenghan's retort.

"Oh, aye? Then why do you yet breathe, hmm? Whose life did it take to bring him back, if not yours?"

"What?" I said, struggling to make sense of Lenghan's question.

"It does not matter!" Casdar shouted. His cry reverberated around us, demanding attention.

Lenghan and I turned to him as one. He had crawled to Gabrián's side, where he was now sitting, his mangled hand cradled in his lap, an emotion too unfathomable to name upon his face. When he spoke again, his voice was quiet. "He is dead."

The words knifed through me, sharp and swift.

"No," I said, hurrying to Gabrián's side again. I wrapped the tendrils of my unnatural power around his heart to find it still as stone in my grasp.

Nay, he could not be dead. I would not allow it.

"Àil i blethìn," I prayed, as I had done only a minute before. *Let him live.* Over and over, I repeated the words to no avail. My spirit was not loosed from my body. The river did not swirl around my feet. He was gone, lost to a world I could no longer access. As I floated through the nebulous cloud of my grief, a single thought pierced through me.

"What did you mean?" I said, rising to round on Lenghan. "If it was not my own life I took?"

He blinked at me, incredulous. "You don't know?"

"I was prepared to sacrifice every last shred of my soul for him."

"Yet still you live."

I shook my head in confusion.

"By the Black, you don't even ken the spell you worked. It isn't a piece of your soul *you* sacrifice to bring a person back from death, Clìana. It is life itself."

The words came to me as if through water, garbled by the ringing in my ears. Surely, I misunderstood what he was saying. Surely, it couldn't be true. To work power at the cost of my spirit was one matter, but . . .

"A life for a life?" I whispered.

Lenghan nodded grimly.

"Whose?"

"The one they loved most," he replied.

The horror of realization assailed me. Sósia's babe. I had slipped into the Dark Between to steal the bairn from death; and when we'd stumbled back into life, Sósia had been dead. I recalled her once more, lying cold and empty-eyed upon her childbed.

Oh, Stars.

The air pressed in around me, an unrelenting hand upon my chest. What had I done?

And yet . . .

"If that is true, then why do I yet breathe?" If I'd traded Gabrián's life for the one he'd loved most, then surely I wouldn't have lived long enough to treat him.

"Perhaps he didn't love you as well as you loved him."

I shook my head fiercely. "He had found his light in me. He had *grieved* for me, for what we could not have. Nay, the only other he loved so dearly was . . ."

I turned on my heel, seeking out the only other person yet living whom Gabrián had held in such high esteem. Casdar blinked back at me, his eyes wide with understanding.

And yet we both drew breath.

A thousand heartbeats seemed to pass as we stared at each other. Then Casdar sprang on me, his unbroken hand tightening around my throat. He propelled me back until my head cracked against the rough stone of the Sanctuary wall.

"I will kill you for what you have done," he said.

Instinctually, I thought to use my power on him, as I had the morning before. But there must have been some sliver of my humanity left, because self-loathing was twisting in my gut. I didn't want to hurt him. I never had. I had only ever wanted to protect Gabrián—and even in that, I had failed. If it was my life that Casdar wanted, then it was my life that he deserved.

He shook me violently for a moment before releasing me. Stumbling back, Casdar clutched at his chest.

"I told you not to touch her," Lenghan said as I sank to the floor, gasping for breath. I knew at once that he was holding Casdar's heart in the palm of his power. "Let us go, and I will give you your life."

"I would rather die than see her go free," said Casdar.

"She didn't put the arrow through his throat."

"She is a witch."

"She is a fool!" Lenghan shouted. "He suffered at her hand, I will not deny it. But if you wish to take revenge upon your emperor's killer, then you will need to step beyond this Sanctuary—and you will need your hand made whole."

Casdar twitched, his face a mask of pain and anger.

"Well, then?" Lenghan asked. "What will it be? Will you let us go? Or will I have to kill you?"

A long beat passed in silence. Candlelight flickered across the twisted contours of Casdar's face.

"Get out," he said at last. "Go! Get her out of my sight!"

Lenghan's grip was firm around my arm as he drew me to my feet.

"No," I said as he led me toward the Sanctuary's doors. I needed to see Gabrián one last time. To touch his face. To feel his skin against mine. I couldn't leave him, not like this. But the weight of grief slowed my senses. I fought against Lenghan's hold with weak limbs, mindlessly lashing out against him. And in those last moments, time became insubstantial once more. I remember Casdar gasping in relief as he held his healed hand aloft. I remember the bright flash of light as Lenghan opened the Sanctuary doors. But most of all, I remember that one last glimpse of Gabrián, shrouded in blood, his hazel eyes staring lifelessly at the glittering ceiling of the Grand Sanctuary, a wretched mimicry of the Stars above.

# CHAPTER 37

Lenghan whisked me out of the city on horseback, winding through dark alleys and forgotten streets. I remember little of the journey, lost as I was to despair. It was only after we'd passed through Carastile's gates and turned north toward the port cities on the Waking Sea that awareness gripped me. The spires of Alamada Palace rose in the west, each spearing the brilliant Istanelan sky like an arrow. All at once, the day's events assailed me, image after gruesome image stirring panic in my chest. I must have begun screaming and scrambling, striving to claw my way out of Lenghan's grip, for I remember him cursing and the horse drawing short.

"By the Black, Clìana," he muttered, and then the world went dark.

It came to me as I drifted through endless, unholy slumber. The one Gabrián had loved most had never been a single person—not his lover, nor the man he'd called brother.

It had always been a people. A multitude.

An empire.

It was the only explanation for why Casdar and I yet breathed, for Gabrián had loved no one else so dearly save Sósia. But then, if he had loved his people most, what fate awaited the soul of the Astral Empire?

At first, I awakened from the depths of Lenghan's power slowly. Then my gorge rose with sudden insistence, and I rolled to vomit on the ground beside me. Long tendrils of thick yellow bile dripped from my lips. I must have spluttered, choking on it, for someone pressed their fingers into my mouth.

"Holy fires," Lenghan cursed, clearing the muck from my throat as I'd once done for Sósia's babe.

Gagging, I tore his fingers from my mouth and heaved the dregs of my wame onto the grass. Crouching on my hands and knees, I dragged in several ragged breaths. The chill night air cut through my lungs like ice. I stilled when I realized that I hadn't felt such cold for many weeks.

"Where are we?" I bit out, eyeing Lenghan suspiciously.

In the thin half-light of the moon, his face was shadowed. "At the Brennish border."

*"Brenmere?"*

"We'll climb the pass home to Aversere tomorrow."

Horror-struck, I scrambled away from him. "You would take me back there?"

"Where else would we go?" he snapped.

"What did you do to me?" I asked, disregarding his

question. "The last thing I remember was . . . It would have taken *days* to travel here."

"You were mad with grief, Clìana. I needed to calm your mind for a time, to give you rest so that you might once again think clearly."

*"Clearly?"* My head swam as I staggered to my feet, the Stars wheeling high above. "What does that mean to you, hmm? Do you expect me to come crawling back into your bed after all you've done?"

"I'm not the only one with blood on my hands," he said as he stood.

"You killed my sister!"

"Do you ken how I ended Ailis's life? *Quickly*, Clìana. A clean break of her neck, swift and merciful. But you? You *tortured* the man you claimed to love."

I saw my hands grasping the shaft of the arrow and Gabrián's anguish as I pulled it from his throat. "I was trying to save him."

"You were wasting yourself upon him!" Lenghan roared. "His body was irreparably broken. You nearly lost yourself striving to stem the flow of his blood."

"I only wanted to—"

"You tortured him. *You.* So do not dare think yourself better than—"

I slapped him across the face, a violent echo of the time I'd done so in Carastile's Grand Sanctuary. Only this time, he clenched his cheek for but a breath before grasping my wrist and dragging my body near. "I allowed you to strike me once in your madness. I will not allow it again."

"Oh, aye? And what is it that you'll do to me? Hmm? Put me down as you did Ailis?" I scoffed. "You could not do such a thing." Lenghan had invested too much in me, idealized me as a precious possession in his mind. Nay, he would not harm me unless I needled him into reckless anger. I took a step nearer still. "He was a better man than you could ever be," I said.

A vein ticked in Lenghan's jaw. "And daft for loving you, I should think."

I spat in his face.

He wiped the spittle from his cheek with the back of his hand, slow and careful. I could feel the tension in his chest, the anger he was barely holding at bay. "You are tired, Clìana. I think it time you took another rest."

I opened my mouth to argue, then knew no more.


Sometime later, I became aware of the light and shadow that danced across my eyelids. With great effort, I managed to open them, blinking against the harsh light of day. I was propped up against a tree, the grass damp and cool beneath my fingers. Hearing me stir, Lenghan crouched down before me. "You need to eat," he said, pressing a small crust of bread into my hands.

I looked at the food as though it were nothing more than a tuft of wool.

"It's been days since you've had anything but water," he said.

"It would have been better spent drowning you," I replied, crushing the bread in my fist. My body was weak, but what did that matter? Lenghan was right. I *had* tortured Gabrián—in more ways than one. I'd betrayed his trust and dampened his convictions, never mind the suffering I had prolonged in the last moments of his life.

Aye, I had been trying to save him, but he had never wanted to be saved.

Lenghan peeled my fingers away from my palm, revealing the mangled remains of the meal he had offered me. "Eat it, or I will force it down your throat. So help me, Clìana."

I stared at the bread, unmoved. "Perhaps I'd deserve it."

Lenghan caught my meaning. "And give me the satisfaction?"

He snorted as I tore a bite from the bread with my teeth. It tasted like ash, but I ate every crumb.

There was a chill in the air I was too numb to feel as Lenghan drew behind me in the saddle. I saw it in the frost that coated the ground and in the way my breath clouded around my face. It was the beginning of autumn, in a place far from the searing heat of Carastile. I shivered, still dressed in the thin linen of my Istanelan garb, though Lenghan had wrapped a woolen cloak about me at some point during our journey. It had likely kept me from freezing in the night. I wished it had not.

We climbed the pass into Daorender slowly. The ground was steep and muddy, and the horse struggled to bear our weight on the difficult terrain. Halfway up the pass, Lenghan dismounted to ease the horse's burden, leading it ever upward by its reins. He glanced back at me often, as if worried I might bolt from the saddle and flee. But what did it matter? There was nothing waiting for me back in Brenmere or the world beyond. And Lenghan's words were once more true enough. I didn't want to give him the satisfaction of using power against me, be it physical or unnatural. In that way, allowing him to lead me back to Aversere was an act of rebellion. Yet the realization quickly soured. Perhaps I *should* run. Perhaps I deserved whatever fate was most punishing. But weak as I was, I didn't have the strength to seek it.

We crested the pass sometime after midday, stopping to eat a little beneath a towering pine. As I chewed, I stared up at the peak of Ben Tevis, where the Kelkevie lads had gone stalking on the day of Imbela's dawning. I remembered suturing the youngest Kelkevie lad's cheek, Erune's voice filling the room around us. The memory slithered in my wame, unsettling as poison. Stars, to think of standing before Erune again—of telling her all I had done. I hid the crust of my bread in the brush, too ill at ease to stomach another bite.

We began our descent into Daorender soon thereafter. Some way down the pass, the road arced to the left, and suddenly there it was: Aversere, stretched out before us, a blot of ink in a sea of mossy green and brown. It seemed almost cold, a cruel disruption in the landscape. I shuddered at the sight. Suddenly, each plod of the horse's hooves seemed to be a stamp of guilt, the crack of a rod. This was what I deserved. The torment of returning here, to all my ghosts. I forced myself to bear the journey, even as tension knotted ever tighter in my chest.

There was an icy tributary coursing toward the Serenault in the foothills outside the city. Lenghan stopped there to water the horse, his touch almost unbearable as he lifted me from the saddle. As he tended to the horse, I turned eastward and began to walk. Half a minute passed before he noticed me.

"What are you doing?" he called, his voice rising above the gurgling of the burn. I could hear his footfalls squishing in the mud as he stalked after me, his determined strides eating up the space between us. I didn't try to run from him, knowing the effort would be fruitless. Lenghan didn't seem to care as he grabbed at me, swinging me around. "Where do you think you're going?"

"I ken the way."

"Clìana, you cannot—"

"Enough!" I tore my arm from his grasp. "I've allowed you to bring me this far. I'm here, Lenghan, in the highlands as you wished. Now leave me be."

I staggered eastward once again, with Lenghan trailing beside me.

"And where will you go, hmm? How far do you think you can travel alone? You're not well, lass. You must—"

"Do not touch me!" I shouted, shirking away as he reached for me. "Do not speak to me. Do not let me hear you say my name. I am not yours to hold."

He shook me by the shoulders. "And who are you without me? You wouldn't have made a name for yourself without that grimoire. You wouldn't have escaped that Black-damned Sanctuary! *I* am the one who made you, Clìana. I am the one who saved you. And if you had but an ounce of heart or good sense left in you, you'd be on your knees with gratitude." His face was so near, so dark and twisted with Shadow, that I knew he must be standing at the edge of his resolve.

"Go on, then," I sneered. "Break me."

His snarl was feral, his gaze boring into mine. "If it is death you want, I will give to you. But I will hear you beg for it." With a shove, he released me, flinging me to the earth.

"No," I spat, wiping the mud from my cheek.

"Beg," he insisted.

I shook my head.

"Beg!"

Still, I refused him.

*"Beg!"* He crouched before me, the word an animal shriek. His face flushed with rage.

I pushed myself up a little on my hands, meeting him eye to eye. But before I could utter my refusal again, there came a sound like distant thunder. Lenghan heard it, too. He turned to look over his shoulder as a small cavalry spilled over the crest of the nearest foothill, moving swiftly toward us.

Lenghan rose to his feet. I remained where I was, my attention fixed on the man who led the company. His eyes were blue as cornflower.

"My lady?" said Lord Ulmhar as the company drew to a halt around us. He cast a brief, dark look at Lenghan before dismounting. When he knelt before me, his voice was soft and careful. "Are you unwell, my lady?"

I felt Lenghan's searing gaze upon me as the cold, wet earth seeped through my clothes. But it was the pale moon of Lord Ulmhar's face that filled my vision. His broad jaw. His poorly set nose. The glass eye he now bore where once there had been a leather patch, the shade of its iris so well matched that one might almost think his wounded eye had been made whole.

"Alone," I said, forcing the word between dry, cracked lips. "I wish to go somewhere I can be alone."

# CHAPTER 38

Lord Ulmhar took me to a wee hunter's cottage on the far side of Loch Argan, a simple, well-kept abode tucked neatly against the northern hem of the glen. His hands were warm on my waist as he helped me dismount, holding me steady long after my feet had touched the ground. It wasn't an intimate touch. There was no glint of passion in Lord Ulmhar's eye as he watched me. Rather, his expression seemed almost paternal, brimming with concern he didn't voice. He offered his arm before leading me into the dark mouth of the cottage, settling me on the edge of the small bed before lighting a fire in the hearth.

Still crouched low, he turned and asked me gently, "Do you wish to speak of it, lass?"

"Of what?" I replied.

"Any of it. All of it. Whatever it is that's stolen you away."

It would have been easier to speak to him if I *had* been seized, if some villain had deprived me of the life I had known. But there had been no villain in my story, not even Lenghan. Monster that he was, he hadn't betrayed Gabrián's trust, nor had he forced the one he'd loved to endure a fate far worse than a clean death. Those were my sins. My shame.

"Nay," I said, unwilling to meet Lord Ulmhar's eye. My fingers picked idly at a small tear in the linen of my dress.

After a long pause, Lord Ulmhar grunted in acceptance, a familiar Daor noise I hadn't heard in months. Slowly, he rose to his feet. "The pantry should be stocked enough for some days," he said as he crossed the cottage, pausing at the threshold. "You've a kettle to draw water from the loch and several cords of firewood."

He appraised me then, as if searching for some answer in the weary bend of my spine, in the lankness of my hair or the hollow of my eyes. When he spoke again, his voice was gentler still. "I'll post a man outside the door. If you have need of me, or any other, you need only ask."

His tenderness should have been a balm. Yet it grated upon me, scraping at the guilt I fed like a flame in the dark. "I do not deserve such kindness," I said.

Lord Ulmhar's mouth thinned into a soft, sad smile. "Whatever has happened, whatever it is that you've done, lass . . . I imagine the good far outweighs the bad. Bear that in mind, aye? And ken that you need only be alone here as long as you wish to be."

With a hesitant nod, he stepped over the threshold, shutting the door behind him. And so it was that the walls of the wee hunter's cottage closed around me like a tomb.

✦

I had asked to be taken somewhere I could be alone so that I might determine, without another's input, whether I wished to live or die. That was the simple truth of the matter. It would be easy enough to end my life, should I wish it. The hunter's cottage abutted the loch. I could fill my pockets with stone and wade into its icy waters, an echo of the fate so many of my Goddan ancestors had suffered. It wasn't a river pool, but it would suffice. Still, there was a certain terror in the act of drowning that I found I could not stomach, even if it was deserved. But the chill embrace of Loch Argan wasn't the only option available to me.

As a physician, I knew as many clever ways to kill as I did to heal. All one had to do was nick the right vein or slide a blade just so between my ribs. Then there were the ingredients of my trade—the herbs, roots, and flowers that could, in small doses, work wonders in a healer's hands. A dose too heavy for one's weight or condition, however, could prove fatal. But the lethality of an element did not speak to its expediency. A large tincture of nettle grass taken by mouth, for example, could produce a slow bleeding of the wame that would ail a patient for days, leading to no small amount of vomiting that often ended in the patient's death for want of water.

Nay, if I was going to end my life, then I wished for death to come swiftly. Perhaps it was a mercy I didn't deserve. But in a moment of excruciating torment, I didn't wish to risk that I might administer some life-preserving measure to myself. Aye, it was better to be done with it as quickly as possible—if I indeed decided that I no longer wished to live.

As for the ingredient that could aid my departure, I found it quickly enough along the shoreline of the loch. Even with the highland winter rapidly approaching, its dark, slippery leaves grew abundantly in the loch's shallow waters, drifting like shocks of loose raven hair. Blackweed. I shuddered as I plucked several strands from the icy water and carried them back to the cottage.

As a master healer, I knew blackweed well. Its leaves were often used for medicinal purposes, dried and ground before being mixed into a variety of tinctures, tonics, and salves. Some property in its strands calmed the minds of most patients, making it an ideal compound to stir into dreamwine or administer to those with nervous conditions. In higher concentrations, it was often used to ease a patient into a deep, dreamless sleep before surgery. But a heavier dose yet, with the leaves boiled into a viscous extract black as Shadow? It was as swift and lethal a poison as they came. It had a horrid scent and taste, but what did that matter to me? All it would take was a single long swallow, and I would slip into an easy death within minutes.

I hung the leaves from the rafters to dry, the tendrils dripping water dark as blood upon the floorboards.

The blackweed needed two days to dry before I could grind it and boil it to syrup. During those long hours, I held nothing back. If I was going to end my life, then I would end it with clear convictions. I would know, beyond a sliver of doubt, that the choice was a matter of justice, not a craven attempt to escape the guilt that burrowed deep inside me, riddling me with the inescapable ache of despair. And so I allowed memory to assail me.

I recalled Sósia first, lying pale and bloodied on her

childbed, her expression distant with death. Casdar Belorán followed, crumpling to the ground as pain seared like fire through his veins. Then there was Gabrián, furious in light of my betrayal—and worse still, the tortured look upon his face as I pulled the arrow from his throat.

Though I flinched against the horror of each memory, I made no attempt to smother them. Shame and indescribable grief assailed me, and I let them, permitting myself nothing but the truth of the pain I had wrought. It was a trial, a well-deserved reckoning. Yet as I sat before the hearth fire and stared at the flames, Lord Ulmhar's words rose to mind: *Whatever has happened, whatever it is that you've done, lass . . . I imagine the good far outweighs the bad.*

Unbidden, I recalled Sósia's bairn crying out when only seconds before his lungs had been still. I remembered Casdar sitting astride his warhorse, not a day after he'd nearly bled out under the fiery Istanelan sun. And then there was Gabrián in the dark of a prayer room, rising from the cold stone bench where he had nearly died.

These were the memories I fought to suppress. I didn't want to think of the ways I'd wielded bloodcraft to positive results. It wasn't fair to do so, not when the same power had demanded my spirit and caused such irreparable pain. Yet those were not the only heartening times I recalled. Had I not freed the tiny wooden sliver from Lord Ulmhar's eye, potentially sparing his life? Had I not nursed Casdar from his fever at Granara, tended to dozens of courtiers during my time at Alamada Palace, and stitched the wounds of as many soldiers on the battlefield? Did I not have something to offer this world that, if taken away, would make it a lesser place?

Days passed, and the blackweed dried.

As I ground the now-brittle leaves to dust, I did not think of Gabrián or Casdar, of Lenghan or Lord Ulmhar, of Sósia or the Bright Court or the soldiers on the battle-field. Instead, I thought of Ailis. I thought of the way her body had failed her, seizing her muscles with exhaustion and her joints with pain. I thought of the way I'd used to dig my fingers deep into the flesh of her calves and thighs, fighting the atrophy that gripped her when her condition was at its worst. I thought of the sigh that had often escaped her as I worked, the blessed rush of relief that would ease the tight purse of her mouth and the anguish that twisted her face. Could I not offer that same relief to another? Could I not ease suffering as surely as I had so recently prolonged it?

I boiled the dust into syrup, the extract growing thick and black as tar as I sat before the hearth fire, thinking.

Aye, I could be of service to the world. There was no denying it. But who was I beyond the skill of my hands and the sharpness of my mind? Who was I beyond the oath I had sworn to my clan? Was there any good in me beyond my training? Anything beyond my healing prowess that made me worthy of reprieve?

A quiet voice echoed in my ear. *You are no mere consola-tion, Clìana.*

I decanted the blackweed into the smallest cup I could find in the cottage's small storeroom. It swirled in the bottom of the vessel like the dregs of some bitter spirit. It would only take a single swallow. Maybe two for good measure, if I could manage its foul taste.

I held the cup aloft. Taking a tentative sniff, I recoiled.

*I ken this world, my lady, and it is cruel,* I'd once said to Erune.

Her reply came to me then, swirling soft and warm in my chest. *Aye. But it can also be kind, if you let it.*

For so long, I had viewed my life through the lens of grief. Ailis had been my purpose for years, my sole reason for rising each morning. Then she was gone. In her absence, I had closed myself off to deep feeling. I'd kept Erune at arm's length—and Lenghan, too, in the days before I'd known the truth of him. Already, I'd hurt too much. What good would it have done to make myself vulnerable to further grief? Instead, I'd sought safety in the arms of glory, pursuing mastery of my craft and a commission at Carastile. But then there had been Gabrián, and soon I could no longer deny the light I'd found in him. He had cracked me open in a way that had terrified me to the marrow of my bones. I hadn't been ready. The lens of grief had still been clouding my vision. I hadn't been willing to bear the possibility of another loss. And so it had been fear—not power or greed—that had driven me to the edge of monstrosity.

How might those final days in Gabrián's life have played out differently if I'd allowed something kinder than fear to drive me? Perhaps he would still be dead, but could I have offered him comfort while he took his final breaths? Could I have gifted Casdar some form of solace in his grief? Could he have even done the same for me?

There could be no unmaking of the pain I had caused. Yet, perhaps, I might offer something more tender to the world in time—and maybe the world might offer the same to me, if I was willing to receive it.

I took one long, last look at the blackweed syrup

growing thicker still in the bottom of the cup. Then I cast it into the flames, gathered up my cloak, and left the wee hunter's cottage behind me for good.

I cleansed myself in the icy waters of Loch Argan, scouring the last remains of the sticky Istanelan heat from my skin. When my body was clean, I untangled the feathers from my hair, carefully setting them aside before combing through my nest of curls. With my hair unsnarled, I returned the feathers to their rightful place, saving the tiny emerald plume for last. Gingerly, I held it aloft. It had been the aim of so many years of toil and trial, a feather that had once promised greatness and glory, a legacy to be built. I ran a finger down its spine and felt the cool, downy blades against my skin. Greatness, I had learned, was a double-edged sword. For in achieving greatness, one wielded the power of good and ill. But then, could the same not be said for any with the agency to make a choice?

For a time, I had chosen violence and suffering. That time was through.

Weaving the tiny emerald feather into my hair, I stood and looked out across the loch, toward the familiar towering keep that beckoned on the horizon. Putting one foot in front of the other, I began the long walk to Castle Tarne.

I found her in the kailyard, her gnarled hands knuckle-deep in the loamy soil. "Erune," I said softly.

Her eyes found mine, warm and round and bright.

Then she appraised me, and her brow furrowed. Wiping her hands on her dirt-stained apron, she drew near. "Come here, lass," she said with arms held wide, and I fell into the soft comfort of her embrace, at once new and feeling of home.

She held me until I could weep no more. Then she caught my chin between her forefinger and thumb. "Now then, lass. Let there be nothing more unsaid between us."

We walked along the bank of Loch Argan, in the opposite direction of the hunter's cottage. Erune listened quietly as I told her of all that had come to pass, holding nothing back. By the time I was through, the first Stars had appeared in the night sky. Erune regarded me with nary a hint of disgust or disdain.

"What grave Shadows tempt us in this lifetime, aye?" she said. "But you've found your anchor now, haven't you? And in the finding, you've begun to make yourself anew. Aye, lass. All is well." With a small, knowing smile, she looped her arm through mine. "All is well and shall be made whole once more. Just you see."

Castle Tarne grew ever larger as we made our journey home. As we drew near the kailyard's gate and the last tendrils of light slipped over the horizon, I found the courage to acknowledge the tremendous gift she had given me, which I was determined to one day believe I deserved. "Thank you, my lady."

Leaning near, I pressed a warm kiss to her brow.


Winter weighed upon me heavy as a poultice, stiff and warm, slowly easing the troubled wounds within. I didn't return to the guildhall at Aversere, nor did Diarnan

Larmach ever call for me. Erune had likely spoken to her cousin on my behalf, though that realization did not occur to me until some months later. Instead, I slept in Castle Tarne's tiny surgery, wedged between worktables and shelves that held a thousand tiny jars and vials. I took my meals in the great hall at Erune's side and filled my ears with the boisterous sounds of the Kelkevie boys' antics. I bound cuts and stitched wounds, eased coughs and set bones. I awoke aching with every sunrise and healed a little more with each pain I soothed before dusk.

On the frosty night that the Lady of Fire, the Bright Star Imbela, once more rose above the horizon, a delighted laugh bubbled up from deep within me. To this day, I cannot remember the source of my amusement. Perhaps it had been the wiles of one of the Kelkevie lads, or something in one of Erune's unexpected quips that had surprised me. It didn't matter, for once I'd begun to laugh, I found that I couldn't stop myself from weeping with joy at the sound—the bright, round thing that seemed to swell up within me, promising so much more than I'd ever expected to feel again, and more than I had felt in many a year.

Later, as Castle Tarne's courtyard filled with shouts of wonder and the distant thunder of the city's drums, I glanced up at the sky. Imbela's fiery eye was shining high above; and there, in that moment, I decided that the world could indeed be a tender place and that I was happy to be alive within it. Erune brought me a glass of wine to warm me. One of the stable lads took up a merry tune on his tin whistle, his melody faltering briefly when a bonny kitchen maid began to dance. A minute later, Lady Kelkevie appeared on the steps of the keep, her newborn bairn in her arms. She'd had a girl at last, the first babe I'd helped deliver since bringing Sósia's lad into the world. The bairn gurgled happily, her ruddy cheeks peeking out from the woolen confines of her swaddle.

Aye, the world could be a tender place indeed.

The muffled sound of hoofbeats preceded the arrival of a rider then. I turned as Lord Ulmhar passed through the castle gate, a broad smile upon his face—and a knowing glint in his cornflower eye.

# CHAPTER 39

There is beauty in pain. Not the elegance of polished pearls and gems or chips of ivory, but the grace that is woven inextricably from suffering in the tapestry of life. It is sunlight on a sickbed, the fruits of a mother's labor, the cut that frees the body of an ill-gone limb. After all that had come to pass during my time in Istanel, it was a beauty I now sought as surely as my next breath. For in the end, it is the only beauty we are truly promised—and in that promise, there is more joy than one could find in any gleaming jewel.

I found that wonder now, several weeks after Lord Ulmhar had ridden into Castle Tarne's courtyard in search of me. I'd written him a letter only the day before, thanking him for his kindness upon my return to Daorender and urging him to mind his bonny blue eye once Imbelaine had begun. He'd not bothered to reply. Instead, he'd sought me out in person to once more offer me a commission among his companies. This time, I'd readily accepted.

The great green expanse of Strath Cernaid unfurled below us now, lush with springtime growth. It was a welcome sight after our bloody encounter with brigands in a darkling glen the day before. A cool breeze cut between the bens around us, washing away the musk of riders and horses. I inhaled deeply, grateful to yet be alive.

"You did well yesterday," said Lord Ulmhar, his mount plodding alongside mine as the company journeyed south toward the lowlands.

"Och, 'twas naught but scratches," I replied, though the compliment warmed me all the same.

"Aye, but I don't imagine you're accustomed to being assailed. You handled yourself well, my lady."

Lenghan's face flashed in my mind's eye then, twisting in anger before a sudden rallying cry had pierced the air and the distant clash of blades had begun. I could still see the Belorán soldier sitting high above me in his saddle, the tip of his sword glinting as it arced toward me. The shattering of his bones still echoed in my ear. It wasn't the first time that day in southern Istanel had risen out of memory since yesterday's attack, but my duty in the wake of both assaults had been the same. Amid Daor moss and fragrant heather, I'd stitched half a dozen wounds and pulled an arrow from the meat of a man's shoulder, remembering the arrow I'd once freed from another man's leg—and from the throat of an emperor. A fierce pang of grief had torn through me at the thought, but it soon dulled into a quiet ache. I carried the weight of it with me still. But I bore it with tenderness and hope, and it did not consume me.

"Nay, not accustomed," I said to Lord Ulmhar.

I felt his gaze upon me, as if searching for answers in

the lines of my face. To his credit, he'd not attempted to pry the truth out of me since the day he'd delivered me to the hunter's cottage. Every day that passed without a word of curiosity was a surprise. He'd been so inquisitive on the road to Marnos, so insistent that I share the joys and pains of my past. But he had seen me on that day in the foothills, emaciated and engulfed by my grief. And while he did not treat me now with conspicuous delicacy, I thought perhaps that he still considered me a fragile thing. In some ways, he wasn't wrong.

"We'll all sleep abed tonight," he said, as if deliberately changing the subject. Behind us, one of the knights took up a bawdy tune, something about a lass and a field of heather; and the others joined him. The air of joviality was welcome after the sudden onslaught of the day before. "There's an inn not far from here, if memory serves me well."

"Glad tidings, that," I said, raising my voice so that Lord Ulmhar might hear me over the repetition of a particularly provocative lyric. "My spine is of a mind to commit mutiny these days."

The lord protector chuckled. "'Tis good to hear you jest again, lass."

"Careful, my lord. One might say that speech had an air of sincerity."

"Perhaps I've sobered in your company."

"Perhaps you've been sober all along."

A thoughtful noise bubbled up from Lord Ulmhar's throat. He tugged his bonnet low over his new glass eye, the first having been lost in some bet or another. Who could say? The story changed with each retelling. "I thought I'd known Shadow the day my mother died. And again, the night I lost my eye. But I hadn't seen such Shadow as when I saw in you that day in the foothills. I trust that you would tell me, lass, should it ever come crawling back to you."

"I would," I promised, trusting myself to accept Ulmhar's kindness now. "But you've no need to fear."

The words rang bright and true in my chest. Aye, I still mourned Gabrián and all the many pains I'd inflicted. Part of me would forever carry the knowledge of the harm I'd caused. But I was no longer ashamed of my use of blood-craft. I understood the lass whose fear had led her to call upon it, and I'd forgiven her. She was deserving of that compassion, as were all those who hardened themselves in defense against sorrow. To remain soft and warm in the face of torment was a greater battle than many believed themselves strong enough to fight. But I knew now that pain would be suffered regardless—and that shielding myself from its touch would deprive me of the only good this life had to offer. So I let myself be soft and warm, and I welcomed every bit of beauty I could embrace.

Lord Ulmhar and I fell into an easy silence, enjoying the men's carousing and the warmth of the rich spring air. Now and then, a beam of sunlight broke through the passing clouds to glimmer on the river of Strath Cernaid below.


Not long before setting out with Lord Ulmhar's company, I'd been walking down the Òengar Road, making my way toward the guildhall to seek permission to accept his commission. That was when I saw Lenghan, walking with his father across the busy market square.

The two men were bent close as they spoke in low conversation. Lenghan must have felt the press of my attention, for he glanced up and drew short at the sight of me. When I saw his lips form the beginning of my name, I shook my head once, slowly.

Lenghan's mouth clamped shut, the set of his jaw hardening.

In the end, I was glad I had seen him. I hadn't known until that moment how much I'd needed to do so, how important it was that I make peace with myself in his presence. One day, I would forgive him for what he'd done, but never again would I hold him dear. For now, it was enough to look him in the eye and stand firm in my convictions. To know that the greatest form of vengeance was simply the strength to hold my head up high.

Contented by this knowledge, I had turned and walked away.

In the long months before that spring day in Strath Cernaid, I'd heard only one piece of news from Carastile: At the age of eight-and-ten, Bright Prince Leomar of the House of Vendegal had been enthroned as the Radiant Astral Emperor. The realization curled tight and sickly in my gut. Perhaps the Astral throne would mature the prince I'd known in Carastile, or perhaps it would only fan the flames of his malice. I couldn't help but think of the power I had worked in the Grand Sanctuary—a life for a life— and the one Gabrián had loved most.

*A people.*

*An empire.*

Would Leomar bring about their undoing?

Several years passed before I learned that Gabrián's ashes had been mixed with crushed diamond and stone, the sparkling tile embedded alongside those of his father and his sister in the dome of the Grand Sanctuary. Likewise, I later learned of the man in the prison cell—the former brightsword whose family had turned traitor, whose heart bore countless sorrows, and whose visions forebode that we would one day meet again.

On the night before I left Castle Tarne to join Lord Ulmhar's company, Erune had called me into the court-yard and pressed a book into my hands. My heart began to pound, though I'd long ago given Ailis's grimoire to fire. My fingers darted across the surface of the soft brown leather.

"Go on, lass. Open it," said Erune.

Unknotting the cord that bound the book, I found each page of parchment blank. Puzzled, I met her eye.

"Once, you bore a book of destruction," she explained, placing her palm atop the pages. "Let this one be a place to scribe new healing."

A broad smile curled my lips. Many physicians kept a journal, a place to record the knowledge one could only acquire from a lifetime of learning. Where once I had been given a parting gift that tempted me with power, this book offered me the humility of a healer's journey.

In the years to come, I would fill its pages with insights I could never have uncovered within the walls of the guild-hall—or even within the high glens of Daorender. But I made my first note within the book that night at the inn in Strath Cernaid that Lord Ulmhar had promised. Seated at a dining table beside the roaring hearth, I cracked the book open and dipped the nib of my pen in ink. There, on the first page of the journal, I cataloged the flower that Gabrián had once pressed into my palm in the spice gardens at Alamada.

*Aathani.* A balm to heal all wounds.

# COMING SOON

Clìana and Casdar will return in *Before the Morrow Dawns,* the next installment in the *Dark Between* series. For updates on my writing progress, subscribe to my author newsletter at kristenelliskieffer@substack.com.

# ACKNOWLEDGMENTS

I dedicated this book to myself to honor the immensity of the courage and resilience I needed to reach this point in my writing journey. Nevertheless, I couldn't have published *Beneath a Mourning Sky* without the support of some truly wonderful people.

My editor, Sara Letourneau, deserves a world of praise for helping me usher this story into its full magic—no unnatural cost required. I'm also grateful to editor Isobelle Lans for her early feedback on the book's opening chapters, Misha Kydd for her proofreading prowess, Miss Nat Mack for designing such a stunning cover, and Allie Fernfield for teaching me how to properly apply diacritics to Istanel's Spanish-inspired names. (Any flubs therein are entirely my own.)

My mom was privy to the lowest points in my relationship with myself and my art, and she never once expressed anything but unshakable belief in my capacity to make this dream come true. Mom, thank you for being you.

I'm also grateful to Jess, Vikki, Mike, Dana, and my many friends in the online creative community for their boundless support and encouragement over the years. Miss Rodden and Mrs. McCullough are also angels for bookending my grade school experience with such unexpected and empowering calls to creative action.

To my new writing group—Sarah, Neerali, and Jacki—thank you for cheering me on during the pre-publication process. I can't wait to continue working with you as I bring Casdar's story to life.

Finally, to Aunt Jean, I'll never forget your generosity at every Christmas, birthday, and Scholastic Book Fair. Thank you for fueling my love of stories. You are dearly missed.

# A Note on Subject Matter

This book contains detailed descriptions of violence, injuries, medical procedures, chronic pain, self-harm, physical and emotional abuse, grief, drowning, pregnancy complications, stillbirth, death during childbirth, torture, warfare, and suicidal ideation, as well as brief mentions of childhood neglect, sexual assault, and castration. Please read mindfully, and take care of yourself.

# ABOUT THE AUTHOR

Kristen Ellis Kieffer is a fantasy author and creative coach who lives for art that unflinchingly explores our hurt and hope as human beings. A proud AuDHD artist, she lives at home in South Jersey with her mom, her dog, and the wild things growing in her garden. When she isn't creating, she can be found walking through meadows, staring at the stars, and waxing poetic about the creative work that has most recently captured her attention.

instagram.com/kelliskieffer

bookbub.com/authors/kristen-ellis-kieffer

amazon.com/author/kristenelliskieffer